A TALE OF KINGS

To discover oneself is to leave the door open for tragedy

Chapter 1 - A Hollow Fate

Out across a desert of snow and ice, home to fell and remote winds of a freezing and forgotten age, vacant glaciers under a gray sky sat over far reaching white capped mountains. The raging winds blew small flakes of snow over the frozen tundra, an army of little white droplets headed to their uncertain destination and blanketed everything with hail. Through the denseness of the blizzard, lapis reflections of the chilled faces of mighty glaciers stared ever intently out beyond the frozen wastes at the top of the world. The land was bare and void, with no trees or vegetation there to grow, only in the far south of Antara could the old oaks be found but here the land was nothing but the long fields of snow and the silent mountains and glaciers that stood in quiet contemplation as they had for thousands of years.

Through the howling gale and creaking ice, soon, the subtle sound of snow underfoot could be heard. "where are we?!" a young voice echoed

"You know where we are!" a second accompanied it. Older and grittier with experience.

"And you know what we're looking for!" a third said, wearier with age and almost silent as his voice was ripped away by the wind.

"Maybe but I don't know why I agreed to come with ya! I'd wager ain't no one been this far out north in centuries!" the younger voice said.

"Oh shut up and get over here I think I found it " the

older voice said. Out of the vale-like mist came a young boy, dressed in the brown furs of various animals, his rat-like face was nearly frozen because of the weather. He thought himself lucky he hadn't already lost a nose to the frostbite and thanked his bearskin cap which he clutched tightly to his head. His counterparts were older men, both with thick beards and stranded, matted hair. One had brown hair; the only thing that made him visible through the sheets of snow that blanketed all of them with a layer of thick frost, layering their fur garments and weighing them down.

"That ain't it!" the young boy shouted, his voice swelling around him.

"It's the closest we're gonna get for today, make a move, now!" the oldest voice of the gray ranger shrieked.

Their gaze was carried to a massive glacier with a small cut out in its bottom-center, barely visible because of the biting flakes that hit their eyes and withered their skin. Life times out in the snow and cold of the frozen continent of Antara hadn't improved their temperaments but as rangers, as was the occupation of so many in the snow wastes, they were the greatest navigators their land had produced, able to tell just where they were, knowing every glacier, every ice mound and frosted mountain, yet this one time in any of their recollections were they clueless as to their location. Never had any of their dwindling numbers ventured so far north in all the thousands of long, grueling years their people had called the harsh continent home. "We need to find shelter, this blizzard'll kill us if we stay out in it any longer!" the old ranger croaked over the white out, his gray beard swaying in a frenzy.

As they approached the complex, they felt a sudden feeling of being watched, their eyes darting to see what was omitting the predatory sense. But once the three had reached the dark opening in the glacial wall, they relented and drove themselves to go in. Shelter from the wind promised more in reward than the sense of being eyed by some mysterious force.

Soon the cave was lit with the light of a campfire, its brightness reflecting off slippery, glass-like walls that glowed a soft blue in the fire light and sang like harp strings as they moved with the earth. All three rangers felt safer knowing that they were behind these walls of ice, carved beautifully. "I thought you said that the Great-Seer said we'd find something out here, what?" the young boy uttered to his superior. "You also said..." the boy was silenced by his better.

"I know what I said but that doesn't make me right!"

"You bet your arse it doesn't. We were supposed to wait for the other group to join us back down at Brittle Crag and we went ahead without them, just like you said and now look where we are: lost" the boy criticized, pointing a furry, gloved finger at the man. The two were ready to start arguing, after days of treading through ice and snow, finding nothing but half eaten animals and the cold to keep them company, their minds and bodies starved.

The middle ranger stood to the challenge, snow falling from his shoulders as he rose "lost or not, boy, question my methods again and you'll be walking back to Vaskuul with more than cold feet"

"Ah will both of you shut your mouths!" the elder shouted, his voice radiating around the cavern. "Get some sleep. We return to Vaskuul in the morning. The Great-Seer still wants his report. Something's certainly out there, I can feel it, have done since we left last month. This storm's lasted an unnatural amount of time for mid-year" he continued, lowering his head onto an ice-cold slab.

"Like what, exactly? Only thing we've seen are a few snow

bears and they were enough to divert us those few days" the younger challenged.

"Well snow bears would make a boy as green as you wet himself wouldn't they? But mark my words, boy: worse things dwell this far north. Our land, Antara, is an ancient one and many a dark and mysterious power has called it home in its time. There's nothing to say that power has diminished" the older one grumbled as he warmed his hands over the few licks of flame.

"You two are as crazy as you look if you believe these things. No wonder you spend so much time with the fishwives, I imagine they feel relieved to have found someone who talks more than they" the boy mocked.

"You won't be saying that when we *do* find something…or when something finds us"

"But we haven't found anything yet, " the boy moaned. Hearing the stories of his predecessors invigorated him to use his youth in search of mystery. The three were mere rangers but all of them knew the ancient tales of the great explorers of their people who trekked through the land of eternal winter never to be seen again.

"And we're not likely to, so shut up and sleep!" the eldest commanded with a cranky and weary voice. He tucked his old hands between his arms and shut his eyes.

The young boy and the other ranger looked at one another before also seating themselves as close to the fire as possible before turning in for the night.

The oldest ranger awoke a few hours later to find the makeshift campsite empty, with his two companions missing. Realizing, he quickly sprang to his fur covered feet, his breathing increasing as he arose. He looked down to see only flickering embers about the campfire, numbed by the freezing cold. However, the cave felt somewhat...colder. Not just from the lack of fire, but as if it had been made colder than it should have been as though something were forcing it to be. Driven by angst he proceeded deeper into the cavern, its darkness eating up the gray light from outside. Every step sounding like an avalanche in the frozen pit of the earth.

It felt like days, as the old ranger guided himself by just the glimmer of the black iced walls. He felt himself slip a few times, sliding further down, down into the dark. The further he skulked into the lair, the more he began to speculate as to the whereabouts of his friends: had they left him, had something happened to them whilst he slept or were they simply out scavenging for what little scrap of wood could be found around the frozen deserts.

As he thought to himself, the ranger suddenly realized that he had wandered in so far into the cave that everything was now pitch black. Occasionally he could hear the faint drip of melting ice coming from above him, though how high the roof must have been, the ranger was unsure. The room, however, felt spacious, like a void. Endless and cruel.

He began to panic even more now; how was he going to get home without his companions and even if he did, what would he say to his superior: The Great-Seer, residing in the frozen south of the continent in the largest settlement left to them by their ancestors: Vaskuul. Their pious rath would fall on him if he returned alone.

Suddenly the ranger felt his foot hit something hard. Not stone, it was too soft for stone, but too hard to be a bank of snow. The old man turned his sweat soaked head downwards to see a shape, more like a bundle. It's black form, almost human-like. At its sight, the ranger froze, fear in his eyes and rippling through his old body. Never before did he remember being this afraid in all his many and long years. He turned to the light, up at the top of the cavern and as he did, he noticed something. A reflection on the glassy wall. The old ranger could see himself in the mirrored wall and behind him, peering from the shadows. Their bodies contorted. The bodies of the other two rangers. In the ice the old man could see the young boy had had his jaw completely wrenched from its socket and the other ranger lay next to him, his skin white from the cold, blood dripping from the corner of his mouth, both of them stared at the eldest with soulless, white eyes. Both appeared to have been dispatched together and by something both powerful enough to take on two able bodied and hardened rangers and something terrible enough to drive a face of pure terror into their final expressions.

The last living ranger gasped as he bolted for the exit, his footsteps echoing behind him. As did another sound--guttural and disembodied as it stirred. But the running of the man was in pathetic vain as he felt himself stop. He couldn't move his legs, though not of his own volition. He had simply froze. He felt this magic grasp hold of him and turn him round and that was when he saw it. A figure. At Least he thought it so as it pulled itself out of the darkness into the gray. It was tall, taller than any man he'd ever seen. Clad in old, ancient armor, undamaged in its silvery look. Its epaulets were scaled, wrought, iron made to be rigid and violent and by powers unknown to the world since the first days and draped over the armor was a knotted, gray cloak and hood that had withered in ages past, they blew in the draft as pale flags. The armor covered all but what would have been the front of the thing's face. But there was no face. Least no human face. Perhaps it had once been a man or something representing one, judging from its cold, ashy, gray skin that clung to an almost skeletal face, gaunt and unchanging. Void of any sign of human emotion. It watched him for a moment, towering over him. And the eyes: two reflective, black, stones set in its skull with glimmering, yellow pupils at their center and dead, blue, veins stretched from around those eyes to the wraith's cheeks. A sight that stopped the old ranger from breathing for just a second. Its presence was cloaked in a dark and ancient magic and it boasted a malicious smirk barely noticeable. It twisted the fingers on its metal gloves in glee at the new prey that wandered in its lair.

The old man screamed, unable to do anything else. He watched as it drew a sword from a decorative sheath. It was long and sharp, serrated down both sides of the blade, perfectly crafted for such a twisted and powerful thing that held it. The saber must have been the same height as an average man though much older than the race of men themselves.

The ranger could do nothing as his eyes followed the blade down and the cave was filled with the noise of cold steel slicing flesh. Till all fell silent as the snowflakes landed. The cave floor dashed with blood.

Finished with his three distractions, The Great One began walking with stern and ordered steps out of the cave that had been his ancient fane for centuries come and go. His metallic feet leading him with methodical thuds to the entrance, his dark armor shimmering like silver in the sun. Upon his approach to the outside world the wind suddenly picked up, blowing a gale and launching flakes of snow in every direction. The weather had come to life.

When the creature found its way to the frozen desert above ground, he turned his featureless face up to the sky and froze, almost examining it: the gray noon clouds holding back the pale sunlight. Then, with one sudden movement, he threw his hands into the air, the great long, metal nails that had been grafted onto the gloves poked into the wind, bending it to his will. For a moment all stood silent. Until. A large rumble came from the glaciers, not one, but all of them for miles around began to rumble and produce faint cracks. The frozen earth moved its cold bones and shuddered as it awoke. The shuddering stopped and the ground stood still once again, as if nothing had happened. Then, from the frozen deep, a boney hand smashed through the ice and snow, grasping for something to pull, as if drowning below. This repeated itself until there were at least several thousand hands pulling their masters back into the cold world, awakened from icy slumber. Eventually the hands showed themselves to be attached to people, just not ones of the living. Some looked almost human, with stretched gray skin and withered hair, their faces bleached white by the sun, eyes gray and glassy: dead. Others were just skeletons, hollow and gaunt.

The land became a series of moans and distorted groans until every single body had been pulled from the mass grave. Again they went silent and all turned their twisted heads to their master, who raised a single armored finger to the rolling white hills of ice beyond them. With no horn to signal them, not even a voice to call, they began to march, with centuries old axes and swords in their hands, well preserved from being entombed in the ice. The Overlord too followed behind his army, his tattered cloak trailing behind him. His otherworldly armor, engraved with dark and odd symbols, clacked together as an unliving army began their march.

Far across the cold and empty plains of Antara, hundreds

of miles from the awakening, sat Jorrvanskar. The small settlement of the Antaran people. Crafted from wood and thatch hay, its buildings were as their people were: simplistic, sturdy and tested. At the center of Jorrvanskar, built into a small hill, was the temple of The All-Maker, the only construct of stone found in most of the town. Within its cold and ancient walls braziers and fires flickered gently within the temple. At the base of the largest of them lay an elderly man, sleeping under the flames. It was as if a force unseen jolted him from sleep as he shook with fear and terror as it became clear across his face, the echoes of his deep breathing shrilling around the old, cold ruin he was in. His homely blue eyes grew wide as he awoke, stretching across his wrinkled and chubby cheeks, he brushed his hair off his face and itched his long ,white, beard that ran to his chest. Alone he was in the temple, he realized as he sat up, yet it did nothing to stop him from frantically whispering to himself "it's started"

He rose to his feet, struggling to overcome the weight of his fur and pelted clothes. The old soothsayer made a dash for the ancient doors of the temple, reaching out to grasp the large stone rings that acted as handles to the carved doors. Heaving the massive clumps of stone that scraped along the cobbled floor, nearly slipping on the small and secretive black ice that he had almost become used to from his many years in the temple; considering both the stone and ice of the temple were confidants of his, often confiding to himself, letting the walls listen to his doubts.

outside he could hear the wind bitterly blowing on its stone. Thrusting the doors open, revealing the settlement of Jorrvanskar in its limited detail. An insignificant number of hay-wood huts dotted the interior of the settlement, lit by small campfires inside, creating the illusion of warmth in such a cold, remote place. Beyond the walls of thick logs, tipped sharply, was nothing but a solid, flat surface of snow. The hamlet held no more than a few families and even fewer resources between them. A few meagre gardens of ice moss that grew from the cracked and crumbled soil, frozen with the weather, it was food cultivated by the Antarans and only found in the holds of their people. The old man recognised a man he knew as one of the watchmen ``get the women and children!" he cried with a raspy tone, anger and fear mashed into one. "Winds have arisen, we need to make for Vaskuul! Jorrvanskar is already lost! Vaskuul is the only refuge now!" he added, approaching the watchman like a madman.

Around him the small handful of grim looking women and half-starved children stared at their leader; one of the All-Seer's assigned to guide and protect their people, as the All-Seers of Vaskuul had done for thousands of years. They were the world's oldest and, depending on who you asked, most respected soothsayers in the world. This one: Gravis, was the oldest among their ranks, the only one not changed by lingering age.

The watchman paused for a while, weighing the credibility of his friend's proposal. This was their home, one that had stood for hundreds of years, never shaken by time or disaster, to leave it would bring shame. Relenting, the Watchman turned to the perplexed people ``gather your things folks! Make for the gates!" he ordered loudly but not frantically enough to scare the people. Quickly, they began to bustle and gather food--ice moss, stale bread and salted fish and suddenly jugs of milk preserved in the ice came popping up out of nowhere by the hutwives, though soon panic began to set in as people pushed and shoved their way past one another and through the wooden settlement gates. People were shouting and several small children were crying as their mothers picked them up, tucking them to their breasts or pulling hoods over their delicate heads. Within minutes the settlement's puny populace had formed a gathering just outside the confines of the bending wooden walls. Once they had all gone Gravis stood just outside the stone temple, alone. The old man looked at the settlement: already empty and abandoned in a matter of minutes. Its people left, though they didn't know why but Gravis did, or at least suspected. Something was coming for all of them, a threat colder than any winter and darker than any night. He looked back at the desolate huts, fires still burning inside them, the temple looked as lifeless as ever before, with its priest gone. It was no temple of great stature, or filled with riches or fine tapestries to their god as the All Maker would not wish for such lavishness but the stones and mossy steps, the cracked wooden chairs as old as Gravis himself and the brazier at the center, the source of Gravis ability as an All-Seer. But as All-Seer of the All Maker, Gravis had to lead them to the relative safety the wilderness could provide.

"Gravis!" the watchman shouted, at the threshold of the gates "come on! We need to leave, it's a two week 'n half trek to Vaskuul. Let's go my friend" he added as he approached Gravis and wrapped his fur covered arm gently around the elder as they began to re-join the group. As Gravis looked back one last time as an ice-cold tear ran down his face. Panic had momentarily subsided and calm was allowed. The collection of people parted gently, unraveling, as their spiritual leader, one of whom was held with great trust, who had raised half the people in the colony, drifted through them. The old man was almost as confused as his people, he didn't know what to think, everything had happened so fast. But he had been warned by his own teachers, decades before, what such a premonition warranted. Written by the first settlers of the land, those who followed the All Maker and took it upon themselves the great duty of lying watch for such a perverted return.

Gravis and the watchman both turned around and looked at

their solemn people, now at the mercy of the biting cold and wind that whipped up the snow in great mounds and flung it at anything in its path. They had once been protected by the thick, wooden walls of their settlement, built to protect them from such a thing and for even those like the elders, it was the first time many had ventured so far from their home-- sitting out alone on a frozen desert. The people of such places had known nothing other than those curved walls, the adults were as confused now as the children, wandering aimlessly in a world unfathomed.

Gravis raised his hands in the air, like in one of his sermons that he would offer to those at the temple to enlighten them to how best to live from the land as their Lord wished. His fur braces covering everything but his finger ends, making them numb and painful in the wind of the land of eternal winter.

"We have to make for Vaskuul, our capital!" Gravis uttered loudly, competing with the great wind for dominion "We have to warn them, we have to get word out. Something is coming! I have seen it this very day! Just as the scrolls have foretold! Something within me knows this, feels it too, in my heart! We need to be ready and prepared for when it does! This is the duty of the All-Seers and a test from the All Maker! It is his world that this power threatens, his people who will be struck first! Keep strong and remain in the All Maker and we shall find the way! Come!" The All-Seer issued as he turned away, looking into the white out--hiding the vastness of Antara and the emptiness of its lands. Gravis breathed deeply, the frozen air filling his lungs with their perfume of ice.

Thinking hard and fast, Gravis nodded to the watchman who ushered all the people to follow him. And, like a sheep following its shepard, the people shuffled behind Gravis as he led them out into the storm that seemed to consume the light of the sun, leaving the population of Jorrvanskar in a permanent twilight.

As they all trekked through the snow that rose almost to the adult's kneecaps and almost buried some of the smaller children, the watchman said to Gravis in confidence "I do hope you're right about this old man. These people barely have anything to their names except the clothes on their backs, we can't leave our home over nothing, we may not return. I've seen some of the toughest most experienced rangers get swallowed up by this place"

Gravis looked at his friend, brushing the final nostalgic tear away as he smiled at the watchman's concerned remark. "We need to get to Vaskuul, the colder months are approaching and the All-Seers have had the vision, just as the old scrolls said. If it is what is to be believed then no axe or sword will protect us" Gravis answered, not worrying if anyone could hear them because of the howling gale encompassing them.

"Well. You've had 'the vision'. You should hope Fanatiker and the other All-Seer's have"

"I have every confidence that Fanatiker will have already had the vision, he is the master of our order, I wouldn't be surprised if an envoy is already on its way. But we need to leave Jorrvanskar, it's not safe here, not anymore. It's now the furthest northern settlement ever since Hjolm burned last winter. Which means it will be the first hit" Gravis kindly replied to his friend's doubt.

"Everywhere in Antara is dangerous. Why by the All Maker's name did we come here all those thousands of years ago?!" the watchman cursed to the wind and land.

Gravis smiled, pulling a fur hood over his head as the gale intensified "to stop the thing we're running from now."

The watchman's face turned to fear as he heard the grim sentence. All children of Antara had heard the tales of the first great men who discovered the mass of ice and snow thousands of years ago and in discovering the frozen continent, also found strange and untouched things on their exploration, things that lead to the founding of the mysterious All-Seers, other things that consumed some of these great men and left them...altered. Or so the story has been told for thousands of years.

The watchman scowled off into the wall of mist and snow, murmuring, "it's a long way to Vaskuul and the sun seems to be setting faster now. We'll only have a few hours per day"

"Then make them count" Gravis grumbled as the two of them led their own through the raging storm. With miles between Vaskuul: Antara's religious capital and headquarters of the All-Seers, they now faced the perilous weather and beasts of their dangerous, frozen continent.

Chapter 2-Kingsport

Far to the south-western region of the world, hundreds of miles away from the frozen wastes of Antara and separated by the Galenic Ocean, lay the mighty and arguably most precious and important continent in the far-reaching world of Manaheim: Kond. And at its heart, along the eastern coast, the capital city of Kingsport lay in packed layers. Touched by the Bay Of Gales on the east that bled out to the Sea of Swords and boxed in by large, open fields and a ridge to the north and west that spliced the early rising sunlight through its peaks. Ever did light beat down on Kingsport and it was only through the blessings of one of their eight Divines, Arcturus, that they received any rain at all for the capitol was warm and humid almost all year.

Out across the plains surrounding the city, farms and small huts lay dotted behind a small stone wall that had crumbled and withered to almost the size of a hedge, there the city's poorest would wander in drunken stupors to harass the local miller and farmers. A layer behind, continuing across the Summerplains to the foot of its only hill was the housing districts, the largest portion of the city. White stone making the hundreds of houses that encircled the city, topped with tanned tiles, sliding off their roofs. Ramparts and towers, houses and cramped streets all comprised together, forming a noisy and vibrant city.

At the very summit of the capitol, at the top of the hill was The Kings Keep itself, taller than any other building on the continent (except for the mysterious Black Vigil on the borders of the northern realm. Whose creator is not known) with its many stone towers rising high into the clouds like crystalline knives. For the keep had been made by the well paid and now extinct artisans of Ebon, who had combined into the regular stone and mortar, alabaster and a fine yellow moonstone, native to their own island, which gave the keep an almost sleek, golden look against the sun.

The way to The Kings Keep was by a long and winding road that hugged the hill as it ran around it, with houses placed along the road on either side of its white cobble's. Into the hill itself, shop stalls and small markets had been hitched into and dug into its sides and stretching half-way down the mainstreet, from the bottom of the keep to the main gate of the first wall.

Never was the city quiet as children laughed and cried in houses and animals such as sheep, goats, dogs and the occasional cow turned the market into a haven of noise. Along where the walls to the central city were highest, beggars sat in its shadows, under tents of old rags, keeping them safe from the boiling sun that focused on the city and turned it into a gleaming metropolis of wood and stone and steel, though on the hottest days, producing a vile smell of the city's sewage that ran into the sea gulf.

As Capital of the eight realms and the governing body of the continent, it acted as the seat of the High King as it had for nearly two thousand years. But many things had changed in the order of Kingsport, a new family sat on The Gilded Throne and it had changed the course of all eight realms. For better or worse. A particularly new line had taken refuge in the painted halls of the keep, in place of one that had just been vanquished; the Quarthands. The last relics of the isle of Kydrim and the only rulers the realms had ever known in a united fashion. Their final days were rather shrewdly played out as after the death and killing of its last High King, Morryg, the realms had fallen into the pits of civil war for the following three years.

Reaping the bounties of his civil war, overlooking his city from the terrace of an open room, the new High King stood. Six years he had reigned, three of them being in the war because of his 'wrongful' ascension after the death of his predecessor. There he stood, his long black hair falling in thick strands and cut at shoulder length, his face was sharp and slim with a perfectly trimmed, black goatee over his thin lips that always seemed to curl into a malicious smirk. His blue eyes were just as piercing and always narrowed when watching the hundreds of thousands of people below him in the city, as he often did in times of boredom or depression. His golden epaulets shimmered like the belly of a proud fish, frolicking in the free waters and his tunic and jacket of a fine woven red moved effortlessly with every turn.

The High King: Cythees, was always clad in semi armored clothes. A chestplate over a fine, leather doublet was his usual look and helped remind himself of his self anointed position and others of how few a battle he'd actually fought. Cythees smiled before returning inside to the shade of the room, where a long table of dark brown oak lay. On one of the carved chairs to the table sat a woman, as youthful as Cythees. She was the Queen consort; Saura, young and glamorous as were most of the women of her house.

Her hair was as black as her husbands, curled and running down to her waist and holding a small silver tiara on her head. Her face was a delicate thing, but deceptive, though she may have been beautiful, her eyes were cruelty hidden behind false benevolence. They were the eyes of a cat, slick and seductive but uncaring and vengeful. Her violet dress fell down past her feet, as it trailed behind her when she walked. At her neck was a short silver necklace with a rearing horse embossed on it: the sigil of her family.

The Queen sat, legs crossed as she smiled at Cythees as he strode in, yet as soon as the High King's eyes left hers, her face dropped as she demurred. Cythees gullibly adored Saura and she, in turn, extended her tolerance for him, despite both being young, stupidly rich and children of southern Konds most powerful houses: Carrsore and Monthell. Their marriage was arranged and far from a love-filled one.

"It's nice, isn't it?" Cythees asked as he sat at the head of the table, reaching for a flagon and pouring from it firebrand Wine, his favorite, into a goblet.

"What is?" Saura asked in return as she arose and briskly strutted over to the flagon and Cythees and poured herself a drink as well, sipping it gently "the fact that we've managed to enjoy three years of peace without war, the beggars are in a minority and the realms are in stability? Or because you're married to the most beautiful woman in all eight realms?" she added, playfully sitting on the High Kings lap. She ran her fingers through the hair on the side of his head as she gazed with familiar and seductive eyes and smirked as did her King. He enjoyed her enough that he couldn't see her aversion for him.

"Maybe a bit of both" Cythees grinned whilst trying to fondle at her dress. He came from a fine line of Kings, his own father was King of The Fold, a kingdom far to the south and his time as heir to that realm had turned him. Molded him into a tool of terrible need that was completed with his ascension, not as King of one realm, but as High King of all of them.

"You must be very proud, my King," Saura said, stroking her husband's facial hair before pulling herself off him. "Eight realms finally united under the eagle of Monthell and horse of Carrsore" Saura said as she pulled a fine, silk curtain back, peeking through it to the city below, as if being wary of being spotted.

Cythees joined her, pressing himself against her, in turn pressing her front against the stone archway. "Now it's just a matter of keeping the realms in line. They owe peace, their lives to us. War makes us all heroes in the people's eyes" Cythees stated wishfully. Wrapping his hands tightly round Saura's waist.

Trying to turn the conversation, Saura whispered seductively "there's a council meeting in the throne room soon, you should be there"

"I don't want to be there, I want to stay here, in this room…with you" Cythees returned, kissing Saura's neck tenderly. The Queen spun around to face the meticulous and persistent High King "Go, Cythees. The realms need their High King and matters need resolving. I can wait. I'm as resourceful as I am discrete" she said, more sternly in her demeanor. Cythees smiled but didn't move.

Just then, from the large red doors of the room, came a knock. Both Saura and Cythees looked at the door "come in" Saura said, at that exact same time, Cythees snapped "Go away!"

The door opened to reveal an elderly man, late fifties, with a long gray beard running down to his chest and brushed as finely as a horse's mane. The hair on his head was just as gray and ran past his shoulders in messy dreads. He wore the signature Monthell armor of black iron plate held together with red belts and buckles, all very expensive looking and refined. He rested his left hand on the pommel of his sheathed sword as he very respectively poked his head into the room "your majesty, my Queen" he greeted, bowing his head "there is a visitor for you in the throne room and the council will be convening soon"

"Already? By the Divines" Cythees sulked, letting go of Saura as he approached the old knight "come Sir Kellor. Let us entertain this guest" the High King sarcastically said as he glanced at Saura once more, before the gray knight, Sir Kellor, and the Monthell Guard with him led the High King to the throne room, at the center of the rising keep.

When the High King and his escorts arrived at the throne room the great, twin doors were wretched forward, creaking and echoing around the spacious hall. The entire room was composed of white quartz, from the mighty pillars that held the arches and roof up, to the floor that reflected dim phantoms, day or night. On each side of the lofty room were four massive glass windows that leaked sunlight through them, bathing the room in a subtle white glimmer. With the fifth window being above the head of the throne and, as fine as any painting, depicted the first High King, the Father of Kond and the Master To The Realms: Roadarr Quarthand. In the stone beams above him, Cythees looked up to see the flag of House Monthell: a golden eagle mightily spreading its wings across a red field.

Below them sat the Gilded Throne itself, supposedly constructed and melted down from a captured idol of the western natives Roadarr had taken during his campaign though other tales told it as being the melted crowns of the Kings and rulers Roadarr defeated and from them he inserted his victories into the throne. Though, since being a boy, Cythees had heard other stories of how it was made-- from the coins that were given to Roadarr as tribute or dowry to leave Kond before his war for unity began. Though forged from a metal as tough as ill-gotten gold, the throne was masterfully crafted, perfectly cut and refined. There were no indents or chips. Its broad and thick armrests were lined with gold and at its top center were three jewels held in the delicate hands of finely carved idols of two women wreathed in flowers and tapestries. They were gargantuan; a large diamond, the same size as a child's skull and on either side of it were two amethysts, just as large.

Despite the cold and hard feel of gold and stone on his back Cythees could never get tired of sitting on it, having to climb steps that lifted the throne up appealed to his indolence. It gave sight over the entire room, and from his perch, the High King oversaw all. Cythees climbed the steps, noticing the several Kings Watch standing around the throne, their armor was silver, from helm to boot. These guardians of the throne had stood watchful over the High Kings of Kond for nearly two thousand years, their order as old as the palace they protected. Cythees could see on their backs--a red cloak with a golden eagle spread across.

"Your grace" the royal attendant greeted as he humbly bowed at the throne and held, with both hands, a fine red cushion, its yellow tassels swaying from the weight of the crown that rested in the silk. The High King's eyes lit up like a child in blissful dim-wittedness as he pulled the crown off its holder and nestled it in his hair. A golden crown; a sapphire in its center with two rubies on either side. His crown. He decreed another to be fashioned from his home of The Forge. He could never have worn the Crown of Morryg II, the man he himself had slain in those halls six years hence and started a civil war to keep.

"Ah your majesty! I did wonder if you would be joining us this morning!" a youthful and wise voice echoed from the doors. It came from the High King's steward: a young and handsome man. He confidently strode down the steps of the throne room, leading the same path as Cythees had. His hair was a fine blonde, short and perfectly combed, with a few strands reaching from his scalp to his black eyebrows. His eyes were small and serpent like, green in color and sharp in demeanor and were the perfect fit for his slender face. On his body was a long jacket of dark green silk with its clips and studs in the shape of writhing snakes. "Darian" the High King hailed.

Darian Darianth; the High King's steward, had served the throne almost his entire life. As had every Darianth before him; a house sworn in service as stewards to the keeper of the throne. "I assure you, your majesty, I can handle matters here perfectly on my own. Though, of course, I would never voluntarily turn down your presence" Darian said, smiling at the King when he glanced at him and returning his face to disgust when not as though a bug of sorts had landed crudely next to him.

"I'm sure you could, however, whether things would be handled in your own vision or of mine would be what concerns me" Cythees returned, clairvoyant to the methods of his councilor.

Cythees looked around the throne room inquisitively "well?" he pondered.

"What troubles you, sire?" Darian asked as he stepped up to the throne.

"Send in this visitor, let me see what menial task I have to attend to" the High King smirked as Darian beckoned the Kings Watch to open the doors once again. The silver fettered knights swung open the great doors and when they did Cythees mouth fell from its smirk to a more stern expression.

Darian hailed the person who walked in " King Corvus Monthell, Lord of The Forge and King of the realm of The Fold" as a tall and elderly man strutted down the quartz steps. He was escorted by two Monthell guards, their steel armor covered by the red drapes of their house. They held great swords in their hands, their sharpened and deadly tips pointing to the roof. The man they escorted in was Corvus Monthell; the father of Cythees and the true power of both house Monthell and the richest man in all eight realms.

Corvus was a broad-shouldered man, in his late sixties, with a round and balding head with hair as white as bone. His face however was barely wrinkled, save for under his blue eyes and his clean-shaven chin. Over the blood red gambeson that he wore was a bronze sash pinned by a broach in the shape of an eagle. His black boots echoed around the room as he approached his son, a stern and foreboding expression on his face.

Cythees said nothing to him until his father had stopped at the foot of the few stairs to the throne. A few awkward seconds of silence ensued before Cythees was the first to speak "father...a pleasant surprise" the High King uttered, sitting arrogantly in his power. He adjusted himself in his seat His father simply scowled before he uttered "The last time I saw you was three years ago. At the victory feast. Three. Years it's been. Which is ironic as since then you've still been more than pleased to accept the funding that the Forge has always supplied the capital and yet for all I have given him, my son does not speak to me" His voice was low, calm and cold.

Cythees sat back and smiled at his father's implication "Well I do apologize for my absence, ruling the realms takes up much of my time" the High King crudely answered.

"Your advisors and councilmen rule the realms in your absence. I know of your daily activities and they are few besides hunting, sparring and cavorting whilst Gods only know who streams into the realms. We are open and vulnerable" Corvus said.

"How long do you plan on staying in the capital?" Cythees asked, ignoring the mention of refugees in the northern realm.

"As long as it is needed!" Corvus spoke, raising his tone "your sister was wise enough to do as she was bid and came here with her husband. I had hoped the two of you combined would be enough to keep the realms in relative control out here. Now look at both of you: she, a waste and you, a craven. She has one son, unmarried, all alone and her head constantly in the clouds. You sit here in this palace all day whilst the realms look to their High King for naught" Corvus lectured his son.

"She's twenty-nine. That's young enough for most fat lords and obsessive bureaucrats. Why, half the men on the continent would give an arm to have her"

"And she has a son aged thirteen"

"I highly doubt that those fools would be slighted by the presence of another man's child. The world is overflowing with his ilk. Perhaps if you hadn't married her to that merchant when she was only fifteen, then maybe you could have used her now" Cythees retorted.

"Your sisters happiness is not my concern and fear not, when the time comes she will marry again" Corvus said, coldly and without pause "what she contributes...what all of you contribute to our family is the only thing that matters. We ourselves are but crude implements in the construction of this dynasty. There has never been a more crucial time for this family than now"

"How could I contribute more, father? I'm High King of Kond! The eight realms bow to me! I'm the keeper of the Gilded Throne! I'm the first of our line, I toppled a dynasty over a thousand years old. You were not even here the day I slew Morryg, the day I avenged the insults paid to us at court. I Am. By. All. Rights. A legend"

"In name not in practice" Corvus said sharply. "And I may not have been here the day you decided to kill him. I was busy ruling, and later, fighting in your war"

Cythees receded. Thinking himself immune to his fathers cruel words, in reality he was only spared them due to his station which Corvus was forced to respect. The High King steadied himself again.

"And what of these Antaran refugees?"

"We will talk about that alone " Corvus commanded, looking at the eight Kings Watch. The plated knights bowed to the High King and left the room, returning to the barrack towers. "That includes you two as well" urged the King of The Fold, looking firstly at Kellor and then Darian both on opposite sides of the throne. Kellor immediately bowed to Corvus first and then to the High King, Lord Darian smiled and slowly stepped down, watching Corvus the entire time with a smile of such falseness, it would have been impossible for one not to tell it was as such.

When both were out of the throne room and the great doors slammed shut and no unwanted ears listened, Corvus nodded his head towards the smaller meeting chambers at the back of the throne room, through a small door.

Cythees followed behind his father. They both walked into the council chamber, Cythees sitting down in one of the relaxing chairs that stood surrounding the circular table where many a boring and sleepy morning he'd been forced to gather there. His father, however, remained standing, gazing out of the open canopy, the morrow's sun shining on the city hundreds of feet below him.

Cythees stirred for a moment, leaning back into the extravagant cushions on the chair. "So why have you really returned father?" the King asked.

Corvus didn't immediately answer, instead he closed his eyes in annoyance. "You always told me you hated the capitol so why have you returned now?"

"Simply put: you're beginning to seem like a figurehead. There are whispers that I'm sure your friend, Lord Jazar, is aware of but has obscured them from you. The Lords and nobles are growing suspicious of your reclusiveness. I'm here to make sure the people stay in line and the nobles keep paying the taxes and the King's know who it is whose ruling them. The Divines gave me the foresight to see that you would need assistance in ruling, not to mention handling these refugees coming in from Antara for unknown reasons. Besides, it's come to my attention that King Toros Lenglore will be coming here to the capitol as well. No doubt to beg for his son to marry your sister and join The Highfelds with The Fold. I matter of which I must preside over" Corvus answered as he turned around and brought himself to sit down adjacent to his son.

"Let them have her. It gets her out of the capitol and out from under my nose. Let them marry, father, if the Lenglores want a wench give them one"

"Your remarks about your sister are unsavory so I'll pretend I haven't heard them" Corvus said dryly "Toros will also be bringing Gryff" he added.

Cythees face dropped at the mention of Lord Toros' bastard son. " Him? why?" the High King asked with a snarl. "Even a fool as Toros is, I should hope he puts more stock in his true born son, Curtis. Even if that is less than equivalent"

"Toros values his bastard son over his true son and I don't blame him, though I don't condone it. Gryff is young, semi-intelligent and good with a blade. Not to mention if his father has his way then he'll be the heir to The Highfelds before long, he is older. I suspect Curtis will be disinherited because of his…

affliction and Gryff will take his place" Corvus fathomed as he twiddled his old thumbs.

"And still it would not be the strangest thing that family has ever done" Cythees slandered, his disdain for the westerners abounded with every mention of their names for they had harrowed him for many years even before the civil war. The Lenglores were blood of the Rakers, unlike their fellow brethren of Kond who hailed from Kydrim, as most did, or from the east as renegades from an empire. The Rakers were of the older and darker ways and had worshiped darker powers once. As a keen student of the histories, Cythees knew this and despised their descendents.

"I imagine Saura will have something to say. He is her half-brother and supposed heir to the Highfelds, we must assume " the High King smirked at the idea of his wife getting annoyed and flustered or perhaps it was just the urge to see another more dire than himself.

Though Gryff's father was Toros Lenglore, he shared his mother with the Queen Consort. Their mother had met a violent end when Saura's father found out about her apparent adultery. The punishment he had bestowed upon his wife was one that had earned all Carrsore's more fear than even they were owed.

"And the other reason was this" Corvus said as he produced a small scroll from inside his pocket and tossed it towards Cythees who unraveled the parchment. From the seal on the scroll he could tell that it was from one of his father's spies. The High King mumbled the inscription to himself "the Blackbloods have been seen gathering near Wolfenrad" Cythees remained ignorant of what the information read as he looked at his father and raised his hands in confusion "is this supposed to mean something?" the High King asked petulantly as he threw the scroll halfway across the table, disregarding it. Corvus glared at his son's insolence as he slowly picked the scroll back up "of course it means something, you fool" he scolded, sounding as sharp as a searing blade. "The last time those brigands were active they became one of the leading causes of the civil war" Monthell explained coldly.

"That was a different High King, one reputed to be troubled and weakened with grief and who couldn't control his own mind at the end. Coward and devient that he was. Hence the whole reason I shoved a sword through his gut" Cythees patronizingly answered.

"Yes and the reason you were able to kill Morryg without all eight realms turning against you was because he was already perceived as weak before his death and thus had already earned himself enemies at court. Your sword was what ended his reign but his slandering of us was what killed him and a High King without loyalty from his subjects is a pyre without fuel. Six years ago the Blackbloods raided from Easthelm to The Fold, Morrygs incompetence in dealing with them was his first mistake which started a series of others" Corvus began to grow agitated as he ranted, his cheeks slowly turning red.

"If you make the same mistake then you'll follow his path, one that will lead to this family's downfall. Something that, as long as I'm living, will not happen" Cythees could see in his father's blue eyes the worry of what would happen to the newly founded dynasty of the Monthells. His father was obsessed and fully dedicated to the preservation of his family's power and guarded it fiercely.

Whatever Cythees did read in his father's eyes was enough to make him recognise the gravity of the potential situation. Cythees nodded in understanding. "We need to be careful, now more than ever, many will be weighing options in their hands and all those options will soon lead to us. They are just waiting and the moment they smell blood in the water. We are the ruling power of the whole continent, but power can fall as easily as the people who wield it. Now we have to deal with all our enemies, the ones in the shadows and the ones in the light and they will come. The eagle shares the sky with no one" Corvus uttered onto his son as he quickly arose from his seat. "Oh, and one more thing" Corvus remarked, pointing a finger at his son. Cythees leaned forward, listening.

"These Antaran refugees who seem to be pouring into the Winterlands. That has to stop, surely, you're capable of asserting enough control over the Forresters to tell them to close the borders, no more refugees into the country. Permanently. If they have a problem they can sort it out in their own time and on their own lands. I won't tolerate foreigners. Set light to the ships if we have to" Corvus added casually. Cythees stayed seated as he watched his father swing open the door, and without pause, remarked "I don't know, father. Do you think I can? Or do I lack the required amount of propriety and sense of earnestness that your favorite child has?"

King Corvus turned with a stale expression of disappointment "It is true Christen brings more value, more so than the rest of you and had he been my first born the realms may have already been in our yolk. Instead the Divines made me wade through a pretentious and spoilt first born, a rebellious and defiant second son, and then a self-deluded daughter before I got to Christen. But we all have a purpose to serve in the survival of this family, non now more so than you" the same monotone and rumbling voice that Cythees remembered in the many lectures as a child spoke to him now like a phantom brought back to memory. "Nothing I ever do will earn your favor, will it! Killing a High King, claiming the throne! I have always tried so hard but it is never enough for you" Cythees whined with his bottom lip almost touching the table. Corvus only soured in response before slamming the door to the council chambers.

**

As noon began to reach its end, elsewhere in the Kings Keep, in a courtyard of sand, two tourney knights were sparing. Their claymores swinging in the dying sunlight that was sinking beneath the waves of the port and barely rising over the high walls of the Kings Keep. As they fought in the arena, kicking up dust and sand as they swung. Unbeknownst to them, they were being watched from a nearby bench by someone, a boy. He sat, his head resting on the palm of his hand, nearly bored by the knights who fought more for show than to kill or maim which bored the youth who had always wished to see the real violence of battle, his mind sometimes played on it in idle boredom but was always cautioned and warded off by the tender words of his mother.

Eventually one of the knights flung the other to the ground, who moaned as the weight of his armor fell on him. The young boy: a squire for the knights arose when his master beckoned him "we're finished now Martis. I've had this poor sod. Grab our gear" the victorious knight ordered the boy.

At age fourteen Martis was a squire for lowly knights who fought for the pleasure of the Kings, it would have been a fitting position for any other boy, but, like the High King himself, Martis was a Monthell; the distained nephew of Cythees, forced to pack up the swords and spears of fatigued jousters every day.

Martis went about collecting the wares of the knights. He quickly assembled most of them and was just about to pick up the last sword, but before his hand could clasp the hilt a familiar voice came from behind. "I thought you'd be swinging one yourself by now" the jovial voice exclaimed. Martis turned and saw the captain of the guard; Sir Kellor. "Don't you have a job to do?" Martis joked as he hugged Kellor.

"I thought my uncle…his majesty, would still enjoy you being under his thumb"

"He always has, from the time he was a boy. The only instruction he ever listened to was matters of swordplay. Nowadays, though, your uncle's uses for me are running thin. So I find myself looking for other things to do" the old and more experienced knight retorted regretfully. Martis sniggered "You must be running low on a challenge if you've come to me, a fourteen-year-old squire, hardly a challenge for the slayer of Zerek" Martis sarcastically said.

"Ha, that was a long time ago, son. I was a young man when I killed that poor bastard. My legend seems to have faded along with me but it's for the best, I suppose. Youth yields to wisdom, in the end. I'm just not sure of how wise I am for it. Wise enough though to spend my days watching over the heirs of The Forge"

"That's not me. I'll never be regarded as heir to anything so long as my uncle has his way" Martis said, his voice lowering into a moan, though he didn't desire the throne at all, Martis was always reminded by his uncle about his place in the world: a squire boy and nothing more.

"That may be so, but the line of lineage always starts and ends with children and you are your mother's son, are you not?" Kellor smiled as he picked up one of the dull sparring swords for himself and threw another at Martis, who shook his head "you know I can never win" he cursed.

"Well, perhaps thirty or so years as captain of the Monthell guard has left me a bit stiff today" Kellor uttered as he raised his sword to his shoulder. Both the blonde-haired boy and the gray knight smiled as they began. Martis had gotten quicker, striking for Kellor's head and legs, swinging hard, but in due time, becoming weedy and fatigued. The two moved with each other, the old man easily keeping up with the youngsters footing. Kellor soon saw an opportunity, without even breaking a sweat. Easily disarming the younger Monthell and taking his legs from underneath him, leaving Martis in the dirt.

Kellor stood over the boy, smiling warmly "not bad" he said as he lowered the tip of the sword to Martis throat "but not good either" he joked, prompting an annoyed response from Martis who swung, almost taking the great knight by surprise. Martis got back up and swung again, narrowly missing Kellor who giggled, a strange noise coming from a man who usually kept a calm and almost stone-like demeanor. Still, however, Martis was again thrown to the ground, this time accepting the hand Kellor offered him. "You're getting better," Sir Kellor reassured Martis, who huffed. "Go on, grab your stuff and we'll…" Kellor didn't finish as something caught his eye; a woman in a fine red dress, strutting towards the two. Martis caught sight of her as well "mother? Oh great" the boy said sarcastically, getting a nudge in the shoulder from Kellor.

Martis' mother; Eleana. approached them with great steps. Her long and curly brown hair blustered in the wind. Yet still did the woman look ever so elegant with sharp and intelligent blue eyes bordered by thin and slick brows. She always wore two strands of her curled hair down the sides of her face and the rest tied or in a braid down past her shoulders. Her slim body was contained in a flowing, red dress down to her feet, held in place by the strings and bows of a fine, white corset. She hiked up her skirt as she climbed the few steps to the ring "I thought I told you, no more sparring, Martis Monthell" Lady Eleana scolded her son, shooting a disapproving look at Kellor whom she knew was his main enabler.

"It was just a small fight mother. I'm not always going to be a squire you know, no matter how much you wish it were so" Martis argued. He quickly read the look of both love and displeasure from his mother.

"Whether I want it or not is completely irrelevant, being a knight is not going to be part of your destiny" Eleana said as she put a calm and stern hand on her son's shoulder. "And I thought I told you not to encourage him," Eleana said, turning to her friend. Kellor shrugged, though Eleana was his sworn mistress, both shared a less-than-serious attitude to most of everything.

"The boy has a point, my Lady. He cannot be expected to be a boy forever, most common boys his age are already training to be some noble lords' soldiers now or have at least been shown lifes true colors. I should know " Kellor announced as he patted Eleana's shoulder.

The young mother smiled at her old friend, one she had known since she herself was a girl. She put a hand on him and then turned her motherly attention to her son, pinching his cheek which Martis quickly swatted away "you understand that all I want from you is the sense to go out into the world and know what you want to be, not some lowly knight and certainly not a sailor.." She was cut off when Martis interjected.

"Wasn't father a sailor?"

Eleana looked at Kellor, the two glancing at one another, as if the question Martis had posed was some form of dreadful insult to the both of them.

"Exactly why I don't wish you to become one. Your happiness is all I want in this world. We mothers want nothing more than for our children to be blessed. All the more if we can bestow those blessings on them ourselves " Eleana smiled warmly.

Martis nodded in submission. His mother: a woman he loved more than anything else in the world, he had only ever known her. For his supposed sailor of a father he had never met was only a fixation for his own mind but he knew not to mention him often as it seemed to draw horrid responses from most of the Monthell family--this phantom whom he'd never met seemed a curse to his kin.

"Yes mother"

"Then go on. Back to your chambers. I'll see if the cook has any of that stew left" Eleana said, trying to persuade her son, both their eyes never leaving each other.

Martis grabbed the remainder of the swords, placed them at the side of the training ring and left, the sun setting on his back, radiating off his red training tunic. He always felt the grandeur of the palace, rising miles and miles above him in its titanic fashion. Martis could feel its goliath presence as one of the largest buildings in the known world and one that reduced simple people to tiny specks.

Once the boy had left ears length, his mother turned to Kellor "what am I gonna do with him?" she asked her councilor as she looked out across the bay, the city's people and houses reaching out to her, just down the hill. Here she had dwelt for many years, moving into a manor house not far from the Kings Keep, even long before her brother had claimed the throne.

"You don't need to do anything with him. He's a boy, and a lucky one at that. He's born into the most powerful house in all eight realms, he has the privilege of opportunity, he has a good heart and he's trying to carve out his own destiny with it. Let him. Most boys his age are already sowing the fields of some Lord or King who couldn't care whether they live or die. He isn't the heir, not to the high crown or the ruby crown but he can still do something with himself" Kellor reasoned, standing loyally behind his young mistress with both arms crossed behind his back.

"I just hope he doesn't turn out like Drake; they seem to act just alike sometimes. And I haven't seen Drake in years. My own brother. I don't know if he's alive or dead all the while he'll probably be off chasing some whisper of adventure in the far flung edges of the world" Eleana said, closing her eyes as the sun finally left the bay, covering the Capitol in a subtle glow as its light ducked beneath the waves.

"Your brother Drake is far from the worst of your siblings, My Lady. I have served your house for thirty years and out of the four of you, you and Drake were the only ones who wanted something different than what was expected of the both of you. Young Martis is no different. Some of us are just meant to choose an alternate path. The more you try to stop him the more he'll crave it" the old knight said gruffly.

Eleana quickly smiled at her friend's council and turned to face him. "I remember when I first came here to the capitol as a girl. I was petrified. My father brought me with him during a council meeting of High King Isen" she said, slowly and barely above a whisper as she stroked her hand across one of the plant pots hanging on the terrace ledge. "Ha. Isen, one of the best High Kings I ever knew and the only High King most knew in their lifetime. Shame about his son. Though I suppose if Cythees hadn't killed him then he wouldn't be on the throne and, in tow, we wouldn't be here" Kellor retorted, trying to convince himself that Cythees was a benefit.

"Don't give my brother too much credit. He killed Morryg because he could, because his ego told him too. Ever since my father brought him to the capital at the age of ten, he did nothing but covet the throne and the royal family, wanted to be like them. Being the heir to the entirety of The Fold wasn't enough for him, I suppose" She answered, gladdened that she was momentarily able to free herself of these thoughts that had played on her for the many years she had lingered in Kingsport. "You think my brother had the realms interests at heart when he thrust his sword through his own High Kings chest? When he kept me here, so he'd have someone to taunt when the war was taking an ugly turn?" Eleana quickly pulled herself out of the quick flush of memories that ran through her mind. She receded, calm and composed "but you have always been here for me, Kellor. And for that I thank you" Lady Monthell said, trying her hardest to smile at the awful recollection of the torment her elder brother put her through.

Kellor proceeded again to stand just behind his Lady, placing his hand on her bare shoulder. "I would follow you to the depths of Oblivion and back. You know that, my Lady. Was it not I who stood guard over the nursery the night you were born? Was it not I who stood vigil on the night of young Martis' birth as well?"

"Yes" Lady Monthell sighed.

"You're still young. Why not leave Kingsport, go back to the Forge, or maybe leave the continent all together, could become a writer in a foreign land. You could maybe become a great adventurer of Mundiil and its provinces, no? Not your style? Oh how your father would detest that idea" Kellor joked.

Eleana smiled, though not because of the joke, as she turned to face Kellor again, saying "I could never leave the Capitol. Cythees will always want someone who isn't one of his jesters or fools to make fun of. And what better joke than his own sister? In his mind, I'm an embarrassment to house Monthell, I have a fatherless son, unmarried and I have to beg him for a share in my own wealth" she grimly remarked.

"You are strong, My Lady. You'll figure something out. I don't think I will delude myself into thinking you will stay here forever. One way or another, you'll get to leave" Kellor said as he lowered his head in a bow and then took himself back inside the confines of the mighty Kings Keep. Eleana stayed. She turned to the small wall, overlooking the city below. In contemplation she watched and thought.

Chapter 3-A Shadow Under Kings

Elsewhere in one of the great, spacious chambers of the Kings Keep--another advisor to the High King stood over a wooden desk, layered with parchment, books of all calibers, carted in from every corner of all the realms and other stately things. The red sleeves of his robe drooped down to the floor as he placed his hands on the table, reading over recent information from every corner of the world. The intelligencer of the High King and a mysterious man, dangerous but reasonable. Jazar, a man known for his calm and collective ways, yet a man whom people, the Kings and nobles alike, were cautious and wary of. His will was as potent as the plethora of assassins in his employ, stretching throughout all the Eight Realms.

His appearance was as ordered as his ways, with a single red robe flowing down from his shoulders to the cold stone floor, his long, brown hair tied into a short ponytail that ended just past his shoulder's, his beard was braided like his hair into three short strands, a very unique look for a nobleman, especially in the finery of the capitol. But the most compelling feature of his were his eyes. Unlike anyone else he'd ever come across, Lord Jazar's eyes were a dark purple; a rare condition that made him stand out from the other counselors. That and his already foreign attire was always his preferred color of deep red, though, that did nothing to wipe off the sneers of the 'blacksheep' he was called whilst amongst his other councilors.

With a new night upon the city, Jazar could hear most of

everything occurring from the courtyard to the outer markets. Its greedy shopkeepers of coin and trade had retreated into their homes, the city only illuminated by the candles in house windows and odd braziers about the cramped streets. To the north-west of the city Jazar could hear and see the bells of the religious Gray Chapel ringing its huge, bronze, bells in the dark. Their cries echoing around the city, its atmosphere becoming somber and almost silent. Its huge dome reached a height almost as tall as the Kings Keep and was just as old. It had been constructed when one of the Quarthands, Sithren, some seven hundred years ago, had converted to the faith. He brought their teachings from their old capitol of Oldinronx in The Fold to the hills of Kingsport. The 'Pious' as he was named by the commoners of his time, initiated the first Faith War of 902 AKC within his own family and the result was a fractured royal house that had lost its control over the faith. Now the keep and the chapel sat idling each other: two brothers vying for dominion over the city.

A sudden rapping on the door disturbed him from his peace. Before answering it, Jazar hastily slid a few papers, lined with confidential knowledge into the draws of the desk. When he did eventually pull open the door, he was met with a familiar face-- the face of his colleague and fellow councilor: Lord Darian Darianth, peering at him from the torchlight.

Darian was guarded by two soldiers from his own house, their helms covering all their faces as much as the darkened corridor they stood in, the vertical slits on the helmets casting shadows on the floor. At his arrival Darian raised a black eyebrow as he asked, "may I come in?" arrogantly.

"Keep your voice down" Jazar murmured in his normal confident and softly spoken tone as he pulled the door fully open, prompting the other noble Lord to enter. Once he had, Jazar quickly slammed the door in the face of the guards, locking it with the latch. He then made a point of going to the balcony of his room, drawing the silk curtains shut, despite the castle being layered by tower after tower. "What have we got this month?" Darian asked in his honeyed voice, sitting on the end of Jazar's bed impudently.

Jazar seated himself back behind his desk, interlocking his fingers on his lap. "It appears that the insignificant flow of Antaran refugees has increased. It would appear they have grown tired of living in that frozen wasteland and that the insignificant have become…significant" he answered.

"They've swapped one frozen wasteland for another, at least ours has better views. Their first port of call will be The Winterlands. Let King Forrester deal with them. It's his concern for now and who knows--maybe he'll deal with unexpected calamities a lot better than his father did" Darian smirked.

"His fathers ending was unnecessarily so. I've asked myself often, how well did you really weigh that consequence? It was a foolish order you gave"

"Everyone's order, Jazar. We all chose a side in the war and terrible things happen in times of conflict, the other house leaders and Kings who supported Morryg were there when I made the decision. He should thank me, I'm the reason he ascended to King"

"I've always admired your boundless sympathies for others and their struggles" Jazar prodded.

"I have sympathy for those who struggle just not the patience to deal with their failures"

"Regardless, the High King won't take kindly to foreigners coming over and if the Forresters aren't telling him…he will have something to say. I've even heard tell some of the northern Lords and nobles are letting them in on account of some of them sharing common blood" Jazar warned as he shook his head at Darian's pacifist idea.

"We'll leave it out of the High King's ear for now. What he doesn't know can't hurt anymore than the things he inflicts upon himself. Anyway, anything else?" Darian dismissed the vale warning his colleague had proposed.

Jazar scowled at Darians apparent insolence before producing a scroll and throwing it, purposefully aiming for the Lord's head. Darian caught it, fumbling with the seal and reading aloud "the dragons have gathered in Ushkin. The Lunar Festival has begun…ten thousand…Osh-Venn soldiers…the Mundilic Empire uniting in a weeks' time" Darian looked up. "So, the Malacenders are choosing another Champion to lead their empire. Good for them, the Sea of Swords lies between us and them as it has since time began" he added.

"Do you face everyday life with this much arrogance and dismissal? I don't suppose much concerns you" Jazar retorted. The spymaster, though tolerant of most things, was already beginning to lose patience at Darian's attitude.

"What concerns me are serious matters against the realms, against the capitol. We are the High Kings advisors. We have eight realms to govern, me and you. We cannot leave it to the arrogant fool who sits on that chair" Darian slandered Cythees.

"The last time the Mundilic Empire gathered to this degree, they produced a Champion Rider, a Harbinger, and invaded. You know what that means?" Jazar asked, arising from his chair and pouring himself a goblet of wine from a pitcher on the desk's corner.

"Ridiculous" Darian scoffed as he too arose and snatched the pitcher from Jazar "the last time a Harbinger was picked was six hundred years ago. One hasn't been seen since then. Whatever power they did have is gone. The dragons are no more, the last one died in that same invasion. And the drakes have been dead even longer. Why should we worry?" he continued as he took vast gulps from the chalice.

"It's something that must be kept an eye on. We can't risk the possibility, however 'insignificant' it may seem to you" Jazar sarcastically advised.

Darianth stopped drinking and slowly looked at his confidant "I don't remember you being this cautious ever before"

"It is only through being cautious have I survived in the court for so long. Both you and I have served a High King before this one, neither of them relatively good ones as far as High Kings are taken. Isen was the best of the three that we served and he's been dead now for nearly nine years. All I want is stability and order throughout the realms, keeping things as they are, as they always have been. Because, for good or ill, the realms are pillars that hold everything up. If one is allowed to crumble it is harder for the rest to do the lifting. But together they easily hold up the continent, even if they don't know it, even if they don't like it" Jazar metaphorized as he began to look over the many pieces of parchment, all containing rumors and whispers from around all eight realms. "And you want to maintain your position," Darian snarkily suggested.

"That to, of course. I'm good at what I do, perhaps one of the best and I would not shirk my duties in replace of where I came from. The slums and smithies are no longer my home"

"If it will settle your nerves then yes, my friend. We'll do something about it. Leave the dragons of the east to me" Darian assured Lord Jazar with a devious smile. Darian then finished the last drop of his wine and proceeded back to the wooden door, undoing the latch and pulling on its ringed handle as it creaked open.

"What? Where are you going?" Jazar asked, confused as Darian had only just arrived and their monthly updates usually lasted longer into the day. The red clad councilor watched as Darian's two personal guards stood to attention as he flung the door open, the bronze metal plates on their armor clanking together as they moved like huge tins. "You're not the only one whose hands reach everything," Darian said cryptically to Jazar, turning and smiling at him, before slowly closing the door.

Jazar stood, once again alone in his room. Confused, his eyebrow furrowed. He sipped his wine once again, before half-heartedly returning to his papers amidst the dim, candlelight

*

Around a dinner table deep in the royal apartments, next to a great burning hearth sat Martis and his mother, Martis was now just in his simple, white bed tunic, his mother still kept her regal red dress on, though she had casually disposed of the corset and unbuttoned the top of the collar. For only in private or in the company of her son did she ever feel comfortable enough to lower her vice and distant ways and be calm and natural to herself.

On the table, steaming bowls of venison stew sat, a misty and meaty aroma wafting from them and rolling over the bowls. Martis could smell their succulent scent and though a boy who held a craving for the harshness of life he did partake in the finer perks of his station from time to time. He tugged on the tablecloth, bringing the bowl closer to him and then tucked in. His mother ate with more grace, using her silver spoon and fork as she watched her son ravage the contents of the bowl "I'm tempted to send you down to the kennels to eat with the rest of the dogs. Cutlery!" Eleana nagged at her son.

"It's the stew. It must be the deer in the Summerplains. They taste better than deer from The Fold" Martis said between mouthfuls of venison. '`Besides…" he added as he chewed

"I haven't eaten all day. Too busy helping the knights and scouting" Martis continued as he suddenly stopped eating, realizing what he had just given away.

Eleana stopped eating as well, placing her fork and knife gently down on the cloth "scouting?" she quoted with surprise. "I thought I told you to stop snooping about the keep, it only takes the wrong person to see you in the wrong place and questions will soon start to be asked and I won't have the answers they want. We are far from trusted here" she lectured, waving her finger in Martis' direction.

Martis ignored his mother's annoyance, trying to convince her of the importance of snooping "I went into the armory today, there are all sorts of things in there, armor from hundreds of years ago, the sword of Sempronius Silver-hilt, the dragon skull itself!" He continued in awe as he named the lost relics of bygone High Kings and their heroes. It was the story of Sempronius Silver-Hilt that fascinated young boys like Martis: a great hero, raised in the slums of Kingsport and risen to the Kings Watch before sacrificing himself at the hands of would-be-assassins even after he was dismissed from his royal charge during an internal scandal after the death of High King Alduwyn's infant son. A children's tale but one still rooted deep enough in truth to be remembered.

"Martis!" Eleana cut in "enough. I'll hear no more of your endeavors throughout the place. And another thing--I need you to stop this nonsense with the other soldiers. If you want to train, fine, but don't do it with common arena grunts" Lady Monthell ordered.

"Kellor says that the arena grunts are the best to learn from because they show the grimness and skill in fighting he says it's not as the story book knights make it out to be" Martis said, defying his mother's wishes.

Since Martis had been a boy he had always looked up to Kellor, as many in the Monthell house had. The old knight had fought and taught two generations of Monthell and his experience showed with strength and a certain valor most wouldn't find anywhere else in the astute, guileful house of Monthell.

"Kellor would…he's a good man…a great friend but…" Eleana was cut off herself when a quick knock came from her door. Both turned to face it.

"Who is it?" Eleana asked to the door as a familiar yet unwelcomed voice came from the other side "It's Saura…the Queen" a smooth voice uttered. Eleana rolled her eyes as she mimed to her son, from across the table "let her in"

"She's never come to see us before, what does she want?"

"How will we know if you don't let her in? And mind yourself, it's still the Queen Consort your talking to" Eleana smiled.

She watched as the door slowly opened and at its corner, the head of the Queen emerged and soon her perfectly fitting figure followed. Both Eleana and Saura locked eyes for a moment, both hiding their true feelings behind false smiles, as both women had quickly learnt and mastered, though why, Martis didn't understand. It was clear his mother despised the Queen and the Queen despised his mother, though the callousness Saura directed at all but herself and those close to her was well known and so Martis thought little of the staunchly alluring Queen as she slowly seated herself in his chair as he was forced to stand for the monarch. Saura threw her curly raven hair over her shoulder as she smiled at Eleana "I thought I'd stop by and see how you are doing; I know you both live quite lonely lives even in such a massive place. The complete opposite of myself. When I first came here, after my wedding, I loved the vast expanding halls and winding staircases. As a girl growing up at Steed Rock I thought the world was on those high cliffs and windy moors' ' she shifted Martis stew bowl with disgust "but here I learned quickly: there is always something or someone bigger. Though I suppose we all have our different…duties to attend to" Saura simpered.

An incredibly awkward silence filled the room as Saura stared at Eleana with a faint smirk on her purple lips. "I haven't noticed you attending court lately. I do hope nothing is amiss" the Queen added.

Eleana smiled back, flipping her own hair behind her as though preparing a toast. "I find court nowadays under a… delicate management. Quite certain, it never appealed to me during the days of High King Morryg so it certainly wouldn't warrant me being there now. Perhaps it's the air in there, or the air of those within" Eleana cleverly retorted, raising her thin eyebrows to Saura, waiting for a worthy response.

The Queen, nearly dropping her benevolent act, contorted and twisted her fingers as her lips pursed for an instant, enraged by the clear insult Eleana had paid her. "Well of course. I assume that raising a boy without a father must be hard enough, but soon if, sorry, when King Toros arrives to beg for your hand in marriage with his son, then poor Martis here will finally have what he has always been denied, well since that boating accident" Saura responded, pointing to Martis, who looked at his mother for an indication of what to do next. All three knew why Saura was visiting, the real question was what she wanted from it. No one was as spiteful or unnecessarily cruel as Saura, she saw everyone as a potential threat and combated all threats the same way.

In the six years her brother had sat on the throne, this was only the second time Eleana had spoken to Saura, the first was at her brother's coronation, of which even then, the two women professed their disdain towards the other. It was in the silence that Saura saw her moment, as she glanced over at her nephew-by-law. She sized him up and noted the obvious about him. "Your husband: Martis' father, was a sailor wasn't he? A merchant Lord?" she asked as she looked over at Eleana, fluttering her eyelashes as she did.

Lady Monthell was dubious "Yes. He...had his accident in the bay when Martis was just a babe" she answered hesitantly.

"And you yourself were only young when you married? I know the feeling"

"Eric was a good man, loyal to his family" Eleana continued though her voice was quiet in anticipation.

"The boy certainly looks like you, doesn't he? long chin, sharp eyes, wonderful complexion…" she paused, as if surveying an anomaly or intrigue "Shame that he didn't get those black locks your family's men boasts, or what your husband did either. Strange isn't it? Blonde hair for a boy of The Forge"

Eleana's face honed, her eyes narrowed as she smirked with confidence and surprise at Saura's guile. She picked up her fork once again and stabbed a small chunk of venison "not at all. My grandmother was from house Green-Wood of Southshire, she had hair as yellow as lemon" she quickly reeled off. Saura sighed in boredom for her chosen victim was shrewder than planned.

"He's a good boy. I see you raised him well. I'm sure the father would be proud" the Queen answered. The words finally slashed deep in Eleana at the insinuation of her son's birth, one she had heard hundreds of times over but to come from such a venomous mouth and yet to travel on such a sweet tongue was what angered her the most.

"I pray to Lady Izaris that she gives you a child, so that you may know the burden and love you feel for one" Eleana nodded. "if, assuming you are capable of such emotion anymore" she added under her breath, her eyes narrowing. Another deathly silence fell over the room, so quiet that only the flickering flames of the fire made noise.

"Good…good. Well I thank you for your prayers, Lady Monthell. I would offer mine in return but I've never been one for religion" Saura said, rather confused at the contempt that she wasn't used to seeing from a usually timid Eleana. She rose from Martis chair. As she walked past the boy, towards the door, she smiled at him. But it was a smile Martis felt no warmth from just falseness and Saura knew it as well. Had the boy not been present Saura would have no cause to hold back her feelings for Eleana, but the Queen Wife of Kond was more snake than the gallant horse on her families' banner.

Just before Saura reached the door handle she stopped. Turning back around, half her face lit orange by the fire, making her eyeshadow seem darker than what it was, she delivered the news she had come to tell, the true cause for her visit: spite. "Oh yes. Your father has asked for a meeting to take place tomorrow morning, King Toros will be here with his son, Gryff. Your boy may have a father sooner than expected" she smiled again before turning and slamming the door so hard, Martis felt its vibration carry through the cream stone wall and into the bed he was sitting on.

Both mother and son waited till the sound of Saura's heels were echoing further and further down the corridor before speaking. "Bitch" Martis cursed. His mother opened her mouth wide in disbelief and fear, her paranoia making her check for listening ears, then remembering only they were in the room; smiled. "Don't call her that again" Eleana said, standing up and walking over to her son, bending over till her blue eyes were level with his green.

"Don't joke, son. This palace is crawling with informants of all the councilors in this place, don't let them hear what you truly think. Even the walls themselves will turn on you if you give them the chance. This place is vile, full of betrayal and lust"

"Then why are we here, is it because of uncle?"

Eleana took her son's head, gently, into her soft hands "One day I'll tell why we're here but for now. Get to bed" she smiled once again, pulling Martis up and ushering him gently to the door. "Make sure you go to your own chamber. No late night scouting and I'll see you in the morning" Eleana ordered. She had caught him before, though had not made him aware of it. She herself was no stranger to the silence and solitude of survival in the capitol.

"Of course. Good night, mother" Martis said, cheekily, thinking how innocent his mother must have thought he was, though, as he believed, unbeknownst to her that the fourteen year old occasionally wandered into the kitchens for a while, returning with one or two young maidens or how he would cheekily spy with some of the other younger knights when the female cooks and washing maids were undressing. But his mother knew well the workings of man, so too did she understand the mind of a boy.

Eleana closed the door on her son, leaving him in the corridor. It was only then that Martis noticed how calm the night was and how dark the confines of the apartment corridor could be when night was at its thickest. The blackness of the torchless hall was eminent. It immensely unnerved Martis who wasted no time in returning to his chambers, the sound of his scuffling footsteps reverberating off the walls and shadowing his haste as behind one of the corners, two innocent eyes watched him from the hollow dark of the halls. He watched Martis, who never looked in the boy's direction, not that he would have been able to see him if he did. He saw Martis turn the corner right to his rooms. Then. As quick as he had apparently arrived, the royal spy ran back into the darkness, seemingly swallowed by the void of night. The ear that sent him beckoned him back.

By now, a few floors up in the royal apartments, Saura was removing her tiara, placing it gently on a beautiful red cushion on the dresser. A small fire was burning, bleeding little shafts of light around the darkened, stone room. Its small yet cozy confines were aerated from the huge open doorways that lead out onto the stone terrace, overlooking the Bay of Gales to the east. There where ships, day and night, sailed into the harbor loaded with all manner of goods and exchange. Though from these heights even the largest vessels were nothing but fleeting shadows dancing over the steady waters. Alone. She stripped off her blue dress, feeling it brush against her as it slid to the floor, the silver studs of the dress glittering in the firelight. Saura stood in the middle of the room, naked. Her feet were becoming cold from the stone as she grabbed a goblet and filled it with wine from one of the hundreds of pitchers around the palace. Her black hair fell down to her breasts in tiny, individual strands.

When suddenly. A loud knock came from the door, Saura rolled her eyes, expecting it to be her intolerable husband, however when she pulled the door ajar, after wrapping her white nightgown around her, she saw not Cythees but Lord Darian. He smiled wolfishly at Saura as she quickly let him in, checking to ensure they weren't being watched. When she had confirmed it, she grabbed Darian sharply by the collar, shutting the door behind him. Darian smiled; this was not awkward nor did either see it inappropriate as the two had done this dance before.

"I didn't think you'd be coming tonight," the Queen said in between pulling Darian's clothes off feverishly, snapping the small chain that attached his cloak.

"Only once this week. Being the royal steward is incredibly...taxing" Lord Darianth smiled, exploring Saura's body with his own hands, nearly throwing her on the bed just as she ran her fingers through his blonde hair.

"Well allow me to relieve you of some of that woe" Saura whispered as she smiled with a devilish grin, her eyes looking straight into Darians.

The two climbed into the royal bed of the High King.

"We ought to be careful" Darian said, pulling back as he turned doubtful. He was cautious of Cythees rage as the High King could fly into childish bursts of anger though, if discovered, his outrage would most certainly be rooted. Darian considered himself adept at avoiding them but even he was prone to drop his defenses when enthralled by a woman like Saura, she was the only one he found himself drawn to again and again.

"Fuck the High King" Saura answered, stroking Darians face as she tried to pull him in further. "We've always been together. Cythees has never got in the way of us before" the Queen moaned into her lover's ear.

As the two continued to kiss and grope at each other's bodies Darian whispered "Give it time and your lord-husband will be out of the picture soon enough"

Saura pulled back, a little disturbed at her lover's statement.

"What do you mean?"

"I mean if he gets in the way of us, our plans, anything"

"Ha you'll do what? Cythees is one of the best swordsmen in the eight realms. Are you going to challenge him in the old ways? Have you ever held a sword before? Men know when to fight, but rulers now when to stay their hand and wait" Saura mocked as she raked Darians back with her nails, making him groan and then snigger, he was as much a sadist as people judged him as.

"Not every man is obsessed with strength at arms, at least not past Grasspoint, a rare few have a gift with the mind. And look what I've conquered with mine" Darian said, before grabbing Saura's wrists, holding them against the bed so tightly that her body left indents in the covers of the bed.

"Let's see what you can do with your other...assets' ' Saura joked, letting her eyes wander. Seduced by the power and promise of a mighty serpent.

The two of them, now undressed, covered themselves with the sheets and proceeded further to intwine themselves. As outside the chamber door the young spy boy who had just been watching Martis, now stood at the corner of the hallway, pressed stealthily against the tanned stone of the keep, but he wasn't alone. Standing next to him was Corvus, who emerged from the shadows, dressed still in his evening clothes.

He dismissively ushered the boy away as he remained, watching the door with sharp and cruel blue eyes. His old and wrinkled lips pursed in rage. He knew who was in the room he stared at, he knew what they would be doing in there, his own daughter-by-law. Corvus, naturally, had headed the whispers and rumors and had made sure his doubts were solidified, yet he didn't intrude. He watched the door in the orange light of the brazier for a while. Before returning to the shadows.

Chapter 4-Fire and Ash

Whilst Kond sat in the west of the globe, its King and councilors plotting, east of the Sea of Swords, far past the island of Kydrim, lay the proud continent of Mundiil. Spreading thousands of miles from the eastern coast to its borders with Argus. Its people ancient, its ways and gods just as old. It was the older sister of Kond as men had first flourished here in the far more tropical regions than ones that could be found in the west. It was a land of many peoples all of which were more ancient and proud and rooted in tradition than its cousin in the west.

This continent had thousands of years on Kond, its people were not shaped by their choices or by each other but by the countries within it. Mundiil was the base of the world's oldest empire, headed by clan Malacender: the great dragon Emperors. The empire's great capital was Ushkin, the jewel of the east. Its walls were old, high and strong, carved by the first stonemasons of history. A sprawling city hosting thousands of civilians, the city stood in the thick of the widespread jungle forest of Tashi. Where once was a simple temple to their dragon God, tens of thousands of years ago, now had sprouted the great home of the dragons and drakes or at least it had been in the past. For the foul drakes of old had long since passed into history's pages and the dragons, proud and godly, were as rare as winter in this part of the world. Protected by thick bamboo canes and vines and poisonous plants of deadly proportions. Its perimeter walls were old and dotted with carvings of ancient times. Its history written and carved into the outer walls of its districts. Ushkin sprawled through the forest floor before reaching a drop off into a deep and perilous waterfall to its east that ran down into the delta, a first bastion of man. To its north and west were its main entrances that leaped out into the world beyond and the south was bordered by a bank of thick, forest mud that most of the city's children played in on most days, away from their mothers, who might have warded them wary of the dangerous beasts lurking outside in the mist.

Ushkin's people were of strong build, standing taller than most others yet were just as welcoming and gentle as a swift breeze flying over the city. And all were warriors. Not a single soul in the city of sun was without a small blade, be it made from iron, steel or even bone. The city's protectors: the Osh-Venn feared nothing and bowed only to the dragon emperors even though the Osh-Venn themselves shared no blood with these people and were part of the ancient clans the dragon kin had conquered. It was an understanding based on trust and strength, formed and nurtured over many thousands of years between the two nations.

Rising high into the green thicket of the trees however was the centerpiece of Ushkin. It stood proudly in the middle of the city, watching over it, once it had held dragons of old, now it held their masters. The mighty Obsidian Pyramid, one of the oldest creations of the old world. Its tip reached out of the leaves of the jungle trees, taking in the boiling sun like an ancient black stalk ascending through the earth. Most in the city told the time of day depending on where the pyramid's shadow landed. Such was the architecture of all Ushkin, it shamed the other great cities of the east even as one of the oldest. The city had barely changed in the thousands of years since its conception in the mind of Stun, the first Emperor and Harbinger both.

Within the pyramid's summit was the large and spacious gallery of scales, its stone obsidian, shiny and shimmering in the light like slivers of midnight molded to the structure. Idols of all six Harbingers adorned different parts of the triangular room as did fine furniture of carved chairs and the Great-Eyed Table, a huge bronze war table centered with a large hole in which a fire burnt from within. From this summit of the pyramid, looking out across the city through an open room was a young man, the young dragon prince: Tarith of clan Malacender, the heir of all Mundiil and its states. Son of Tephus and Cassandra, he was a noble and self-described bravehearted warrior, young in life and kissed by sun, was the way his parents described him. In truth Tarith was a handsome young man, with a chiseled face that even Ornagoth would have struggled to carve finer. His signature grayish-blue hair that had been cause for speculation and he had always paused at the thought but in the back ends of conversation he thought he had heard the reason for his uniqueness in appearance and it was not one of lineage. Tarith had hoped that of all days, his descendance wouldn't affect nor be questioned on today.

He watched the early morning sun rise from Mount Krakcarve ahead with his silver eyes, its golden glow washing over everything. Tarith knew that today was a long-awaited day: the Lunar Festival. Perhaps had he waited for it yet staved it off in his mind. Far below he could see people preparing. Hogs roasted on spits of all sizes, wreaths of flowers were put on posts, stable pens and walls. Tarith even noticed that the Osh-Venn seemed to have increased the amount of flags around the city, everywhere he turned he saw the red dragon head roaring over the yellow field. It filled Tarith with both pride and a certain amount of angst and fear. He knew what the Lunar Festival meant, it was the symbolic choosing of a new champion, usually an unofficial naming of the heir, by the great dragon God, Ornagoth. His idol sat outside the main steps to the pyramid; a great winged dragon, its hind legs supporting it, wings spread out and its front legs reaching forward to grasp a royal scepter.

Before Tarith, his father had held the status of Champion as had every Emperor before him. Rather prearranged, he thought, which may have served to take some of the meaning out of the festival. For twenty-thousand years this festival had commenced and Tarith knew that that night would be his choosing. He observed the people below him as dutifully as a shepherd tends his flock. His silver eyes sweeping over everything in the city, until. He caught a glimpse of a massive bronze bowl, large enough for three people to step into at least: The Dragons Scryer. Around it people placed small flowers of all colors at its basin as he watched as water was poured from as many jugs and sacred pots as there were people in the city itself.

It was then that he heard a familiar voice call him from below. A kind, older voice, full of care and sweetness and a certain strength at its end. The voice of his mother. She called him as she herself climbed the black steps to her son, she emerged as a middle-aged woman, early fifties, with long black, frizzy hair, undone by the humidity of the jungle. Her tanned face was aged from fifty or so years under the sun with the majority of the wrinkles around her cheeks. Despite her age however his mother always looked at him with young, brown eyes that never failed to provide comfort to the young Prince.

When Empress Cassandra approached her son, he towered above her, his hair draping to his chest as his mother's was held neatly by gold chains and a tiara, the chains falling to meet the red, sleeveless dress she wore. She was always the contrast to her husband, the current Emperor: Tephus. Though both adored their only child, both had their own ways of showing it. Tephus taught his son that strength and foresight were one in the same, as was wisdom and intimidation. Cassandra differed as she had taught Tarith restraint and tolerance. "I thought I'd just come and wish you…wish you good luck. The people are behind you for the festival" Cassandra choked as tears of joy welded in her eyes.

"Our people, mother. And loyal they are to stand with me" a smooth and quiet voice uttered forth and on every word did Tarith focus, studied and learned with language and art.

"They are the people of the Empire. Which will one day be your Empire, today will be the first day to which they will witness you as you are: strong, proud and a gentle leader"

"You cut such a fine image of me, mother"

"I never did require much inspiration"

Cassandra held out her hand as she laced a strand of Tariths silver hair around his ear. "I think you're ready…you will make a fine Emperor I think, as good as your father. Maybe even better but we'll keep that between the two of us and these blackened walls" the Empress predicted as she smiled, though her gaze was carried more mournfully. She was a woman prone to easy sorrow if it found her and it was rooted in her care for her family.

"How is father? He hasn't been himself recently, I know he's trying to hide it but the man has never been a liar" Tarith asked, concerned about his ill parent. Tephus was indisposed with a once meager sickness, now its consequences were affecting his body, but not his mind, never his mind.

"As well as to be expected. His age has never prohibited him, but I fear that his soul has finally caught up with his body. He is strong and public as ever before, if anything, this celebration may give him cause to boast further" Cassandra said, trying to console herself with her own words as well as her son.

"What a terrifying thought" the Prince jested.

Such a thing, the naming of a potential Champion Rider, as the people of all Mundiil knew hadn't happened in centuries at least. Not since the great dragon Emperors of old, who tried desperately to invade their cousins of Kond across the sea.

"Your father will want to see you before tonight," she smiled "but before that...I brought you something. I think you'll find them rather relaxing. You always bloody have" she added as the Empress clicked her golden ringed fingers as three beautiful, half naked girls came into the room, all giggling. Behind them were two Osh-Venn carrying a bathtub and behind them two sultry Mundilic maidens with pitchers of water behind them. "Mother this is unnecessary. Father has warned you not indulge me. I don't..." Tarith reasoned though smiling in submission as the girls started to undress him, pulling the yellow sash he wore off. They ran their fingers through his silver hair as his mother took herself and the Osh-Venn to the black steps once again "try not to have too much fun with them, no silver haired children are to be born to these girls" Cassandra joked as she trotted down the stairs with Osh-Venn guards behind her.

It was mid-evening once Tarith was prepared. He stood with a silk toga from his shoulder to his shins, his young and smooth body purposefully on display. His long silver hair tied back into a ponytail and several braids. The prince could hear the thousands of people outside the pyramid, chanting and singing, shouting and cooing and so sheepishly made his way to the base of the pyramid, the journey down the steps and past the bronze idols of past Emperors seemed much longer than he had last recollected and their eyes seemed to watch every step he took down the long and descending halls. He walked past the many Osh-Venn that he'd known and trained with his entire life, he saw smiles appear from under the human skulls they wore on the front of their masked helmets. He made his way to the plaza, in front of the great hall which had its doors propped open to the throne room where the Fanged Throne stood at the center of the room. The seat of every Emperor since Stun and the oldest standing seat of monarchy left from the first era.

The throne room was dark in the evening light and Tarith saw the shadows cast over the chair. The carved wings that served as armrests seemed to stretch and contort across the stone floors and the drake skull at the top of the throne, that had sat for thousands of years, watched with its dead eyes as the Prince passed by it. The stone itself had once been a statue to some ancient, dead, deity that Stun had seen fit to melt down by the roaring flames of dragon fire and had his masons remake the shrine into the Fanged Throne-- head of the Empire. Over the throne itself was the imperial state flag, flapping gently in the warm gusts: a roaring red dragon on a silver background with golden wheat below it and a golden crown above it.

Through a red curtain that lay at the triangular entrance to the palace Tarith could see the evening sun beating through, shining upon his father: Emperor Tephus. Tephus was a proud man, at age fifty-six he was still strong and aged well. His hair was a dark black, now turning gray, dreadlocked down to his shoulders. On his head was a crown of bronze that glittered when he turned. The Emperor's eyes were as commanding as the booming but low voice he emitted, wearing the coal coloured royal eyeliner under each eyelid, Tephus stood out from any man of the Empire. "Father" Tarith uttered as he approached.

Tephus turned along with his attendants as they silently admired the young Prince. Tarith paid close attention to his father's expression of content "you look like the man you were always born to be, my son" Tephus uttered strongly, his hazel eyes met his sons as he patted Tarith on the shoulder "your ready then?" the Emperor asked.

"No"

"good. It should make it all that much fun once it's over. Remember son, your destiny will be one of legend. You will be the herald of a new age once Ornagoth has shown us your purpose" Tephus said as he clasped his son's cheeks as he once did when the boy was a child. "They are your people, you have nothing to fear. Our blood runs in their veins as much as me or your mother. Keep to tradition. I was as jarred as you when they did this for me." his father added as he smiled from under his old, grizzly gray beard

"I thought no man could tell another man of his destiny, Father" Tarith proceeded.

"Portent or not. This is your day, Tarith. For this will be a day that history will remember as the birth of its next great Emperor" Tephus smirked. "Now go. Ornagoth waits for no one and this festival has taken too long to prepare for us to do anything less than enjoy it" the Emperor commanded of his son and then almost pushed his son out through the curtain, nearly tearing it down. Tarith felt the warm air caress his body as he stepped out into the streets of Ushkin, the crowd's cheers became roars and whoops as the prophet of Mundiil stepped forth. A small escort of Osh-Venn kept his sides protected as Tarith made his way to the Dragons Scryer. Steam poured from the hot water inside it and Tarith could smell the bitter scent of all the herbs and ceremonial plants around it. As he got closer to the scryer the people of Ushkin stretched out their arms to touch their prince, their devotion to clan Malacender was always evident and true. As Tarith felt the many arms surrounding him in a warm embrace, he turned to the pyramid one last time; his father and mother stood at the wide entrance, watching him.

Tarith then closed his eyes as he walked the small wooden steps that rested against the scryer. He placed his bare foot into the water, nearly scolding his flesh as the rest of his body followed. The steam drifted into his nose, warming him gently. Tarith looked again to see his parents but the steam was thick enough that he could see little in front of him. The miasma provided a shield from the crowd and the fear Tarith felt in the chaos of adoring citizens was pushed aside as their visibility faded and all images turned warped.

But within moments of relief, a strange feeling came over the prince: inferiority. As he felt something else arrive and consume his fear and vanity. Something had removed all feeling, momentarily. The young man could sense its presence around him. And then it happened. The cheering from outside the column of smoke ceased and all went silent, as if all the people in the city had vanished, as if the city itself had vanished and its noise drowned out with silence. The smoke became too thick to see through, like a fallen flour bag it spread throughout the city. Then Tarith heard a voice, commanding and powerful. It came from above, below and from both sides of him. It echoed around in its layered voice as it uttered its prophecy "dragons will rise in the crater. Wrath. Fire. Tested it will be by a betrayer and by the city of silver. Cross seas to a far great city, undaunted by storms or ice" the final word 'ice' resonated with Tarith, though why he couldn't say as the voice trailed off and snuffed out.

Then. As quickly as the mist and the mighty voice had arrived, so too did they leave and Tarith began to hear the crowd cheering once more as their noise was born again into the world. Tarith could see them, oblivious, they had clearly not just seen what he had experienced, but what followed, all saw. The water in the scryer began to ripple as the scryer itself began to wobble as if the hands of the people had suddenly grown angry and started to shake the bowl. Tarith stepped back, almost falling out as the water suddenly vibrated, the ground shook and the contents of the scryer became a haze of raging and roaring flames. Their lime coloured light reflected in Tariths silver irises as he closed his eyes and prepared for searing pain to engulf him, he had failed. The people gasped in terror and surprise. The Prince opened his eyes. He felt no different. The flames left him untouched, save for a slight warmth. He looked around himself with obscurity. The people looked with admiration, horror and demented looks on their faces. A still silence fell over the city, the crickets chirping now more emphasized. Droves upon droves looked in wonder at this messsiah from the flames. Until Tarith saw from the palace entrance, his father raising his hands, with a shocked face of his own and his wife next to him, and clap once and for a moment it was the only sound the people heard reverberate from those ancient walls and stone towers. In response the whole city erupted in cheers of ecstasy, praise and thanks to the rebirth of the dragon emperors.

It was in this flurry that Tarith noticed that the people of Ushkin began to kneel, tucking their heads low to the ground, falling around the city to their knees, on the streets, from windows, even the Osh-Venn patrolling the walls. Tarith looked out to the sea of devotion, his silver hair let loose in the gentle breeze, his red sash reaching out to the people as it flew like the mighty dragon banners. He stood over them with his brow facing the pyramid. The ceremony was over, Ornagoth had spoken and a seventh Champion Rider had been chosen since the Mundilic Empire was founded as many as twenty-thousand seasons ago.

The flames in the bowl suddenly died out, as if a great mouth had blown out a candle and at once the Prince was hoisted above the shoulders of his people as they cheered and reveled. Amidst the noise and facade of the festival Tarith saw, in a spiral of pale moonlight, his parents, proud and strong in their own right. Around the entire city shouts of "hail to the dragon emperors!" and "long may they reign!" filled the night as the crickets became a distant memory. The great statue of Ornagoth was crowned with a circlet of jungle plants: a sign that another Champion Rider had been chosen. From the steps of the palace Tephus and Cassandra spoke to each other "So, the first part of the prophecy has come to pass...he has no idea how dangerous that is'' Tephus claimed grimly.

"All the Harbingers before him went through this and passed as he did. He is now sown into the tapestry of our history and he links us now, to the past" Cassandra reasoned "this prophecy has been told six times before" she added not moving her gaze away from her son.

"And six times before have the Champion Riders fallen for its temptation. They were mighty in their time but they all fell upon their own blades in the end. I pray the father grants him a more merciful fate" Tephus murmured as he glanced with a sorrowful and long face at his wife and then quickly hid his own doubts and smiled back, warmly, at the few citizens that noticed them on the steps and turned to cheer them instead. As was orthodox after the Lunar Festival--the remainder of the night was filled with feasting, brawling, joking and the occasional whoring, all in good fellowship. Whilst Tephus and Cassandra retreated inside the Obsidian Pyramid. For the rest of the evening Tarith remained outside with his people, drinking Serbothian brandy from the bone-helmet of an Osh-

Venn, whose face paint rained down his face from the tears caused by his inane laughter. A mighty song of the ancient Ushkin people was sung: A lament for Stun, the first Champion Rider, the founder of the Empire. For the few minutes it was sung, the night digressed and grew silent as the lone few sang the saddening, gray tune. Tarith walked among his people, passing by young mothers holding their sleeping children, the men of the city with their families, the beggars who had traded a single day of suffering for one of recognition and Osh-Venn, men of great strength and violence, who shed tears through the passages of the song. Some gathered by mighty Stun's statue at the east of the city to light homely candles that lit the statue's base and knelt in kinship and memory.

By daybreak, the party ambience had diluted into the faint chirp of morning birds and the city was silent, its people stumbling about, drunkenly. The rest lay oddly positioned on street corners and the streets themselves in states of debauchery. A gentle mist rolled in from the tropical forests outside, lavishing over the mossy rocks on the forest floor and sweeping over the bushes and bamboo canes like the sea, stopping just outside the city walls that threatened to dispel it.

For the fear Tarith had felt the evening before, before the Lunar Festival, he had traded it for a headache and a night of drinking and gamble. Strands of his silver hair were stained brown from the brandy, his chiseled features were puffy, as was common with him once he had drunk. The Prince was the first out of the hundreds of thousands of inhabitants of Ushkin to awaken. The first thing the new Champion Rider noticed was that he could barely see the sun-baked cobblestones of the streets for the people laying on them. He smiled blissfully before turning his gaze back home, to the Obsidian Pyramid, the great golden banner with the red dragon head flew over nearly every building, from the small tiled houses to the bakers to the blacksmiths to the barracks, to the senate building and the court house and all the way down to the falls.

His sandals flopped clumsily as he proceeded back through the triangular entrance to the palace, it was incredibly quiet, only the jungle life outside the walls, the toucans and capuchins, were the only things of sound in the vicinity--a cacophony of shrieks and squawks.

Tarith eventually arrived, tired, at the pyramids summit, the sun shining off of every black surface. He smiled tenderly as he saw his mother and father asleep together on a large chaise lounge, it was the first time he had seen his father sleep in months, ever since his illness got worse. Tephus' gray dreadlocks covered Cassandra's face as the two quietly snored.

The Prince gave his parents a few more minutes of slumber before waking them gently. His mother, pleased to see him, smiled as she awoke, whereas Tephus groaned as he rolled back over to sleep, more interested in his long-sought slumber. "You're up early," Cassandra smiled.

"I never was a nightly person. I rise with the sun" he smiled as he seated himself on a cushioned puffet. " I was hoping to discuss with you about last night," he asked.

"Of course, anything. W-what do you want to know?" Cassandra nodded.

"The voice that spoke, who was it?"

To her son's question, Cassandra squinted. As though the simple question Tarith had posed was some great riddle unknown to her. "What voice?"

Tarith returned his own look of incredulity at his mothers

reply. To him the answer was obvious. "The one from last night? The one that spoke of a crater and the crossing of the sea. The mist? Surely, I didn't imagine it, everyone saw and heard the voice and what it said? Mother?"

Cassandra's face turned into one of confusion and surprise as she shook her husband awake. Tephus rolled over, uttering strange groans and wheezes till the Empress whispered Tarith's findings and thoughts into his ear to which Tephus' eyes shot open as he himself sprung up, nearly falling on his face as he clambered off the chaise lounge. The Emperor, once he had regained his balance from a night of sleep and an evening of light drinking with his friends in the senate, he took his son by the shoulders ``Where are we going father?"

"To a man with all the answers we now seek" Tephus beamed, leading the two of them down the obsidian steps. Whilst Cassandra remained, almost in a meditative state, gazing out of the large open room terrace, two flags of Clan Malacender flapping either side of her. She now knew what this meant, as if the fine lines of twenty-one years were finally adding up and everything made sense-- if what she assumed was true.

Tarith held his father's hopeful cause, keeping an eye on where his father led him. Past the armory as big as one of the great halls of Konds castles, past the indoor pools that belched steam high into the stone rafters and deep down into the heart of the pyramid they went. Tarith recognised their location when he saw the ancient dragons painted high on the wooden ceiling above him, their huge wings stretching out to cover whole portions of the room, and the beams of light that shone through carefully cut holes in the pyramid's side and reflected off of crystalline lights hanging from ancient chains: The Great Library of Deor, the fourth Emperor of Mundiil, a man of knowledge, wisdom and foresight, even for his young age that he was when he died.

Tephus, still in his night robes, pulled his son through aisle after aisle of dusty old tomes and the many magnum opus of long gone Mundilic scholars and historians, even a few of the past Emperors. When at last the Emperor and Prince arrived at the center of the library, as one could tell because it was brightest in the center, where the sunbeams hit a huge map of the known world that spanned the entire floor, from the far reaches of Argus in the east; old and strong, all the way across the sea to the great realms of Kond in the west. The paint was chipped and cracked in a few places along the huge floor, a reminder of the library's extensive age and the archives of knowledge it held within its crumbling walls. On the odd table or two Tarith could catch a glimpse of one of the old archivists hunched over one of the many books in Deor's Library. "What's down here father? I admire this place, its arts and architecture, but research has never been my thing. I know some of statecraft but swinging a sword well...that's something entirely different and please don't remark that you spent your share of time down here also because I'll be inclined to call you a tale-spinner" Tarith joked, remembering the sword strapped to his waist, its hilt forged with gilded steel and at both sides were small, roaring dragon heads, its blade of sharp Ebonrim steel that glimmered in the bright sunlight.

"There will be no sword swinging around here, my son," Tephus grumbled, though distracted and not paying full attention as he searched for someone else about the library, his head turning from left and right to peer through the shelves.

"Well, well. Both the Prince and the Emperor have graced me with a visit, I should be honored your benevolences" a croaky, mad and old voice said, making both Tarith and his father jump slightly. The voice belonged to an old man, so old that when Tarith looked at him he knew, judging by the multitude of wrinkles on the old man's face, that he must have been older than some of the books in the library. However, from the Emperor's quick smile, Tephus immediately recognised the old archivist, in his blue, hooded robe that was chained around his waist: Arch Curate Vacile. The loremaster of all Mundilic history.

The old man smiled at the Emperor, his old and close friend. As Vacile had served in Deor's Library for almost eight decades. His age was clear, from the sagging of his neck and the shaking of his old and weary fingers as he reached out a hand to clasp Tarith's own. The young man looked down at him as he clasped the curates dry hands with a twinge of discomfort at Vacile's lack of a sense of personnel space.

"I judge you have come here seeking my expertise. As you always have, as your father, here, did before you when he was named Champion. But it would seem you were named Champion *Rider*, the Harbinger, very different, yes very different. I know you know, the dragons never lie" the almost senile old man said, pointing at the ceiling.

"Yes well, Vacile, I need access to the Vaok Diin" Tephus stated, inconspicuously nodding to a barred off section of the library. It took a while for Vacile to realize what the Emperor obviously hinted at, nodding gormlessly for a few moments before waddling over to the small barred gates. Tarith and his father watched as Vacile fumbled with a chain and a ringlet of keys, unlocking the gates and throwing them open, slamming them against the neighboring bookshelves. The old man disappeared for a while, returning soon after with a large book. Its pages were yellow and tattered, and its leather cover appeared to have been sewn back on several times over the course of its life. Vacile slammed it onto a table, producing a thick plume of dust to rush from the pages.

Both Tarith and Tephus drew in closer to see the contents--ancient and parts written in ancient Ashié, making it hard for Tarith to decipher. "What is this, loremaster?" the Prince questioned as he squinted his eyes.

"This is the Vaok Diin, my Prince. A collection of the names of all seven Harbingers of Mundiil and their histories, what they did, their achievements and their failures, your benevolence" Vacile said with a certain level of joy, flipping the pages to the most recently written: six-hundred years ago.

Tarith mumbled "Fotia Iron-Crown. Famously tried to invade Kond with her brother Barrok and their dragon Ithilax. Killed by Tomwyn Red-Wood of Grasspoint"

"Yes. All six Champion Riders, but since your father has brought you down here to me, well, maybe another is set to join their ranks?" Vacile smiled.

Tarith looked, bewildered at his father and then at Vacile as he sputtered "Me? In there?"

"Perhaps. Assuming this is all true and not a falsehood or misappropriation of the stars. As the seventh Harbinger your name would be recorded here too one day" Vacile explained.

"What needs to be recorded in there?"

"Your life…and your death"

Tarith's face turned to slight horror at the simplistic way Vacile said it. "So just like in the ancient legends? No. No? These are children's stories" the Prince protested.

"All stories, be they true or false, all start with a glimpse of fact. Make no mistake, my Prince, dragons were very real once. Why, this pyramid itself was constructed by the first of your kind and his dragon: Numinex. His breath was so hot and the dragon so large that he could carve holes into entire mountains" Vacile said, in awe of those beautiful creatures.

"Dragons, my son. Every Champion Rider marks as a herald for the return of the dragons and since the last Champion Rider was some six-hundred years ago; this will be... a great honor for us-- your parents and your city. I can barely believe that it's all true myself. I may hold my doubts but truly, in my heart, something tells me that you have a tremendous part to play" Tephus said, skimming his finger over the page as he read the words to himself, when a particular name stood out to him. The Emperor grinned as he looked at Tarith.

"What father? Something you know about this?"

"Something I suspected, son. The trek must be made. I've heard tales that that's where all Harbingers had to go but to read it for myself, after all this time... and yet it be so obvious"

"What? Where? Father, is this the illness, it numbs your mind doesn't it? This is all delusion" Tarith asked, making light of his father's ailment. Tephus brought Tariths hand down on a name, engraved in black ink, written thousands of years ago, the birthplace of all dragons. Tarith recognised it as he murmured the words: Dragontooth Crater.

"Where fire is undone and made, where stone turns to sand and fades" Tarith recited a portion of Ashié text he had once read about the crater. "We cannot go running off with an expedition, into the blue" Tarith exclaimed. Tephus looked straight at his son, glaring through him "son, this is something that goes beyond us. This hasn't happened in centuries, how could we be prepared? But mark me--this is no illusion, no side effect of sickness, this is something that goes back to the founding of the Empire itself, by God, even before that. This is tens of thousands of years old so trust us when we tell you that something greater is laid out for you to take. I just need you to believe it"

Tarith paused and pondered. He had never seen his father this desperate, even when under the influence of his herbs that he took to dull the pain. This was excitement in a man who was as staunch as stone. He took a breath, deeply, before he spoke "I...this cannot be. Father, naught but a day ago I was Prince and nothing more or less of it. Now because, what, a bowl set itself on fire I'm some mythical Harbinger?"

"How will we know whithout first having gone to this place to see for ourselves"

"You are talking about a pilgrimage that may end up bearing no fruit whilst the eyes of the entire empire watch me and our enemies wait to see me fail. I would much rather deal with those fools in the senate than this"

"So you would walk away from what has been set for you? To spend your life as I have: ineffective, hollow? I may have bought myself a century, at best, of remembrance. My rule has amounted to little save for some minor political intrigue after a falling out with the senate when I was young and the bolstering of our army"

Tarith clasped his fathers hands as he stood taller than him, trying to shelter his words from reaching too many ears. "You are more than that, father. You inherited near two-hundred and five years of peace, any fool or 'ineffective' ruler may have destroyed it but you prolonged it"

"I still walked away from my own destiny, son. You must learn from me. You cannot make the same error as I and I refuse to give into this illness until I see you take your place in your own story" the Emperor uttered with more surety and sincerity than Tarith had ever heard before. The Prince sighed, deeply. The sweet scent of the bannana plants calming him slightly. Enough for him to say what his father had wished to hear though he did not belive fully in the words himself: "Then that's where I'll go. But I do confess that I know not the way"

"Well what better person to come with you. Vacile, you will ride with my son and the Osh-Venn to Dragontooth Crater. As I understand it hails somewhere in The Red Plains, just beyond our territories. From there, Vacile will be your guide. I suggest we get preparations underway" Tephus ordered.

"A voyage to The Red Plains?! It'll take a week just to gather resources for the trek" Tarith protested.

The Red Plains were a vast waste, a country-wide desert. Its beasts were fearsome and deadly as were its famous sandstorms.

"We don't have a week, you will leave in a few days, we mustn't keep fate waiting" the Emperor decreed, confidently. It was the most joy he'd shed in what felt like years.

Vacile smiled, realizing it would be the first time that he would have left the confines of the hollow passages of the library in a quarter century. Tarith trailed behind his father, who led the two of them out of the pyramid and into the outer training grounds where some twenty Osh-Venn awaited them. As they walked Tarith could feel the doubt starting to play on his mind, gnawing on his contempt. "Father?"

"Yes, my son"

"Do you believe all this? For all that is to come, to be a revered part of our history. Do you truly? I don't..." Tarith was stopped mid-sentence by his father.

"Tarith. From the moment you came into this world, the moment I saw those wisps of starlight hair, I knew you would be a... different kind of Emperor. And for twenty-one years I have awaited this day to tell you that. I remember when my father, your grandfather, Haknir, told me of the mighty Champion Riders. The great dragon riders, no one can stop them. And then when I heard what they all had in common, which the rest of our line does not"

"What?"

"Look at me, my , and tell me what differences there are to us"

Tarith knew what his father eluded to, though he felt he knew a much colder truth for its reason at the back of his mind. His father and mothers appearance wasn't his to share, both of them were tanned with years under the sun with dreaded black hair. Their son was far from either.

"Truly. You wouldn't chalk my looks of light skin and silver eyes up to fate?" Tarith asked.

"Only a fool would look at us without question but that fool would not be a student of our history either. Like your grandfather and his grandfather and his grandfather before: Tanned skin and black of hair. all except the six , who, like you, all had hair of gray and eyes of silver, bright in features and most handsome. Trust me when I tell you, my son, your fate was decided long before you were born. One day you will take my place and, if he decrees, guarding over you will be a child of Ornagoth. How can it not be true?" Tephus shook, putting both his hands on either of Tarith's shoulders. It was the first time the Prince had felt this much attendance and interest from his father in a long time and he almost felt starved for it. Tephus had always been a stately man, ruling always took up much of his time.

"Now come. General Lo'atal is already gathering his men. He'll be wanting to see you. I know you and he have always been close. Oh, and make sure to say farewell to your mother or even Ornagoth and his winged demons won't stop her from coming after you. And your city will await for your return" Tephus chuckled as he led Tarith back out of the library, leaving Vacile to pitifully try to clean up the dust from the tome. "Finally your purpose in this world can be laid bare for everyone to see. Revel in it, Tarith. If not for the Empire, if not for your family, then for yourself" Tephus commemorated his son before parting from him"My son is a Champion Rider!" the Emperor shouted back, his voice booming from every corner as he walked up a flight of stairs back to the armory. The Prince smirked at his father. It all was starting to make sense to him and bit by bit was unraveling before him and yet, Tarith was far from certain of what he wanted. He felt the tiny fire of doubt, fueled by his fear and unsurety and dimming the occasion. To be a Champion Rider is to be revered and worshiped but is also to be alone, alone with the expectations and quivering fears of so many.

Chapter 5 - Hardened decisions

In the farthest northern reaches of Kond, half a world away from tropical Mundiil and over six hundred miles from southern Kingsport, lay the snow-swept fields and moors and mountains of The Winterlands, the most northern realm in all Kond. Bordered on the north by the Galenic Ocean and the south by another of the realms: Grasspoint, the largest and central realm of Kond. The Winterlands were held by the great family of Forrester, old and proud. Their castle: Ironmarch, stood sandwiched between two rocky peaks of a small snowy ridge that ran from the Winterlands western shore to a mighty lake in the east of the cold country.

Ironmarch itself was a medium sized castle, a hundred meters wide and a hundred meters long. Its large square walls keeping the main keep and the housing district separate from the desolate fields. Outside the keeps confines were where the windmill and a handful of huts and houses that lay, spread out inadvertently across the hardened snow and soil that curved down into a hill, leading into Frost Fang Forest. Most of the actual keep was stone and thatch, unlike the southern castles of limestone and steel, for Ironmarch had stood in The Winterlands for a millennium and a half. A gray sky always seemed to lurk above the landscape, ill-boding with snow or sleet. The winds were cold and hard, wrapping around the rookery tower of the keep and blowing the odd strand of hay across the muddy streets of the Snow Quarter that adjoined the Stone, Grey and Iron Quarter, all in a square formation around the keep itself. At the back of the keep was the legacy of House Forrester, the mighty Enk Forest of song and legend, leading for mile after mile of tall frostwood trees, their bark strong and far sturdier than average wood. A well sought-after resource that had earned the Forrester's right to place the great frostwood tree on their brown and white banner that flew over the castle.

There the people differed from those elsewhere in Kond. All helped. Not out of kindness but as an understanding of survival; children pushed heavy goods off the back of carts for their fathers to catch, the old blacksmith was helped by his two apprentices and even the guards, in their sturdy, old and ugly armor, were respected and spoke with civility towards the citizens. Ironmarch's defenses were strong and its fires burned warm inside, beating off the cold that flew over the peaks and over the seemingly endless moors. As the snow blew silently over the land, King Forrester watched from the wooden balcony of the great hall. He was a young man, only in his early thirties. Tall and broad shouldered. His short hair, like winter hay, blew in the wind as clumps of snow gathered in it. He sported a slight stubble from his frequently growing beard. He was tough in nature and was molded by his land, being prone to moments of self-imposed solitude, yet he was kind and affectionate to his people and kin. His gloved fists rested on the wooden balustrade as he cast a steely look down onto the town, creating quite a brooding spectacle as his fur cloak blew gently behind him. He was used to doing as such, whenever he felt confused or unsure of something or simply when he wished to be alone, though he knew that was never for long. He stood in contemplation, adjusting the straps on his cuirass.

"What do you imagine yourself doing down there, Ulfrik?" he heard a familiar voice behind him ask. It was a voice he had heard every day of his life, the first voice, the voice only a son could recognise--his mother: Abigail Forrester. Ulfrik smiled as he turned to see the face of the one who guided him and who stood by him.

Lady Abigail was shorter than her son, graceful in her age of nearly fifty years. A lifetime of living in the cold and frigid temperatures of The Winterlands showed on her wrinkled and weathered cheeks that seemed to become youthful once more whenever she smiled and had not lost their color. Her eyes, like her sons were a piercing blue that burned almost as brightly as her ginger hair, tied into a single ponytail and thrown behind her, befitting of a lady who looked and moved with grace, always dressing in her thick, blue gowns that fell to her feet and topped with a bronze brooch in the form of the frostwood tree.

"I always find it comforting watching them. Their lives seem so fruitful and calm. And yet they are what keep The Winterlands alive, their blood flows through it as much as ours. Gives life to every seed of grain' ' Ulfrik said as he turned back to the balcony that hung only a few feet from the castle's main entrance. Abigail smiled as she joined her son, standing next to him. "You view them as kin because they are our kin and those behind these walls will always be ours. Their lives are just as hard, even harder actually. I should know" Abigail nodded as she was not from a noble house of the northern realm, the woman who was the foundation of House Forrester was once a simple girl born on a farm who had met Ulfrik's father in some odd twist of fate or maybe even by the decree of the Gods as he belived.

"I've noticed you've started spending more time 'leisurely gazing' of late" Lady Forrester mumbled to her son.

"I know. I wish father had told me all the duties of being King of The Winterlands were so taxing at times. Suddenly sitting on a big chair in a large hall doesn't seem to have as much appeal as it did to a ten year old boy"

"So, it's the boredom that's getting to you?"

"It's the waiting. Waiting for the next problem to befall us. Fathers gone... and now it's me. But I still feel like something is coming. Like a debt we've not paid yet. Forgive my melancholy. I know it's one of my vices" Ulfrik confessed as he stared blankly into the cold mist that was forming on the moors.

"Every ruler, every person, be he lowborn, commoner, noble, Lord, King or even the bloody High King, they all face their problems. What matters is how they deal with them when they come. Whatever the problem is, if and or when it comes, we will defeat it. A farmer needs no less reason to fight for that than you" Abigail said, offering the wise council Ulfrik knew she would. For his mother was not prone to flights of fancy or rashness. She considered all sides and was sneered at by the many lords and nobles for it. "As for any debts we owe. We owe non, how many of our men perished in the war for that high fool in Kingsport to keep his crown, we are paying nothing to anyone that hasn't been paid a hundred times over before. Come on" she nudged her son kindly "it's time for the monthly council. The other noble and Lesser Lords are all waiting for you. They all arrived. Even when you said they would not"

"And as you said they would. Good. Hopefully, it'll break the boredom of sitting here, waiting for the winter snows to come," Ulfrik joked as he led his mother back inside.

The inside of Ironmarch's great hall looked as ancient as its exterior. Old, dark brown wood and gray stone held the lofty ceiling up with the hall itself taking on the same square perimeter as the rest of the castle. Though the hall was more than large enough to support the populace of all The Winterlands nobles, by the standards of the other great houses of Kond, the hall was minute. Old, frosted and small windows lay on every side of the hall, letting in dim blue light from pale blue panes. A large fire sat in the middle of the room, belting out nurturing heat and embers. The fire was surrounded by three long tables on the east, south and west of the hall with the northern side being the large doors that lead out of the hall to the ground level.

The Lords gathered on two of the tables as Ulfrik and Abigail sat on the center table. "Where's Laya? She was meant to be attending" Ulfrik whispered to his mother. To Ulfrik's' consternation his wife, once again, had prioritized the meeting as below whatever she was doing at that moment. "Perhaps she's been kind to us all and left indefinitely" Abigail dryly said. Ulfrik shook his head at his mother's sarcastic reply. Never had Lady Forrester ever wanted her son to marry Laya Snow-Shod, the girl was brash. Strong, but brash. She always boasted a fiery spirit which always enticed her husband and repelled her mother-in-law. "I would've hoped that after almost eleven years of marriage and two grandchildren you would've put down your grievances with mine own wife. Do I have to issue a royal command to get the pair of you to talk?" Ulfrik hissed.

"You may do as you wish. I would take her as you see her... when I'm cold in the ground" the Lady of Ironmarch retorted.

"Shall we begin, your grace?" an attendant asked Ulfrik. The King looked around for his wife. Not seeing her in any corner of the room, he diffidently nodded to continue, prompting the attendant to gather the attention of the Lesser Lords. Once the Lords' shouts had been quelled Ulfrik arose, the lords seated. He prepared to utter his speech and to have his annual report of problems in The Winterlands and he would have if it weren't for the doors swinging open. The whole hall turned in conjunction as they saw who entered: Queen Laya Forrester.

Ulfrik shook his head in disbelief, he always expected such impertinent behavior from Laya, though he loved her dearly, she wasn't serious. His wife's short frame strutted in. The strands of her long brown hair that wasn't in a plait fell into the fur collar of her cloak and it moved robotically as she walked. Her eyes were a dark green; two emeralds set evenly into her head that were as pale as the snow outside as were her lips that boasted almost no color at all, except a faint pink tint. Her body, like her Lord husbands, was protected by the thick leather of an armored corslet that hid under a heavy cloak of winter. She was fair and buxom, which correlated with her ferocity to make her the desire for most men and the envy of most women. Her hands were gloved and balled into fists at most times. As the woman approached the long table, the Lords bowed, respecting the strength of their Queen.

Ulfrik didn't say a word as he watched her climb the steps to the table and take a seat next to him, smiling as she did, seemingly oblivious to her lateness.

Abigail sneered as Laya sat and Ulfrik, for just a moment, smiled as his mother and wife were seated on either side of him. "My Lords. You've all been summoned for the discussion of the current problems and reports of the north" Ulfrik announced. The other Lords murmured amongst themselves, the room became more of a vessel for debate as the first Lord, Hearthly, arose and spoke "beg pardon, my King, but I ask that more reinforcements are sent to Greywater Grove. The Warborn attacks are becoming a growing plague and I fear they may spread up the entirety of our eastern coast if left unchecked. Summer may be nearly ended, but even the constant snows of winter may not stop them if they come in force. They may winter in the old fortresses out there where they could hold them" he pleaded.

Ulfrik leaned towards Laya as the Lord continued to speak, however his voice became dulled in Ulfrik's ears. "Where have you been?" he asked his wife impatiently.

"Hunting"

"Before a meeting of the Lords? Have you no regard for appearances?"

"If the day has come where appearances are our utmost concern then we may be the most successful rulers who ever lived" Laya retaliated before smiling back at the chattering Lord, pretending to acknowledge what he said. Ulfrik quickly turned back to the Lord and also smiled humbly "of course my friend, I will send twenty of our best men to keep Greywater safe and patrol the rest of The Hawkways as well. I'll have Captain Dullever see to it" Ulfrik nodded, hoping for a quick end to the conversation. Though Ulfrik held great respect for all the people of The Winterlands, having known a great many of them since the time he was a boy, however he was never satisfied with any mundane concern, only the threat of the Warborn tribes, who had always been the gravest of concerns to the Kings of The Winterlands since they were established a thousand years ago. Ulfrik had paid attention and had heard more and more of the Warborn and noticed how truly violent and emboldened they were becoming, like a deadly tide, first testing the beaches before the crash. The Warborn claimed to be the first disgruntled settlers of the continent and the true victims of Roadarr's unity. After being forced to retreat by the first Kings of Grasspoint and split from their long extinct cousins, the Hillsmen. Savages they were, with faces painted with green swirls, matted hair and beards and never wearing armor, fighting in the shadows of the forest in guerrilla attacks with war cries on their lips. Since the Forresters had ruled over The Winterlands so too had the Warborn lived under their rule, always causing havoc and spilling Forrester blood. In recent months they had taken to attacking the very outskirts of Ironmarch itself, firing their crooked arrows of ancient make, over the walls at the people inside. Ulfrik had tasked his good friend, Captain Dullever, to take the fight to the Warborn, as an experienced veteran, Ulfrik trusted Dullever more than most. The battles of Tide Mark, Fishermans Forde and The

Siege of Baramuel had shown the both of them what each other was made of and it had solidified their confidence of each other.

The Lords moved onto their next matter; one Ulfrik again was concerned about. Another Lord, fat and white bearded, stepped forward. "My King. On your orders we've also been trying to aid the Antaran refugees who keep arriving on our shores, but it seems there are too many of them. Though they only started crossing the ocean but a few weeks ago, for some unknown reason, they are taking up space and with winter coming we won't have enough food and shelter for them. We barely have enough for our own" the noble implored.

Ulfrik calmly sighed, he knew that this problem would arise but not as soon as this. King Forrester opened his mouth to reply, after thinking on his answer for a few moments, however before he could utter it onto his nobles, a courier came running through the now open doors to the hall. He looked exhausted from an almost three week ride from the capitol. The court stood silent as the courier cautiously handed the letter to Ulfrik who stared at him with accusation at the interruption of his speech.

The first thing he noticed on it was the royal seal; a golden eagle with a crown above its head. Ulfrik sighed more depressingly this time, knowing that it would be something important in the mind of High King Cythees as communications between the capitol and the neighboring realms were always kept tightly at a minimum.

Ulfrik read the letter to himself before sniggering. Then he held the letter out as he proclaimed "well my Lord, it appears that your quarry couldn't have come sooner. The High King wishes to know why we're all allowing…" he looked back at the parchment "'foreign savages into the lands of the High King without royal consent' signed by 'Darian, loyal steward to his majesty: Cythees Monthell, High King of Kond and Keeper of The Eight Realms'" the hall erupted in fury as shouts went up, cursing the High King and his steward who was just as despised as Cythees in The Winterlands, maybe more. For the six year span since the last High King, the Winterlands had grown to hate the public figures of Cythees and his steward, Darian. Darianth's family had caused the barbaric deaths of many Forrester men during the civil war because of their well renowned cruelty and cunning in their desire to win. Though it was a plan of admirable plot it was, at its fruition, dastardly and splitting for all the realms.

Abigail gestured for the noise to quell and out of respect for the Lady of House Forrester, the Lords ceased. The chairs of the hall creaked and cracked as they seated themselves and looked to Ulfrik for an answer. The King offered one as he arose himself from his large chair and speaking proudly said "my Lords! In the nigh on four years that I have served as your King my only concern has and will always be for the people of this realm. The men and women of this kingdom. Our men guard the northern shores so that the other seven realms that make Kond can go about their lives, the wood from our forest, Enk Forest no less, lines the roofs and walls of the other realms' houses. Here in The Winterlands our strength built it, our blood sustains it! And it is because of these reasons that I accepted my father's mantle, which also means doing what I deem necessary for the survival of our independence!" the lesser lords all sat, hushed to await Ulfrik's final message "And what I believe to be right is that I must go to the capitol, speak with Cythees personally! I know many here dislike him and many here hold their honor to The Winterlands as high as they do to their High King which is admirable. I will speak with Cythees and agree on terms to allow the refugees of Antara safe passage into Kond and safe living for the ones already here"

Again, the hall erupted, this time in an argument. Some agreed with Ulfrik, others, however, either didn't want to allow Antaran refugees in The Winterlands or held their loyalty and oath to the high crown more preciously.

Laya sat listening, the noise making the inside of her head feel as if it were contorting, she detested the muling and mundane sitting down and discussing, a pointless noise, she thought. It became clear when she frantically stood up, nearly knocking her chair over "Enough!" she shouted.

All the lords froze. Looking at Laya who stared at each of them with her large, green eyes. "My husband, your King, has given a command. We are now inclined to follow him as he is given to follow a decree from the high crown. Lord Great-Shield alert your men at Icehand Caps that all Antaran Refugees are allowed safe passage into The Winterlands. I will see that my father is ready at Fort Mistveil, it guards our southern borders. We will be needing it if Cythees feels inclined to remind us that we're part of *HIS* eight realms. That will do for today my Lords, the court is concluded!" the young Queen ordered. The lords didn't move, looking at each other with doubtful faces. Questioning Laya's orders. "Out!" she repeated. To which all within the hall quickly gathered themselves and began to exit the hall in a great herd.

The lords arose for a third time as they discussed with themselves, muttering and some complaining as they left. Ulfrik, though publicly agreeing with Cythees behest, was torn between his loyalty to The Winterlands, who despised Cythees, and loyalty to the High King who his father had died fighting for, believing Cythees to be a greater choice than the then current High King, Morryg of whom had lost his mind after his own father's death. Morryg's madness was the excuse Cythees had given when he killed the High King in an 'honorable duel for the throne' a doubtful excuse at the least.

When the lords had left Ulfrik was pulled aside by Laya who whispered to him with concern "so do you really plan on going all the way down to the capitol to talk to Cythees? Like he'll agree to let them into The Winterlands"

"I have to try, Laya" Ulfrik said, gently caressing his wife's pale cheek as she smiled. One thing that surprised Ulfrik was how he had never stopped loving her. Marriage for them was not the curse others made it to be and through it the two had a trust the even time couldn't shape.

"You'd better be prepared then. Cythees is as entitled as a ruler can get, even for a Monthell. And I've never even met him, though, from what you told me when you were at his coronation, thank the eight divines. But you can't go alone"

"I won't be going alone. I'll take Dullever with me. That man could fight all the beasts of this land and still complain for lack of a challenge" Ulfrik replied just as he felt a tap on his shoulder. A frantic and heavy tapping. He turned, impatiently, to see one of the Forrester soldiers in their dirty and unpolished, metal armor from head to toe, their visor covering their face "My King. There's been another Warborn attack" the guard reported quietly, not wanting to air any more trouble.

"Where?" Forrester asked, grasping the handle of his claymore.

"Kings Grove," the soldier answered through desperate pants and coughs.

Ulfrik looked at Laya, the two of them understood. If the Warborn could attack Kings Grove they were getting closer and closer in greater numbers to Ironmarch as the grove was only a few miles from The Winterlands capitol.

"Go. Take Dullever. Slaughter any of those savages that you find and... come home in one piece. Every time you leave to go after them you come back bloody or nearly dead. Its so menacing and...quiet handsome, but...just come back. It would be even better if you were a good swordsman" Laya pretended to joke but still hid her worry for her husband behind her humor.

"Ah. It just means I'm getting good at it" Ulfrik smirked as he pulled away from his wife "I love you" he stated before he and the guard, along with a small escort, ran to the courtyard stables.

Dullever was saddling up the horses when Ulfrick arrived. Several other soldiers reigned their mounts and were already underway as Ulfrik approached the grizzled captain. Dullever was a broad shouldered man, frizzy unkempt, brown hair lay on his head, looking similar to the birds' nests in the frozen winter trees. The shoulder guards on his coat of armor were smooth and untarnished, simple northern steel. His steel chest piece was worn from the many years of service and his torso was covered by a thick leather corslet that appeared to have been slashed so many times that some of the leather was stranded and almost falling off. His brown beard was thick and short and clung to his aged and short face, keeping the bitter cold out. He noticed Ulfrik approaching in his own armor, cleaner and more polished than the rest. "My King" Dullever greeted as he gave a respectful half-bow.

"Kings Grove it is then, Angus" Ulfrik said as he clambered onto his black ardennes, flicking his white jacket over the saddle, finding it hard to move in the huge, iron shell he had strapped onto every limb and every opening.

"Filthy bastards. Should stay in their holes like the rats they are. Having said that, tracking them in the open is much easier than tracking them in the forests and their huts" Dullever confidently uttered as he pulled himself up onto his horse with his gloved hands. And confident he could be. Dullever was the most experienced man still living in Ironmarch when it came to dealing with the arguably justified barbarism of the Warborn clans. He had served as master of arms for several years when Ulfrik was a boy, under the rule of his father, Randall. He had never seen fit to take a wife as the third son which had earned him the title of 'womans bane' from his elder brothers. It was a name he regrettably would never escape.

The afternoon mist hung over Ironmarch as the small company of men departed. For the three hour ride to Kings Grove all the men spoke of was their disdain for the 'heathen savages' whilst some defended the Warborn as they were the first human inhabitants on Kond, thousands of years ago. A simple people who fractured themselves into four tribes. Two were annihilated in seperate wars, one was assimilated into Kondish culture. The last was the esteemed group that awashed The Winterlands and were now the under-scourge of civilization pushed out by the Uniter, Roadarr Quarthand, and then segregated and molded by his trusted second, Farthor Forrester. But all knew to fear them and their savage rage-- strange and unruly figures creeping over the cold hills of the Winterlands.

By the orange hue of the evening sun spreading over the snowy fields of the southern parts of The Winterlands, Ulfrik and the Forrester men arrived. Their horses peaked over the hill to see Kings Grove. The steeds stood in the gloom, stamping their hooves glamorously as their riders surveyed the scene in the valley below them: Kings Grove blazed. Looking off at the town under the low, evening light Ulfrik could make out tiny, little, black specks ran through the snow and were chased by others on their tail in all directions, scattering to the winds like a flock without course. As soon as the sight met the Kings eyes, he drew his sword "spread out, surround the town and kill any Warborn you see and, by the Eight Divines, Keep the people safe and don't fall to these animals, not today. Lets show these goat-fuckers whose land this belongs to" the King ordered.

The horses reared up as their riders charged into the village. Immediately Ulfrik found himself separated from his men and engulfed by black smoke that surged out of the buildings. The strong smell of the wooden houses burning and thatch smoking and the scent of blood in the air all wafted up Ulfrik's nostrils as he almost found himself distracted with recollections of the war, the field at Brookside. Not even the animals of the market were spared with their heads and innards painting market street. Ulfrik dropped down from his horse, unable to ride further, and looked around himself in a daze. Kings Grove was the last untouched village aside from Ironmarch that had not been violated by the savages, save for the settlements in the farthest northern and eastern reaches. Now even its peaceful walls had been breached, its house's burnt and it populous killed, raped or worse. These horrors were only lessened when a Warborn emerged from the smoke like a phantom born of ash, raising their sword in an attempt to strike Ulfrik, who blocked the initial attack and then batted the sword away from him with his own blade. The Warborn screamed in a blood rage as he tried to attack again, this time with more fury yet Ulfrik equaled it with his own. Their hatreds clashed again and again as the Warborn, bearded and wild, did not relent. Until Ulfrik slashed his sword across the warriors' neck, pulling it across his esophagus like a rake through soil, spurting a fountain of blood everywhere as, with a gurgle, the warrior sunk to the ground.

Ulfrik looked on, he could only see the vague silhouettes and shadows through walls of thick, black, smoke and orange flame that ripped through half the houses in the settlement. King Forrester reseated his horse and drove the war stallion through the fire that wrapped at the horse's hooves, kicking up fresh embers. Before Ulfrik re-joined Dullever he cut through half-a-dozen more Warborn till his sword was dripping red and the white gambeson jacket he had thrown over his armor was stained a messy crimson.

He found Captain Dullever in the charred remnants of the square with three other Forrester men, fending off at least ten other Warborn. Their eyes were wild, and Ulfrik could only distinguish the barbarians from the green face paint they smeared carelessly onto themselves.

Dullever slashed at one of them but the Warborn still proceeded, like starving dogs to the promise of meat. Until Ulfrik stepped forward. The Warborn all took a few steps back, the King was a legend among the northerners, where fighting was concerned, and a potential prize to the Warborn, who screamed as half their warriors went for him. With only his sword, Ulfrik had cut down two of them before the other three had a chance to attack. Forresters didn't fight with twirls and smart or fancy movements of the blade, but with simple skill and strength. Killing the other three one at a time as they, though wild berserkers, were not disciplined in martial fighting.

Dullever and his men, their hopes restored, cleared the rest up soon after until the Warborn lay dead, in the wreckage of their own destruction. Though short, the town-wide scuffle had been bloody and its numbers high.

It was long into the night when the flames had dulled and vanished, when only faint orange embers clung to twisted remains of carts, stables and the poultry amount of houses.

Every cobble was blanketed by ash, snow or blood and many villagers, humble and common alike, lay on those same stones.

Ulfrik stood alone for a moment. Sword now sheathed as he listened to the crows now feeding off the remains of the dead and lingering over the town as small spirits in search of a cold, black sorrow. This had been the largest Warborn attack he had ever seen and he doubted that even his father, the great bear, before him could recall an attack more brazen than this.

The smoke was still rising when Dullever approached Ulfrik "I've had the lads gather the remaining villagers, they'll stay here to protect them and fix as much as they can but... this is going to take months to rebuild" Dullever paused as he looked to his King who turned a stern face towards him, the rebuild was not what concerned him, his mind was set on further things. "What do you want us to do with the bodies?" Dullever asked gruffly. Dullever was more so a stoic bear than a man in his ways and it showed, though ever was his concern aligned with Ulfrik's'; with the people of The Winterlands, or as he had always hoped.

"Let the people mourn their dead and see to them in their own time. Put the savages on stakes outside the settlement. It should ward the rest off for now. As for reconstructing-- we don't have enough lumber without cutting into our own winter supply and the mason's around here are already overworked" Ulfrik conceded, still looking at the charred buildings with daze and disbelief.

"I could send word to my kin. Cragwillow is always at your disposal. Our mines produce more than enough for the materials and we could send a few wagons of stock wood" the captain offered.

"Of course. Thank you, my friend. I'll send word to the Arlys as well, they can help you with the supplies and Ironmarch can provide the rest but this is still going to hit everyone in the area. Hard too, when winter arrives" Ulfrik said as he looked down at the ground. All of it boiled his blood with the audacity the Warborn had in their growing numbers and coupled with the death of his own people and the rage that filled him warmed him against the cold of the land. Dullever waited a moment, sharing his friend's concern briefly, before reaching into a satchel on his belt as he regarded his King "Ah. The lads also found this on one of the Warborn warriors. Never seen it before. They thought it's some sort of relic or trophy, no idea as to its ilk and it's certainly not from any of their feeble smithies. I've seen many handcrafted knives in my time but nothing like this. It's old, very old and it may be ugly but it was made well for its purpose" before producing a small blade, nearly impossible to see as night was drawing in. It was a dagger. Black in color with both its handle and blade curved into a thorn shaped impression, as if it had been met with fire and warped. Ulfrik grasped it and immediately felt the hilt mold into his hand, a perfect fit for its bloody purpose "I'll have it looked over when we get back to Ironmarch. Surely one of the curates will have an inkling" Ulfrik answered as he saved the dagger, sliding it into his belt.

"Get saddled. We need to head home and try and find out what this is and form a plan to combat these...terrors. And see to it that a cart of food finds its way here at first light, villagers need to stay fed, these poor sods have lost everything" King Forrester ordered sternly. He wavered for a moment and it was when he gazed into the wreckage of one of the houses and saw the charred bones sitting in the corner of a blackened room that he lost his modest stoicism "Dammit! We should've seen this coming, Angus. All through spring we heard the whispers! I heard them on the tongues of traders and travelers! Nothing! We did nothing" throwing a stone into one of the smoldering homes.

"You reacted the same way you always have: concisely,

efficiently and calmly. There are too many village's to safeguard personally. The guardsmen here did all they could. It could've been anywhere they hit: Here, Masser, Bulfreks Town, Ironwater Way. Some things you can't plan for. Some things have to happen so good men like you can respond accordingly. That's the best we can do" the captain comforted. Dullever nodded before he escorted his charge back to his horse outside the settlement.

With the cold wind now picking up, the ride home was much more peaceful and silent as the men tried to reserve themselves and without the voices of the roguish and brave few men who stayed behind, the journey was more sorrowful. With the now recognised threat that the Warborn posed against the people of The Winterlands. The dark caves with voices in their depths and the inner forests were now much more closer to home.

Chapter 6-Blood On The Land

The cold wind of Antara knifed the trekking group of Jorrvanskar as they marched over the wisps of snow and the thick sheets of ice and sleet, intent on escaping a hard fate. The sun shone desperately through the great raging blizzard, a few fractals of light reached through and kissed the faces of the poultry population. It was bitter. The weather and the mood of the people, freezing, half-starved and ready for the desolation of Antara to claim them.

The women held the young children to their sides, tucking their heads into the fur poaches of their coats and held the infants to their breasts, wrapped in woolen blankets, like small sacks of precious vulnerability. The men, on the perimeter, had their hoods pulled firmly over their heads, fighting off the harshest part of the storm. They held torches up in the air, producing a dimmed orange glow that helped beat off the cold.

Gravis was suspicious of this storm. Winter was still a few more grueling months away and even for a land that was frozen all year round and void of a summer, a storm of such merciless power as the one they were in shouldn't have arrived yet. The inhabitants of Jorrvanskar could barely see, their eyes were plagued with snow and their fatigued limbs shivered and quivered from exhaustion.

"We must find shelter!" the Watchman screamed over the howling wind at Gravis in desperation. The old ranger, who had called Antara home all his seventy years, looked about, knowing every hill and drumlet of the land, every snow-capped mountain, every frozen crevice that stretched past the

Barrow Ways. Yet somehow, from delirium or old age, Gravis knew not where he was. He only knew they had gone south, towards Antara's capitol: Vaskuul. Gravis turned back to the Watchman in reply "There is no shelter! We must push on!"

"Where?! This blizzard cloaks everything! We'll freeze if we don't get out of this haze! It will claim us all!"

Gravis was about to reply but felt a tickling sensation at the back of his throat, forced by the cold. He tucked his head into his cloak as he coughed and then as he reemerged he noticed something. Something in the distance. As his eyes brought it into focus, he could see a shape, out in the blizzard. It was alone whatever it was.

A single hand went up in the air and halted the group and whilst the people took rest for a few moments, Gravis kept looking, with nothing but the sound of the raging wind to muse him.

The shape was almost human, but hunched and broad-shouldered, walking on two stumpy legs. Its arms were stretched away from its body to an almost ridiculous proportion but hung down to the creature's knees and were dragged along the floor as it shuffled. The closer it drew the more defined it became and soon appeared to be covered in some type of fur or clothing as Gravis could see large hairs flick up off the creature's body whenever the wind picked up. The old man squinted as he noticed it was hobbling rather quickly in their direction. Gravis pulled back as the shadow became clearer, now only a few meters away. He noticed the all too familiar feature on the creature; on each hand it only boasted three, large, claw-like fingers. "By The All-Maker" Gravis murmured.

"Gravis?! What's wrong?! What's happening out there?!" the Watchman asked and got no reply as Gravis turned to him, eyes wide, wider than the Watchman had ever seen on the calm old priest "troll!!" Gravis screeched as he turned again and met the face of the troll as it charged. It was hideous. Matted grayish fur covering most of its face except its two pointed ears and the sides of its head. Sharp and uneven teeth sat like meat hooks underneath two small slits that acted as a nose. But its eyes. The creature's eyes were green, no pupils, just a pale, murky green, the ones on each side of its nose that gazed like fish, with vacant, dead twitches. It stood a few inches taller than the old ranger but was far stronger than any man. It let out a blood curdling screech that gurgled at the back of its throat as it picked Gravis up and threw him a few feet back into the snow and dirt.

The men around Gravis drew their brittle swords of iron and rushed the beast in a furious rage. But the swords did little against the hardened hide of the troll who batted two of the men away as it grabbed another, pulling him off the ground with its powerful and gangly arms and sinking its jagged teeth into the man's bare neck, puncturing it, making a spray of blood rush up out of the rangers mouth as he gargled, choking on teeth and blood. The women screamed in horror as a few other men tried holding the beast back as it roared again with a terrible and piercing shriek. Pounding at its chest like some perverted representation of an ape.

Gravis wasted no time. He snatched a fallen torch from the frosted ground and whilst the troll was distracted, thrust it into the beast's fur, igniting it immediately. The troll turned and screamed in anger and pain, it lept towards Gravis with its claws outstretched, ready for the kill. The flames, however, engulfed its back. It turned and swiped clumsily, knocking Gravis once again to the ground. Bracing himself in fright, Gravis opened his eyes as no searing pain of claws ripping his flesh rushed over him. The troll twisted and spun as the flames refused to dull until the flesh began to burn and bubble like a pig on a spit. The animal did, at first, refuse to back down even as the flames burned away at its hide. It thrashed and spun, knocking rangers across the snowy terrain like string dolls, flung about a room and cast, with ease, aside. It paused its wailing for an instant as its half-blind eyes locked with the old mans who could not dissuade the feeling of pity for this poor creature that was, itself, trying to survive the blizard. Eventually, through its screams and attempts to put out the flames, the troll collapsed into the snow, producing a loud and solid thud. Its quick but brutal reign of terror over.

"When the fuck did trolls travel this far south?!" the Watchman shouted, his voice dripped with exhaustion as he panted, helping some of the other men back to their feet.

"They haven't. Ever. This is the first time I've ever heard of it. Even these poor beasts feel the shift in the land. Something unnatural is at work here" Gravis answered as he crouched down, inspecting the furry corpse before looking over his shoulder "Get the people steady, bury the bodies! Come spring the animals will have taken most of them back to the All-Maker" he ordered.

"Then what? Do we push forward?" asked the Watchman. He had to almost ppress his mouth against Gravis' ear to speak, quietly, not wanting to send the people into another frenzy of panic.

"Let us see what the All-Maker thinks" Gravis smiled as he stood back up and stretched out his hand into the storm. He reached out with the bestowed power granted to him by The All-Maker, as all priests like him had been.

The All-Maker was the patron to survival and hardship in Antara and as a Great-Seer, Gravis tried admirably to sense or to ask, even though he didn't know most of the time, for shelter. Closing his eyes, he felt the storm lift for just a moment as his voice called to his God. The cold seemed less alien and more familiar. He felt the storm abate for just a second, lifting its deceptive haze to reveal their sanctuary and all, for him, became clear once the light found him and the winds called him to listen to their subtle whispers. In the distance, a ground barrow lay, half-buried by the encompassing snows-- an ancient preaching hall of the Great-Seer dug into the frozen earth like a crypt for their ancient traditions. "There!" Gravis pointed as he led the people of Jorrvanskar down the almost snowed-in steps that spiraled down to the entrance of the circular barrow. It seemed, at least to him, that once again the father of Antara had not abandoned his people. Or maybe it was just intuition, a subconscious knowledge of the halls existence.

Once inside torches were lit and jammed into the cracks of the ancient and cold stone. The children sat around them like desperate moths to a kindling flame. From what Gravis could see the barrow was one long passage under the shallow ground, with adjacent rooms running the whole way down. The people huddled at the entrance, the men clutching the women to them and tucking their arms around the children. Gravis sat himself on a large mossy rock, wrapping his thick cloak around him and tucking his cowl. The Watchman gingerly approached him and whispered to his old friend "We're already running low on preserves and we still have a week before we reach Vaskuul and thats if the weather fairs us well. We won't last lest we turn on our own"

Gravis, in response, gave a look of incredulity as he sniggered. He knew his people, half of which he had seen come into the world and was determined to not have to see them leave it before himself.

"Have some of the lads bring that troll in here. Skin it, flay it and cook its meat. It tastes like shit but it'll do for now. Use the heart too. Trolls heart is good for the body" Gravis smiled as he picked up a torch.

"Where are you going?"

Gravis turned with a spin "To look ahead"

"And when will you be coming back? we need you here"

"When I've looked behind " Gravis joked as he ventured down the corridor and from behind, the Watchman smiled at his friend's sustained sense of confidence in their chance of surviving the perilous way.

In every room Gravis went in, he checked. And every room was circular and bare and the further he got from the group, the emptier, larger and colder the rooms got. Until the old ranger reached the end of the hallway where a small, carved iron door stood. Looking back, he could see all the people of Jorrvanskar, all clearly illuminated by the fire's orange glow and chatting whilst huddled around tiny and pathetic flames. Then he turned back to the door, pressing against it gently, expecting it to give way on its hinges, then slightly stronger as the door seemingly had not moved in centuries and whomever crafted it had done so very well. A small crack appeared as stone grated on stone, giving the old man room to push himself through the interstice and sneak inside. When he entered he found the space was just large enough to fit him in, with a shaft of pale light shining in through a hole in the roof and the sound of the howling wind outside. The room was freezing and damp in the air, overcrowded with ice moss.

In the column of light sat a plain and simple altar, carved from stone. On it sat a bowl full of water. Gravis stood over it, the cold wind hitting his eyes, making them run. He could see something at the base of the bowl, it was small and dark, hidden in the murkiness.

After a few meager moments of thought Gravis struck his naked hand into the frigid water. The Great-Seer had seen seventy-eight winters in his time, but none were as cold as that water as it wrapped around his fingers in a cruel embrace, stinging them. Gravis pulled the object out and to his surprise, saw a relic he had never recalled hearing or seeing in any archive book or scripture. It was a small piece of some sort of circlet, a fragment of it at least. It bore a wolf's head on its band, jaws wide open in a snarl. He peered at it, looking it up and down in confusion. The crafting was refined and to a much grander degree than any of the few rough and wasting smiths that remained in Antara.

It was during his investigation that he heard a commotion from back at the entrance. Gravis rushed back, nearly slipping on the icy stones. He arrived at a scene. The Watchman was sitting on the floor, holding his chest whilst an elderly woman tended to him. The doors to the barrow were wide open and the snow brought itself in, uninvited. "What happened?" Gravis asked the people, of whom most stood in shock. The old woman replied as she tended the Watchman "some of those bastards attacked poor old Bjorn here and then made off with most of whats left of the food. There were three of 'em. Some of the boys ran after 'em but they've already gone I reckon. Weak-willed hay blades"

Gravis seethed angrily as he stared out the door into the cold. He would never have surmised that his own people would have turned on one another and so quickly at that, to be so weak as to leave at the first sign of trouble. Hope was fading for the people of Jorrvanskar. "Get him seen to" Gravis whispered to the wise woman before announcing to the rest of the group "We make camp here tonight. We have enough food for a few more days. Now it's still a long and perilous journey to Vaskuul but hold faith, friends. In both The All-Maker and in yourselves. We will find safety at Vaskuul...I swear it, trust in yourselves and yourselves only. We've seen worse than this before but if we keep moving, keep pushing then I swear we will see those tall gates at the other end" the people, though they didn't cheer or clap, were greatly moved by Gravis' speech as he saw small, somber and silent smiles creep across their faces instead. This gave the old ranger hope as his people, even in the far and desolate corner of the world, castaway from their home and void of any promise of saving, had come together in a need for survival--the characteristics of any true Antaran, he thought.

By the time dusk had dawned on them, or so they thought, having judged the amount of light coming through the cracks in the stone, all had taken up rest, slumped on the rock or sleeping on what few bedrolls they had taken. The foul and vexingly thick troll meat had been begrudgingly eaten and only its bloodied bones remained scattered around the entrance. The torches were dimming, casting long and dark shadows down the hallway of the barrow. Gravis however sat on the cold stone of the floor, facing the iron doors down the hall that were now shrouded in the dark. He stared, facing it in ponderous thought. His hands rested on his knees as he sat with his legs crossed, meditating. Something about the wolf's head had caused a yearning for an answer he could not solve alone, he reached out, using all his teachings to be shown the All-Makers way. But what he got, the quick flash of a vision he received in his minds eye, could not have been from a being as caring and benevolent as the All-Maker. Gravis saw before him a hand, clad in crude, ancient and twisted armor that creaked as it reached forward to touch him in his reflection, as if it were there in the barrow with them. And a sightless void that followed as Gravis heard a sharp and guttural exhale, which seemed to echo around the chamber, though only audible to him. He quickly snapped from his contemplation of the situation with a gasp and rose up, panting in shock and slight confusion, his eyes just as wide as his realization in Jorrvanskar. He sat against the stone, cold enough to feel through his fur clothes and cloak, stroking his thick white beard as he gathered his thoughts. The Mind Stalker was ensnaring him though, of this, he did not know at the time.

The old man spent the final hours before daybreak staring into the fire, anxious to leave now his people had gotten well needed food and minimal rest. Not only could the weather turn at any moment, but Gravis had never once forgotten the first vision he had back in Jorrvanskar, whatever had arisen would soon find them if they didn't hurry. The storms and snows were beginning to turn to its command as the old sage could sense it growing in the air: a power that only the earth herself had witnessed, long before man.

When the worst of the blizzard faded, Gravis set to work waking everyone up and by the time the sun had surpassed the mountain peaks of the southern ridge, they had left the barrow behind. With only their footsteps showing marks of once being there.

Elsewhere, in Kond, in the courtyard of the Kings Keep, Eleana Monthell wandered around the gardens that sat high in the shade of the great tower. Surrounded by pillars that held up the tiled roofs of the open corridors and ribboned with the royal standard flag of a golden eagle, a shrewd taking of the Quarthand flag which boasted the white hand over the beating sun on the same purple field. Though that flag and all its memory had been stricken years ago.

The gardens themselves were open, with the sun baking down on a center peachtree that sat in the heart of the shrubbery that had been carefully tended and molded into the shape of a great X. Eleana neatly perched herself on a marble bench as she sighed. Many a time she would wander around the gardens in idle boredom, this she had done in the sixteen years she'd called the capital her home.

She tucked her red skirts between her legs as she pruned the roses growing on a bush. Her ear's lifted to hear the gulls of the harbor a mile away, squawking obnoxiously with their high pitched yells against the bells of the Gray Chapel, not far from the palace, tolling in the morning, an alarm to summon people to their daily chores. This was one of the few places in all of the capital that Eleana felt at peace. She shut her eyes in comfort. Her brother and his Queen were flung from her mind as her troubles ceased for a moment. The junipers and their sweet, homely smell reminded her of the far south in all its summer glory. She could remember the large juniper tree that grew in the gardens of The Forge, the place she yearned for most: home. The Forge wasn't as monstrous as the King's Keep, not in size anyway. The weather was much tamer too, the heat in the capital was sometimes unbearable with its uncomforting humidity. At home, however, she knew it well. The huge, gray, towers of stone rising against the cliff side and across the fields, overlooking the city of Eagleton and its mines below on the beach and the Neon Sea hugging at its shores. However, her momentary solitude was interrupted by the sound of a twig from the peach tree crunching. She turned sharply, snapping open her eyes with a cold look. Till she saw who it was. She smiled when she saw him trying so very hard to fane innocence, as if he had not been spying on his mother.

"You seem to be getting rather good at sneaking, though it's a shame you stand out like a dog in a cathouse," she joked.

"Sir Kellor says that stealth is a key concept when fighting as 'your enemy can't fight you if they cannot see you' that's what he says" Martis answered as he joined his mother on the bench.

Though his mother came to gaze at the foliage, Martis found it intolerable and didn't sit quietly for long. "Kellor says my sword skills are coming along. He was joking yesterday that I'd be as good as Sempronius Silver-Hilt" he said, trying to start a conversation. Yet his mother saw through the false formality "What do you want?" she dryly asked.

"Why do I need to want something? I thought I'd spend some time with my mother"

"You hate this place, Martis Monthell. You only ever bring yourself here when you want something or rather when I'm here and you want something from me. As well you should. Don't feel condemned to this place as I am" Eleana smiled as she put a hand on his face and gently stroked at his soft, white, cheek."How I long back the freedom youth instills, no cares or troubles that time can't solve. So what do you want?" she added as she let go, looking up at the blue, autumn, sky that still showed signs of the warm summer in its wispy clouds painted through the air.

"The Queen Consort. She came to me to tell you to come to the council room. Some King. Toros and his son, Gryff, will be here soon and grandfather wants to speak to you first" Martis said, sounding rather rehearsed.

Eleana's face dropped. She knew what this meant; her father was arranging for another marriage, this one she could tell would be less joyful than the last. She turned to her son "listen.

If the Queen should ever approach you simply smile and ignore her, don't make it look as such, for she's adept in dishonesty, more so than you will hopefully ever be but certainly don't trust her. Don't trust anyone in Kingsport. Here at the top you will find most got that way by treading on others. They climbed the ladder by stepping on the heads of those before them…but…they forget they will meet the same people coming down it" Lady Monthell passionately stated. Though she hated the corruption of the capital she had no other home, if she returned to The Forge it would only give her father more reason to try and marry her off. To sell her to the next. To rid himself of horded goods. She felt it necessary to remain there, not just for herself but for Martis who had never known any other place than Kingsport, besides the idle holidays he'd taken at The Forge, whenever his grandfather allowed it and they were few after Martis had proven to be as stuborn as his mother and refused audiences with several nobles at a banquet the year just past which had slighted their name. He had, instead, chosen to flirty amorously with some of their daughters without proper introduction but then refused matches with them when laid out for him. It did not suite him.

Eleana stood up proudly. "Come along then. We must entertain our guests" she smiled falsely, as she led Martis alongside her to the throne room doors that stood just in front of them--a lion's den. As they approached the large doors leading into the royal hall, Martis heard his mother whisper to him "I know you don't like your uncle. You are not alone. I know the lengths of his cruelty, it is nothing like the slight tantrums you have seen him throw, it is something else entirely. But be careful what you say around certain people. Your nearly a man grown and they will treat you as thus and when they do then you will have to stand alone. Watch. Listen. And learn"

Martis scoffed at the advice, not really understanding or caring for the consequences of uttering the wrong words to the wrong ears. In his mind his uncle may not dare or care to scorn a boy of fifteen who made it his effort to stay clear of him.

The great doors opened, slowly, as the thin shaft of light grew in size and spread throughout the hall of the throne room. Martis and his mother entered casually. Their footsteps echoed around the place, off the marble floor that cast dim reflections. Eleana looked up, her brother, the Queen Consort beside him. Lord Darian and Lord Jazar, both together and standing just behind Saura like leashed hounds and Sir Kellor, behind King Corvus; lonesome and by himself to the right of the throne, watching with his emotionless eyes. All watched the two intently. Martis felt quite uncomfortable being stared at by very unfamiliar people such as Jazar and Darianth. His heart drummed in his chest so hard he thought it might break free and yet his mother, who also didn't relish the idea of being silently watched, stood vast and proud, holding her skirt just above her blue heels which rang about the hall with every step, awkwardly. Her eyes met her brothers as she drew closer until being stopped by the silent and silver wall of the Kings Watch. She looked at them and tried to see the faces of the greatest knights in the Eight Realms, one chosen from each, but the fancy and expensive helmets did well in concealing their wearers faces. Such a council was the one that governed the realms and its head's glared at her with judgment in their eyes and hearts but still doing nothing to break her resolute composure.

"Your late" Cythees uttered, conceitedly.

"It's early morning, brother. I would say I'm here as best as the daylight permits" Eleana retorted, immediately seeing the look of annoyance that her father gave her.

"Your majesty" Cythees spat with narrowed eyes.

"Pardon?"

"I'am not your brother here and now. You will address me by the title the Divines bestowed on me"

"Of course...your majesty" Eleana curtseid and then pulled herself away from the awkwardness of the situation "You wanted to speak to me about something before my wonderful intended arrives here?" she pressed sarcastically.

Cythees sat forward, imposingly, yet still he was dwarfed by the shadow of the Gilded Throne. Now slightly annoyed at his sisters' belligerence, he uttered "Yes...the Queen has noticed you seem to be troubled in your duties as a mother and has come to me for aid" the High King smiled. Everyone in the room understood that this was just another petty ploy for Cythees to taunt his younger sister.

Eleana glared at Saura, who returned a smug smile. "Oh...did she...how very kind of her majesty. To think there are those in the realms who doubt her intentions" Eleana said, still staring at Saura.

"Yes...well. Being the High King of the Eight Realms requires generosity towards subjects and I have elected to assign a few troops to guard you and your...son" Cythees simpered as a struggling smile cracked across his thin lips. Eleana glanced at her boy, next to her. They were both smart enough to understand that Cythees hadn't disposed of these guards onto her for generosity. And at Cythees word, as he clicked his fingers, four Monthell guards approached, seemingly out of nowhere, and surrounded Eleana and Martis. "Well...your majesty. Thank you for this gift. It's so nice to see how much value you place on your most loyal of subjects" Eleana returned sarcastically, giving a mocking half-bow. "Will that be all, brother? Sorry...your majesty?"

"I do believe father wants to speak with you first"

Eleana turned her gaze to her father, who stood just next to the throne.

"Yes. Await me in your chambers. I will join you shortly. We've just received word. The Lenglores departed Cloudspear on the last turn of the moon, they will be here by tomorrow, you must be ready for your suitor. Wear a more decent dress" Corvus ordered, giving no time for his daughter to reply as he asked Cythees "will that be all, your majesty?" as if a father must ask his son for blessing or a man as rich and influential as him had to ask the High King for permission.

"Yes, I believe it is. That will be all for now. We'll reconvene later!" Cythees stated as the court shuffled off to their own various bits of business.

Eleana turned to Martis and held him by the shoulders as she gently murmured "go back to your own chambers whilst me and your grandfather speak"

"But mother w…"

"No arguments. Go on. I'll find you when we're finished. I promise" Eleana smiled as she let her son go, kindly letting him leave.

Eleana always tried to keep Martis away from her father's wrath as whenever she spoke she knew her father would have something to counter whatever she said, always leading to a vicious argument, something Eleana tried to keep her son from, despite him being of the age to have seen most harsh truths of the world she knew her fathers words could be as deep cutting as any blade or trauma and she was tired from the exhaustion of this constant fighting. Yet perhaps it was why he too refrained, only when arguing with her, not the other siblings. He saw in her his own fire and such a pertinacious resistance to any change that was foisted her way.

Eleana noticed her father staring coldly at her. The two led themselves to the high tower of Eleana's chambers. When they arrived they were greeted with a lavished site. On all the stone walls of Eleana's room were paintings and tapestries of all sorts, imported from the far reaches of the world, others she had brought with her from The Forge. Many of which Corvus had ordered her to take as he had proclaimed that he was never one for flaunting their riches on art or any other thing for that matter. Had it not been for her or her mother, The Forge would have been as despondent as its King.

Eleana went and stood on her balcony, covered by a canopy of silk, whilst her father positioned himself at a table just inside the actual chambers. Lady Monthell kept her back to her father, staring out at the Bay of Gales, the mighty boats sailing in from Mundiil and Argus, loaded with spices and silks and strange oddities. "So, you wanted to speak to me?"

"Yes. Your marriage to Gryff Lenglore, we need to discuss how best it would be to seize on this union and your new life with the Lenglores" Corvus said simply.

"My new life? Father, I will stay here with my son, where we belong, where I have lived for nearly sixteen years. I will not marry that half-bred son who stands to inherit nothing but his fathers admiration for his own lust"

"The boy is heir to The Highfelds, recently legitimized by his father why do you think that is?"

"I don't know. Though clearly you do, for all your gloating" Eleana shrugged. Corvus frowned.

"Don't be insolent. Toros would never leave his realm to his true born son. Not with his affliction. The Gods gave him another chance to correct that mistake"

"Is that what they call it: an unnatural profinity for boys. I can think of worse crimes than buggery"

"Regardless. Gryff is now heir. He has beaten his brother out of his place, rightful or not the lords and nobles of The Highfelds did not argue when it was put to them. You will help to fill that place"

"No. I won't do it"

"Oh yes you will. You cannot expect to ask the heir of the Highfelds to lower himself and lessen his station by joining you in this cesspit. No. You will go to him. When Gryff and his father arrive tomorrow you will impress him and if you're successful in that pursuit then you will leave with him on the day to begin your life in The Highfelds as a future Queen. It's high time you were married" King Monthell firmly stated.

"No. I won't. I have no desire to be a bastards Queen and I already let you marry me off to that merchants son and that was two years of hell and then I've spent the last fourteen years trapped in this gilded cage. Six of those years my own brother has made sure that every time he sees me to humiliate or degrade me for no other reason than because he doesn't want me here and I have to stay here, regardless of my own thoughts, for Martis. And now you want to send me away to the Highfelds? No. I won't do it" Eleana ranted as she turned to face her father in a moment of anger.

Corvus rose from his seat abruptly "No more! I will hear no. More. On the matter. You will do as instructed and cast your selfishness aside. If everyone based their lives off of wants and wishes then they may find their lives rather hard to overcome" he said as he concluded the conversation and headed for the door. As he reached for the handle Eleana entered the room from outside "and what about Martis? Hmm? What about your grandson? The current heir to The Fold? What about his 'wants and wishes'? Or is he just fodder?" she asked as a single tear started to weld in her eye. "Will you use him as nothing but a pawn as well? You hold nothing sacred, nothing! People are just tools to you. Even your own family. Mother, who followed your every word at the cost of her heart. Cythees: the golden boy, spoilt as your first born. Me, who you've used from everything between a bartering chip to a broodmare and then Christen, who worships you and is the only child you ever wanted" she yelled as her voice became raw and unkempt. "Drake was the only one out of all of us who saw you for what you were. Before your plots could swallow him up as well"

"Silence!" the King of the Fold bellowed without even turning to face her.

"One day you and Cythees will see that all of this was worth nought in the end" Eleana cursed.

Corvus had already regained himself and calmly turned back to his daughter and with no remorse said "the boy will return to The Forge to live out his days as a potential heir and asset to the house of Monthell. His time of clinging onto you has far exceeded its limits. You have a duty. And so does he, to our family, to ensure our superiority is unchallenged. Now is perhaps the only time we will have to peacefullly ensure the continuation of this dynasty and I will not have you jeopardize that on account of your weakness" as he pulled open the green door by its ringed door handle.

As it creaked open and Corvus placed a foot in the stone corridor Eleana spoke a final word to her father "I won't let even you--the mighty Corvus Monthell take the only thing of value I have left! You and Cythees may be set in your pursuit of power or control, it doesn't matter to me! The success of our family doesn't matter to me! Whoever sits on that bastard throne or wears that fucking crown doesn't matter to me! None of it!" Eleana flared as she felt her voice crack and quiver.

She knew it was inevitable and that her father would get what he wanted but the same resistance of her youth burned within her as it did Martis and her exiled brother before them-- a kindled fire set loose.

Corvus shut the door behind himself, never turning. As if his daughter had never spoken and uttered such iron -wrought words and as the door shut behind him, Eleana dropped to her knees, pinning her fine red dress beneath them as she began to cry. She held her golden, eagle necklace close to her, remembering her mother whom had gifted her the pendant. The grief of all the years had swelled within her to an almost unlivable level and she felt its cold and merciless grip tighten on her. She saw no other way out and, as hope faded, she cast the necklace away from herself, over the balcony. Her resolve sunk within her and settled on a hollow bedrock of despair as the truth dawned on her: she had never been aught. Not a Lady of The Forge or the daughter of a King, save for the tool of her father in his designs. A life wasted in service to anothers ideals and ones that had gripped her all her life and yet she accepted it time and time again. This time, she thought, it must not be so.

Chapter 7-Dark Clouds Ahead

Evening light glowed down on Ushkin City, across the tiles of houses and through the many different flora of the jungle around the city. Thin cracks in the trees let through the final glimmers of daylight onto the Obsidian Pyramid and washing off the other side, making a long and dim shadow glide over half of Ushkin. Already, the surrounding land had become an orchestra for the nightly birds and insects to play their tunes.

Whilst most of the city's inhabitants still lay in their houses, with the streets empty, Tarith and the Osh-Venn were setting out to Dragontooth Crater, ancestral birthing ground for all true Harbingers and anointed Champions. The young Malacender had clothed himself in his traveling armor; a thick, black chest piece was strapped to him with a roaring dragon head in its center, as were his iron gauntlets shaped like fire about his wrists. His white forearms seemed to be the only relic of his humanity besides his face as even when traveling the people of the Empire went with their strong armor, ready and prepared for the ruthlessness of their land. He wore thick, leather boots and knee pads, capped with steel. His ptergues covered the majority of his lower half, with each stud on this exquisite piece of armor resembling a slumbering face.

The Prince's silver-blue hair had now been placed in the traditional dreadlocks of his people and was no longer the fine sheet of silver gray he forced it to be on the daily. It barely blew as the first gentle winds of the day arrived. He observed from afar, watching weapons and food previsions being loaded into carts and covered with tarpaulins. He approached one such cart, asking its driver "is everything readied? This journey is to be a long one"

"Yes, your benevolence. It was a bit short notice but when the Emperor commands, what choice do the Osh-Venn have but to answer? All the things we can take with us, including luck, we have" the driver said as he turned to face Tarith, his voice muffled somewhat through the skull mask he wore over his head, with just his eyes showing from out of the sockets like some fearless mockery of death as was the desired effect of their traditions.

Tarith nodded, he would finally be leaving the boundaries of his city, something he had always wished for. Of course he had accompanied the Osh-Venn on scouting or hunting missions where he could be the first into the fray but nothing so singular and unique. The furthest he had ever reached was a few miles west to the river trading cities of Veros and Celmn'en, known for their carnivals and great tapestries of lore and history that stretched back tens of thousands of years.

As he surveyed a small number of other Osh-Vennisian soldiers, throwing in some last minute sword training, he heard a booming and gruff voice speak from behind him "well, well my Prince. Blood-friend to Osh-Venn and Harbinger at just twenty-one. You just couldn't stop drawing attention to yourself. The selfishness of royalty"

Tarith smiled, recognising the voice immediately. He turned to face this person, drawing his sword as he did and pointing at the person's throat. "I should have your tongue for such slanders" Tarith smiled. The man smiled back. The great brute was General Lo'atal, an old friend. At just a few years older than Tarith, Lo'atal towered over him; he was big, even for an Osh-Venn. He was a muscular man, covered in gray body paint from head to toe which, in the constant heat of Ushkin, had dried and cracked, making him look just like one of the stone idols of his people. Lo'atal showed very little emotion, save for a small smile he would produce whenever his good friends were nearby. His matted, black hair was tied in a bun and held together with the leg bone of a snapping turtle. He wore nothing on his top half, showing his strong chest and abs that framed his body and his lower half was covered by a red skirt, decorated with crushed jaguar bones.

"But yes, it would appear that now even Ornagoth himself has taken an interest," the Prince said, lowering his sword slowly from Lo'atal's throat. "How many march with us?" Tarith questioned.

"About ten score in total. We don't want to leave Ushkins defenses depleted"

"Good. Good. Gone are the days of the legion I suppose" the Prince tilted his head as he watched half an ox being loaded onto one of the supply carts.

"Having the legion like the days of old would take the pressure off our own homeland. Maybe when you ascend you can see to it"

"Not if the senate have their way"

"Well you just let me know when you want them executed and we will serve. I don't know how the Emperors of old stomached the idea of having them all sat in that building conspiring to who knows what end"

"You mean to say you hold no trust for politicians?" Tarith smirked.

"Well the way I hear it Emperors and their offspring arn't much better" the General joked. "Well, your benevolence, we march when you give the order. It's a few week's trek to Nadenia and from there we will cross through the Goldbrand River and into the Red Wastes where the crater lies, if the maps are to be believed and if we keep to our course" Lo'atal explained.

Tarith nodded in understanding "I have a few things to deal with first, see to it the final preparations are made"

Lo'atal obeyed, greeting his Prince before continuing with the haul.

The Princeling wandered back to the palace steps where he soon found Vacile sitting on them, fumbling at books and oddities in his satchel. "I almost mistook you for a vagrant, was about to have you flogged" Tarith taunted the old man.

"I suppose I have always lacked the grandeur of a conventional historian in place of a beggar, then" Vacile smiled warmly. Like a caring grandfather, Tarith had always felt comforted by the odd and half maddened man, his loyalty was trusted and backed by servitude to the clan for decades. Though Vacile was always one to stay away from the royalty and preferred more his lore and ancient languages to study.

"So…" Tarith continued awkwardly, fumbling with the studs on his skirts. "All these stories…I…can't, I haven't even started to believe it yet. It's as if this is all some strange dream, an invention of the mind and any moment I'm going to wake up and see I'm still back in bed with some girl. Though I would have few reservations about that"

"Your benevolence. You are much more than what you believe

yourself to be. Ornagoth knows this, he knows your heart. Learn to follow the strength he's placed within you and then your path will be as clear as fallen rain. My knowledge can only go to certain lengths. You will have to carry your own torch though" the curate consoled. He placed a wrinkled and shaky hand on Tarith's shoulder before he whispered a few gravely words into the Prince's ear. "You should bid your parents farewell. They will wish to see you before we leave"

"Of course. Thank you, Vacile" Tarith smiled sheepishly. He slowly pulled himself back up and lingered in anticipation. He would have eventually plucked up enough courage to bid them goodbye, he was sure of it. However he was beaten to it as he soon saw both parents declining the stairs from within the palace. Tarith lowered his head at their approach. "Mother, Father. It is time"

"That it is, son" Tephus smiled, grasping his son by his shoulder. "I cannot say what you will find, I fear my limited wisdom would fail you. Then again, you could always survive without it. Ha, but I will allow you to go with my blessing and remember if this is indeed it. If we are right as I have hoped since I first saw you come into this world, you are the one. As Stun was and its his blood that courses through your veins" the Emperor smiled. The two men embraced and, for the first time in a long time, Tarith felt the shallow void between himself and his father close. He looked out from over his fathers shoulder to his mother, she smiled, though it was clear Empress Cassandra had more to say than she could permit herself. The sorrowful look she had in her eyes was enough to tell Tarith how little she wanted him to leave, how much she had wished that maybe Ornagoth was mistaken and hadn't cast her son into the world with seemingly impossible expectations.

"Your good people, the best. The creator himself couldn't make better parents, rulers…friends" Tarith finally uttered. He felt the words leave his mouth and tremble with the subtle hint of fear. It loomed over him more than ever before. "I will return, I promise. I do not know what the nature of that return will be but I swear I will come back. Whether it be a truth or not"

That final whisper was enough. Tarith released his father, their eyes never leaving each other. "We love you, Tarith" he heard his mother say as he finally pulled himself away and began to slowly walk backwards, back down the steps, keeping his eyes on them as if scared of them suddenly fading from existence itself. Behind the Prince, Vacile bowed to his Emperor and led Tarith away. "Come, my Prince. We must stay on our course. It is done. Your journey must differ from theirs now and where we are bound, they cannot come"

"Get the men ready. It's time to move. Our course is set. We mustn't keep Ornagoth waiting" the curate ordered to the General who had by now finished with his final packings and was awaiting the two, holding the reins of their mounts. Lo'atal bowed before bellowing orders to the men. In this moment of solitude, Tarith clambered onto his stallion and as he did he looked, with great contemplation, at his surroundings. The yellow flag with the red dragon head flew over the Obsidian Pyramid and on the walls of the city like markers on a map, leading to the senate building at the far edge of the city. He felt the thin drops of moisture from the towering trees and palms fall onto his skin and nourish him and though he wanted to move beyond the confines of the colossal city there was something, he felt, that was pulling him back before he had left. An unidentified force that he couldn't explain was wanting him to stay, saying he could still have a good life as the Emperor of Mundiil, but a larger part of him knew that no Harbinger before him had ever shrunk from their anointed destiny and he did not want to be the first in twenty-thousand years to bring a gloom to their legacies or memory. He felt their eyes on him as he turned back and met his fathers eyes whom welled with a single tear though, luckily, he was too far for his son to notice.

Lo'atal rode up alongside his prince on the back of a massive, three horned rhino; a special present from Lo'atal's own parents who ruled the warrior-breeding province of Dush'Uul, far to the north of Ushkin. Their beasts made the animals of Ushkins great jungle seem trivial when compared with the immense size of most of Dush'Uuls immense animals.

The large rhino snorted and grunted as it trotted up to Tarith and his war horse. The two animals dressed in their cultures' chains and armor about the body. "I hope this journey proves useful, your benevolence. The Osh-Venn aren't suited to such treks"

"Oh come now, Lo'atal. I had always heard the brave men of Dush'Uul were born with swords in their hands and shoes at their feet"

"Yeah and if your God was as smart as is claimed he'd have you born with wings. Save us marching half a world away" the General bantered back.

"Do you truly believe in that? Dragons. Half the stories are nothing but goat piss and I can't afford to be wrong" Tarith doubted.

"It dosn't matter what I believe, your benevolence"

"Tarith, General. I'm not Emperor yet, you can still treat me like a human being" the young Malacender said, whipping the reins of the war beast as it began to pick up speed. "And as for belief…" he added "we all have to believe in something. Ourselves, our gods, our chosen destinies"

"You think our destinies are chosen?"

"Why wouldn't they be? Why would Ornagoth show me such things if it were not to be part of history?"

"Why would a God have any need to do any of this in the first place?" Lo'atal answered as they began to quicken into a gallop towards the main entrance to the city, passing by the orange and blue tiles of the stone and thatch houses.

He had not noticed at first but as they passed through the city there came a chatter and quiet clamor as people suddenly came to their doorways and windows, stepping out onto the streets or moving from them as the royal escort rode by with triumph. Their looks had changed--the peoples. Never had they presumed to look upon Tarith with such a reverence and terror and a look of sheer bewilderment as a piece of living history paraded down the streets.

Tarith watched and heard as the towering, bronze gates were drafted open, creaking on their large and ancient hinges as they rode through their threshold. The Prince made note of all the great carvings of ancient Malacender hero's engraved in panels, illuminated by the sun sinking over the twin hills to the west. The company of two hundred Osh-Venn and their charge left the city under the cover of early morning shade, the people uttered no more cheers as they had the night before as now they looked on, even from the towers and inns and balconies of establishments and from the lookout of the pyramid, alone in the sky as she had rushed to see him, the Empress watched her son cross from the safety of the city and out into the ever reaching lands of their empire that she now caste him out to.

Cassandra smiled humbly as a singular tear fell from her eye. Behind her stood her husband who placed a comforting hand on her shoulder as they both saw their only child, the future Emperor, disappear from view through the thick bars of the jungle's bamboo. As the black clouds of an encroaching autumn storm loomed over the city

Twilight had now come into its full effect over the capital as night shifted and morphed into day. In the council chambers, a thick shaft of young light came through the stained glass window of the hall that consisted of large, marble pillars and a wooden table which curved inwards fashionably. Sat at the council table was Corvus, Queen Saura, Sir Kellor who stood guard next to the table and the High King himself. They sat awkwardly as they waited for the three main subjects to arrive. First came Eleana, she swanned in, holding her white skirts as she walked down the steps into the chambers. All the way in she glared at Cythees and her father as she took her place in front of the table, facing them. Eleana refused to speak to any of the council, choosing rather to stand in silence, waiting for her intended, distastefully. She controlled the silence. Now the time had come, no longer could it be waylaid despite her protests against it.

The feel of the room was uneasy and awkward as the five sat in awkward silence. Or at least they did for a while before Cythees took in a deep breath, about to make a provocative comment toward his sister when the doors opened again, silencing the High King in his cruelty. Corvus, Kellor, Saura and Cythees turned to see who was in their wake, whilst Eleana stood staring at one of the stone pillars, protesting silently as she clenched her jaw together in a mute rage.

Two men came in with an entourage of troops. The colouration on the troops revealed them to be from The Highfelds, with their studded corslets dyed red and pointed, steel helmets capped with black bear fur. The men they escorted in, one in his late twenties, with sharp, jet black hair and an arrogant look about him and another man in his early fifties. Eleana knew the two, the younger one was

Gryff Lenglore, the Queen's half-brother, the result of an affair between Saura's mother and the older man; King Toros Lenglore.

One thing that Eleana and the Queen had in common, perhaps the only thing, was their disdain for Gryff. His arrogance joined the two together in an equal despisement for him.

Gryff was a renowned warrior, cold and merciless in the field and a charm to most harlots and the like and with a charisma that few men could match. He was tall, athletic but slimly built, with a puffy, pale, face that seemed to pout constantly. He was lightly armored and he strutted in with an air of feigned confidence only a life of privilege and pomp could instill. His father however was the soul opposite, as if somehow they'd been crafted in opposition to each other-- different cats of the same litter.

Toros was a cold and brutish man, though not in appearance. He had a rather welcoming, square shaped face and thick jaw, with a constant stubble that lingered around his mouth. His hair was mostly a dark, raven black, though the telling of his age was at the gray sideburns reaching down to his lower jaw. His hazel eyes were always vigilant and aware, and they quickly honed in on his rival, Corvus.

The young Lenglore attendant was the first to speak "your majesty, may I have the utmost honor of presenting King Toros Lenglore, ruler of The Highfelds, Lord of mountain and ash and castellan of Cloudspear!" she said.

Cythees narrowed his eyes, suspicious always of all the Lenglore's. He despised trickery and any other form of betrayal that wasn't immediate and obvious, he hated their cunning and smarts and how they always sought to negate and undermine his minor efforts of ruling. And they hated him just as much, a passionate disdain stoked between the two sides, ever since the closing days of the Civil War in which the High King had cut short one or two of their kinsmans lives.

The royal attendant countered "Your grace, you stand before High King Cythees Monthell, annointed guardian of the Eight Realms of Kond, keeper of the Gilded Throne and protector of the holy faith"

"Your Majesty" both Toros and Gryff addressed as they bowed respectfully.

Cythees once again went to talk but not before being cut off by his Queen this time "We've been here for some time" Saura stated bluntly, smiling pretentiously at her half-brother. It was always hard to tell what went on behind the many faces Saura put on and even harder was guessing the intent behind the words that came from thoses faces.

"My apologies, my Queen, we traveled as quickly as the roads allowed" Toros answered as honestly as he could before his son interjected "I wish we could have arrived sooner if I'm being honest, my Queen, I do so love the women from further south. They seem to have an unnatural talent for seeing things rather...differently" Gryff mocked with a smooth and husky tone, smirking as he did.

"Oh, I'm sure they would agree. Many of the women here in the capital alone need a big strong warrior to whisk them up and carry them away...but men like you have to supper instead" Saura simpered, her tongue ran vague insults like a cotton weaver. Even staunch sir Kellor had to smile from the corner of the room at the Queen's remark.

"Well. This problem is soon to be solved" Cythees said, showing his relief at finally being able to utter. "Toros allow me to introduce my...beautiful sister; Eleana Monthell, Lady of The Fold" he added, looking sharply at his sister as he said it.

Toros, remembering the debt of respect owed to Corvus for

past discrepancies, lowered his head in respect for the young lady...even if she was a Monthell. "Ah, my lady, it is a pleasure to finally make your acquaintance. My uncle always spoke highly of you ever since your meeting at the tourney of spring some years ago " the King of The Highfelds said, smiling faintly as Eleana, who was unfazed and unaccepting of Toros' kindness, stood with a blank and emotionless face. "I must say I do not recall your uncle. I was only ten and six at the time" she replied, barely even meeting his eyes.

"Though I had thought I was to be married to your son, not you, King Lenglore. Though I welcome the flattery. I can see it must be an incredible boon to be with such a man" Eleana retorted, casting an awkward shroud over the hall as Toros receded and behind them--her father seethed. Their royal guest nudged his son sharply on the shoulder, prompting Gryff to slowly approach Eleana, the way a lion taunts its prey before the first bite. He grabbed her hand, quite forcefully as he kissed it with his smooth lips and she could smell the fine scents he bathed in; rose. "You are everything your father promised and more, my lady. I never did didain from an older woman. They offer more...equal challenge" Gryff whispered in her ear as he smiled. Yet Eleana stayed stood, uncoerced and uncomfortable. Though she could feel the vile words pouring into her ear and her disgust was almost overthrown by the sense of her stomach slowly sinking when she recognised Gryff's implications. She stepped back, away from him. Sickened.

Saura noticed her sister-in-law's discomfort and, without pause, taunted "come my dear, I do believe that your...suitor is fond of you. Would be a shame to let another one slip away like the rest" she said, smiling falsely.

"As your majesty wishes" the Lady of The Forge retaliated.

"It is a pleasure to see you too, my sister. It has been rather lonely at Cloudspear. The last time we saw each other was at that feast in Bavrellion. You looked as exquisitely stone faced then " Gryff said, looking towards the Queen, his eyes narrowed as a small, crafty smile curled in the corner of his lips. The Queen stared coldly at her half-brother, colder than Corvus looked at his daughter, her green eyes, almost emerald, glared at him, piercing his ego like flame onto flesh. Saura, equally, was ashamed of Gryff who, as she saw, was an insult to House Carrsore and a reminder that even her parents, as pious as both faned, could make foolish and petty mistakes that cost them, hauntingly. Any other fool she would have snuffed out but due to his station, Gryff's wick was harder to dull.

Cythees was smart enough to notice the strained, if not non-existent relationship between his wife and her brother and stood up, the golden chain and pin that decorated his fine, red, tunic pretentiously glimmered with the sun as did the golden rings on each finger. "Well my King? What do you make of this union? I for one would consent to this match if it would please you and yours as well. I mean, these are only the first days but I believe that both my sister and Prince Gryff, as now befits his title as I have been made aware, can prove to make something from this alliance. The two would be welcome to a private chamber if needed" he smiled cunningly as he delivered his short ultimatum masked as suggestion.

"That will be unnecessary, your majesty. It has been a long ride and we, right now, only wish for rest and food. However, I do think like you. That the two of them could build a much stronger and more beneficial bridge for our houses. And of course, it would be an honor to be connected with the high crown. Especially through such a fine woman that we could hope to heal the wounds between us" Toros uttered, absent of his son.

"Indeed. Then it would not be that your uncle and father both died for nothing on those fields jsut outside" Cythees dared to mock. He found it stimulating most times. "Then it is settled. My King, I will allow you to make the arrangements for a marriage, should you want to be wed in Cloudspear. I'm sure my sister would be delighted at that prospect. She has always spoken of her love of the other realms and a desire to see them in and out"

Eleana may have held her composure up until that point but the mention of an eminent and quick marriage and in a place she'd never been, terrified her tremendously. "Thank you, your majesty" Toros said as he and his son bowed before turning for the door but soon stopped by the authoritative voice of Corvus "Toros. May I speak with you alone?" he asked, as if it were an actual request. Toros nodded calmly, signaling Gryff to stay as the rest of the council emptied the room too.

Eleana felt nauseous. The feeling of betrayal twisted her insides as she stormed towards the doors alone, pushing past the kings watch as her brother and his wife spectated from the other side of the council room and were prideful of their achievement.

To the other side of the hall the old Kings wandered off to a smaller room connected to the lofty council chambers, whilst Gryff stayed outside.

The arrogant young man stayed pressed against the stone as if one of the pillars themselves may fall down and whilst there he noticed the Queen change course from walking linked-armed with Cythees out of the door, to him. She bade her husband to leave her as she then approached the pillar, her heeled steps echoed about the hall as she marched towards him.

"I thought you would have come. Like a dog in search of its next hunk of meat" she said, clasping her hands to the front of her waist, elegantly.

"I'd have married Cythees but he was taken," Gryff jested.

"And I thought it was your brother who preferred the company of men"

"Half-brother. Besides…not all of us are as lucky to marry the High King…" he paused, as if finished " and yet still make time for others into this union" Gryff smirked. Saura became slightly enraged at the obvious jest, inching closer to her instigator.

"You will withdraw such a filthy accusation"

"I accuse you of nothing. I have no leg to stand on when it comes to our devotion to morality or the Gods laws, unlike our mother"

"My mother"

"Indeed. But we sit as two pieces on the same board. Both working towards the same goal. You use your uses as a woman to make it so whereas I must play politics in these courts and halls"

"Your father plays it for you, you mean"

"As yours played you. First as a Princess then as breed stock to a man you despise"

"It is a shame, Gryff, that after all you've accomplished: repute, riches and fine looks, you still haven't found the right woman. Until now of course. I do hope that old, used, haggard makes you happy, though I don't imagine so. She's not your type. For all her naivety she still possesses more wits than you. Her last husband met with a tragic end that the good Lady Monthell was simply heartbroken over. Right up to the moment he drowned" the Queen stated with a burning look.

"All women are the same, sister: spiders that sting and suck men dry. But fear not, we are siblings, we should be allowed to know each other's secrets without fear of them being spread and yours is more than safe with me. I assure you" he taunted.

His voice was smooth and subtle and his words poured over their intended as sweet and as heavy as fresh honey.

Saura smiled dimly at the comment as she stared right through Gryff.

"Tell me," she exclaimed, linking arms with him as the two began to walk away from the office. "You're a fighting man. Have you ever heard of the Gillens of Steelgate?" the Queen asked cordially.

"I've heard them mentioned, sister. Why?" Gryff answered, trying clearly to draw a larger reaction from the Queen but to no avail as she proceeded.

"Well house Gillen was one of the supporting lesser houses of The Furtherlands, before the Tyrens took their place after their own exile from Easthelm. They were inconsequential, really, but they were still a Lesser House of whom served...some other Lord of my fathers. Lord Gillen was always a, shall we say, friendly rival of my father. He always tried to exceed him in any way he could. He attempted for years to best us in anything, trade, crop growth, livery, you name it. Much like the Mallorys of The Fold who sought to challenge and question our good King Corvus, the Gillens constantly tested my father. Constantly. But they never got their chance...until my mother betrayed my father... and had you. Well when my mother was on the run she came looking for help at her old friends' keep: The Gillens. I think my mother thought she would be safe, or at least she was until my father was informed that she was hiding there by another friend" Saura smiled, turning to Gryff, halting the two as she did.

"Do you know what happened to the Gillens?" she asked as her smile quickly fell away, replaced with a cold, menacing look of expectancy.

"They were killed off" Gryff answered.

"Yes. Killed. Though, I think, in this instance we could use a stronger term. I prefer the word annihilated myself. Every. Single. Thing in Steelgate was put to death. Women, children, cattle, work horses, everything. Under charges of treason and potential sedition. The place was a ghost town for years after and it's only just started to spring back but more so as a prison for the worst in our kingdom than as a city. And my mother... do you know what my father did to her?" the Queen giggled, cruelly. As if taking pleasure in revealing such things, though it was obvious that the death of her mother had both altered and continued to haunt Saura.

By now the young Gryff was perplexed and confused, he raised his black eyebrow, awaiting an answer.

"Well. My father stripped my mother naked and had her beat about the castle before having her thrown off the cliffs at Steed Rock. Hmm. Have you ever seen a body when it hits the cruel waves and the rocks just beneath it? All that flesh just rips and splits and its contents lay bare and pressed against the stones and jagged rocks" the Queen remarked, showing no smile this time, no pleasure, nothing but her hatred towards her half-brother, the embarrassment and reason for her mother's death, a mother who she loved above all else.

Saura leaned closer towards Gryff, clasping his hand in hers as she pretended to dust his shoulder with her other hand before murmuring in a voice so devoid of emotion and so simple that it seemed eerie "if you ever presume to relate yourself to me again, in public or private, I'll have you flayed alive. Regardless of the esteem that oaf of a father holds you in. You are the second, half-breed, son to a family of confessed traitors that live only because my husbands house decreed it" before smiling quaintly, as if no such words had been said, before letting go of her subject to rejoin the council and her maids, who trailed away down the hall. Gryff turned around to look at the thick oak of the door his father had gone into, intent on telling his father of the menacing threat made and then remembered how he didn't want to test and see if Saura was indeed bluffing for she was never a one to make idle threats. In truth, perhaps, she reveled in indulging them.

At a desk inside the stone office, Toros and Corvus sat at a smaller wooden table, both already holding a goblet of wine. "That seems to have gone off without a hitch. I thought you said that she would have had more resistance in her" Toros praised his associate.

Corvus didn't smile at the jest, he barely even moved, straightening himself up "Oh she will. Just not yet but give her time. Eventually they give up, though. This'll only be her second marriage which the priests have assured me can be overlooked in the eyes of the Divines. A joining of both Houses Monthell and Lenglore will unify the realms anyway. With my son already married to the Carrsore girl the south is in full control as well as the west" Corvus murmured in a low and guttural tone, more to himself than Toros. "What are your thoughts on the wedding?" he suddenly asked as he stared with two serious gleaming, blue eyes.

"Oh come Corvus we both know you couldn't give a wet shit about when the wedding is and who attends or what color the bunting is or the flavor of the cake. So long as one of yours marries one of mine and you Monthells get to go on seeing yourselves as the strongest house, whilst we stay where we always have; under your boot" Toros smiled. He truly understood why Corvus had arranged the marriage, to control or at least aim to control House Lenglore and wrap his golden tendrils around it even more. Ever since the ending days of the Kondish Civil War, when the Lenglores had tried to swiftly seize control and were soundly defeated. They had hoped to catch the Monthells unaware after their victory over the Quarthand royalists and reassert themselves as the conquerors they belived themselves to be. Now Corvus had Toros calmly under his thumb and Toros knew it, humiliatingly.

"As I recall you put yourselves under that boot. Your choice was to betray us and march on the capitol to claim a crown that wasn't yours and it is by my choice that you aren't stepped on by that boot " Corvus mercilessly stated. Both their faces dropped as did their acts and pretentious tolerance, for just a second before they regained their motives to see the other one loose.

"And your son claimed a crown that was his? He challenged Morryg in the old ways and won and is hailed as the High King. My family attempts to reclaim our birthright and we are denounced as rebels and savages" Toros protested as he put aside the goblet for a moment.

"Your birthright? Ha. Remind me again whose gold it is currently being used to rebuild your realm at this very moment. Your people were savages from Antara whose whole claim to the throne lies on a slavery crusade you enacted almost eight-hundred years ago. My family were here just as long as the Quarthands were. Your uncle, Istlod, and your father overstepped their bounds and lost their heads because that is the way of things: one family displacing" King Monthell jabbed with a calm and calculated retort. He was almost joyful in recollection of the Highfelds debt to him.

"This alliance will continue. After all it is far too valuable to you than you would admit. Though it remains unpleasant, but do not be fool enough to think we have forgotten. It has only been three years since the end of the war. I watched Cythees strike down my father right outside on those fields and heard how you ordered the death of my uncle after our surrender" the King of The Highfelds was cautious in his words but fearless in his usage of them.

"Men die in war for all manner of reasons, it's irrelevant. You're lucky we didn't have you all executed for such treachery. The war was almost over before delusions of grandeur got the better of you. We could have enjoyed the peace after a relatively short war and your father and uncle would most probably still be alive, hating us and loathing our fortunes" Corvus said before sipping the wine. "And you are right. This marriage is of no concern to me so long as Eleana does her duty…and Gryff does his"

"My son will do whatever he can for a woman. She is a beauty I'll give you that"

"As Promised. She is only one and thirty years of age"

"With a fifteen year old son" Toros added.

"He will not be getting under yours or Gryffs feet, I assure you. When I'm finished here he will accompany me back to The Forge. He can learn from his uncle how to rule and how to be a Monthell seen as how his mother has coddled him since he left her womb"

"Touching, truly. I have heard very detailed reports about this boy…and the suspicions some hold as to his heritage" Toros relaxed back into his chair with a shrug.

Corvus smiled, realizing Toros' false flattery. "Do you know?" the old Monthell started, standing from his chair and proceeding to a canopy. "I've heard the most intriguing rumors, myself, about Gryff and the Queen's younger sister: Ilana? I think the girl's name is" Corvus uttered, smiling to himself.

"You are aware that it would be considered…distasteful for Gryff to be intimate with someone of his own blood" Toros answered as his eyebrow furrowed.

"Well you westermen do have queer customs. It would not be hard for people to believe. Of course we know Gryff is from the female side of House Carrsore and Ilana and her mother married into it. 'By blood' there would be nothing wrong with it. However..." Corvus pressed convincingly and then slowly turned, his face stone, his eyes fixed on Toros as he slowly walked towards him "I do hope the boy remembers his duties as a husband and future King before his duties as the play thing of the Carrsores" he idly murmured to Toros, before taking a sip of the Firebrand wine.

"It almost feels as if you're going to make a point," Toros retorted.

"There is no point to be made. Save for this: do remember where your true loyalties lie. A bastard and a King are two very easy things to replace. It would be most unfortunate if the realms had to be reminded who saved you from yourselves all those years ago"

"Be careful Corvus. Not all take kindly to insurrection" Toros stated, putting his goblet down firmly.

"Not all," the old eagle repeated.

Toros watched as a ragged piece of parchment fell onto the table in front of him. He read the look in Corvus's eyes and childishly picked it up, unraveling its contents. "Let me guess, bridal arrangements?" he mocked, rolling his eyes before even reading it. Corvus could tell however when Lenglore had read the parchments message as he saw the look in his eyes change, like a swift and sudden storm breaking. Toros' face fell, looking rather concerned as he scowled into the paper. He looked at Corvus "The Mundilic Empire has named itself a seventh Harbinger. Is it true?"

"Of course, it's true. They hosted their primitive festival a few days ago, that's when they chose him"

"Him? Whose him?"

"Their Prince. He goes by the name Tarith. Young boy, you know what that means. He'll be as brash as a newborn bull and if the tales of the Harbingers of old are true it can mean that that brashness will eventually come to a head. A fiery, unstoppable head"

"Its not possible. You don't truly believe all those stories about monsters and great armies? It was nearly six-hundred years ago since anything but tales came about the Champion Riders"

"I believe I've seen the skull of a dead dragon here in this very Keep. I believe I've read the accounts of the attacks and battles from the sky and if something occurs once then it possesses the ability to happen again" Corvus impatiently answered.

"So, what do you propose to do? We can't seek open war with Mundiil. Its Empire is five times the size of Kond and if the return of the dragons is true and these creatures are at the helm then…"

"Why would I risk open war? You Lenglores and your lust for battle, not to mention your warped sense of honor. Not all wars are swords and fire. Wars can be fought in the mind and be waged just as deadly. We shall defeat them through time, influence and this great game of governance" Corvus interrupted sharply "for now we will wait and see what the 'dragons of the east' do" he said as he turned, again, to the canopy "something is rising. Something…dangerous" he murmured to himself.

"You'd best hope that this little laying in wait game pays off. Even a man as calculating as yourself can fall into the trap of overconfidence and I do not wish to see fire fall from the sky as it has before" Toros warned, arising from his chair.

"I won't allow the fire to fall" Corvus grimly stated as Toros headed for the door.

"We shall see" King Lenglore said, reaching for the ringed door handle, pulling the door open to join a still bewildered Gryff outside. The two Lenglores were now ready to leave and return to the mountain fortress of Cloudspear. They had both had their fill of Kingsport and could not stomach the sight of the looming walls and lofty galleries of the keep any longer. Their pride and jealousy was a subconscious one but it swelled and beat to the drums of war everytime they cast their eyes on the city or its nobles.

Chapter 8-Ancient Origins

Young Toby Forrester sat by the simmering fireplace in his room. The flames rose high, filling the cold air of the stone castle with a blazing warmth as the embers bashed against the iron fireguard. A book laid out in front of him; A Histories of the Northern Realms, by Curate Jeriyll. Though the poor boy found it incredibly dulling, he could feel his young eyes drooping, both from the relaxing heat of the fire and exhaustion of a day's play. In a lazy drowse he looked up to the crib on the other side of his room, tucked away in her own corner she lay still in the cotton sheets: a little bundle of squeaks and groans that he knew was valuable to all. He could tell the way the midwifes and maids still tended her and though he himself was just a young boy of six, he knew what she was. He laid his head on his hand, almost asleep, before he was startled by the creaking of his door.

He jumped as he looked to see his grandmother, Lady Forrester, peering through the crack in the door. "Aren't you supposed to be practicing your reading?" she asked warmly, letting herself in, her long, blue, gown falling to the floor. She placed herself on an oak chair, smiling at Toby the whole time. "I am, grandmother. Look" the six year old said naively, handing the book to her.

She took it from him and examined it "Ah. Curate Jeriyll. He's been around for some time, I read that when I first came here many years ago" Abigail chuckled. She looked at him: her son's son. Toby looked every bit like his father, young and fine, blonde hair untouched by years in the cold. His eyes were his mothers but his face was his fathers. The son of Laya and Ulfrik, sat peering with sharp familiar green eyes. Abigail disdained them. They were the eyes of that immature woman whom Ulfrik had been taken by. Had the boy not looked to be his fathers spitting image then perhaps his grandmother would've found it hard to rear him and his sister whilst the parents were away.

The boy was as well dressed as any six year old lordling in the Winterlands could be--fine clothes made of northern cotton wrapped around him to keep him warm, with the shirt's fur collar kissing and rubbing at his neck and the wool frills on his sleeves that blanketed him away from the persistent cold.

The little boy innocently looked up to Abigail "But haven't you always lived here, grandmother? The men say our house is old and mother says you are as well?" Toby asked, respectfully ignorant of the insult he'd paid to his grandmother.

Lady Forrester looked slightly offended at the remark but swiftly let it pass. She knew if anyone was to say that it would be from the mouth of the mother. "No, I haven't always lived here. You know all the lesser houses of Kond? I should hope so otherwise the lessons with Brayla clearly aren't working " she asked. Toby nodded in reply. "Well I didn't come from any of them either"

Toby played a face of utter and childish shock, with wide eyes and an open mouth, with one or two young teeth already missing. "No" Abigail laughed "no I wasn't, can you believe it? I was just the second daughter of a pig farmer when your grandfather met me whilst he was on a hunt for his eighteenth birthing date. On a speck of land not far from here. I think you would've liked your grandfather. I know he liked you. Both of you, " Abigail said as she caressed the thick strands of Toby's hair.

"I would've liked to have seen him" Toby murmured with his young words. Abigail brushed his blunt and round, little, nose.

"I know. He would have loved that. He always spoke about wanting to train you and teach you how to hunt, oh how he loved to ride out into those woods and not come back for days or even a week at a time. And he was very doting over you, almost as much as your father when you were born. You gave us quite the scare"

" I'm sorry"

"No, silly boy. When you were born we were told you may not survive and yet, miraculously, here you stand. Proving the strength of your father and grandfather lives within you" Toby's grandmother smiled as she clutched his tiny, stubby hands in her warm and soft palms. She swiftly carried her gaze over to the carved crib on the far side of the room, slowly getting up and quietly creeping over to the pen so as not to wake her. She looked in at her granddaughter; fragile and weak.

"Everyone says she's going to die too. I hope they're wrong" Toby whispered delicately. Abigail couldn't bare it. The tiny girl before her was only just a year old and near gripped by death. She saw on the side of the cot that both Ulfrik and Laya had left tender gifts of straw dolls and small mundane gemstones. "I hope so too. Little Lydia is strong, just like her brother and her father. You keep an eye on her, she's your sister. Remember that. One day it may just be the two of you" Abigail reached down until her ginger locks bristled the younglings nose as she wiggled at the friendly touch and stroked kindly at Lydia's pale face as she slept. She could remember the night well. The snows had not let up and the midwives' methods had almost run dry when Laya's labors had begun. Even Abigail could not have held up such a stern demeanor against her in that desperate moment of such strife that she had feared for Ulfrik that they would lose both mother and daughter. "She will be fine. I just know it. And I will keep praying to Izaris and Mephala for her. Those God's of youth and fate must carry her now" Lady Forrester sighed, turning back to Toby.

It was in doing so that the book once again caught her eye. She casually picked it up, squinting as she idly read a few words, she had forgotten how embellished the curates and scholars could be. "Ha. Jeriyll claims to have seen all sorts. I remember once, in some of his later writings, I read somewhere how he thought he'd met a snow elf. Old fool" Lady Forrester slandered the writer as she looked at Toby for a response, forgetting, for a moment, his age.

"What's a snow...elf?" the young Forrester struggled.

"Snow elf, my dear. They were the first people who lived here in Kond. Thousands of years ago they were the only ones here. Elegant creatures. With paper white skin and hair, the color of starlight. Their capital city was said to be in Enk Forest somewhere, just behind where we are now. But they haven't been seen for centuries, gone without a trace, like most of what Jeriyll claims to have seen" Abigail smiled, raising herself up from the creaking chair and tossing the book onto the bed.

As she reached for the handle of the door she heard Toby ask "So where have they gone, nana? Nothing just disappears"

She turned to see her grandson grinning, though he was young he wasn't stupid he had his fathers intrepid wit and knowledge. Toby could see the world with the truthful eyes of any child but could ask questions about it that would stump its adults.

Abigail thought of an answer that wouldn't leave too much question in the young boys mind "Gone. Like many other things, my dear. For the world is not as young as it once was and the things that made it wonderous have long since fallen into the pages of books such as that one" she smiled, before opening the door with one hand and offering the other to her grandson "come on. You can finish your reading after breakfast." Lady Forrester ordered as Toby grabbed her hand.

"What about Lydia? Is she coming?"

"Um. No. Best to let the healers and diviner's tend to her. perhaps tommorrow" she answered, pinching his cheek and then led him down the broad corridors of Ironmarch, cold and lofty.

A minute later the two entered the great hall. The night guards, weary and sleepless, had already seated themselves at the two vertical tables and had begun their meals whilst the only horizontal one, the King's table, was empty: his father was not back yet. He watched the men shoveling bowls of porridge into their mouths and eating sausage and cooked bacon by the fork load. Both grandmother and grandson were greeted stalwartly by each guard, maid, kitchen hand and cook as they took a seat at the Kings table. Whilst Abigail fretted over Toby, trying to tuck his loose shirt into his ragged trousers, she noted the attendant scanning the room bashfully and then noticing her and proceeding to make his way to her.

"forgive me, my lady, but King Ulfrik has returned," he said. The words hadn't fully left his mouth before Abigail had set off down the hall. Two days had passed since Ulfrik rode to save Kings Grove from the Warborn, but time was of little consequence to his mother. She flung herself round the stone corners, ducking under fiery torches and passing cooks as her shadow flickered in and out of existence as she passed through the shafts of opal light that poured in from the blue window panes. Her hastened footsteps echoed down the halls to see what manner of return her son had made. They had said those same words to her when her father-in-law was taken by Warborn and the same repeated when her husband was taken by treachery.

When she made it to the courtyard, Ulfrik was already unsaddled and making his way up the steps to the keep when Abigail flung the doors of Ironmarch open. Both Ulfrik and Dullever saw her, standing atop the steps with her dress blowing softly in the cold Winterlands breeze and the stone structure of the main keep stood proudly behind her. The King sighed as he looked at Dullever "Home sweet home" he laughed.

When he made it to the top of the stairs his mother greeted him with the tightest hug, only one given from mother to son. One that Ulfrik had felt many times before when returning home, no matter how long it had been for.

"I thought you were only going to Kings Grove, what happened?" his mother asked in a hurry as she held Ulfriks face in her hands as though he were suddenly a babe again.

Captain Dullever answered for his King. "We spent most of yesterday tracking the remnants of the attackers on the grove. But I think a few stragglers made it out"

"Did we lose any men?"

"Not a single one. Davis fell off his horse coming back but I assume thats more down to his fondness for mead than anything else" the captain smiled "I think we arrived quicker than the bastards expected us to, my lady" he added before he bowed.

"Good. Good. Well come in, you two will need rest. Come on, I'm sure Toby hasn't eaten anything"

"We'll join you in a minute," Ulfrik said, prompting his mother to return inside. "Go on. Tell Toby his pa's home, I'll come and see him in a bit" he added as he urged his mother back inside. "Oh..." he stopped her in her tracks "how's the little one?"

"She's fine. She made it through another night without the healers"

"Ha. She only ever seems to when I'm away" Ulfrik joked.

"Don't say that"

"You know I jest. She's strong"

Dullever appeared from atop Ulfriks shoulder "Aye. Always said that she took after her mother"

"Go on, mother. Inside" he ordered. Brushing off his friends blunt remark.

The King and his captain waited until Abigail was out of earshot before they spoke. Thanks to the autumn breeze, their words were cloaked.

"What the fuck are we gonna to do about the Warborn if we're a thousand miles away in that rats nest of a capital?" Dullever hissed, he had almost forgotten about the trip to appease the High King.

"I'll speak with Laya about it"

"And the dagger? We need to know what it is"

"Steady, Dullever. One thing at a time my friend, one thing at a time. No need to go and cause hysteria over a rusty blade" Ulfrik cautioned, leading the way up the stairs.

The hall's doors flung open as Ulfrik entered a room full of proud faces smiling back at their King. The people's loyalty laid bare and clear as they whispered and congratulated Ulfrik on his return and praised him, their King, under hushed breaths. And Ulfrik, he merely asked one question, raising his head up to the rafters as if looking on his home with new eyes, as though the stone was not a familiar friend "Where's my boy, where is my son?" the King smirked with glee as his pale eyes hunted for Toby.

"Pa!" a little and sweet, young voice answered from under one of the tables where he played with his wooden toys. Toby crawled out from the table and stumbled for a moment like a tiny calf finding its steps, he ran to his father, wrapping his arms around his calves "Oh I've missed you too, son" Ulfrik greeted, running his gloved fingers through Toby's hair.

"Did you kill the nasty hill men? I heard the cooks saying thats where you'd gone"

"Oh really?" Ulfrik picked his son up and held him up to his own face, pale green and pale blue eyes meeting with familiarity. "Well perhaps we should have a word with the cooks about what's discussed in private and what's idle gossip" the King answered in a playful tone that coated their true meaning.

"I'm glad your back, Pa. I've been reading just like you said"

"Oh yeah?"

"Yeah. About the brave men, like you"

"Oh I don't know about bravery. Foolish sometimes, more so than brave as I'm sure your mother and granny would agree. How is little Lid? You been looking after your sister?"

"I suppose" Toby scowled.

"Come on. She's your sister. Your younger sister, which means its your job to keep her safe and happy" he smiled, trying to coax the same reaction from his boy but to no avail. "Now, pa has some things to do if that's okay, now go on. To your room. Take your breakfast" Ulfrik laughed as he placed Toby back down. "Go, get. Or I'll throw you to the monsters out in the forest" the King added as he threw his hands out like claws, pulled a rather grotesque face and mimicked the growl of some animal. Toby ran from the hall giggling at his fathers jest, as a trail of nursemaids followed after him with smiles under their white cotton veils.

"Go on, son. Enjoy all that freedom and bliss whilst you can because you'll not like the aftermath. Not if you end up like me" Ulfrik murmured quietly, to himself.

By the early afternoon Konds sun was glittering over the snow of Enk forest when Ulfrik called his mother and wife to meet him there. There where privacy was in abundance under the ancient, cold branches. Enk Forest stretched for mile after mile, from Ironmarch to the cold mist of the horizon to the north where thousands of broadbark trees, the very trees that had granted house Forrester its namesake and banner. They grew to enormous proportions, some of their tips reaching out and vanishing into the low banks of cloud, with their branches capped with wet, silver, tips of snow and ice. The forest's heart was the Elder Tree, the largest growing thing in Kond. Like a parent surrounded by thousands of children, the Elder Tree stood hundreds of feet taller than all the rest. A single branch from the tree could've held most of Ironmarch and it was underneath one of these snow kissed branches that the foursome convened. The two women trudged out, Abigail in her blue dress and tucked fur collar and Laya in her thick, iron armor, her bear fur cloak hiding most of her body as she took large, cumbersome steps through sheets of cold, heavy snowbanks.

"What is it, my love? Could it not have waited till noon. What are we doing here?" Laya asked, folding her arms in a desperate attempt to keep herself warm.

"Believe me I wouldn't have called you both here without a good reason" Ulfrik announced.

"And what is that reason? It had better be good, Ulfrik. You forget how cold things are without the light" Abigail said, sounding rather unimpressed at her son's choice of location.

At the prompting of her question, Ulfrik produced the strange dagger they had found at Kings Grove, unraveling it from a piece of cloth and tossed it to his wife. Laya caught it by its handle, looking perplexed at her husband "what is this?"

"We found it at the grove. Dullever seems to think it could pose merit if we know what it is. Its certainly no normal dagger. It was brought so we would find it. If you'll do me the honor of finding out what it is and why the Warborn would choose to use it and with the message it came with" their King asked. "The Warborn are a growing plague so I need people here, in our home, bringing the fight to them whilst I'm away. For over a thousand years our people have been at war with no real outcome. We have to do something now to quell the bloodshed before our enemies outnumber us" he added.

"You can trust us then?" Laya asked.

"No one better" their King guaranteed. However, Abigail was in a different state of mind. She remembered Haldon, Ulfrik's grandsire, the carnage he inflicted on the Warborn and the ultimate price he paid when he was killed on the field by them. Being dragged off into the mists to be drawn and quartered in their huts. as she asked "why now, son? You're only going to Kingsport, why have you become so enthralled with the Warborn?" with a confused tilt of her head.

"Because I know Cythees. Or I know what I've heard and those I've heard it from I trust. He is power mad, always trying to assert himself. His court is no diffcrent. Lord Jazar, cunning, deceitful, known for his lack of loyalty and sneakiness. Then there is the Queen Consort, Saura, a woman as ruthless and vicious as her father and the rest of them and then of course her lover, conveniently the steward and trusted lakey, Darian Darianth, traitorous murdering bastard we know him to be. He'll try and twist things to blame us and we need to be...we need to be ready for whatever happens. It wouldn't be the first time a Forrester left the safety of our lands and was killed for it. Our only true allies are those here with us now. We must count those close to us and do what we can. Or more will have to be sacrificed" Ulfrik answered, grimly, as he glanced at Dullever who nodded.

"Don't be foolish. Cythees has no cause to do any such thing" Abigail scoffed.

"Beg pardon, my Lady, but I wouldn't put money on those words. The High King is quick tempered, rash, not to mention one of the greatest swordsmen in all eight realms and the way I hear it, he loves to prove it. And his resilience to allow the Antarans refuge or asylum which has pushed us further away from his good graces" Dullever said.

"So, they say" Ulfrik quickly butted in, smiling as he clutched the pommel of his sword.

"Careful, Ulfrik. Don't travel south with these intentions. Don't ask me to bury my son as well as my husband, do not. We can't do anything without reason or provocation less we be seen as the aggressors" Lady Forrester ordered.

"Mother, I just need you and Laya here. I trust no one else to deal with the Warborn. Believe me, I have no wish to remain in the capital any longer than I need to and I have no wish to leave you here with them longer than need be either" Ulfrik assured his family "Now. Me and Dullever will leave tonight, after a bit of rest, for Kingsport, it's a two week ride so the quicker we leave, the quicker we can return and things can finally get on the road to normalcy" he added as he hugged both his wife and his mother, whispering into both their ears "be careful who you speak to for the nights will grow long" before gathering Dullever and a poultry amount of guards and leaving Enk forest. Their deep footprints soon covered by the many, gentle flakes of snow. Laya and Abigail watched him leave, saying nothing to each other until Ulfrik was well inside Ironmarch's back gate, leading into the archers training yard.

Laya was first to speak, rather distantly and disdainfully as the two women held no mutual liking for one another. "So, What do we do with this?"

"How should I know? It appears to be Warborn, that much is certain, it appears to be made from some type of black iron. As for where to start..." Lady Abigail paused in thought.

"What? What is it?"

"Toby's book. The Histories of The Northernmost Realm. I might..."

"You're basing your first mode of investigation into a sacred and dangerous weapon of the enemy using evidence from a children's book?"

"All books tell stories for those who read them. You should try it sometime when you're not busy negating others words" Abigail mocked her daughter-in-law. Though the two weren't malicious towards each other they were cold at times and their differences were a welcomed border between the two.

Laya relented and followed suit. Trudging through the snow at Abigails side "Why does he always insist on leaving me with you? I could do this alone" she murmured.

Soon the history book was laid out on the table of the quiet great hall. Abigail quickly flicked page after page, so fast some of the pages almost ripped from their cracked, leathery bindings. The words became blurry as she brushed over them with her eyes. A few pictures had been sketched, mainly Warborn huts with their triangular roofs and ancient castles of the Winterlands, most of which were now ruins or were only half inhabited where once thousands of men had gathered. Until. When one page was flicked, an etching of the same dagger that Laya held appeared on the page of the book. Abigail read to herself then mumbled the blades ancient name "Nettle? The blade of sacrifice, the initiate?"

"That's this? Why would a simple Warborn be carrying a sacrificial dagger?"

"It's called the initiate. It's the start of something I'd wager. The start of something horrid. It was clearly given to the Warborn with the intent of us finding it, though why, I cannot say. Some sort of primitive rite?" Lady Abigail fathomed, standing up to look out of the small balcony doors in the hopes the cold chill would alleviate the bemusement.

"now what?" Laya asked but got no reply. Abigail stared out of the open shutter doors with a confused look on her face. "Abi. I said, what do we do now?" Laya repeated, getting frustrated at her question being ignored. Again, Abigail didn't answer, only looking out across the snowy moors, beyond the mill, at the border between the moors and the southern forest, where Ulfrik and Dullever had ridden not but an hour or so before.

Something had caught Lady Forresters eye. A figure, standing at first alone under the shade of the autumn trees, then joined by another and another, all lining up at the forest edge. Abigail stayed, watching. Standing, confused and shocked, she did not know if it was just the branches and brush swaying in the wind. All the wet autumn limbs and leaves of red and brown swung about in the wind, revealing only quick flashes of movement. It was only when she saw the hunched backs and ragged clothes gathering slowly under the many golden trees did Abigail's mouth drop. Laya followed her gaze. "By the light of Oldir!" she announced as she drew her sword, running to grab a few guards. Abigail stayed, only for a moment before she could make out the figures on the forest edge a little better.

She saw them, with their green face paint, the swirls of the old, forgotten tribes: The Warborn. About fifty barbaric warriors stood at the foot of the forest, brandishing axes, daggers and swords all clustered together from previous raids or simply made by their own low craft, tattered and rugged monsters in the woods. As they gathered together, Abigail could hear the guards of Ironmarch, who had noticed the enemy outside the walls, begin to shout as they ran towards the parapets and grabbed spear, bow and sword.

"May the eight take them all" Lady Forrester muttered with contempt to herself. The castle horn blew its single, low and impending rumble that boomed between the crag. For battle.

Outside in the courtyard Laya had gathered the remaining guards of Ironmarch and had escorted the miller and his family inside the keep. They stood around her as she gave brief orders ``Don't be alarmed boys! These vicious little snow rats are nothing but the scraps from Kings Grove and they were defeated with a few horses and a couple good men. We'll have them easily! I want it quick and bloody, have their guts on the floor before they even know what's happening! Our King may not be here but we will fight for him all the same! Take em!" Laya exclaimed as the young and stoic warrior emerged under the oak archway, her mother-in-law watching from just above on the balcony. Ironmarch's archers were ready. In unison they knocked their arrows and, upon orders, let loose, pelting the Warborn with hundreds of arrows as they fell like rain, knocking down most of the Warborn attackers before the Forresters had entered the field.

The Warborn had begun their unorganised charge up the frosty hill, their boots kicking up dew and patches of snow like rampant bulls, snorting and wild too. "Open the gates!" Laya raged at the draw master. The chains to the portcullis creaked and groaned with age and cold as Ironmarch's mouth opened and the drawbridge fell across the rocks like a huge tongue, unfolding to reveal Laya and her men, armored and furious.

Abigail and scores of other citizens of Ironmarch looked out to see yet another clash between the ancient enemies. The Warborn were not organized like the Forresters but they fought with anger and wild rage born of hundreds of years of persecution and injustice. Where once their hands had been made to carry the stones to build the castles of the Forresters now raised to pick up swords against them. The cries on their tongues spewed their violent and hateful words with passion at the 'occupiers'.

Laya had already cut down several in a few short minutes and her men were fighting just as efficiently. The Warborn were used to fighting in smaller groups but in the forests where they were in control, out in the open field their advantage was robbed. Laya brought her sword down over a Warborn's head. It splintered with bits of skull and tissue as she carved her way through. Another volley from the archers came down, ending the lives of more barbarians as they bit into their tunic and shirts. The outer fields quickly became a violent and bloody array of screams, roars and shouts, pain-filled and wrathful. Neither side receded immediately, bodies fell and were sooner used as walking planks that squelched over the wet grass and mud. From above the scene, Abigail was amazed at how quickly she lost Laya in the swarm and even more amazed at the sudden sense of dread that followed it. The bear cloak she wore, however, soon resurfaced, stained a dark red, as Laya was seen leading the final frontal push that cut the Warborns defense in two. Splintered and fractured, the hillsmen soon receded until, finally, Laya and her armored giants slaughtered the last of the pack.

The attack was of shock value and served only as a reminder to the Forresters of the still very eminent threat of the Warborn. As Laya had wished, however, the attack was short and bloody, the two wolves of the north had clashed, and one had won with the other running away to lick its wounds.

Laya sheathed her blade as she sighed deeply, the adrenaline was beginning to wear off. She sat herself down on a little rock as the men around her gathered themselves, picking up the few dead and a dozen wounded and cursing the Warborn for them.

It was then that Laya caught a glimpse of a bloodied piece of paper lying alone in the snow. She wouldn't have noticed the paper at all if it weren't for the fresh blood streaking across it and staining the crystalline snow, poisoning it crimson. She leaned over and picked it up, unraveling it. It was a letter of orders, short and quickly scrawled. A name stood out to her. As the letter had asked the Warborn to attack Ironmarch, the request had been asked by 'Torrold Stone-Fist' a name Laya had heard screamed from Warborn who had been captured and quickly introduced to the tender mercies of the torturers. Torrold Stone-Fist was the chosen iconic figure of the Warborn, the leader of their largest clan. A man of fearsome repute who seemed now to take an interest in Ironmarch and its inhabitants. He passed through the shadows of the many trees in The Winterlands forests, spilt blood on every stone and, as the tales prepended, was as skilled as any hillsman could be with a blade or ax.

Laya glanced up at Ironmarch, sitting inside the crevice of the snowy, stone hills. She knew what she had to do. She had her first lead and though her doubts were almost insurmountable about whether she thought herself capable of dealing with the Warborn alone her confidence was lifted every time she saw the ancient structure, taking in the awe of the kings of winter-- her family now by joint blood.

The heat of the hall's fire felt bitter and hard on her reddened face, chilled with the winter breeze. The hall sat empty, save for young Toby and his grandmother who both stood by the large spit in the center of the room, its bright flames flung up into the air and twisted like molten rock, casting two shadows towards Laya. Toby quickly spied his mother and ran to her. She hugged him tightly, her arms both embracing her son, warmly, and shielding the heir to the winter crown.

Abigail stood behind Toby; an impressed look was on her face. "Quick and rough?" she remarked.

"Sounds like the first time with Ulfrik" Laya joked as she walked past Lady Forrester casually. Abigail appeared shocked at the unnecessary revelation.

Laya clasped Toby's head in her hands as she kissed his forehead. He smiled at her with the tender innocence of a child ignorant of the outside. "Now are you going to take good care of your grandmother whilst I'm out?" she whispered.

"But you can't go, mother. I need to show you my book"

"Oh and you will but right now I need you strong, son. As strong as the big tree's. You must be here, watch over your sister and granny. I have to go but only for a little"

"Why?"

"To stop bad men who want to hurt little children like you. Nasty, evil men and I don't know when I shall be done. Now I love you, more than anything that the God's ever put on this earth and that is something you can't get away from" the young woman smiled as she felt her heart soften. His face was the most delicate thing for a place so harsh and it easily blew away all her worries in an instant. Laya felt her eyes begin to water and quickly shielded him from the sight as she hugged him, clutching tightly at his clothes and arms.

She couldn't bring herself to stay longer after that, not even getting out of her armor, she ordered several men to accompany her back outside. She barked orders for horses to be readied and men to gather weapons. She brought together the keeps greatest rangers for The Winterlands wilderness was only navigated by the few who knew every road and path.

"Where in the name of Oldir are you going? You've only just got back inside. Come, we need to find out what those animals want from us, not to mention this game of riddles with that bloody dagger. You can't go galavanting off on some revenge spree now" Abigail stated as she followed Laya about.

"Why do you think I'm leaving? I'm going to find out what the Warborn want and what this 'bloody dagger' means because I know where to find the someone who sent it" Laya said, impatiently, turning and planting the small noted order of the Warborn into the palm of Lady Forrester.

Abigail looked down and squinted in disgust as the blood, now sticky, clung to her fingers, making them gleam red. She examined it with a particular confusion "What is this?" she asked.

"Well, isn't it obvious? It's a secret recipe for apple pudding" Laya snapped sarcastically.

Abigail didn't rise to pay heed and flipped the parchment open and mimed a few words. She stopped for a moment and asked Laya, without removing her eyes from the letter, "this Torrold Stone-Fist; You've heard of him before?"

"A few times. He's the leader of the Warborn, a great bear of a man from what they say"

"Then why are you going with so few? We need to think on this"

"There is no time for thinking. I have a lead and I need to exact on it before it dries up. Please, Abigail, stay here where its safe and look after the children. Please"

"Well. If you have to go, I'll trust in you to show the Warborn that the Forresters have killed worse than bears before" Abigail said sternly, handing the letter back to Laya who seemed surprised. "That's it? No more stern words about staying here. Family, duty, tradition? Is everything alright?" Laya asked as she crumpled the letter into a side satchel on her belt.

Abigail smiled as she gently grabbed Laya's hand and held it in her own. An action Laya had never seen from her mother-in-law and was quite confused by. " I understand the two of us may have disagreements. Disagreements about practically everything. My concerns, however, are aligned with your own, I think. Though at times we are rivals we are mothers first and so we love our sons with the kind of love that men will never understand so we know what it means to see them suffer and we do anything to prevent that. That hall up there is my home and has been my only home for the better part of my life. It's where my children were born and one day it will solely be in another's care. If my son thinks that you can be trusted with protecting our lands then I have to stand by him" Abigail said, as Laya could feel the wisdom behind the mothers words. "Besides I'm sure you'll do much better out there in the wilds, fighting, than sitting in the court and listening to the dronings of nobles and lesser lords. Best to postpone and leave that sort of thing to the…older and more experienced generation" Lady Forrester joked for the first time in a long time. Laya felt almost unease by the apparent rise in Abigail's mood though it wasn't a feeling that lingered, her smile was wise and warm, a sign of her patience. Laya had savored the moment, though it would never occur to the stanch woman to show it, a want that she had always tried to keep concealed as her mother-in-laws appreciation was a gift hard to earn.

The snow queen smiled, confident and somewhat surprised that she may have earned the respect of the Lady of Ironmarch after nearly a decade of marriage to her son "Be safe. And come with words of victory and the hope that we may be rid of those barbarians…forever. There is enough terror plaguing the world as it is" Abigail uttered as Laya made her way for the huge, oak gates of Ironmarch once again. Laya exclaimed as she continued to walk towards the horses "I won't come back till Stone-Fist is dead…or wishing he was!" before assembling her loyal, mounting her horse and leaving the fortress in a trail of beaten earth, mud mashed with the pulped bodies of the insurgents. Daylight hung above the party with a gray haze as they set out into the cold reaches of the Winterlands, through Frost Fang Woods and turning east to the wilderness of the Hawkways and its many forested roads.

Two moons later and eighty miles to the south, Ulfrik and Dullever passed through the old and ragged, iron gates of Fort Mistveil, the great castle designed to protect The Winterlands southern borders. It stood alone at the head of the Grey Ridge, black and cruel and wreathed in fog with its stone thick like huge, earthy fingers. The two men crossed under the last stone bridge of the fort that lay squeezed between the frozen peaks. The horses moved begrudgingly, occasionally slipping on the dirt and losing their empty-headed composure for a moment. The path was wide enough for two horses to pass one another and slid down into a wide open flatland, mapped with small marshes that wreaked of the damp and moss and every step the horses took flung dirt down off the path onto the muddy swamp around them.

"The last time I crossed these borders was when the civil war broke out. God's--six years ago" Ulfrik called to Dullever who rode opposite him.

"Aye. Dreadful time that was. Though what was even more dreadful was watching you on that battlefield. I can remember, during the battle at Great Wood, I turned to see you fighting. I can remember thinking to myself as I stood in that burning field; how the fuck did I train this boy? He swings a sword like a hunchback with clap" Dullever joked, before breaking into a fit of laughter.

"Bastard" Ulfrik chuckled, his laughter echoing down the flatland and through the cold mountain pass that he could feel sliding under his padded chestplate, steel braces and thick leather coat over them.

The horses trotted down the dirt path and through the marsh for what felt like days. A few miles along and the feted marsh grew into a ridge, reaching into the low hills and mountains. Ulfrik and Dullever rode the path, diving up and down like winter swallows in the trees. After a few miles along the ridge and as night was slowly beginning to creep down from the sky the two could see the mighty fortress of Swords-Wrath, the home of the King of Grasspoint, the home of the Stormblades, as honed and proud as the Forresters though not as ancient.

Swords-Wrath lay out in the middle of the horizon, standing in the winding floral tundra's, windswept and lonely. To its right was a large hill that hosted a few trees that choked the evening sun as it tried desperately to peer through and to the left was the Red Water River that stretched from there: the center of Kond, all the way down to Kingsport in the far southeast and fed into the Rivelin River. Grasspoint was idyllic in its appearance, fresh, autumn flowers running down the banks and sides of every road and each bush hosted an orchestra of chirps from crickets and songbirds.

The beautiful site prompted Ulfrik to turn again to Dullever "do you know in all the years I've known you I don't think I ever asked--have you ever been to all eight realms? Man such as you, I'd expect so"

"Ha. My gray hairs would say I've seen some awful shite but no. Not all of 'em, my King, but most of 'em. The one and only benefit of war is that those who had never left their homes got to see what the outside world was like. I don't think I've ever been to The Fold or The Furtherlands or Easthelm, that's too far south for me and it's full of the most insufferable twats the Divines ever suffered to create"

"Aye. Too many of us are born to live and die in our own corner. If the Divines are good they'll send me somewhere else. Ironmarch will always be my home and her hills and moors will always call me back but I think, before everything's over, I'd like to see some of what's left of the free world instead of marching through it" Ulfrik answered.

"Well it appears we may yet. It's a long and winding road to where we're going so I expect you'll see your fair share of sights before the end," Dullever smiled. As the two were reminiscing they heard subtle flaps of large feathered wings above them, clearly audible in the still air. Both men turned their sights to the sky as a large eagle glided over them. Every flawless brush of its wings against the sky carried it further away as it almost seemed to float more so than fly. In its sharp beak was a large tree twig that it clung onto as it flew above them and into the distance. Ulfrik watched the bird fade off over the horizon as he told Dullever "We'll take the BlackWood Pass around Swords-Wrath, I don't want the High King knowing we're coming till we're past Mootling"

"Don't you think that's a bit risky, your grace? The pass is unguarded and the only ones who use it'll be Lenglores and their lot, of which I'd rather not meet this early into a trip "

"Come now, Dullever. If Cythees wants us there he'll get us. Just not the way he wants. Besides, the Lenglores may be a bunch of ruthless schemers but so's the rest of the realms. I've noted their absence in most of the courts since the end of the war though I suppose that's up to the fact they couldn't even stand up to Cythees alone in the last war" Ulfrik smiled cunningly, a look Dullever had rarely seen on the young King. A look that Dullever thought didn't quite suit the upfront warrior, probably due to his lack of it in those recent dark years.

"Where are we stopping then?" Dullever asked, his eyes flickering from the eagle to Ulfrik.

"We'll stop at Mules Town tonight" the King ordered. "It should keep Lord Jazar's spies on their toes" he added.

"You want to be careful, your grace. That fiery attitude may be warranted on the battlefield but the south of Kond has a much different view on strength than us. Oh, and when…if we meet him, try not to cause confrontation. The war hasn't been over very long and I've seen battles and wars start too often over two mens hatred. It's as good a thing as any to push boys off into war but right now we don't need another" Dullever pleaded.

"You mean Darianth, the man responsible for the Betrayal of Inns and the death of my father, your King? The traitor who had our kin butchered? The traitor who turned on his own High King and watched as their kin were raped and butchered? Him? Oh no, that's been completely forgotten, bygones are bygones and all that hollow shit" Ulfrik scoffed. Dullever nodded, slowly.

"No one is innocent in war. Not us, not them. And yes. I understand. I loved your father as much as you, I'm sure. I followed him to the depths of oblivion more than once and…if Oldir and his divine host appeared to me, right now, I wouldn't hesitate to ask to take his place in the ground. But we're not coming all this way for the Darianth's, we're here for the High King and at the High Kings request we shall remain. Please" the captain said.

Ulfrik stayed silent for a moment, weighing his choice of words. "Don't worry. I don't want another war as long as I live. I've seen its horrors; women raped, children beaten and orphaned, blood in the air and chunks of limb scattered everywhere. Not to mention the countless men slain on both sides and all for what. But that man is responsible for my father's death and I'll make sure he knows that before our visit is at an end" Forrester smiled childishly as Dullever huffed.

"You sure?"
"As sure as the sun rising in the morning"

The two eventually came to the end of the ridge as it lowered down into the tundra that was littered with poppies and daisies hiding in the tall grass that gave Grasspoint its name. Few trees grew on the land, save for the crescent of small oaks that marked Black-Wood Pass. There the birds played longer and higher tunes than in The Winterlands. As a boy, Ulfrik had come to Grasspoint with his father, generally at the invitation of Grasspoints King: Igmodd Stormblade, father of Kaullus who sat the throne. Here was where Ulfrik thought he could have lived if fate had been different. The land's history was just as rich. From the last battle at Harrow Watch with the Rakers Of The North to push back the enslaving invaders to the felling of Empress Fotia Iron-Crown, the last Champion Rider.

By the low light of dusk the two passed through the first arch of Black-Wood Pass' tree's and stumbled across a sight that didn't fit the scenery; around a small encampment, hiding underneath the low hanging leaf's was a group of four Monthell soldiers. Ulfrik recognised their perfect armor, their slick shoulder plates and the red garment threads they covered their armor with, not to mention the golden eagle embossed on their shields and the feathers engraved on their visors. The two north men stopped to a halt as the soldiers stood up, looking as wild eyed as the horses. It was then Ulfrik realized they were not alone, the soldiers, they had with them a not so willing woman. She looked like an average farmer's daughter, dirtied and oddly clothed in sown rags and a cotton cap tied about her head in which a few strands of wet hair ran through. They could see from the puffy blotches that were the new editions to her face, it was clear she had been beaten since she had been snatched and used as the soldiers' thing, being tossed from one to the other. The Monthells dropped her when the two north men approached. "Hail friend! What is it that you want?!" one of the soldiers asked, annoyed, clearly from being interrupted.

"I want to know why it took four brave men to take down one young lady," Ulfrik retorted as he got down off his horse. Dullever's eyes rolled at how quickly his instructions and advice seemed to wash off Ulfrik's mind as they always seemed to, even when the King was just a brash boy learning to joust and fight he had struggled with keeping his passion caged.

"Oh. Her? Just a goat farmer's daughter. We gave him the choice--all his goods or her. You can tell winters on the way" he laughed as he looked back at his comrades who also sniggered crudely. "Don't worry, we always let 'em live. Ain't savages" the soldier sneered vulgarly.

"Oh, how kind of you. And what is it that has dragged four enlightened Monthell's into Grasspoint? That's mighty far from The Forge or Kingsport or any oath swaying company" Ulfrik strutted into their camp.

"Ah. Well the High King sent a letter to the King of The Winterlands a while back and it seems the bastards not replying. We've been sent to escort the royal prick down to Kingsport" the soldier stated.

Ulfrik turned and smiled at Dullever, who anticipated what was coming as he himself got off his horse, spritely for a man of middle age.

"And just how quick does his majesty believe someone can travel from north to south?" Ulfrik sneered as he confidently rested both hands on his belt strap as the soldiers gazed at him with confusion.

"What's it to you?" one of them asked.

"Just curious is all"

"Yeah well. Best move along, friend. These roads can get real dangerous after dark"

"The Divine's blessing for your concern" Ulfrik turned, feigning to get back on his horse and pausing just as he reached for the saddle horn. He turned back to the Monthell's who were all stood tensely around the tiny embers of the scout-fire. "Well, gentleman, it just so happens that you've run into your 'escort' I'm Ulfrik Forrester and this is captain Angus Dullever and you still haven't let that girl go yet" the King said, reaching and clutching the handle of his sword.

"You? Oh no. You're the fucking King of the Winterlands?" the soldier laughed as he sobered up.

"That. I. Am. I have the privilege of saying. Now I'll be leaving now, alone, and I'm taking that girl back to her home. Nearest town from here is Mules Town which just so happens to be where we're headed and it's where I'll assume you snatched her from" Ulfrik ordered brashley, almost growling as he spoke, stepping towards the girl. The soldiers tensed up as Ulfrik spoke. "She isn't going anywhere and now neither are you" one of the Monthell's defied

"Guess again" Ulfric sharply retorted, watching the last Monthell pick up an ax from the side of the small campfire that sizzled away. Carefully, one of the men held his hand out. "I think we'll all come with you, your grace, you, me, the lads, the girl and that gruff bastard who's gotten you this far. It would be a shame to have to harm any of you and we weren't sent to kill a King" he said.

Ulfrik sighed in regret. "You southern boys just don't listen, do you? Men like you aren't bred to kill sheep lest not Kings and again…you've not let that girl go yet"

The soldiers looked at each other apprehensively. "Step back, you bastard" their leader snorted, reaching for his blade as the others approached Ulfrik.

"Pity, fella's. No one needed this" the King murmured, Looking down for an instant before, like a springlock, he drew his sword upon the soldiers getting too close, smashing a nose into the pommel and instantly knocking him to the ground with a bloody crash. The other soldiers drew their weapons as one threw the girl into the dirt. In seconds Ulfrik had already cut one of the four down as they rushed him. Another swung a mace straight at his head, it glimmered as it caught the sun and clashed with Dullever's sword. The captain threw the man to the ground before thrusting his sword into the soldier's chest, with enough force to break through his armor and leathermail, cutting deep, down into his heart. "We'll call that one self defense, yeah?" he joked whilst grappling with another soldier. Ulfrik smiled, this sport was what he'd been needing for a while. "Call it what you want" he laughed back.

Two soldiers remained, both standing parallel to the two northern warriors. Ulfrik grimaced as he lunged at the soldier, knocking his sword out of its stance. Dullever too attacked the soldier with the bloody nose, slashing his sword across the man's bare face as he yelped, falling to the floor. The King continued to fight his opponent for another second before managing to grab a handful of the rapers hair, using it as a handle and planting the mans face into a nearby tree. The men looked at each other, Ulfrik glared into the bloodied eyes of the stunned and shaken Monthell for a split second before he drew his sword down across the lad's throat. A gush of blood spurted over Ulfrik's face as he barely seemed to notice the quick, warm splash of lifes water.

Dullever held his sword against the throat of the last soldier, who lay in the dirt, bloodied and beaten. "Thanks for the noble escort and service to the realms. Have a good think about it when you wake up" Dullever mocked. He waited for the Monthell to grasp his implication before delivering a quick and sharp kick into the man's face. His teeth clacked together like the jaw of a wooden doll as he thudded into the dirt and didn't get back up.

Ulfrik sheathed his sword, now all four Monthells lay, dead or incapacitated. "Bury the dead ones. Bodies attract crows, crows attract search parties and search parties attract unwanted attention" Ulfrick ordered.

"What about this one? He's gonna tell everyone about this after he has his little nap" Dullever pointed toward the unconscious soldier lying peacefully on the ground, his head resting against a log. Dullever looked at his King who nodded slowly, he knew what he meant. The Captain sighed with regret as he once again pointed the tip of his sword against the man's throat "hell's fire" he muttered through his prickly beard. The blade quickly introduced itself to the flesh of his neck and as it retreated it left a precise flow of blood that trickled out of the gash. Dullever nodded to Ulfric "it had to be done" the King answered and no sooner had the words left his mouth and the heat of the fight left his body did he then remember the girl who was frozen in fear, pressing herself against a fallen tree. The King of The Winterlands reached out an armored hand "I'm sorry that you had to see that, miss. But you'd have seen far worse if we hadn't come along, I'm sorry all the same though" he said. But the girl didn't move, paralyzed by fear. Her wild eyes skimmed the tree line, darting back and forth like bottle flies. Ulfric inched closer. The poor girl looked at him frenzied, primitive fear consuming her. Ulfric was almost within reaching distance as she sprang up. Like a newborn deer, not sure how to walk. She ran in frantic panic past the King and his captain, who looked at one another, slightly confused but expectant. They watched her find her way onto the path before Dullever turned to Ulfrik "I'll get to work on those holes" he muttered.

"Yeah" the King sighed. "I truly did not wish for that. Stupid fools. All they had to do was walk away" he then mutered to himself "they never walk away"

A mighty evening sun beat powerfully down over the bamboo forest of Ushkin, flickering through their cracks that carried on up as tall as most of the trees. The horses plodded through the waist-high grass that shook each time the breeze blew over it, cooling the company of Tarith Malacender as they wandered from the borders of the capital province of Ushkin to the imperial province of Nadenia.

On horseback all the smells of the native plants seemed amplified as the mind was taken off of wondering where to next put your feet or risk being stabbed by barbed teeth in the grass. In all twenty years of his life, Tarith had never seen a land as rich in jungle flora, more so than Ushkin. On the border between the two provinces life seemed to have gone unchecked, with no village or city for miles either side, nature had retreated and there she had made her home in the bars of bamboo and the thicket of trees around the border country.

"Where's the next inhabitants, General? Feel like we've been wandering for eternity already. I don't know how you Osh-Venn do it over those volcanic wastes" the Prince asked, rather weary from the near week long trek. He had taken off most of his armor because of the monotonous heat that lingered in most hours of the day with its mark clear as to how shiny Tarith's tanned face had become with sweat. His grayish-blue dreadlocks were matted with moisture and dirtied from the road air. He only wore his armored skirt and steel shinned boots and even they seemed to be causing the lower part of his body to become rather warm. The Prince had even undone his silver chain from around his neck as the fine metalwork and dragon head pendant turned hot in the searing sunlight.

"There's a settlement of Nadenians in a few more miles, you'll know we're near when you see the skulls hanging from every tree" the General joked, looking back to see Tarith's reaction.

"When you hear yourself telling those sorts of jokes, do you sound funny?" Tarith bantered.

"Relax, your benevolence. You've dealt with Nadenians before. They may be reclusive and a bit strange but I thought that of your people when I first met them"

"But the Osh-Venn have always been friends to the Malacenders, your best warriors protect the capital. As you have for thousands of years, ever since the last legion was disbanded. The Nadenians, well, let's just say in the twenty or so milenia the empire has existed in all its forms, Ushkin and Nadenia haven't had much to say to one another"

"But they're still part of an empire. An empire that is made of several different cultures and that will never change, your benevolence. Once, your people held no trust for mine and hence the imperial legion was needed, now the legions are gone and the Osh-Venn protect the heart of the country. Your people pray to Ornagoth, the God of will, crafting and such, they dwell here in the jungle. My people pray to Sal Uran, lord of the sun and the Blood God and we make the ashlands and volcanoes our home. The Nadenians believe in the three headed snake, Kirva, who will one day come from the sky and devour this world and most of them dwell in the eastern deserts and the surrounding areas. And whoever is in charge gets to decide who is the right one? It's the fear of all who live in an empire; that their own history may be swept away" the General answered wisely. Tarith narrowed his eyes in thought. He had not judged Lo'atal to be as philosophical as this . "And yet despite our differences we've been part of the same empire for thousands of years. Though I'm sure that when dragons and drakes flew the skies it was enough to keep most in check" the Prince suggested. He thought back to the age of Champion Riders and their dragons, beasts so large they could cover the many cities of the empire with their wingspan. Before even that it was the drakes who had flown in the skies, more shrewd and less majestic than the dragons, to be sure. For the drakes where not a gift from a God, they were of human make, crafted in the enchanted caverns of the Scale Lands to the south and turned into lizards that could fly though most were unable to conjure the great fire a dragon could, or live to be a great age and non grew within even a fraction of any of the dragons sizes.

"If this pilgrimage ends well or that Vacile is correct, your God will reward you with such a thing: Fire inside flesh," said Lo'atal.

"I'll be the first Harbinger in six-hundred years. It doesn't feel like a reward just yet. I really shouldn't be here" Tarith said, his voice dulling and becoming quieter.

"Really? Such gifts are power, my Prince, and those who wield it can either build a new world or destroy the old one. Why not you? Someone must be the harbinger of either good or bad and change"

"Why not do both? For the purpose of a better world?"

Lo'atal smiled, sympathetically to his Prince's naivety. "Many have tried and so few have succeeded, your benevolence. Most of them leave the world in worse conditions than what they started with" the General answered. For a brutish warrior of the hot reaches of Mundiil's north, Lo'atal had seen much in his thirty five years and the experiences had honed him.

As they spoke, Curate Vacile rode up next to them, his blue hood covering most of his wrinkled and cracked face. "Are you prepared, your benevolence?" the old man asked, kindly. He remained oblivious, perhaps lost in excitement, Tarith thought, as to how the Prince himself actually felt about the quest. Maybe he thought the dragon clan to be immune to doubts.

"Prepared for what?"

"An audience with the Sultan of Nadenia. Should we reach their capital city: Arden. Your father would want you to be cordial with the province ruler...and wary of him"

"I've never met the man in person. I know my father rarely spoke of him. Why wary, Vacile?"

"The Sultan holds a... delicate disposition when it comes to Nadenia and its place in the empire. It would be prudent of you not to mention Nadenia's bond with the Malacenders unless unavoidable" the curate advised.

"Is that a diplomatic way of saying not to bring up the fact he's part of an empire? For fear of his reaction?"

"Yes, your benevolence. It is"

Tarith nodded in understanding, however, questioning how many of Mundiil's citizens truly did wish to be aligned with the Malacender Empire. His whole life he had lived in Ushkin hearing nothing but the dogma of his forefathers. "Fortunately..." Lo'atal presided "if we take the sand passes then we won't need to go within a hundred miles of Arden" he yanked the reins of his rhino to jolt it onward as the beast slowed.

"Heh it's been a long time since even I traveled. I do miss it. Who was ruling then? I don't know. It may have been your grandfather. Or was it your great-grandmother?" Vacile recounted, more to himself than anyone actually listening. In his service the old curate had served four Emperors who had all enjoyed long reigns themselves.

Vacile was about to continue when Lo'atal's hand shot up into the air. The line halted, stopping like dominoes one by one. Tarith drew his sword, it sang as he drew it from its scabbard. "What is it, General?" he asked.

"We're being watched," Lo'atal growled as his eyes darted around the forest. Every branch, every cane of bamboo seemed to come to life with a thousand eyes and mouths as the group watched cautiously in the silence. A lone hornbill cawed from a palm tree, reminding them as to the jungles constant presence.

No sooner had the words left the General's mouth that a quick rustling came from the trees above. As soon as the vanguard looked up another force of attackers emerged from the bars of bamboo from their sides, seemingly from out of the canes themselves.

Tarith charged one of the hooded assailants, cutting his shoulder as he rode by. Another pounced on Vacile, knocking the old curate off his horse as he groaned whilst he was held to the ground. By this time, Lo'atal had already dismounted and drawn his sword, though made from bone and reinforced with iron, it was sharpened to a ridiculous degree. He swung at one of the hooded fighters, who moved like a swift breeze, knocking the Generals sword out of his hand with their spear and holding its point to his throat. Lo'atal gulped, not expecting the reaction, staring intently at the stalker. They leaned in closer to him, unafraid, and hissed "do not think I won't kill you, Osh-Venn, it would be as quick as blinking"

"And I'll return the favor" Tarith's voice whispered from behind the assailant's ear as he pressed the tip of his sword tightly against their back. In the confusion he had gone almost unnoticed as the stalkers made through the Osh-Venn, disarming them and forcing them to the ground. Men from the back of the caravan noted what was happening and were rounded up as sheep are to hounds long before the message had a chance to travel down the line. As far as the river, these strange rangers emerged and took hostage of their weapons and supplies.

"Order them to drop their weapons. Now!" the Prince

commanded to a slender figure who stood close by. He saw the gold cap on the tip of her green hood and recognised her to be the officer.

"And just who are you that commands me?!" their leader shouted as she lurched forward and pulled Tarith off his hostage, nearly slicing his throat with a concealed dagger as they spun around. The two wrestled among the grass and dust, till Tarith threw off the hood of the leader, pinning them against the floor and feeling delicate wrists underneath his palms. To his shock, the leader and seemingly skilled fighter, was a woman, about his age. She had beautiful tanned skin, glamorous and youthful. Her round eyes were a piercing green that lay on opposite sides of her small nose that was dotted with a few meager freckles and a small scar, the shape of a scythe above her left eye. She scowled at Tarith and Lo'atal with a strange fury as if enraged by Tarith's audacity. Her hair was raven black, blacker than any night sky Tarith had seen as it lay resting in the grass like ink spilled onto the paper. Even the clothes she wore: an armored corset and boots were all made from the finest Nadenian leafmail, bronze and gold like the scales of summer serpents, perfect for agility as she had so easily displayed.

Tarith held her to the ground, his long, silver ropes brushed her face, as he spoke to her in her own tongue. "Duviel Blaz. Nej'el. Al ok Suna?" *stay yourself, immediately. Would you strike the Prince?*

At this introduction, the woman's lips parted in shock and disbelief. She wriggled as she was let go by Tarith who pulled his forearm off her throat.

"Is this true?" she asked.

"True enough that I won't have you killed, girl. Just who are you. Speak! Now! Before I reconsider and oblige my friends here"

"My apologies, my Prince. I'm sorry my first meeting with you is under such circumstances. We weren't aware it was you and..." she said as she held her hand so her people could see, ordering them to release the Osh-Venn.

"It's fine, truly. It's good to know you people keep watch of your borders. A very close watch I might add" the Prince smirked, sheathing his sword and collecting himself, admiring the woman's skill.

Lo'atal grunted as two rangers hoisted him to his feet. "And who are you that you seem to have had such a change of heart so quickly?" he asked, growing more savage in his confusion. The woman seemed hesitant to reveal her identity, glancing at her men and women around her, her mind asking what they would think if she revealed her name to the intruders. "I am a ghost of the sands, Osh Venn. And of the leaf and stone, as are all my brothers and sisters here" she turned to Tarith "Come, my Prince, bring your men, I'll take you to Arden if that's where you seek to be going" she answered.

"How do you know where we're going?" Lo'atal questioned, still incredibly suspicious of the new stranger.

"Why else would a pack of Osh-Venn and their Malacender master travel through these lands? There is little of anything here for you except dust and bones and poison" the woman flirted.

"We're not going to Arden. We have no business in the 'citadel of a thousand toxins'. The sand passes will take us where we want to go" the proud General interceded again, breaking the woman's audience.

"And you will all be dead within the fortnight if so. A hundred, two hundred men all crossing the sand passes? If the weather doesn't wither all of you down to nothingness the ash vipers and dust men will. Arden lies to the south as do all our major settlements, they are safer and the route less perilous. It would also be our honor to host the Prince. If only for refreshments and replenishment" she replied. Lo'atal receded, silently admitting defeat in the easier choice. He had heard of the dust men: strange creatures, rumored to be haunting spirits of the dust, taking on a human form in desperation to see themselves avenged. Though plenty within the academics order and the many mage guilds could differ on the actual makings of one. Even an Osh-Venn General would be wise to avoid such creatures, should they even exist.

"I would not wish to intrude. We can find other ways to pass" Tarith smiled "though you have my thanks" he did not wish to meet this Sultan of Arden, especially after such introductions to his people.

"You would not be intruding. Besides Arden is the most direct path through Nadenia. Depending on where your going"

"That is not your concern"

"Lo'atal..." Tarith cautioned the impatience of his friend and then resaddled his horse, as did Lo'atal and the rest of the rather confused vanguard as the Nadenian rangers awaited them. Tarith nodded with a chuckle "Perhaps so, then. I see no reason why not"

"My Prince..." the General hissed over to him. He was unsettled by the Nadenians, he always had been. They were beautiful beasts, spiders in wait, they were politicians who played with poison. Regardless, he voiced no more of an opinion that may have casted slight and within minutes of the Prince's reply, the Nadenians had begun to escort them, spears visible and sharp that spread across the remainder of the bamboo forest-- deathly blades of grass concealed deceptively within leaf and on every branch. As they crossed Tarith found himself drawn to speak to the leader once more. "I thought word was sent to Nadenia that we would be embarking this way not but a week past. Is that one of the famous Nadenian greeting party's?"

"We received no such word, your benevolence. I was told that an unknown and potentially hostile force was entering our land. So we were sent to apprehend you. Had I known it was you and your...companions I would've spoken against the decision"

"Who told you to come here?" Tarith asked, his eyes narrowed as he rode next to the woman.

"Our Sultan. I'm rather confused now. I can't imagine he would be incorrect in the information given to him"

"Perhaps not in the receiving of the information but in the executing of it, yes?" Tarith replied "And who is it that I'm currently speaking to? No offense meant, but under those garbs and hoods you all look the same"

"Amira. My names Amira"

"A pleasure to meet you, Amira. Though I would appreciate less tussling and fighting should we see each other again" the Prince joked, looking down at Amira as the two's eyes met. As representatives of their own countries who'd always hosted rocky relationships in the past the two felt as though they should've been less forthcoming with each other, though their bantering came almost naturally.

The Nadenian's took the company past their original destination of the smaller border city of Dayaso Peaks, which, despite Tarith's predetermined imaginings of a great city sprawling off into the desert, was but a handful of stone houses centered by a small citadel of green and aged brick. The whole city was barely visible as they passed over the last hills a few miles south. The jungle forest soon dried out after that and turned to the famous ashen sand and soil of Nadenia that Tarith saw something only ever described to him by the tongues of warriors, travelers and traders of Ushkin. It stretched beyond the horizon; the heat shimmered off the barren land of which they trekked for another three days before Tarith gazed upon it: The great Nadenian Plains. Mile after mile of orange rock and scorched earth. At its heart were the distinguishing four, white towers of Arden, stretching into the sky like a goliath's crown. A walled perimeter was woven between each tower, encasing them and the city itself in a safe box, away of the desert. Tarith could see, from horseback, the hundreds of thousands of houses, bathhouses and other buildings that lay behind Arden's walls, most covered with tarps and curtains of all different colors to escape the raging heat. A roaring musical of people's voices raised up out of the city and carried itself out into the dunes.

The city seemed to be the total opposite of Ushkin. Arden was composed of thick, white stone for its walls and towers, at its southern side was the Sultans temple, its golden dome rising out of the white, carved stone. Its temple was rounded and circular, shapes Tarith had barely seen; he was accustomed to the triangular form of The Obsidian Pyramid and the low, carved walls of his home city.

When they approached the main gate, Tarith and the others felt the cool shade of the doors' shadow shield them from the desert's sun. "An old city, this place is, oh yes. Arden has stood almost as long as Ushkin herself and will probably remain just as long" Vacile whispered in Tariths ear as the two admired the structure of the large city, its architecture. The construction of the city was something the western dwellers of the empire had never seen. Lamps had been built into the bases of the pillars that held up the temples and houses of the mid district, their light shone through the stone with a muffled, orange hue. Arden held in her grasp the finery of Mundiil's eastern culture: its people with their leather armors and cuirasses and their headscarves of all different colors. All bore the same tanned and darker skin as Amira, the same beautiful eyes--shining like light on the horizon and all worked, unloading spices, working stalls, soldiers on patrol. It was truly Ushkins sister-city, thought the young dragon Prince as his eyes wandered the streets. He could smell the hot leather of their armor, beef cooking on large outdoor fires, burning sage that blew from every household's window to ward off foul omens, the dry scent of freshly woven, dyed fabrics and carpets and then there were the less inviting smells like horse dung and the smell of warm blood from the butchers though they did not mar the majesty of this great city.

Embossed and carved in the white marble of their structures were scenes from Nadenian folklore and history all jumbled together. Camels and their riders rode on by, their shadows casting over the group as they passed over the dusty mainstreet.

Lo'atal remained vigilant, not allowing himself to be seduced by Arden's great beauty, he saw what the others didn't: the look of suspicion the citizens paid them, the look of distrust for a potential outsider that cast him back to his first days away from his homeland. The General kept his hand close to his sword and himself close to the dragon Prince "I don't like this" he whispered to Tarith who gave the General a look of nieve surprise and then soon took his friend as seriously as he had always before being lost in these new and strange pleasantries "keep a sharp eye" the Prince ordered just as the company and their escorts arrived at another set of gates, these were smaller, bronze gates hinged with black iron. They led into the Sultans temple, it seemed even larger now they had gotten closer to it, almost blocking out the skyline. Tarith heard from above, cries in Taviri: the native language of Nadenia. He understood most of what was said, hearing the commands for Amira to be allowed in.

"It's been a long time since any from the Malacender clan came to Arden. I would imagine the Sultan is pleased to see you" the forest assassin stated to Tarith.

"Is that why he changed your order's without your knowing?" the young dragon Prince remarked, raising a silver eyebrow to Amira, who scowled at Tarith but remained silent, understanding his trepidation and doubt. The dragon Prince knew he could expect less of a reception than was promised. The gates creaked open, barely audible over the bustle of the city's market. Amira proudly led them up the pathed steps to the monastery, stopping just outside the main door. The large company halted behind her. Tarith turned to see that there were that many Osh-Venn with him that even when they had been herded into pairs of three, standing next to each other, the line still reached from the top of the monastery's steps to the main entrance gates of the city. " How could you not trust an armed host pouring through your door? Come on, anyone could be mistaken for thinking the two nations held a discourteous relationship" Tarith bantered.

Amira smiled, impressed at Tarith's wit and his defiance to pretend that there was a harmony between Nadenia and Ushkin instead of an unsteady relationship. She could tell both shared a complete disinterest for politics.

"No, your benevolence, but I must ask that you surrender your weapons before entering the palace"

"You have a lot of nerve, Nadenian" Lo'atal growled from behind Tarith, standing over him-- a watchful guardian.

"Just your band. I would not ask the future Emperor to disarm himself in front of his own subjects. Just you" Amira demanded. Lo'atal could imagine a smile creeping across her face from underneath the hood and bandana that covered her mouth.

Tarith nodded to his confidant, who bowed his head in submission, dutifully ordering the men to drop their weapons. The Nadenian guard quickly swarmed the Osh-Venn, making their way down the lines and gathering their weapons, knabbing them up and taking them to be piled in the guard tower like some twisted, gnarled impression of a huge crown laying in the center. The doors then swung open, allowing Tarith and Lo'atal inside. Immediately, the scent of sweet perfumes and different smelling sages blew past them with an amorous scent. They were bitter and rich with scent and smell. Most were of plants that Ushkin had never seen--from the far, southern shoreline of Nadenia where the sweet smelling ealmesh seemed to be a popular and prominent scent for the Sultan, same as jasmine.

The interior of the temple was a maze of curtains and stone pillars and at its center was the ruler of Nadenia himself. He was laid in a nest of silk cushions topped by a canopy over his head. The Sultan differed from what Tarith might've expected. He was no great, beastly hero of sand and stone, as had been told about him from the time of him being a young Prince himself. He was bald, sweaty, fat and rather short in height. The only hair that seemed to be on his head were the two gray, bushy eyebrows above his brown, glazed eyes. He seemed to be wrapped in a blue robe that fell just before his feet, the ceremonial dress was not only covered in all sorts of food stains but was incredibly tight around his rotund waist. Around him, in different positions and states of undress, were several harlots. Some slowly danced, others pressed against the pillars seductively, casting looks of fancy towards the strong and muscled Osh-Venn. 'Truly this is not the state of an imperial ruler? Most certainly not a great Sultan. How could she draw herself from this?' Tarith questioned himself.

"Father" Amira announced "I bring before you, the Prince of Ushkin. He's on a pilgrimage. He has indeed been named…Harbinger as our…friends in Ushkin reported" the Princess added, awaiting her father's words with submissive eyes.

Tarith's head shot to Amira as she hailed herself as the Sultan's child and the revelation of her foreknowledge of him being the Harbinger. "You? A royal Princess? When…"

"I suppose it would be best to tell your men that an assassin beat you instead of a Princess. Forgive me, your benevolence, but secrecy was not just yours to hold" Amira quipped as she stepped towards her father as Tarith and Lo'atal gazed at her with a new look of reverence and shock. "It would appear that the senate should be addressed upon our return. Some tongues have been waggling" Tarith turned his head to the General but kept his eyes on Amira and her recently revealed father.

"Don't worry. We'll cut them out when we get back. I told you; trust non of them" Lo'atal grumbled back.

The Sultan, who was about to place an entire bushel of grapes into his mouth, suddenly dropped them and froze, staring at the Prince. "Harbinger you say, my, my what a gift of grace you have brought to me. My darling daughter. My only child" the Sultan smiled, twiddling his sausage-like fingers. His voice was sleazy and low, crafty in both his tone and ways.

"A pleasure, your royal highness. My apologies for coming unannounced, we were not destined for Arden originally. However we're here seeking passage through the city and into the Red Plains. I was told this was the quickest and safest, not to mention most scenic, way" Tarith said, trying to reciprocate the kindness the Sultan feigned

"It appears you'd have enough men to go through the city with or without my permission"

"I thought, or rather, your newly revealed daughter convinced me to show cordiality and less dishonesty and ask politely to travel through the city. Unfortunately she was less than willing to reciprocate that honesty" the Prince mocked. He saw the small glimmer of anger in The Sultan's eyes at the mention of his daughter from a rivals tongue, as though the words were poison or hex.

"How very un-Malacender of you" The Sultan answered. He raised his fat hand into the air and clicked his chubby fingers, all clad with rings topped with all sorts of gems.

Several girls approached Tarith, each placing a soft hand on his shoulder. He smiled at them as he would a stranger in the street, passing by.

"It has been a long time since a member of the imperial family made their way here" the Sultan grumbled, fumbling with the thick, ropey belt about his waist. Tarith shrugged "Well the grace and beauty of Nadenia certainly doesn't fall short of all the stories told of her. It is a worthy and appreciated member of the..." he stopped as he caught himself.

"What?" the Sultan asked "member of the great empire? That's what you were going to say"

"That was not how I was ending that sentence" the Prince answered, his lip curled as he could already sense and tell, from the Sultan's raised eyebrow and condescending tone, they would be no friends. Vacile, alleviating, stepped between the two, one on his bed-throne and the other with his army at his back. "Forgive us, great Sultan. We are guests. As your tradition dictates we would like to invoke invaak: guest right. In return we would be happy to…"

"I do not need a lecture on my own culture and customs by a shriveled bookkeeper who sits at the side of the Prince" the Sultan brazenly cut in with contempt which sent Vacile coiling up and awkwardly retreating back to his host and from behind him came the Prince, to his defense. "I would ask that you speak to the people of my bringing with the same respect as you would with me: your Prince. Anointed by the priesthood of Krakcarve, son of Tephus, heir to the empire " Tarith hailed himself.

The gathering all stood silent at the foot of the cushioned throne for what felt like yearning hours until the Sultan raised his soft and plump arms and smiled welcomingly "of course, my Prince. I forget myself. Please stay the night. Let us postpone fate for but a day. Enjoy yourselves. The girls will tend to your needs and on the morrow you can leave on your most noble quest. As always, an honor to finally make your acquaintance, your benevolence" the Sultan said, pulling himself up, with the help of several servants.

When he had finally been hoisted to his feet he glared at his daughter. Tarith caught the icy look but said nothing, not wishing to prolong the already awkward encounter. "My daughter. May I speak with you?" The Sultan said as he spoke directly to Amira, who nodded in submission.

The Sultan then turned back to his Prince, smiling appealingly "please enjoy yourself. This palace I gift to you and your men for the night, as I would the city" he bid as he and Amira left the room for a more private balcony outside. Tarith, however, was quickly whisked away by the girls into another, smaller, curtained room, very similar to the Sultan's throne room, lantern-light and white with green and blue tasseled carpets strewn about the floors and the scent of jasmine and grapefruit to steam out the scent of greed and untamed pleasure. Tarith smiled behind his shoulder at Lo'atal who stood, confused as to what to do. He looked at Tarith for guidance, the Prince simply nodded as the girls pulled him into the room.

One Osh-Venn approached Lo'atal, bowing his head "General, what shall we do?"

"We won't be leaving anytime soon; the Prince is…distracted. Go on, Mekk, there's a whole city out there with enough things in it to keep you and the rest of the boys happy. Keep a few on guard here at the palace, I'll stay too. Of all the provinces and people of the empire, I distrust this one the most" Lo'atal said, ushering the captain away.

Outside on the temple balcony, Amira stood with her father. As she walked out onto the overlook she could feel the warm wind push past her, flicking grains of sand against her face "What is it father? You seem unsettled" she proceeded. At first the Sultan didn't answer, he ran his stubby fingers across the carved rail as he looked down into the desert sands that laid pressed against the white walls in great piles. "Every time I think you've disappointed me, how is it that you find a new way to redefine those terms?" he asked, harshly, not taking his eyes off the boiling sands. Amira removed her hood and bandana; her hair flew in the breeze like a black flag of radiance. The sun flickered off the carefully crafted, bronze chainmail on her chest piece. "What do you mean?"

"I mean why is it that when I send you to redirect these imperial tyrants you bring them straight to our door?"

"You're lucky I didn't kill him. Thanks to your orders. Perhaps, whilst we're here in this moment, you can explain why you said our eyes inside Ushkin said a foreign threat may be entering from the western borders and why you had our troops throughout the country on alert. As one of the commanders of our armies and your daughter, don't you think I should be given this information? I could've killed the son of the Emperor of all of fucking Mundiil! What were you thinking playing such deception? That is not our way" she lectured her father, a fiery spirit that Amira usually kept hidden, though on occasions letting loose for her father to see. Like the high flames of a summer fire washing against a large desert boulder.

"Enough!" the Sultan screamed, sweat starting to drip off his head, making it glisten in the sun. "All of this. This...this betrayal, simply because I make arrangements to wed you to Suladan"

"What? How could you..."

"I arranged this costly marriage for you and you threw it back in my face once before. Now you bring the Emperor's son here, who you tell me is now Harbinger which can only mean one thing! Well! I can tell you, my daughter, that this little trick of yours was in vain. You will marry Suladan, even if you escaped that fate once before it has only hastened his...hunger, for you"

"I will do no such thing, be wary of that. And do not forget who will rule as Sultanah in your stead, old man. Keep your politicking. I knew not about the Prince, thanks to you"

"Such poison dripping from your words. Just like your mother" The Sultan snapped at his daughter, rage and insult deep in his face. He grabbed both Amira's cheeks in his hand, squeezing her face. "This little ruse will not work nor will it stop my plans of which I have sacrificed too much to let go of now and I still have some things left to sacrifice, remember that. Soon the 'Champion Rider' will be gone and when he is there'll be no more hiding, my dear. This scheme of yours is done, failed. Suladan holds the largest single army in Nadenia and you will help me take it so we may then use it or rather I will use it. He will use you" he finished, wrenching her face free, before walking back into the palace.

Amira turned her back to her father. She could feel the anger and hate growing in her, wishing something would happen to allow her to release it, to set her off and then there was another feeling, one she hadn't felt in so long, so long in fact that it was almost foreign, unease and powerlessness. No poisoned blade or tilted spear could pause it. She stared up at the peach, evening sky, not a cloud sat in the skyline. The Princess gave into her thoughts and allowed but a single tear to fall from her cat-like eye and drift down her face and then, quickly, being quenched by her hand as she wiped it away. She was Nadenia's strongest warrior and fighter. A leader of both shouldn't show such weakness and lack of control, she told herself. She let go of her rage as she ungripped the wooden rails, opting to return back into the temple-- a layer of serpents she didn't know how to tame.

In her haste to remain calm and collected in front of their guests Amira had neglected to see Lo'atal pressed tightly to the corner of the doorway. His eyes scowled underneath his body paint as he watched the princess leave. His ear had been turned to the words of her father and they heard what they had wanted to: deception from an ancient enemy of the empire.

Chapter 9 - Winds Rise And Fall

In the gaze of the far off and distant moon, Kingsport sat, straddled by the Bay of Gales, it sat with little noise playing into the late night. If it weren't for the lamps, candles and brazier's scattered around the city and lighting it with a gentle glow, the capital would've been immersed in total darkness upon the hill and across the Summerplains. In the sky the heavens roiled and the clouds twisted like waves as a small storm began to brew, unleashing loud crashes and rumbles as the sky took a deep breath.

Beneath the blackened heavens the Gray Chapel conducted the nightly sermons, their hymns echoed out of the spacious stone walls of the chapel, spreading across the city with low tones of praise to the Divines.

From inside the Kings Keeps, on one of the higher balconies, Eleana stood listening, her curled hair let down and left to flutter in the mild breeze, for a modest woman, she was irresistibly beautiful in her brooding, with her hair free and her fair skin kissed by the breeze, pale blue eyes looking down upon the masses. Autumn was closing in on all eight realms of Kond and she hated the autumn, it served as a harbinger for the biting cold of winter and the darker, lightless, evenings.

Her white nightgown clung to her slender frame, naked against the moonlight. She had been asleep previously, but something had woken her up as it gnawed at the back of her mind: a concern. Her concern was for herself and her son. She pondered many things in the tedious, dreary-eyed and dark hours of the night and one that kept calling to her was the idea of leaving, taking Martis and leaving Kingsport, leaving Kond for good. She thought how her father would erupt in fury if she did and though the thought gave her a slight ounce of joy it also warned her not to leave just in case.

She wandered over to a small glass table and grabbed the silver pitcher filled with firebrand wine. She poured a sip into a goblet, she hated the stuff, and gulped it down in one. The taste was too bitter for her but it was a perfect numbing agent that was helpful in distracting her mind from its torturous thoughts and dreams that seemed just as cold as that opal orb drifting through the heavens above her. Sunlight was her comfort and from its warmth she could find a slight peace but Eleana hated the light of the moon; silver and cruel and a reminder of the nights dark edges.

She sighed deeply and turned around, attempting to get back into bed and hoped for a few short hours of sleep but she nearly collapsed from shock when she saw Jazar stood in the doorway. He had somehow opened the door without her even hearing, despite only being a few meters away from it. It was then she saw the freshly forged key sticking out of the keyhole that she knew one of his many secrets and knew to be wary of the castle smith from then on."What in the name of Oblivion are you doing here at this hour?" Lady Monthell hissed, angry from being both interrupted in her privacy and scared by the shadow that watched her in the threshold.

"Cannot sleep? Myself too, I'm afraid. Though I can order for the alchemists to remedy that if you want. I used to have the same problem but I find that prairie poppy extract is most calming these days but it is only...provisional" Jazar said kindly, always his first move in any conversation.

"Do not waste your falseness and your honeyed words on me,

spymaster" Eleana whispered as she quickly shut the door behind Jazar, trying not to make a noise. "And just how did you get past my 'security' that my brother 'gifted' me?"

"I know many things, Lady Monthell, you of all people should know this. And one of those many things is the times of which the guards leave that door unattended whilst they change shifts" the spymaster said as he smiled cheesily, flicking his red cloak onto a chair as he sat.

"So, what exactly do you want?" Eleana asked impatiently.

"The question isn't what I want, it's what you want" Jazar said in his calm and smooth voice, which seemed never to raise in tone. He looked at her with those odd, lilac, eyes that one could never tell what thoughts occured behind.

"Don't toss your riddles at me"

"This is no riddle. It's come to my attention that the four Monthell escorts sent to bring Ulfrik Forrester down to the capitol never reported back to their garrison, they were found this afternoon: dead. Someone had tried to bury them but they either didn't have enough time or the weather was against them, a farmer noticed them on his way to market. Whoever killed them is someone who holds a grudge against the high crown. Enough so that they would risk a bounty and a death sentence for killing Monthell soldiers"

"And why are you telling me this?" Eleana questioned, becoming more annoyed, more to her own confusion than to what Jazar was saying.

"Perhaps I trust you" Jazar answered, leaning closer to Eleana. His purple eyes shining like amethyst set into his skull.

"And you expect me to reciprocate?"

"Oh no. Trusting me would be a very unwise thing. I may act on principle but principles can be altered if the cause for them is threatened and I have had to alter them from time to time"

"A man who sacrifices whatever suites him--"

"Is a servant"

"Then how is it you wish to serve me? To seduce me?"

"Nothing so crass, my lady. You want to leave this place. I see in your eyes, a longing. You don't belong here. That much is a given. You're a flower. Growing in a garden of thorns" Jazar told Eleana.

"Some flowers grow better alone"

"And there generally the ones that wither first" Jazar answered back quickly before continuing. "I need your help to steer Cythees away from any rash actions towards Ulfrik when he arrives. My spies in Mules Town say he's stopped there, which, depending on what road he takes, means he'll be at the capital in the next half week" Jazar implored, now sounding more desperate, so much so that he removed his hood. His ponytail dropping past his shoulders once more.

"If you want someone to talk sense into Cythees you'd have more luck asking his horse. For a spymaster you're not very well informed, Jazar, I must be the person Cythees trust's least in this world"

"Yes, but you are his family which guarantees that you stand the best chance of being around him for the longest. Besides, you are also resourceful. Your father's adroitness for planning and politics hasn't been wasted on you, my lady. Though he may think so. You need only let it show" Jazar complimented, getting up and walking to the threshold of the canopy. The moonlight sliding over his face, casting a vague shadow on the stone floor.

"So even if I could keep Cythees from being himself how can

you help me? You are a clever man, Lord Jazar, but you're just a boy playing a game he only half understands and you haven't seemed to grasp that you're not the only one playing it. In a few days' time I'll have left Kingsport for The Highfelds, he'll see to that--that I'm sent to those moldering mountains for the rest of my life"

"In a few days' time Ulfrik will be here. All you have to do, my Lady, is wait till then. Once the negotiations about the Antaran refugees have been sorted and any other problems have been addressed, I'll organize your leave of the city. Tensions are high but if we act now we can bring about…well, not a peace, but a stalemate. Listen, I have some contacts, sailors mainly, they own a small spice running fleet, one of those ships regularly visits Kingsport and sails between here and Lightning Bay in Jea'Ika. If you help me I'll see to it that you escape both this marriage and your brother and father into the bargain" Jazar raised his brow in anticipation.

"And then what? Will we all live happily ever after?" she jested, throwing her hands up.

"No. Contentment cannot be achieved so easily, sacrifices must be made for that. But it will null the tension for now. The realms have enjoyed three years of peace and relative prosperity under the eyes of the true rulers of these lands"

"Meaning you…"

"I am merely an observer who tries to tilt the board into a direction that will suit as many as possible and I think you and I can both aid in that effort. What do you say?" the spymaster asked, clearly anxious to hear an answer.

Instead, Eleana demurred for a moment.

"I don't think, in all the years I've known you, I've ever asked where you came from" Lady Monthell stated, raising her eyebrow. Jazar seemed puzzled yet he indulged Eleana's canter.

He sat upright and straightened himself out and placed both his arms on the silver table as he began a rather brief tale "I've lived in the capital all my life. My parents came from Argus, Oshika province to be precise, as fugitives of one of its many crime families. They were good-hearted people but incredibly nieve. They became cobblers, I was never interested in such a lifestyle. I quickly came to realize what so few do on the streets: secrets and hidden words have a lot more value to them than shoes" Jazar fumbled with his long sleeves as he briefly paused, folding them around his wrists like huge drapes. He plucked a grape from the bowl next to him and tossed it into his mouth. He waited to finish chewing before politely continuing. "Started offering my service to all the lowlives of this place-- coin in exchange for secrets and soon that...line of work got the attention of Morryg's father, Isen. Twenty years ago,"

"Three High Kings in the span of twenty years, not bad, Jazar" Eleana complimented. "But still a dangerous game to play . Sacrificing so much for so small a prize"

"Satisfaction and harmony are no small prizes, my Lady. What have I sacrificed--I gave my life to these realms. I turned my own hope and dreams down to give someone elses a chance because perhaps theirs is more needed than mine. I live here, in these vast halls I worked my way up here, climbing every tedious hurdle so I'm content to keep it this way but I can still help others climbs steps of their own. I know what it is to be sneered at by some noble or lord or not even acknowledged at all and I know the resentment that builds by being told to live your life in service to those who care not for you"

Eleana stared at him in thought. This confusing concoction of a man that had all the warmth of the early morning sun but the same unpredictability of a winter storm. He had lied when he claimed he could never seduce but, instead of advances, Jazar used persuasion and suggestion to garner the minds of his lieges.

"So now that I've indulged your interests, what say you about my offer?" Jazar inquested.

Eleana paused for a while, weighing what few options she had in front of her. She turned away from Jazar, looking at herself in the dim view of her mirror, half of her was cast in the shadow, the other illuminated by the frosty light of the moon. She turned again, to face Jazar "alright. But I make no promises and I will not be responsible for anything Cythees may do. I'll try to sway him, but I wouldn't hold much hope of success. And we will see which runs out first: his temper or my resolve"

Jazar smiled in relief, he got up from the chair, his objective complete as he turned for the door when Eleana grabbed his sleeve "if this works, you'd better hope you live up to your end of the bargain, my lord. If I'am to be thrown to the dogs I will do so pulling another with me" Lady Monthell hissed, a look of warning set in her eyes. Jazar bowed as his hand pulled open the door "My lady" he said, shutting the door behind himself.

Eleana breathed in deeply, holding her hand to her forehead as she thought. She knew her brother well, she knew that for her to try and change his mind about anything would require a great deal of skill

***

The last few dregs of night fell over Antara's western landscape, plunging everything into total eclipsing darkness.

Gravis still led his people to Vaskuul. He knew it wasn't far, even with the storm, which had plagued them since they were forced from their home, bearing down on them. A few of the villagers had not survived the trek going on from the barrow. They had lost some going through the Spear Pass, mostly children, and then some over the Rakeshaw, mostly the elders and two injured from the troll. Their numbers now dwelt at twenty or so as they pulled each other through the knee-high snow that bit at them coldly every step they took. Each person only being able to see the one in front as they all blindly clung to one another, frozen hands holding onto frozen shoulders and weary eyes being pelted with ice from all directions. Gravis headed the small group, trying to find Vaskuul. They had been trekking south and west now for nearly two weeks and Gravis knew the capital settlement should be close, yet for all his effort to try and peer through the snowy vale, he couldn't see anything except the moon's light that cast a blue reflection from the icy ground, creating a glowing effect from inside the storm itself. The flakes danced on this glowing ballroom and skidded over its surface in large wisps.

The old ranger stopped in his tracks, now determined to find Vaskuul, he squinted his eyes, holding out his hand into the gale, concentrating. Again he focused, the prayer in his mind, pleading to show him the way. Suddenly Gravis felt a presence, not a divine one but an overwhelming one, a proud one, that cast aside the storm just long enough for Gravis to see the great stone temple and the freezing ocean at its back. Ancient Vaskuul, lying on the coast. Its walls, though low to the ground, were still higher than Jorrvanskar and its huts, though still made of thatch and rotten wood, were wider and its mighty stone temple was constructed out of the same stone as at Jorrvanskar except this one had a much taller, stone spiral at its top, reaching out into the cold, snowy air.

"Almost there" Gravis said to himself. He turned back to the group "come on! We're almost there! Just a little further!"

"Where?!" the Watchman asked, his voice torn from him by the wind. Gravis pointed a gloved hand to the spiral of the All-Seer's temple that was raised out, into the moonlight.

The wind, in a desperate attempt, seemed to pick up, ravenously, trying to pull the villagers back into the snow, given one last chance to break them. When upon a sudden, a loud blast of noise came from Vaskuul, the sound of a horn, Gravis recognised it, it was the singular blast, low and long and eerily sounding off through the storm--they had been spotted. Gravis looked ahead as he saw the gates of Vaskuul slowly inch open as a single man came trudging out, his face covered by a thick, fur hood so that Gravis could only see the thick beard that grew on the man's face.

"Who are you?!!" the gatekeeper questioned as the group finally collapsed outside the walls.

Gravis was slightly confused and angered at the gatekeepers' lack of concern for a group out in the freezing cold. He hesitated before answering "It's me, Gravis, tell The Arch-Seer, Fanatiker, I'm here. My people…we need help, had to…abandon Jorrvanskar!"

"Very well! You may enter!" the gatekeeper shouted back.

Gravis led his people into Vaskuul, he, himself waiting till everyone was inside the confines of the capital settlement. It had been years since he had last set foot there and Gravis quickly noticed that the place hadn't changed a bit, like the order of All-Seer's that lived in the temple, Vaskuul seemed to have clung to tradition; not wanting to change anything about its ways. The old ranger was also astounded to see that inside the walls, the storm was merely being brushed off the stone like a ripple of water in a river, though Gravis soon reasoned it was doing so because of the magical resonance of Vaskuul, hence why the order of the All-Seer's was founded there and why the Arch-Seer's had always made their home where the snow met the sea and the cold waves crashed against the frozen shoreline and the muddy, clay beaches.

The others in Gravis' charge also took to looking around the oldest settlement, though their attentions were drawn towards the warmth of the fires and the sheer magnitude of Vaskuul compared to Jorrvanskar, for some the poultry amount of younglings that remained, this was the first time they had ever seen stone instead of thick, wooden logs and thatch. Even the old herbalist women of Jorrvanskar were amazed at the amount of ice-moss that Vaskuul was able to grow, an entire quadrant of it was laid out at the back of the settlement, enough to feed the people of Vaskuul for weeks, giving the ice-moss time to grow back. Others gazed in wonder at the cows and goats that stood grazing in abundance whereas to the far north you would have been lucky to see but a handful. Whilst the ancestors of Jorrvanskar pined away in Antara's far and coldest reaches, Vaskuul based itself and sunk its stone roots deep into the solid earth of the land. The docks sat still and stagnant, half-hidden in the ocean mist. Once they had boasted ships, inconsequential to any but them, but now even the ships had stopped in their frequency. No pilgrims, few supplies, though that was attributed to the abandoning of Rackshaw, an island lookout that sat half a mile out in the ocean.

Gravis had little patience and was more interested in the temple of the All-Maker. He looked up the many mossy, stone steps that lead to the great door, he sighed, much more in disbelief at the fact he was even alive to be there than a feeling of regret about the amount of stairs. It couldn't have been a more fitting feeling. There was something calming about

Vaskuul, though aged and iced it was wide and held the many peoples of Antara in it, the closest they ever came to a city save for the ancient lost settlements high in the northernmost hills. Perhaps it was the mere sense of safety in numbers that gave Gravis some comfort, perhaps it was due to the presence of the All-Seer's there. Their ancient scrying powers and abilities to foretell time radiated out of the city in a way Gravis hadn't felt in decades. He wondered if he was the last they had taught of their methods of fire gazing and dreamwalking, he hadn't heard of any initiates or apprentices in years, much so to how costly the path of an All-Seer can sometimes be in its solitude.

The old ranger slowly proceeded up the stairs to where the large, circular stone door was, beckoning him in. The last time Gravis had been inside the chief temple was decades ago, that much he could remember, it was just after he had completed his training as an All-Seer, a tedious and hard path to follow for those without patience. When he reached the top of the steps he had to stop and remember the way to open the door. He found himself reaching out his old hand, not for a handle, there was no handle, but to ask permission to open the door, as if some power controlled who could and couldn't enter. Gravis left his hand resting on the stone as he felt the door begin to shake, he looked up and saw dust flutter down as the circular stone split in two, opening laboriously. A familiar sight greeted him as the doors hit the walls with a solid thud. Another brazier, like his at Jorrvanskar. The blue flames inside it flickered just as he remembered, and he knew the power that was marshaled inside them. Despite the flames dancing in the bowl, Gravis could feel the cold wind rush through the temple, which he had noticed was rather empty. Only the wind blowing through the large, carved hole in the temple's roof was creating noise, a dreadful, sorrowful moan on the air. This, Gravis could remember--the quietness of the Arch-Seer's temple. So many souls passed through this hall over thousands upon thousands of years now lost to time. He perched himself on a cold, mossy chair that had been carved from the stone of the temple itself. Tapping his fingers on his leg in idleness, he waited patiently and rather awkwardly, looking around and seeing that nothing had changed in the temple, mostly due to its lack of things that could potentially change. The stone was ancient and cold, cracked and mossy, the large pillars holding up the roof were just the same. As for decoration, there wasn't any, no fine carpets woven of foreign yarn like in other parts of the world, no bronze, silver or gold statue of their God, for the All-Maker was no God and to describe him as one was a blasphemous offense and so it was unseemly for them to paint him as something he was not, he required no tribute. Just stone and the brazier, plain and ancient.

It was during his recollections that Gravis saw the person, or rather, people he had primarily come for: The Arch-Seer and his council. Both were clothed in red robes made from specially dyed, red fur, supposedly from sacrificial blood, as Gravis could remember his old father telling him. Their sleeves were raked and bits of yarn were plated at the wrists like a large carpet on each arm. Their hoods were capped at the midpoint, hiding their faces, mostly-- dark, looming, crimson shadows. Gravis paid them a disdainful look, not one of arrogance but of annoyance as he knew that no doubt a conversation would occur between him and one of the priest's that would surely contain their opinions on the old ways.

Then came a voice, older than Gravis by a decade or two, croaky and shrill with a heavy nordic accent, as befit most of the Antarans. If the cold wind had a voice it would have sounded like that, Gravis thought. "Well, well, Gravis Cold-Spear finally returns to our great temple, the same temple he once spoke so lowly of" the voice said, casting off its hood to reveal The Arch-Seer. Gravis sneered at the face he hadn't seen in years, one that seemingly aged every day. His hair was long, gray and stranded, running down to his horse-hide belt. His eyes were sunken in and gray but always gazed hungrily, like a starved wolf. About his lips and chin was a scraggly beard, curly and matted with the wet conditions from the moss growing inside the temple and resting above the lips was a crooked nose that looked windblown at an angle or melted to his waxy face.

"Fanatiker. It's been a while, old friend" Gravis greeted, trying to sound warm as he hugged his old teacher.

"Oh? Friend now is it? Strange the last time you visited here was many years ago. You held a different view about me then, didn't you 'old friend'?" Fanatiker coldly proceeded, flicking his wrist for the other red priests to leave the two alone, in confidence.

"Times change, Fanatiker"

"Yes. But people do not. Tell me--why have you come here, now, with winter nearly on our doorsteps?" The Arch-Seer questioned and for the first time in a long time Gravis felt lessened in his want to speak, though he didn't particularly like Fanatiker for his opinions on looking after the people, it was the old and dingy priest who had taught Gravis many things. Things like reading ancient Antaran, deciphering prophecies and scrying from the braziers. Once it had been master and apprentice but now the rivalry ran deep.

"Something is out there. I have felt it, through the flame, a power that only grows stronger. I don't know what it is but...its fashions are far from benevolent. Have you not seen? Even the weather has changed, never have the storms been this fierce outside of winter" Gravis explained with desperation hinting in his eyes. Fanatiker drew back, a look of surprise and doubt was spread over his ancient face. Such mindless conspiracy coming from the mouth of one of his own students.

"So, you've moved your entire settlement, people under your protection, in the middle of a blizzard here to Vaskuul, a two week journey on foot, because the weather has changed?" The Arch-Seer asked, looking confused and somewhat disappointed, the way one would with a child telling fantasies.

"No that's not all. I saw something, weeks ago. Three rangers from here. They were on a mission, warranted by you. I saw it in the fire. Have you sent any patrols that far north recently?"

"So your scrying capabilities are still as strong as ever" Fanatiker sniffed.

"Was it on your orders? Did I truly see that?" Gravis pushed.

Fanatiker stepped back away from Gravis at the proposal of the question in an almost exaggerated manner. "No" he answered, in a rushed and frantic tone "I know of no such patrol"

Gravis looked suspiciously at his one-time master, though his concern was with his people and their survival, so he didn't dwell on Fanatiker's strange answer for long.

"And what else was in your vision? Anything except the rangers?" the old priest asked whilst trying to hide his concerned look by facing one of the walls.

"Yes. I saw something...someone, well, something. I don't know what it was, but it has a cruel grip upon life. It wasn't human, whatever it was, and it held the dead among its soldiers" Gravis answered, sending chills down his own body as he mentioned the men and women returned to life.

"Ha. I think you've consumed too much ice moss, come I'll have the herbalist look you over, it usually shows itself as..." Fanatiker was interrupted violently.

"What?! No! Fuck the ice moss! I have left my home of seventy years and brought my people here for help because there is something out there! Call the other settlements here, Vaskuul's walls are the only ones made of stone. Now, there are ten more settlements in Antara, summon them all!" Gravis raged, angrier at not being understood then being taken for a fool. Though he knew to expect this and knew it to be a fool's errand to tell the Arch-Seer about the mystics of Antara, they were men set as deep into their ways as their very temple was to the ground.

"I'll do no such thing. Winter will be upon us in a few short months and it'll take a month at least to gather all the settlements" Fanatiker resumed.

"A month? It should take longer than that to gather all ten settlements! Antara is thousands of miles wide. We have people from here all the way to the Troll Claws"

"There aren't ten settlements anymore, fool!" The red priest revealed. Gravis' mouth dropped agape at the news, hitting him hard. A cold feeling washed over him, like the feeling he experienced when retrieving the wolf's head from the barrow only this time it radiated throughout his entire body. He was right. "What do you mean? There aren't ten settlements, what is there more now?"

"Less. And it's been decreasing every few months for the last two years. Only five settlements remain that we know of" Gravis at first thought perhaps Fanatiker was playing an incredibly cruel joke with his already agitated mind but soon remembered Fanatiker would not know what the definition of a joke to be, cruel or otherwise. He watched in shock and disbelief as the priest continued as he pressed his back against a mossy stone pillar "Helgeg was the first settlement that went missing. Two winters ago, we sent supplies up there. A month later scouts returned, still with the supplies. They said that the settlement was still there, but it appeared abandoned. No women, no children, no guards not even the settlements All-Seer. We thought at first they'd simply moved. Helgeg was to the far north-east so we thought they'd have moved because of the weather or game but we haven't heard reports of any of them since"

"Why in the name of The All-Maker was I not notified of their disappearance? Why were the other settlements All-Seer's not notified?" Gravis asked as he stood up in amazement, flinging his hands in the air in disbelief.

"Because you did not need to know, " Fanatiker answered, looking angered at Gravis' intrigue. "Panic sets in quickly here. Our people are desperate, sickly. This would have resulted in the loss of their faith to us" The old priest narrowed his eyes as he ordered "now you and your people will be allowed to remain here till winter ends and after, you will return to Jorrvanskar!"

"How can they keep faith when it is embroiled in lies?"

"Because it is how the All-Maker wills it"

"The All-Maker? Or you?"

"There is little diferance these days" the red clad priest finished as he turned his back to Gravis and returned to the lower, deeper parts of the temple.

Gravis, himself, stood in shock and despair. He felt it creep into him, as unwanted as the cold winter's wind. He stood, alone, the wind blowing flakes of snow through the large caverns in the roof, letting in faint glimmers of morning light. Examining the room to make sure no one watched, Gravis slowly proceeded to the brazier, its everlasting blue flames picked up as they sensed the almost symbiotic presence of an All-Seer. Gravis reached into the flames, not feeling their heat nor pain from their touch. He closed his eyes, resting yet concentrating, he tried to see, though not with his eyes. A quick flash erupted in his mind and a whisper trailed through his ears, speaking in a language he had never heard before, the voice was distorted and disembodied, echoing around the room. Then he felt it, the presence of that same power he described to Fanatiker: a cold, looming presence, one that seemed to dwarf everything in existence. In the dark, Gravis could feel the sense of foreboding in his own mind as everything began to suddenly close in and a terrible and guttural laugh echoed about the caverns of his mind. He quickly let go of his concentration, snapping back to reality, back into the temple.

He stared up at the sun that was now creeping from behind the white clouds, turning the snow into glitter. Yet the star provided Gravis no solace for his mind was fearful and confused. The fire revealed many things to The All-Seers, Gravis knew this, but he couldn't decipher whether what he heard was a warning of the present or a prophecy for the future.

Chapter 10-Honor of The Sword

Night was at its thickest over Arden--the capital city of the imperial province of Nadenia had finally started to quieten down from its hectic demeanor Though many of its pleasure house's and taverns still hosted the now drunken Osh-Venn the city had digressed somewhat, the subtle glow of candles in windows and braziers in the streets being the only illumination. The sands coughed powerfully over the white city, blowing dust onto its streets and scattering what few remained on the streets with it. The great temple stood tall among the towers and houses, like a watchful parent over its many children, starlight intertwined with the crystalline spires on its dome. Inside its walls the guards stood like dormant statue's, not moving, their deadly spears raised to the open sky.

From inside one of the small lavish bed chambers Tarith and the girls had finished their few hours of pleasure, provided by The Sultan as a distraction. Emerging from behind the doorways curtain, Tarith lazily put on the bottom half of his armor, his chest still on show and covered with scented lipsticks and bite marks. He ran his fingers through his hair, releasing it from its tangled mess though a few dreadlocks remained roped together. As he approached the antechamber, intent on finding something to eat at this odd hour, he saw a shadow, hiding behind a corner, trying to conceal itself within the dark stretches of the hall. Remembering he left his blade back in the room where the girls were still sorting themselves out, giggling to each other as they recalled their drunken ecstasy, Tarith and the shadow kept their gaze on each other as the Prince cautiously stepped to one corner of the room "Whatever it is you want: a conversation, a joke or just sex I'm afraid I'm out of all three. Those lovely ladies back there have seen to that"

"Glad you enjoyed your time" a familiar voice stated. Tarith moved closer, as did the figure, into the light of the torches on the wall. The bulking figure revealed itself to be the General. "What do you want? I thought you'd gone with everyone else. I never interrupted you when you were with that harlot from Zysho City that you were following around all that time. You picked a good one though, those back there were okay but..." the Prince crudely answered before he felt Lo'atal's large hand cover his mouth, nearly blocking air from entering his nose as well.

"We're not welcome here. I would advise we leave now, not first light, now. We pack our things and leave before anything happens" Lo'atal whispered. Tarith read the concern in his friend's voice, taking heed from it as he peeled the Osh-Venn's steely hand away from his mouth. "What makes you say that?"

"The Sultan has hidden more from us than he has revealed. Then I had expected. Even for a Nadenian "

"Like what?"

"His disdain for you has increased tenfold since we came to Arden. The fat fucker thinks that his daughter brought us here on purpose to ruin some arranged marriage" Lo'atal explained rapidly, checking to make sure no one was listening.

"How do you know all this, Lo'atal?" the Prince asked, both puzzled and concerned before his mood immediately shifted back to his usual informal and casually minded as he grabbed an apple from a nearby fruit bowl on a table and bit into it ravenously.

"He wanted to speak to his daughter about it. I thought I'd go check the place out. I don't trust these Nadenians . Never have and it would appear for good reason"

"Well so much for your honor and not 'sneaking in the shadows'. I take it that's how you uncovered these true feelings of our host?" Tarith said, almost looking disappointed at the out-of-character action his friend had taken.

"My occasional lack of honor may save you a lot of trouble, especially this time. We need to leave. I don't like this, and neither should you. This Sultan is truly a serpent, this nations love of those things plays well into their nature" Lo'atal said as he grabbed his Prince's wrist and pulled him towards the staircase that led outside and down to a small side gate in the city's wall. "I'll get your things. You get to the horses. I'm sorry my Prince but when it comes to your safety I outrank you in terms of authority. Let's go" the General whispered again.

"Go where?" another voice asked from the dark shadows, in the opposite corner from where Lo'atal stood waiting for Tarith. Both the General and the Prince turned in surprise, Lo'atal drew his blade before the person had even finished. Its black iron barely glimmering in the direct moonlight.

From out of the opposing darkness. Amira stepped forth, her black hair let down, falling to just above her waist. She still wore the tight, forest coloured stealth suit with some of its strings undone, showing her arms that held small but clear tattoos of Kirva, the three headed snake, running from each wrist, up the underside of the arm to her shoulder. "You know in a certain light you look a little less deadly" Tarith joked as he kept a straight face aiming at her in admiration. Until he saw the streams of black and green running down both sides of her face, no doubt from the malachite powder she used as eyeliner. Both Tarith and Lo'atal looked at each other, awkwardly, as they realized. The look on her face was certainly unsettling, a woman of her composure having streams of black ink running down her tanned face seemed out of place and somewhat eerie "What trouble's you enough to make a great warrior such as yourself weep?" the young Champion Rider asked.

Amira quickly wiped the streaks away, leaving smudges across her cheeks. "Nothing, your benevolence"

"It's a crime to blatantly lie to an Emperor"

"I apologize, your benevolence. This is nothing"

"Don't be sorry. I'm not Emperor. Not yet, anyway" Tarith humbly smiled, trying to find some joy in a woman he thought possessed an attitude of almost stone. Despite only having known her for only a handful of days.

"What troubles you, Princess?"

"Nothing. I simply love the stars in the sky, how bright they shine. I am very nostalgic of all those hot nights training out in the desert with friends. My emotions sometimes get the better of me. I'am still a woman, your benevolence" Amira answered, trying to sound convincing even though she herself was struggling to believe her act.

"Of all the things you lack control of, I don't get the sense your emotions are among them. Even if you are, as you put it, a woman, which I fail to see how the two correlate" Tarith produced a welcoming smile. "And what's this about your father making you train in the desert?"

"No, it was my choice. All warriors of Arden train in the harshest elements as a form of initiation. I saw no reason to remain absent from that. Not if I'm to command them one day"

"Well whoever trained you must've been an absolute master with a spear. I've seen Lo'atal bested once or twice but never in that fashion" Tarith said as he heard Lo'atal let off an almost animalistic grunt in response.

"The man who trained me? Ha, his name was Sadeeb, he was a good man, a gentle man. But no force any deity could muster was as quick as him with a blade. He would listen to me even when my own father…well Sadeeb was always there" Amira stuttered, feeling more vulnerable with every word spoken.

"I knew of this man," Lo'atal interjected. His face suddenly lighting up for the first time since introduced to Amira "He bested a few of our arena fighters in his earlier years. My cousins always spoke of him during the summer pit fights. So much that was honored with the rakya. He was certainly good with any manner of weapon. Though I always heard his death was less than fitting and recent"

"Fairly certain no one deserves the death they are given but it comes just the same" Amira quietly answered.

"I suppose it is," Lo'atal replied. He understood the ways of fighting, the finality of it as did she. Their cultures were not as opposed as both the Osh-Venn and the Nadenians pretended. Both had been underdogs and pilgrims who seized land that was not theirs, both had warrior ways of ancient and beautiful makes but arts and architecture that rivalled the ancient Ushkinians. One was of the northern volcanic ashlands and southern tropical jungles, the other was of the far east and its widespread deserts and canyons.

"How did this man come to die?" Tarith questioned with intrigue.

"Suladan" Amira answered through barred teeth.

"Suladan?"

"He's a local warlord, loyal to my father, wants to marry into the lineage. My father offered him the chance to take my hand and I denied it. So Suladan enacted one of the ancient laws of Nadenia. By decree, any man who wishes to marry a woman must first prove his strength in combat"

"Sounds rather macabre," Tarith said, raising an eyebrow.

"It is our ancient tradition that goes back to the founding of the province. I would not expect outlanders to understand. Sadeeb agreed to fight to uphold me from any marriage proposals and... eventually he won the duel. But Suladan prefers deception over honor. I had to watch as...as he stabbed Sadeeb in the back infront of so many onlookers who just stood and did nothing. Nothing as such a great man was ended. My mentor, my friend. A dishonorable way to end the life of the greatest warrior of Nadenia" Amira cursed.

"So that's who is coming here? This Suladan?" Lo'atal asked.

Amira turned her attention towards the General, smiling. "I knew my eyes were not lying to me when I thought someone was watching" she said "but yes. He will come and he will win and then I will, by all the laws of Nadenia, be his...his wife" the Princess despaired.

"You don't have to," Tarith stated simply. Both Amira and Lo'atal turned and looked at him, both confused.

"Unless you would fight for me," Amira joked, sniggering to herself.

Tarith firstly remained silent at the joke but couldn't help but smile at the thought that came into his head. Lo'atal, attuned to Tarith's sudden ideas, noticed the devious grin "No. No. If you're going to suggest it, no. I can't allow that. We're not here for this and your father will have my people eradicated if harm comes to you" he sternly boomed, though feeling what little authority he had slowly slip away under Tariths toothy grin and his bright, silver, eyes shining with glee.

"No, your benevolence. It's not...forgive me but it's not your place. These are our customs, our traditions, I have to follow them. Plenty of marriages have been built on tears"

"You can't build on water, you drown in it. Why would you follow those traditions down a path that will end with you being stuck as wife to some warlord? Or would you prefer to follow something else? Something of your own making, whatever that might be. Because, like me, we seem to be pawns of fate. The difference is-- if you follow this path you know where it'll end whereas I do not" Tarith reasoned, stepping closer to Amira and looking into two set emeralds that glimmered up at him. He could see the conflict within her, playing inside her eyes like a theater of confusion. "I'm sorry, your benevolence. But this is my path alone" she whispered, entranced suddenly, catching even herself off guard, as if Tarith advancing closer to her had made every focus of hers switch.

She snapped out of her stupor and pulled herself away from the young Prince with some difficulty. "I have to go now. I have to get ready for his arrival. At least I'll finally get out of here" the warrioress smiled before turning on her heels and proceeding back into the palace's halls.

Tarith simply watched her with a blank and emotionless face, as if pondering something.

By the time the early morning sun had crept over the dunes and back onto Arden, Tarith and the rest of the Osh-Venn had mostly gathered and formed a large assembly in the center of the city, just outside The Sultan's temple. Like a mass of hide and scaled armor, capped with bone-made helmets. They seemed eager to leave, few of the Osh-Venn trusted Nadenia, probably because most of them had never even seen it before, they rarely ventured from either their own province of Dush'Uul and the imperial city. Thousands of years ago the provinces had warred and though so few still recalled such days of death, the blood-memories remained for the brutish Vennisians certainly differed from the Nadenians when it came to discipline.

At the bottom of the temple's steps Lo'atal had readied the mounts of both himself and Tarith of whom came down the steps to join them, fondling the straps of his leather braces. "You're up early. I take it you want to leave as much as the boys?" the General asked as he looked up from dealing with the horse's saddle.

"Our destiny calls us. I cannot delay, my friend, despite certain…situations. It would seem that fate favors testing us in more ways than one but the Princess is perhaps right: we can't get involved with their internal polotics and raise further tensions" Tarith said, regrettably as he pulled himself onto his short-haired stallion.

"What of this warlord and his army that the Sultan wants to enlist?"

"Something for the senate to decide upon when we return"

"And the Princess?"

"Amira? Maybe it is not up to us what we do about her. Who's to say?"

"The safety of this quest"

"Well the one thing I can't deny about her is that underneath all that brooding and steely looks she seems to have a good heart, I can admire that about someone, can't I, Lo'atal?" Tarith asked, tilting his head as he looked at the General with a raised, black, eyebrow.

"Oh yes of course, your benevolence. I've noticed you admiring her 'good heart' particularly last night in that dress" Lo'atal retorted sarcastically before raising his own eyebrow, beating

Tarith's argument. The Harbinger was about to answer, as his mouth opened in annoyance, but no words came out as they were beaten down by the noise of the city gates opening. Tarith couldn't tell whether it was the massive gates opening or the amount of horses that came pouring through it that caused the ground to shake slightly as the great desert stallions flicked up dust from the streets and pathways as if carving an entirely new road for themselves. Their feathered leashes and saddles flew in a bright array of many foreign colors. At the helm of this cavalry was a man like no other in the city. His tanned skin was glabrous and smooth from a lifetime of wealth, his eyes were sharp and cat-like as Amira's were and made up with the same malachite powder. Another reminder of his apparent wealth were the silver rings placed on every finger on both of his hands and the silver circlet he wore on his shaved head. His muscles were large on his arms, winding up to his broad shoulders. He was dressed for battle, not armored head to toe but covered in only the vital places of the body in the finest silver armor. "Who the fuck is that? He's got more metal on him than a blacksmith's bench" Lo'atal bluntly stated. For the Osh-Venn do not see the need for so much armor in combat, it can slow them down and deny them a good death.

"I'm fairly certain that that's Amira's intended: Suladan and that is some of his army" Tarith answered as the two men watched as the warlord stopped his company before Tarith's.

The horses grew unsteady as they approached the Osh-Venn. Both Tarith and Lo'atal stood, aware and waiting and unwavering as two pairs of eyes met.

"This is quite a gathering of...Osh-Venn, my, my, what would bring men like yourselves this far east?! Ran out of cows to fuck?!" Suladan shouted over the hundreds of Osh-Venn who all stood with either blank or unimpressed faces whilst his own men and guards laughed, stimulated by the daringness of their master. The warlord studied the men from the far northern province, the same way one studies an animal of rare find.

"Are you aware you're blocking my way?!" the warlord added, sounding more impatient as he called up to Tarith, standing high at the top of the temple's steps.

"Are you aware of who you're speaking to, desert dweller?" Lo'atal jumped in. To the question Suladan pulled his head back slightly, as if inspecting the one who asked him. The General, however, didn't give him a chance to respond as he introduced the Prince to the warlord "this is Tarith, of clan Malacender. Son of Emperor Tephus and Empress Cassandra, The Dragon of The East. Heir to the Empire, the seventh Harbinger"

"So, the rumors about your...dragon God choosing another had merit after all" Suladan scoffed, mockingly, as a thin smile crept along his full lips. "I must say I never thought my path would take me to the 'seventh Champion Rider' what a pleasure it is to make your acquaintance, my Prince" the warlord stated as he bowed his head.

"The pleasure is mine, great warlord. It's a privilege to be in a city so beautiful" Tarith said, not taking his silver eyes off the pompous deathbringer.

"You'll find there are many beauties in this part of the world. I'm about to go and claim one myself, if you'll excuse me" Suladan said. And with that he turned his cavalry to the right as they rode to the west of the city, where the large and ancient arena stood, its sandy bricks rising high into the air, meeting the Sultans temple in terms of size and dominating the west side of Arden. It was ancient and old, maybe even older than the Great Pit of fighters in Jea'Ika province, with man-sized statues depicting everything from bravery to erotica on every pillar.

The horses flicked and kicked their hooves as they brashly

drove around and through the gathered Osh-Venn and citizens, their riders cooing and wooing and yelling as the pack crashed through the city. Tarith watched with conflicted eyes as he asked himself what he wanted to do.

"Well" Lo'atal's deep voice broke the Prince out of his thoughts "we should be on our way. Vacile tells me it could be a few more days before we reach the crater and most of those days will be walking through the vast expanses of The Red Plains. So, shall we get moving?" he added.

"Keep the men here. We're not leaving yet" Tarith ordered as he handed the horse's lead back to Lo'atal.

"Where are you going?" the General asked. Tarith didn't turn to answer, his eyes fixed on the arena as he spoke "If I'm not back soon, come find me at the arena" before stomping down the street, alone.

Lo'atal rushed after his charge as he panicked but soon lost the vexing Prince in the droves of city dwellers on their way to the pit, all being herded by the guards.

Tarith pulled his black hood over his head, cooling him from the sun and hiding himself amongst the city's denizens, molding into the crowd of attendees who proceeded to the arena. It would have been a strange and dangerous thing for him to blindly waltz down any street, especially Arden where its people would sooner capture their Prince than converse. The Harbinger didn't stop walking until he got to the coliseum, following the hoof prints of Suladan's host and the crowd of people who were pushing and shoving themselves into the large arches in the arena walls by the thousands. The arena towered over any other building in the city with its enormity, bullying most of the other houses and towers to one side of its bulk.

When Tarith himself got to the grand arch he could either carry on with the rest of the populus into the arena stand or turn left into the small armory. He knew then what he was going to do as on the walk there he had been debating it with himself. This sneaking was nothing new to the Prince, many times, as a young boy, he had snuck around Ushkin city for various reasons, despite his royal stature he had always had an uncanny ability for blending in and becoming one with everyone else. Once he was inside the small and rather dark armory the first thing to alert the Prince was the smell of the hard leather used in their light armors and hot steel, baked after a summer's day of fighting.

Selecting a helmet that would cover his face and changing his black, hide torso armor for a simpler leather chest plate, he drew his sword and pulled a shield off of a wooden rack. He examined its weight before sliding its wristguard onto his arm and arming himself--ready. He did feel quite cumbersome though, the armor was a strange assortment and badly completed, straps hung out and buckles ran undone.

As he approached the tiny wooden door that led out into the arena, he looked out of the cracks between the old beams of wood. He could see the crowd already amassing inside, filling the stone seats. Until. In the high stand, surrounded by the Arden guard and shaded by silk curtains, he saw Amira and her father. The Sultan had changed into a purple robe, probably in order to hide the wine and grape stains as his wide waist nearly pulled open his belt. Next to him Tarith saw her. He didn't know what it was inside him that couldn't let her go, a fixation maybe, he pondered. She was rather unlike anyone he'd ever known and of all the exotic women he'd cavorted with, she was something else, she had something else: resilience.

Her hair was flowing down, not being held back, it blew swiftly in the breeze. She was dressed in a way Tarith had never seen her, yet it still intrigued him. Instead of her unorthodox armor, designed for stealthy fighting among the canebrake, she wore a simple bronze bralette that was coupled with several chains leading to carved bracelets and a green skirt that settled gently on the floor and about her head was a tiara of clustered desert flowers. The Prince watched as The Sultan awkwardly arose, having to have two of his guards aid him by picking him up by his soft and plump arms. He heard the maddening voice announce Suladan and the royal opposition. Tarith watched as a side door on the other side of the arena slid open as Suladan emerged, wielding two large, silver daggers. He had removed his circlet of silver and his cloak of fine eastern silk, allowing for quick movement in battle as all Nadenians aimed for.

The competitions lasted an eventful amount of time, as befit such a celebration, long into the early noon. All watched the warlord tassel with a pompous bull first, the striped cats of Balghir and even the maned lions from the far south. Until the beasts limped back to their cages of wrought iron or didn't move at all. Suladan's days were spent fighting the toughest of beasts: men. Anything less was inadequate. The Prince of Ushkin, however, had only ever battled those who dared not to strike him or killed a beast from a range with the bow but he was quick as he knew he would have to be.

He froze as the Sultan then asked if any in the arena wished to take the royal opposition's place. He knew. He could either rise or shrink from this, perhaps if he were to leave now no one would know, he pondered. This act would not be recorded in any history chronicle or book that may follow him after death. But he knew, it was not in his blood to leave. Placing the shrouding helmet over his face, concealed by the belief he was no one. He drew his sword, the two dragon heads roaring on either side of the hilt. But before he could fling open the door leading to the arena, Tarith felt an incredible wave of doubt wash over him, almost crippling him to the ground as he felt his breathing intensify, his senses bolstered as the adrenaline coursed through his blood. He knew the laws of Nadenia enough to know what happened to the loser of such duels but, remembering his father's advice during his many younger years of training, Tarith slowly pulled aside the wooden door as it left a sliding trail in the sand, into the arena and the smell of baked earth and the blinding, white, light of the sun outside.

The applause from the Nadenian crowd roared from every direction for half a mile until they realized a fighter had actually entered the arena to challenge Suladan and soon the claps and cheering became muffled into silent stares. All hoped this formality would begin and end swiftly so that the engagement party could begin. Tarith saw, through the dimness of the helmet, that the thousands of people in the arena, once maddeningly chaotic and in uproar, were staring intently at him--this masked figure. Both Amira and Suladan appeared surprised at the newcomer, all whilst the Sultan stood, hands pressed against the stonewall of the overlook they were sat on as he leaned in, asking, his voice projecting around the entire arena. "And who are you that would seek to stop the uni...contest of matrimony?" There was a pause that filled the air of the arena with an eerie silence as thousands of of eyes and ears turned from the Sultan to the nameless volunteer.

Tarith paused for a second, looking at Suladan, who appeared more than ready for a fight and no less tired from his previous battles, and then up at Amira. For a moment, the Princess appeared to be concentrating on this mysterious figure until she silently realized, her eyes widened, and her mouth opened in shock but still she resigned herself back to her seat, in keeping with tradition. She had no choice. Looking back at the crowd for a second time, Tarith sighed slowly, he felt his breath shiver in the helm.

Confused as to the unplanned arrival, the Sultan called down to the pit "and who is this? A challenger to the mighty Suladan?!" so the crowd may hear "and not part of our arrangement" and then so the crowd couldn't.

In response to the Sultans question, the warrior's helm was quickly torn off. The Prince had need to speak. Half the arena gasped, the others looked on, slightly confused and unaware that the Prince was even here. Some had whispered that Ushkin had invaded but given how they were let in others were not confirmed who was in their city, until they were. The Sultan's face turned from annoyance to pure aggression as he bit his lip so hard that a tiny pin drop of blood formed on his lower lip. The Sultan turned to Amira with anger on his face "I take it this was all part of your plan? Well done" he hissed at his daughter.

"Father I had nothing to do with this I sw…" the Princess was interrupted by her father as he spoke directly to Tarith. "Your benevolence! Though I'm honored to have you here in our very own arena, I must protest, not only was this spectacle not scheduled but these are our sacred traditions you interrupted!"

"I assure you, great Sultan, this is no spectacle. I come here to accept the challenge though I alter the terms!" Tarith announced to both the Sultan and the rest of the arena as his silver-blue hair was released from the helm in a tangled mess. "If I should win I ask that Princess Amira be free of all arrangements. If I lose then Amira will follow your will to go ahead with this engagement!" the future Champion Rider stated, with a smile.

"You are aware that the loser is traditionally injured or killed in fight's such as this?! I don't want to cast war on both Nadenia and Ushkin over a simple fight of our tradition! Stand down! I have never known such insolence" The Sultan said, trying to charm the young man that stood a hundred feet below him.

"Let it be known that I accepted this challenge willingly and a message should be sent to my parents to inform them of my death should God deem it so!" Tarith answered.

"I'm afraid that won't do. I simply can't allow the obvious

threat to a royal's life!"

"Don't worry on my account! I know most of you would not cast a slight on my demise" Tarith replied. "We all know that's what you believe" he then muttered to himself, tossing the helmet away as he stood in his stance; shield casually down by his side, a challenge, and his sword pointing at Suladan who smiled with enjoyment. "It is a pleasure to fight a member of the imperial family, but you'll forgive me if I don't hold back, I have a bride to marry" Suladan announced as he approached the Prince.

"Would she want the same thing?" Tarith asked with a provocative smile. Suladan's eyes filled with a sudden anger, like a tiger with sight of its prey. He swung like lightning with the dagger that was dodged by Tarith. Another attack followed as Tarith parried his sword to stop a stab in the chest from Suladan's knives. Again, and again Suladan would attack and again Tarith would redirect the blow and then strike himself. Being around the Osh-Venn since childhood aided the Prince immensely as the Osh-Venn themselves prefer to fight with quick, sharp blades, though often made of bone. He swung skilfully as Suladan retaliated, blocking when he could, though struggling slightly with the shorter blades. Tarith quickly realized that though he possessed more skill, Suladan was quick and agile, a fearful trait of most Nadenian fighters. Many of Amira's fighting techniques from the day she captured the company, Tarith recognised in Suladan. The Nadenians struck like the serpents they worshipped and some with just as much venom which gave the Prince thought to make sure Suladan's blades did not even graze him.

The two locked sabers for a moment, giving the warlord a chance to speak "only the best warrior will win 'my Prince'"

"Only one's going to stand at the end. The other will be in no

A TALE OF KINGS

position to argue" Tarith retorted. The warlord roared as he took Tarith's sword into the air with one dagger and slashed at his unprotected thigh with the other. Tarith grunted as a thin line of blood seeped from the wound. Panic was overridden with rage as Tarith stood straight and true. In the high stands the Sultan realized the wound delt and smiled manically, though it was buried under his chubby cheeks "I see he's not the only one with a 'plan'. You will drag us into a war with the rest of the empire if he dies down there. There will be no silent rebellion. No gloriously forced democratic succession. They will rain hellfire down on us!" Amira stated to her father in disgust. Her father didn't reply. A moment later and Tarith gained the upper hand in the duel once again, bashing Suladan with his shield, the warlord arched back in a daze as Tarith took the opportunity to cut across his opponent's arm. Suladan screamed as he dropped a dagger. In a moment of desperation, he swung the other dagger at Tarith's face, but the Champion Rider was anticipating and tilted his head to the side and in one swift motion, slicing his dragon blade up, grazing the warlords silver armor and cutting a bloody gash into his chiseled chin.

But the warlord of the east was not as easy to fell as Tarith might have hoped for. Suladan did not, at first, relent. He was rage-filled and driven by pride, it fueled him to continue as he thrashed and stabbed once again at Tarith. The two men locked together, dragged each other to the floor, rolling in the dirt and dust--two lions fiercely in combat. They punched and kicked, at one point the silver warlord had the audacity to sink his teeth deep into Tarith's hand, the Prince yelped as he let go of his shield. "I've never had the chance to kill a Prince before. I hope it's as delicious as it sounds" Suladan growled, mere inches from Tariths ear.

"You won't get to savor it" Malacender said as he pushed Suladan off of himself, kicking his jaw and rising above him, sword poised to strike but a blunt fist to his knee sent him back to the ground.

"Get up, young Prince. You want spectacle? You shall have it" Suladan taunted but his overconfidence had blindsided him as Tarith, from the ground, sunk his swords tip deep into the flesh of the warlords calve as he approached.

The warlord fell to the ground in defeat, pain and immense humiliation as the crowd chanted. The Prince kicked both twin daggers away from Suladan, so as to avoid any deceptive moves from the warlord who frantically looked up to the high stand, first at the Sultan and then at his intended. Reading the look in Amira's eyes which were cast onto the silver haired victor, Suladan turned back to Tarith, he knew the look she gave him, one of admiration, relief and surprise. "Kill me" he asked the Prince. Tarith tilted his head in confusion at the strange request.

"What?"

"You have won, you have to kill me! I've failed her, I've failed my clan, my father and his father before and I have disgraced myself above all else. Kill me. Kill me!" the warlord pleaded desperately through chipped teeth and bloody drool. Tarith could almost feel what he thought was sympathy for his opponent. The same sympathy one would feel at the sight of an injured or dying animal needing to be put out of its misery. The Harbinger lowered himself, squatting in front of Suladan "I won't kill you. That was never part of my deal. I've won, yes, but that only means that now she can choose what she wants for herself" the Prince murmured before pointing to Amira. A few hundred heads turned, following the Prince's direction. Tarith stood back up, wary of the rage and anger he saw begin to swell in Suladan's eyes, keeping a close eye on the warlords daggers that lay a few feet away from him. The Sultan rose again, this time able to pull himself up in sheer fury. With regret and disdain for the Prince of Ushkin, the Sultan announced, "the terms are clear...my...my daughter is free to do as she pleases!"

The crowd, Tarith, Suladan and The Sultan now all looked at the Princess. Amira was, at first, embarrassed to have so many eyes on her till she saw the look of her father, his chubby face now turning a bright red, almost looking like the cherry tomatoes he had in a bowl next to him. She smiled at him spitefully as she placed her hands on the stone baluster "it is with sound mind that I free myself of all arrangements to marry the brave warrior; Suladan, who though lost, will be remembered for facing the mighty dragon and we shall see is widely compensated for his valor!" she shouted--strong yet humble. The arena erupted in a mixture of happy and angered shouts, some citizens giving praise whereas the more traditional and elderly cursed the dragon Prince for ever arriving in Arden and interfering in their ways, hurling food and other assorted waste towards him. The guards even had to hold back the lines and aisles that swept towards eachother in riot.

"You come into our lands, you interrupt our traditions and now you think you can just walk away with the Princess?" Suladan murmured as the heat started to penetrate his weary and exhausted mind. Tarith turned away from Amira and back to face him "if that dissatisfied you, warlord, we may fight for our own reasons. If this is what you wish"

Suladan receded and sat back down in the sand, exhausted, had he not been so worn he would have gotten back up into the fight, as stubborn as he was and as loathing a man as he had been raised to be.

"Good, good" the Sultan muttered, only able to smile rather maliciously as he tried to keep a grip on his temper. hatefully staring directly at Tarith, a hate that now grew stronger than ever before, his distaste for clan Malacender had boiled into contempt "captain, seize my traitorous daughter" he commanded prompting one of the masked guards to restrain

Amira, grabbing her wrists and forcefully trying to place cold, metal shackles onto them. "What are you doing? You heard the..." but Amira was cut off by her father's sharp and shrill voice that dripped with relentless disappointment. "It appears I have you to thank for all of this...daughter. I should've suspected that after the old swordmaster got himself killed you would not stop until you achieved the same end, and simultaneously tainting my plans. But did you really need to stomp on our sacred traditions to get there?"

"You didn't care for Sadeeb and you never cared for our traditions you only cared to see me shipped off for the goal of securing an arrangement for our 'independence' and hidden behind that--your assent. Take a look, this is the price of independence. They will never let us go" Amira argued as she tried to wriggle free of the guards.

Tarith looked up in time to see the commotion in the high stand. He pointed the tip of his sword at the Sultan who was watching as the guards restrained Amira "enough!" the Prince cried, his voice radiating off of every brick in the arena. Something about it sounded different, more powerful and booming and not the young boy who had arrived the day before.

"You may be the future Emperor, but you will not dictate our rules and customs! Too many of your ilk have done the same!" the Sultan shouted back. "We have allies and friends. Friends in your corner who will back us!" The arena stood silent for a moment. Waiting for a reply. One came but not what anyone there was expecting. Tarith, about to speak again, opened his mouth but was silenced as the side doors, of which the citizens had entered the arena, swung open violently as their barricades were wretched from their locks. In their wake Lo'atal and at least fifty other Osh-Venn swept through the gate, knocking aside the Nadenian guards, tussling with them for control of all the entrances.

Tarith smiled at the support, knowing he wouldn't have to face the Sultan alone. He turned once again to the ruler of Nadenia, standing high above him. "I'll ask only once more. Let. Her. Go" Tarith scowled. As he spoke Amira suddenly managed to free herself from the guard holding her, delivering a painful blow to his crotch. The other guards tried to corner her, their spears pointing mere inches from her face. Tarith watched as the Princess stood on the baluster, hands still shackled behind her back, and then, in a moment as quick as air, cast herself off the near twenty foot drop. She arched herself as she formed into a backflip, landing graciously in the dirt and hay of a cart as softly as the feather off a wing. Both Tarith and Lo'atal looked impressed at the display of Amira's acrobatics and of the angelic weightlessness of Nadenian women; their agility and flexibility was stunningly unmatched. In one swift motion the Princess jumped, bringing her bonded hands under her legs before making her way to Tarith in the ensuing confusion.

Whilst Lo'atal and the Osh-Venn held off the guards who began to encompass them, Tarith stretched out his hand as he felt Amira's tight grip "We need to leave! Now!" Tarith shouted, placing his sword between the chain links and twisting the hilt until he felt the weak chains groan. The bonds creaked and then split and, with Amira now free, Tarith turned to his General, signaling Lo'atal to round up the company.

"This what I get for leaving you for all of three hours" the General complained.

"Well, I thought I told you if I wasn't back in a bit. Where were you for those three hours?"

"Looking for you. We thought you'd be in the crowd watching. I should've suspected you'd do something this stupid"

"I'm just trying to make this memorable for you"

"Yeah but I'd like to be around to recall said memories. We have to go now, My Prince"

"What? I'm not leaving, this is my home. If we can force him to surrender I can succeed him. This is your fault!" the Princess stated before she struck the Prince sharply on the shoulder.

"Do you want my help or not? I cannot grant it to you on opposing sides of a battlefield" Tarith said as he rubbed the arm.

"I don't need your help!" Amira answered again, she went to strike him in the face but he was too quick. "You fools, you don't even know what you've started" she smirked with disbelief, pulling her hand violently away from Tarith's.

"Tell that to them," the Harbinger said as he pointed to a large group of guards who had made their way down the steps of the arena and were proceeding towards Tarith and Amira. "If we're going now is the time!" Lo'atal roared as he flipped a guard over his shoulder as though they were nothing but bags of corn, their light armor making a thud as they hit the ground. Amira stared at Tarith, angrily. He smiled as he pushed her and himself towards the gate with Lo'atal and the Osh-Venn fending off the encircling rioters.

"This is gonna lead to war, you know this don't you?" Lo'atal remarked as they fled out the arena gates.

"These two nations have been on a knife's edge for centuries now. You can't blame the rocks for falling when it's the rains that force them! Besides, what's he going to do when he finds his heiress is aligned with us!" Tarith bantered back as they pushed themselves through the market and main square.

"The horses are ready!" the General stated as they ran through the streets to the rest of the Osh-Venn. Looking up at the bridges and guard posts as they escaped through the labyrinth of houses and market stalls, Tarith saw that the other Osh-Venn, at least two hundred of them, were spread about the city, fighting the guards of Arden, on every rooftop and every stairway. Tarith watched as guards were thrown into tarpaulins from the low walkways above, momentarily a shadow of a passing body would blot out the high rising sun. The horses caught Tarith's eye, ready to go, he saw old Vacile, already on his horse, giddily awaiting the signal to leave "where are we going, considering this was all clearly and calmly planned out and executed?" Amira sarcastically remarked as she was quickly pushed onto a spare horse by Tarith.

"I always liked improvising, didn't I, Lo'atal?" Tarith laughed in reply.

"That you did, my Prince, but whilst we have a moment can we use it to leave. We'll discuss your obscure and unnatural love for irony later"

"To the edge of the Red Plains then. We set up camp there!" Tarith ordered, turning to Lo'atal, who nodded as the Harbinger, the Princess of Nadenia, The Osh-Venn General, the lore master and their host mounted their horses, making a fast getaway through the southern gate that Lo'atal had ordered opened whilst he gathered the men during Tarith's distraction.

The General saddled his great rhino: Bharak, named in honor of the younger brother of the last great Champion Rider, who snorted and huffed as his great bulk started to charge towards the gates. A Nadenian upon the city walkway sprinted for the push-lever to the main gates, flicking it in motion just as an Osh-Venn took hold of him. The bronze gate began to shudder as their mechanisms moved and chimed and the escape began to seal. Lo'atal drove Bharak like a honed spear inwards, towards the gates. The beast lowered his head and a sky-shattering crack blasted out of the gate as the rhino's metal tipped horn busted open one of the gates. The horses and their caravans raged out of the city in droves as the last remaining Osh-Venn remained to insure a safe exit.

Within minutes the city of Arden was cleared, the shouting that had spread from the arena throughout the entire city had dulled, as the dust settled and the Osh-Venn warriors drew back, following their Prince, a red mist from the plains outside the city descended on Arden as the hundreds of horses became simple mirages, flickering on the horizon as their army charged into the unknown.

Chapter 11-Dangerous Beasts

Laya led her men into the remote heart of the south-east. There all the great pine trees lay bare, blown in all different directions, their branches twisted and tangled like one large briar bush capped with snow. The ground glimmered as the somber glow of twilight broke through the sky, casting shadows over most things but giving enough light as a harbinger of the early morning sun. Across the entire landscape the hard ground was an array of cold ice and soft snow that was plowed by the hooves of the horses as they were driven forward now that the weather had died down and the snow was falling slower as if gradually thawing from time. It was hard to imagine that even the first Forrester: Farthor, was able to brave such a depressingly quiet land and not turn back. Though perhaps it was more so that he had been pursuing the Warborn north even then and had chosen to make his home in the north so as to watch over it. Even now, over the land, Laya noted the many ruins built by Farthor and his sons as they passed through the forest and saw the ancient remnants of the old watchtowers, constructed in a line that led from the forest up the winding ridge to the north-east. Though time had rotted them and turned their insides black, the relics of the ancient Winterlanders remained.

The scouting crew stayed quiet, not wishing to give away their position, being in the heart of Warborn territory. They were weary, having spent the last few days since their departure camping in the odd deserted hovels they could find.

Every snap of a distant twig and every crunching step the horses took Laya believed was too loud, and with good reason. She knew the enemy, as did all the men with her. The Warborn rebels were guerrilla fighters, attacking in numbers out of nowhere and leaving mutilated bodies behind. Yet there was no sign of them. Even in the south-east, the most forested part of The Winterlands, unkempt and unpruned. Laya was surprised that they hadn't already fallen under attack. She looked around, her eyes darting to every tree to see if behind it was a lurking berserker. Through the cloud of her breathing in the cold, she could see the sun begin to peak from behind the distant mountains that separated The Winterlands from The Pale, another of the Eight Realms. The horses snorted as Laya brought hers to a halt, her men waiting patiently behind her as she surveyed the land, her eyes narrowing to look at every detail, every animal. After a few moments she turned to her men "dismount here, we'll walk the rest of the way and remember; we need to catch the first Warborn patrol we find, I want information about their leader before we kill them. Stay low and only move on my word" she whispered. The men nodded as they quietly climbed over their saddles, their scaled, leather vests and metal shoulder plates creaked as they shuffled heavily.

They crept over the small mounds of frozen dirt and took refuge in a long ditch that ran the width of the rest of the forest. Keeping their helmeted heads down, the men positioned themselves to set up a small fire. "No" Laya hissed "no fire, I don't want every savage and his mother finding us. We won't be here long. Keep to it. We move south to check the clearing and then we pull back to Erikstead" she ordered, pulling her cloak tightly around her as she felt the chill. "We don't even know where they're camped or even if it's just the one camp. These bastards move around" one soldier said.

"But we know that all Warborn attacks for the last few seasons have come from this direction. And there are no villages for miles so it's perfect for these half-breeds to hide here. I'm not asking that the six of us try and take out every bloody Warborn, we just need to capture one and take them back home. I want to know who this 'Torrold Stone-Fist' is and what he's planning to do" Laya answered. She pulled her head above the ditch, peering out into the forest beyond. Even for a stout warrior like herself, there was something inside her that made her feel uneasy under unfamiliar trees, the silence was deafening. No other noise. No birds, no people, not even the sound of the wind slinking over the branches of the trees. Her eyes went from side to side of the forest, taking note of every dark shadow, every leafless bush and every bare and hollow oak. It felt like an eternity passed whilst she sat there, the men unsure of what to do, until something broke the silence. A singular noise, sharp and sudden--the sound of a fallen branch snapping out in the distance. Whatever had caused the disturbance was weighty and large, she fathomed, as a rustling followed. Her men stiffened, keeping their hands on the pommels of their swords and reaching for any other weapons they had brought.

Then the same noise came again, except this time several branches snapped, all consecutively, as if being stepped on. By the speed they were snapping Laya knew that whatever was moving in the darkness of the early morning wasn't a person, it had too many feet to be moving like a human all at once. Then again the sounds rang out, as if, bit by bit, this thing was running a few yards and then stopping after a few seconds. It happened twice again, each time Laya heard the snapping and crunching getting louder. Then her eyes caught movement in the brush. Two orange eyes, adjacent from each other, staring past her. The eyes glowed a deep, demonic hue as the beast they belonged to released a low and frightful growl. Laya could see the saber teeth that clung to the top of the animals mouth whilst it bared the others as drool ran down them. Thin snippets of a spiky ridge of hair stuck up off the animal's body except for its ears which were capped with soft tufts of hair.

Laya examined the beast, realizing that it was looking at something behind them, on the other side of the ditch.

She turned at her men, worriedly. They saw the look on her face and knew that what was able to strike concern into the fearless northern warrioress should concern them all. She mimed the word "sabrecat", a beast all northerners knew but so few had actually seen. A beast of legend and of nightmarish folklore, the great stalkers of the remote places of The Winterlands, of which were plenty. They traveled alone and thankfully so, though their solitude didn't mar their lethality. Huge, cunning and able to take on other beasts as well as men and they were as wild as wolves and just as prideful.

Laya kept her men quiet. She knew the immense hearing capabilities the cat possessed and that even the slight movement of their weapons could give them away. She had only ever seen the results of an sabrecat's attack once before, but that was enough to sicken even her, she remembered nothing but thick blood stains in the snow with only tiny chunks of flesh and meat where a person had once stood. Bones snapped to get at the marrow inside. For a creature so large they could move like streaks of sunlight across the snow and just as silent. As she watched it more closely, Laya tried following the animals gaze, turning her head as slowly as possible behind her but before she could see what the beast was watching she felt a gust of air pass over her head, followed by a heavy but soft object hitting the back of her head, forcing her against the ditch wall. Laya pulled herself up to look at what was behind them and saw the sabrecat had lept over them and was now laying with a large dane ax embedded in its left ribcage. The animal was already lying down in the dirt, sputtering its last as it still continued to try and fight whoever it had seen behind the Forresters. It growled and hissed as it looked up to the superior hunter.

Laya's men drew their weapons and climbed back out of the ditch, intent on finishing off the animal and finding out who'd wounded the beast. But as soon as the company had pulled themselves out of the ditch, they got their answer. Standing over the sabrecat was a large, bulky man, tall and broad. On his head was a leather helmet with curved ox horns on both sides that looped around to his eyes, Laya saw that on his face was a sinister smile, the type of smile one would see on a madman or the face one would imagine a wolf would pull once it had caught sight of the deer. Around his grinning mouth was a thick, beard that ran down to his collarbone, tangled at its ends and knotted around an iron ring. The strange warrior also wore no tunic, no armor, just his ridiculously bulky and muscular body, the likes of which Laya had never seen on a man. More so, she made note of the very familiar green swirls painted across him. Laya needed no more explanation, she had what she had set out for: a Warborn. She charged. Raising her sword in the air and bringing it down on the man's head, having to raise it higher than herself as the man was twice her size. The Warborn ragged his ax out of the now dead sabrecat as he blocked Laya's hit, the sword blade and ax handle clanging together as they connected. "Just what I've been looking for," Laya smiled.

"Couldn't have said it better, little lady," the warrior smirked with wild eyes, lifting up a single finger from the hand that held the ax. At its command, Laya heard rustling as did her men, they turned to see several other Warborn emerge from the bushes, some climbing down from tree branches. All brandishing weapons and all wearing that same green face paint. "Well, well. Torrold is gonna really like you. We weren't expecting this many Forresters to come calling, were we lads?" the mad man asked his band, using the shocking distraction to his advantage, using the dane ax's handle to hit Laya in the nose, bashing her to the ground as blood began to pour from her flared nostrils. "Tie 'em up boys. We're going for a little walk" the large man said as the Forrester soldiers looked at Laya for an order. She raised her hand, signaling them to disarm. She dazedly picked herself back up as both herself and her men were grabbed and bound. "Warborn scum" Laya hissed at the man, blood now running onto her lips and hiding in the creases of her mouth. The large man simply smiled, casually scraping his boots free of dirt. "It's off to Pine Grove with you folks. Time to cut some timber" the large man cheered as the rest of the Warborn laughed with him.

Two horses galloped over the dirty street cobbles of Kingsport, each brick leading off into a separate labyrinth of the largest city in all of Kond and ran through the crowd of merchants and commoners, sellswords and charlatans. Several fishermen, holding their daily catches, stared wearily at the two newcomers, though most of the populus ignored the new addition to the mass and carried on with their affairs, absorbing the action of the outside world like a great sinkhole in the earth. Barely had the city changed, since the days of its founding over a millennium ago.

Surrounded by a foreign people who made him feel incredibly unpleasant, Ulfrik gazed along the streets, his eyes flowing over the smaller houses to the shops and blacksmiths, inns and brothels all leading in one messy line to the Kings Keep, sat high on the hill of the city, sectioned off with a long and high, thick stone wall with the guards marching over it like a legion of ants on the mound. All of such was the likes Ulfrik had not seen for years, not since the closing days of the war where he had made his very first trip to the capitol to swear obeisance and fealty, as one of the Kings of the realms, to the High King.

In the square just outside the main gates to the keep stood the mighty Hero's Column, containing the living history of Kond. At the top of the pillar, reaching twenty feet or so, was a statued idol of the great Roadarr Quarthand, the father of Kond, the forger of the throne and the first to sit on it. His line had always ruled before Cythees ilk. Their history, stretching from the time of conquest, to the present day was imprinted on the column, running down like a tapestry brought straight from the earth. As a student of history Ulfrik recalled many of their numbers who had been heroes themselves: Clovis Quarthand, whom had set back the Malacender invasion by slaying their dragon and witnessing the execution of the Champion Rider--Fotia Iron Crown. Or before that, perhaps, he thought, the great Meric--as Prince had fought to free the realms from the grip of the enslaving and conquesting Rakers of The North. Most of the old royal line cast dark shadows over such a shallow dynasty as Cythees'. For a city of such inequity and clutter, as befit any capitol, the Hero's Column was the brightest point of Kingsport. One that had almost been torn down by the current High King but spared by him on the encouraging words of Lord Jazar who did not wish to see the riots that took hold of the capital a few days after Morryg's death continue.

Ulfrik had only been to the capital twice before, it hadn't changed much in the three years since the civil war. He still remembered The Kings Keep, its many broad or slim towers reaching up to the blue clouds above, casting its shadow on the rest of the city below it with a jealous spite. As they rode along the center road, leading to the first set of gates up to the Kings Keep. Dullever waited till the bustle of the market had enveloped them like an ocean of noise and restlessness to hide in. With their voices masked he said in a raised tone "perhaps we should find an inn first. Cythees need not know we're here just yet"

Ulfrik nodded at the suggestion.

The two then drove their mounts off the center road into a small courtyard, pathed with aged, grey tiles. Ulfrik read the inn's name on a sign hanging from the door--the Crowned Jewels. Ulfrik curled his lip in contempt of the place. He was always put off by the smell of the capital, the salty sea air from the docks to the east, washing over the scent of animal and human excrement as well as the scent of hot magma and slag from the smithy's forge, molded with the smell of hay and cooked food and old, white stones.

The two were soon seated inside, tucked away in the inns corner booth. Ulfrik kept his head down, knowing of the attention that could be drawn if he was to be recognised. He saw by their aged faces, the way they spoke and the way the other patrons sat, lonely and angered, many were also veterans of the civil war, though this far south meant they would've fought on the same side, relations between the Forresters and the Monthells were far from stable. Ever since the founding of both houses centuries ago, neither had seen fit to aid each other as it was more than geography that distanced the two. Not since the Malacender invasion six hundred years before had the two joined forces to push back the last Harbinger: Fotia Iron-Crown and her armies. The great dragon of the east, she was referred to, bringing fury and rule to Kond or so she had believed before being slain.

Dullever sat across from Ulfrik, ale in hand and sword unstrapped from him but left strategically at his side on the other chair. As the sun tried to bleed through the thin curtains Ulfrik looked around the inn. Half naked bar maids as young as sixteen laughed and sang and danced to the tune of a drunken bard's lute. Where the rest of the men watched the girls swinging themselves around and onto the laps of strangers, sailors, sellswords from every corner of every continent. Ulfrik kept on alert, watching everyone in the tavern. Not so surprisingly, no one had even noticed they had walked in, considering that no one in the place knew what he looked like. Every customer, every drunkard and sellsword inside the inn, the King noted, what they did and how they moved, remembering that his father, Randall, was killed during the civil war in a tavern--something he had never forgiven nor forgotten. His fathers own men turned on him, much to Ulfrik's disbelief. Until the war's end the blame was given to the Gullery's for Randall's death until the Darianths had begrudgingly owned up to the atrocity later, driving the wedge deeper between the north and south and souring the wounds between the royal houses. Whether Randall's men had been paid or threatened to renounce their loyalty it mattered not to Ulfrik, the Darianth King, Eckard, had conspired with his son and nephews to slaughter all those men that night. A victory for the war but a dark mark for the family.

Ulfrik made note of a particular man he felt he had seen before though he couldn't name where from. The scoundrel had scruffy black hair like a badger or weasel that ran down into long, bushy, sideburns. His mouth was surrounded by a thin layer of stubble that stretched when he laughed with two girls on either arm as a thin smile crept across his face and his blue eyes watched the girls laugh intently as his hands grabbed and groped at them. He was dressed as though a vagabond would if they tried to impersonate nobility, or more to mock their dress. He wore what appeared to be a well-used blue, leather jacket and a tattered, white, tunic underneath, tucked down his trousers. His high sailors boots were pulled up far and brushed his knees. "Dullever " Ulfrik called attention. The captain turned and followed his King's gaze as he nudged his head to the side, pointing to the man in the corner. "You ever seen him before? I think I have but I don't know where from" the King whispered before taking a huge gulp from his tankard, the bitter ale tingled at the back of his throat, washing down the bread and cheese they'd had upon entry into the inn. Dullever narrowed his eyes and examined the man, making sure he wasn't noticed. He stroked his short beard in contemplation before looking back at Ulfrik nonchalantly "No. Never seen the likes of 'em before. Looks to me like a cap'n of some sort, bet half his crew are in here so don't go starting any fights with him" he answered. Ulfrik tipped his head upwards as he acknowledged what his friend said. Casually, he sat back, taking one last look at the room, he saw someone who stood out, though not enough to attract attention but enough to differentiate them from everyone else. Someone who wasn't there when last Ulfrik had looked. It was a hooded figure, wearing a red cloak that concealed all their body except a brilliant beard, braided into three short tendrils. Both men ogled the stranger who had seemingly taken note that they had been spotted and began to slowly approach the booth the two were in, walking so flawlessly across the wooden floor that they appeared to be floating instead. Ulfrik maintained the visage of drinking whilst he slid his free left hand down to his sword on the seat next to him. "That will be unnecessary, My King. I assure you this visit will be beneficial to all of us" he heard a low and sly voice emanate from the hooded figure, though it spoke confidently now, as they slid the concealing hood away from their head, revealing the profile of Lord Jazar. His face held his usual mild grin of power, an understanding the Minister of Information had about himself, knowing how easily he could move about without being recognised or spotted, despite his weighty position, trusting in his ability to stay invisible. Before the Kings Keep Jazar had known the streets of the capitol first-- his father a lowly cobbler of colloquial repute. However, Ulfrik seemed ignorant as to who the Lord was, though Jazar, taking a seat between Ulfrik and Dullever, looked at the captain and familiarly smiled "Angus" he uttered, as if he were an old compatriot with the great northern warrior. Dullever smiled modestly.

"My King. May I have the humble honor of introducing Lord Jazar of the High Kings royal court. Lord of Ears and Tongues and knower of all secrets, one of the most well connected men on the globe" The captain boasted.

"Lovely titles as always, my friend" Jazar smiled sarcastically at the captain before turning his head to Ulfrik.

"How in Oblivion do you know each other? I thought you said you hated southerners" Ulfrik asked his friend.

"I' am not of the south, your grace, so I assure you, you have nothing to fear from me," Jazar smiled.

Ulfrik shifted in his seat " I doubt your difference in home makes us allies so forgive me if I find your loyalty hard to believe"

"It was he who was most useful in the civil war. Remember the Battle of Fishermans Ford?" Dullever interceded. "Yeah. Our forces were pinned down by the Gullery's and the loyalists"

Dullever smirked at Jazar as he recalled the telling of their victory.

"Well. It was Jazar, here, who was able to send his own spies into the Gullery camps and retrieve their plans and eavesdrop on their commanders to know where they planned to march next. Not to mention, he also made several of their captains... well...go on a long trip off a few tall cliffs shall we say"

"Really? I was never informed of this" Ulfrik scowled with

suspicion at the Lord of Spies.

"Well secrecy was of the utmost and you and your father were busy at Red-River Watch. It would've been dangerous to try and get such messages to you" Dullever reasoned

"I always assumed you served the Quarthands to the very end" Ulfrik scoffed.

"The one good thing I'll say of our High King is he was wise to surround himself with the enemies of his enemies, besides, I could say precisely the same to you. I recall the Forrester's at first coming to the aid of the Quarthands before their betrayal of your kin"

"What Eddis Quarthand did to my niece was more than enough to warrant the loss of our confidence" Dullever growled "his own betrothed. Traitors and liars both. He didn't care for her, never once. He just needed an excuse to be rid of her" he recalled how the news had carried that young Hyacinth had been thrown from that horse and snapped her neck, allowing the Prince to unshackle himself from that corpse bride to win the warmth of another.

"Then I suppose we both did our jobs well enough. There was no need for Cythees to pardon me when he ascended" the spymaster smirked.

"Why so?"

"For it was I who had ensured he left the city alive after he slew Morryg and kept the riots quelled after he returned"

"Morryg was killed in a duel he accepted. Bout the only honorable thing Cythees ever kept to"

"Honorable to some and traitorous to others. I ensured that you rebels were well informed during the war and kept the questions of the Quarthands to a minimum"

"Thus playing both sides? And what have I done to curry favor with 'one of the most well connected men'? I take it this is not a social visit?" The King asked, cautiously sipping his ale, keeping his eyes on Jazar's as the contents of his cup started to drip into his blonde beard, soaking the ale up like a barbed sponge.

"No, it isn't. I'm afraid my visit must be brief. The High King doesn't know I'm here, nor does he know you two are" the Spymaster stated.

"And you want to tell him we're here and spoil the surprise?" Ulfrik interrupted impudently.

"On the contrary. I'm here to warn you that Cythees already has it in his mind that you are the enemy. There is idle talk of potential rebellion. To disagree with him is to pronounce your treachery and confirm your descent in his mind or so he'd have people believe. I'm here to caution you to be wary. I do not know what he has planned but do not make the mistake of thinking you are welcome inside The Kings Keep. No matter what faces they put on"

Ulfrik looked at Dullever, now with more concern and worry.

"And how do I know Cythees hasn't sent you down here to lull us into a false sense of inferiority? What of your own face, Lord Jazar"

"I have no face. An inconsequential servant who has always sought to keep the balance and order of things, here and across the realms. And besides, do you truly believe Cythees is smart enough to organize myself to be here at the exact time you arrive in the city? He is only as informed as I allow him to be, your grace" Jazar retorted, hushing Ulfrik in thought.

"What's this about rebellion, Jazar? That's extreme isn't it? Even for that spoilt oaf on the throne" Dullever whispered.

"It isn't just The Winterlands Cythees is fearful of. The Highfelds are also on edge. Of course the crown has never been as stalwart with them as liked but since the civil war things have been gently simmering with them, it's gotten so bad even I'm finding it hard to communicate with my eyes and ears out westward. The Lenglores have the whole realm locked down and quiet and travelers are wary of the roads and not because of the bandits. That shows naught but ill intent" Jazar murmured, hurriedly. The Lenglores were certainly the most isolated of all eight great houses and their traditional and nationalistic views were apparent to all the realms.

There was a slight pause before the small door to the inn was flung open violently as three men, clad in shiny, silver armor and helms strutted into the inn like proud roosters among the hens. They wore the symbol of the royal high crown on their chest plates and were engraved into the center of their rounded helms. Their faces were on full display, not covered or armored. The loyal lapdogs of Kingsport.

"It's the city guards" Jazar hissed, flinging his hood back on before slowly standing up.

One of the serving girls was unfortunate enough to walk too close to one of the city watch. He grabbed her by her long, red hair, holding her face uncomfortably close to his own as he tried to force a kiss on her. One of the bartenders intervened but was taken by a metal hand and pushed back by the other two watchmen. Ulfrik watched in anger as Jazar slyly slithered past the three whilst they were distracted. Seeing the look in his friends eyes and knowing his quickly riled nature, Dullever grabbed Ulfrik's hand as he saw it reaching for his sword "Not here, my King. It won't end well" he whispered, pleading not to.

"They're all dogs here in this shit pile of a city" Ulfrik cursed as he stood up valiantly. Drawing the rest of the inn's attention to himself. "You gentlemen looking for someone?" he asked, trying to sound as naive as possible.

"Fuck off" one bluntly replied but the Winterlands King was too stern and steady to be shook by words and so didn't back down, instead he stepped closer. He asked again "would you gentlemen be looking for someone?" In response one of the watchmen turned his full attention to these two foreign men ``what's it to..." he stopped as he caught a glimpse of the tree sigil on Ulfrik's shoulder pauldron. A malicious smile crept across the dirty and dry face of one of the city guard "Well, well. Looky here boys. It's not been long enough that a Forrester's come down from their frozen corner of the continent. What for, I wonder? The weather?"

"Very funny. Well it appears you've had your fun, you've ruined a perfectly good morning and you've personally put me off my first meal so, if you don't mind, We'll be on our way" Ulfrik said, noticing the guards had left the girl alone, he signaled Dullever with a smile to grab their effects. Ulfrik knew that if an altercation were to take place he wouldn't come out on top and angering this many of city guard would only end with his death or imprisonment. However, as if trying to provoke a more public reaction, the guard put his gloved hand out in front of Ulfrik, his arm barring the way as he went for the door.

"I hear that the High King himself has been waiting to speak to a certain King. You boys wouldn't happen to know anything about it?"

"Rest easy, Commander. We're here to see Cythees. If you'll be so kind as to allow us to move" Ulfrik tried again, this time sounding more impatient as his level of tolerance always ran low with southerners. The guard didn't move.

"I said he was waiting on a King. I didn't say you. Who's to say that you are the men we're looking for to ensure their safety and not just some casual freeloader, drunk and looking for an audience with a man who shits better than you eat?"

"Oh no one. But if you don't believe us and you throw us both in prison for posing as a member of the royal states, Cythees doesn't get to see us today. Who do you think he'll come for when he finds out it was you who ordered our arrest without his consent?"

The city watch's Commander stared at Ulfrik with his one good eye and Ulfrik proudly stared back, as good with words as with a sword. Sounding beaten and angered, the commander held out his hand towards the inn's door "welcome to Kingsport...my King " the commander said, joylessly.

Both the King and Captain were soon surrounded by the three City Watch, guarding the two guests like trained dogs, pushing aside the common people as they marched through the streets and up the four tiers of the city, stacked on one another up the hill, with The Kings Keep watching all of them from above.

Chapter 12-Negotiation

Eleana watched from the gallery of the throne room, alone, as Cythees took his seat upon the Gilded Throne. She didn't know why, but simply by watching him take those short steps up to the throne almost everyday for the past six years always filled her with angst and the feeling of dissatisfaction would grow within her. What would he say this time, how close would he drag the realms into another conflict, she would always find herself asking. She frowned to herself when she noticed how he had changed into the sharpest, most regal of tunics he had, perfectly decorated and embroidered, the color of blood. She knew that he had done all this to spite all else in attendance in the room, with the high crown on his head and his short, pointy beard combed, Cythees looked like the epitome of a High King of The Eight Realms.

But Eleana knew as her brother did too; appearances were incredibly deceiving and useful against the uninitiated. She saw that her brothers attendants had left him alone for just a moment, though the Kings Watch stayed ever close to their royal liege. As she approached their tall and looming bodies, wreathed in plated steel, she felt an armored hand on her shoulder, holding her back with its strength. She turned over her shoulder and saw one of the Kings Watch, his face covered by the engraved helmet, littered with feather carvings from the brow to the lobes. "The High King does not wish to be spoken to until the entire court is here, my Lady " he mentioned, his voice echoing inside the helm. Eleana, offended by the guard laying a hand on her, turned her entire body to face him "I'm here to speak to my brother, not the High King.

As Princess of The Fold I'm asking you to stand aside" she answered with annoyance. She looked at Cythees, knowing his answer yet praying that something would make him change in that moment, that for whatever reason, he would be more lenient and tolerable of her. To Eleana's surprise Cythees, instead of turning her away as he normally might, half-heartedly beckoned her to him. He rolled his eyes as if he had been forced to acknowledge his sister's dreary existence.

Eleana approached, taking one step at a time up to the throne, she saw its broad arm rests carved from quartz and marble, made to look as if it was carved from the wall of the keep itself. Its stone like polished glass, refined and untouched having sat in those very halls for well over a thousand years.

She stood next to her brother, facing the main doors, maintaining a regal appearance in front of the rest of the gathering court. With her eyes fluttering around the room she spoke to her brother "I do hope that you will treat the King of the Winterlands with respect, today. Even for you, try and hold back. Do remember who it was who fought for us in the northern campaigns of the war and whose people saw the most casualties" she protested.

"Oh I won't forget. Just as how I won't forget who they originally pledged to in the opening days of the war. These 'proud' men and their talk of honor. They backed the Quarthands before me. They talk down to Darian and his lot for changing sides but forget to levy themselves into the hypocrisy" Cythees responded, more so as a grunt. Seeing how her brother had already disregarded what she had requested she quickly changed her diplomatic tactics. Eleana leaned in close, her face almost touching Cythees', something she was nearly cringing at, she hadn't been this close to him in years, even as children she had kept to herself and never played with him about the large halls and galleries of The Forge. She could smell the fine scents he coated himself in to cover up the powerful odor of musk and wine. She warned him "father is attending today isn't he?"

"Yes. Why, what's it to y…"

"He'll be watching to see how we all act, to see if we meet his standards. You plan on meeting them by insulting a King of one of the eight realms, one of your eight realms? Remember what happened to the last High King who insulted father?"

Cythees turned his head as well as his attention to his sister, the two knew the workings of each other's mind the same way a snake knows a mongoose and like the two natural enemies they knew the weaknesses of each other too. Cythees' was that underneath the belligerent rage and mood swings was the compulsive need to appear superior and stronger than anyone, thus had formed his immense skill with a blade and why he was one of the deadliest duelers in all the realms save for a few individual peers. For a tournament at Kings Grove some years ago had seen to that--when Ulfrik unseated the then Prince in a joust, a friendly joust. Friendly to all but Cythees who had allowed it to play and fester in his mind ever since.

As well, was the need to impress Corvus, his father, in any way he could. Since the time they were all children, Eleana could always remember her father pushing her brothers to the brink, breaking one, honing one and twisting the other.

Among the few gathered nobles of the capital, who had turned out to see the King of the mighty Winterlands, the rest of the royal court also stood in attendance as the pieces all took their place on the board: Darian, Saura, Corvus and Jazar, who had seemingly managed to arrive back inside the keep just in time, all gathered around the throne, like moths to flame. Eleana shared a cold glance with Saura as the Queen took a seat on the consorts chair that had been carried out by two serving hands; it was a simple chair, not as complex and carefully grafted as the Gilded Throne. The Queen took her seat just as Jazar approached Cythees, whispering something in his ear. The High King nodded to his spymaster, standing up as he beckoned Sir Kellor at the other end of the room. The old knight nodded as he and another guard grabbed onto the two large, iron handles of the throne room doors, heaving them open. The council and abundance of nobles in the court watched as two men from a far and distant land were escorted by the city guard into the throne room. The entirety of the court watched silently as King Ulfrik and Captain Dullever approached the Gilded Throne, their armor awkwardly creaking with their leather and metal straps. Eleana watched as Ulfrik's pale blue eyes never left Cythees, a small smirk on the Kings face made the High King frown angrily, as if already being defied.

The two stopped at the bottom of the four flattened steps leading to the throne, with Dullever standing just behind his King. The two men bowed their heads respectively, not wishing to air their dislike of the High King publicly. "Your majesty, my Queen" Ulfrik addressed, smirking through the stubble on his face. Lord Darianth stepped forward " King Ulfrik Forrester of The Winterlands, you are in the presence of Cythees Monthell, Lord of Kond, bearer of the Crowned Sapphires, High King of the eight realms and Keeper of the Gilded Throne" he announced to the entire court who gleefully and blindly smiled. Ulfrik simply nodded modestly towards his royal sire, awaiting his words. "You wanted to speak with me in person, your majesty?" the King asked, taking a step closer to the throne and watching as the Kings Watch closed in on him the more he approached Cythees, their visors looming with dark shadows.

"Yes, I did summon you. Quite some time ago if I remember"

Cythees sneered as the corner of his lip raised.

"I do apologize, your majesty, we ran into some minor trouble on the road. But when my liege commands me I obey, and I've seen what happens to those who defy him" Ulfrik spouted. Corvus soon spoke, his voice commanding silence from the rest of the court. "You were summoned here, your grace, to answer the High King as to why you have refused to stop the Antaran refugees from entering your country" the powerful voice bounced off of every wooden beam and stone pillar.

"That is correct, your grace. I do so indeed, with the intention of providing limited refuge for them"

"Though that is admirable, my King, the high crown did ask, keeping its own citizens in mind, for you to stop letting these foreigners into the realms. Winter is but a few short months away and with that we cannot be feeding foreign mouths as well as our own. As King of those lands it should be noted your concern should be primary"

Ulfrik sniggered bitterly at Corvus' remark. The guile of the question threw him and coiled his temper but he knew to accede to his better nature that his own mother had installed in him. "As a King of one of the eight realms, Corvus, did you not take the same oath as myself?" he asked to a collection of surprised and shaken faces as so many of the court watched Corvus for his reply yet he gave non, allowing Ulfrik to continue as he watched with calm composure and a dark look.

"'Until my last shall I defend this realm and her people'. Myself and you as well as the other six Kings all swore that in this very room four years ago, at his majesty's official coronation. Those are also words I was taught to live by, by my own royal father, Randall. A man of which you knew, a man who fought and died for your son and a man who also lived by those words. As has every Forrester since the time of Farthor and the Uniter himself. The Exodus founded many of our houses, though my own was not included, many of our nobles and farmers see the Antarans as common ancestors. For some they are kin, and these people are clearly scared of something in their own home, else I would not have allowed them here. W estill take our duty of defence on the northern coasts seriously" Ulfrik pressed.

Corvus finally released his answer: sharp, short and most effective. "Are you aware, your grace, just how much wheat, barley, livestock and weaponry the capital gives to The Winterlands yearly?"

"Yes, at last count it was fifty-thousand bushels of wheat and barley both, nearly thirty-thousand in livestock and ten caravans loaded with iron and steel. As King of The Winterlands it falls in my duty to know as such. Though I'm sure many here, in the south, would like to believe we are nothing but dense, brutish, ax-dragging warriors. The Winterlands pays back that debt, by sending thousands of tons of wood from our forests to build your ships, from our own mines comes the copper and steel you use in your smelting of coins and trinkets" Ulfrik proudly retorted. The court looked at Corvus who did something no one would have suspected: he smiled, impressed at how organized and skilled the young King was for statecraft. He huffed to himself-- it wasn't enough to stop the old eagles tirade.

"Then you will know that in order to support the refugees we will need to supply an extra few thousand of each, which takes time and money"

"Is that what it boils down to? Money? Coin?"

"It has always 'boiled down' to that. The lifeblood of the realms is coin and it doesn't stop flowing because of a few misplaced vagrants"

Ulfrik stood silent, shocked at the callousness of the royal court. It wasn't long until Saura spoke, coldly. Her green eyes watched the two men before her, stalking them, eyes on the lonesome prey.

"So, can we expect a cessation in the flow of Antaran refugees into the north?" she asked bluntly.

"With respect, your majesty, The Winterlands are under my rule so it falls to me to decide how best to rule those people within"

"Your own people, sir" Saura quickly answered, her voice becoming more raised and jumpier.

"That is most...thoughtful of you, King Ulfrik, however, who will be affording for tents and food for these refugees? If I recall correctly it was The Winterlands who suffered the greatest during the civil war, three years ago, so who do you expect to pay for all these people? Or am I wrong and The Winterlands have caves overflowing with gold the high crown is unaware of?" Corvus inquired. Every word he said was with enough conviction to almost turn Ulfrik to his way of thinking but both Kings were losing their patience for the other.

"Our lands suffered the most in the war because we gave most in the war. To this very dynasty no less" the King of snow answered.

The court stood, intrigued at Ulfik's gall yet unsurprised. He was known for speaking his mind and speaking up against those who clashed with his principles.

" Untold numbers of northmen spilled their blood during the war yet all we are to be concerned with is coin? If that be true then it would seem we both have differing views as to what makes a realm."

"It. Would seem. So" the old eagle said from atop the stairs to the throne, his lips now pursing at the impudence of this King.

"Enough of this!" Cythees interrupted, insolently. Both Ulfrik and Corvus turned to him, sensing a shift in the uneasily calmed atmosphere the two had created for the room. "I will hear no more of this. We won't be providing aid to a rabble of pelt wearing foreigners. Close the northern coastline off, no more ships are to enter into Ice Hand Caps unless authorized by the high crown not the snow crown" Cythees proclaimed with impunity, keeping his eyes fixed on the insolent King and his captain with a vexed look. "Send the refugees already in The Winterlands back home, I will even supply you some of the ships from here to sail from Kingsport to Ice Hand Caps, where you will renounce asylum to these people. Darianth. Draw up the order" Cythees commanded, pointing at his steward. Darian bowed and went to leave the room to begin his condemnation, however before Lord Darian could move he was halted by Ulfrik's words "I do apologize again, your majesty, but the refugees already here will be staying. I will do as you say, though, and shut off the coastline but the Antarans already here are staying put...on my orders. A bird carried those orders to the house of Great-Shield on the coastline before we left our own lands"

"Is that a refusal of a royal command? Is it, Forrester?" Cythees asked, standing from the throne. Queen Saura saw fit to divert the situation and said calmly "how dare you defy your High King. The Winterlands are under the rule of the crown and yet..."

"And under the warding of the Forresters" Dullever intervened. He had managed to stay calm. His gruff face seemed more like a bear from the week's travel to Kingsport, his lips twisted as his short temper began to fracture at the insult of his liege and his face, blotched and splashed with mud, scrunched up with a scowl as that temper flared.

"Now, now. Let us all take pause and relent for a moment. I'm sure his grace, King Forrester meant no disrespect to his majesty" cowed Lord Darian.

"Oh you would know all about the art of relenting, Darianth. The High Kings Steward? You live up to your namesake and banner, snake" Ulfrik cursed as he was confronted, finally, with his fathers assassin and all composure was lost as he felt those words escape him before he had a chance to pause for thought of their consequence.

"The war is over" Eleana interjected. "You once fought together, not that long ago. You wiped out the last dynasty and now you threaten to plunge us into further turmoil for the sake of an old wound made to fester again. Or have you all grown so bored of peace yet?"

"Be silent, this is not your place to speak" Corvus commanded of his daughter .

"No"

"Yes, immediately"

"No. We cannot allow this and I will not be spoken down to by…"

"Silence!" The King of The Fold roared, his eyes bulging as the vein on his balding head began to pop as he released the terrible beast that he kept lurking beneath a calmed exterior.

Corvus surveyed the room, everyone stood with mouths agape or simply watching him with surprised and attentful looks. It was unwise, everyone knew, to cross Corvus for he was known little for his kindness and more so for his ruthless cunning and influence but even more nerve-stopping was his rage when unleashed it as it was so rare, like the lion rushing forth for its prey; unexpected and something you could never prepare for. He sighed as he steadily regained his composure

"Enough! This is treachery and I will not be denied my right… I am the High King!" Cythees roared as he arose from the golden chair, his nails almost breaking as he got up from clutching the gold armrests so tightly. The boy looked to his father, proceeding his response. Eleana watched too, she saw the looks in both their eyes and could do nothing but watch history repeat itself. The eagle was relentlessly snapping and snatching at everything to assert itself, she thought. It could not begin like this.

"Very well. Ulfrik Forrester, on charges of treason and the disobeying of a command of the High King, you're hereby sentenced to arrest until a price may be established for the Winterlands for this act of betrayal. You will remain here till we have passed judgment. Guards! Escort King Forrester and his confidant to the dungeons" he commanded. Though Corvus regretted the less than peaceful decision he still felt no personal guilt; Ulfrik was simply another citizen of the high crown, one who would learn his place one way or another. If he could not be cowed into an agreement then perhaps he could be convinced by a few days in the cells. "Have all the birds tethered. No word reaches The Winterlands until we say" Corvus whispered across to Darian.

Four guards of the Monthell household, aided by Sir Kellor, approached the two northmen, who nodded at each other. As the guards were only feet away both Ulfrik and Dullever drew their swords, the metal sung as it was drawn from the scabbard. The guards and Kellor grounded to a halt and drew their own. The warriors stood at a standstill, with the royal court watching, like gamblers in the ring, waiting to see who would win. "Now!" Ulfrik shouted throughout the gallery. "I will not be imprisoned like some common thief. And I will have say as to how my lands are governed. This is not the end that we all fought for!" his sword raised and ready.

"You are not the only ones fighting. Take caution to remember that" Saura started but was cut off as her husband's hand sprang out in front of her.

"Think very carefully about your next decision. The consequences of what you now toy at will be severe" Corvus warned with booming strength.

"I'll tell you what" , Ulfrik said, brightly. He then pointed his sword to the steward who, though somewhat threatened by Ulfrik's persona and intent, smiled. How ridiculous this King was, as much as Darian remembered about him from their last encounter at court where the King had demanded Darian pay solemnly and in blood for his fathers death. "I will gladly be put under shackles when that man answers for his crimes against my house. When he answers for the deaths of my father and kin, when he admits to his treachery, then, I will go gladly!" The King raged.

"Tragic and terrible events can happen during war, your father was not exempt. I will not apologize for a necessary action that was taken to win the conflict...my King" Darianth mocked.

"Keep quiet, Darian" Cythees scolded his steward.

Whilst the court was distracted Jazar looked at Eleana, nodding his head towards Cythees. Lady Monthell knew that she needed to intercede on Ulfrik's behalf. She stepped forward, the court watched, mostly in astonishment, as the normally quiet and reserved Eleana spoke out "father, is there really a justifiable reason to imprison a King?"

"Is there a reason to defy the *High* King?" Saura answered sharply. Eleana and the Queen locked with narrowed, cat-like eyes. A desperate disdain of each other that it was surprising the whole court in attendance didn't pick up on it as Saura's flawless face turned and shot a callous and mocking smile.

"Perhaps a heavy fine would be sufficient. I see no reason to punish King Ulfrik in this way" Eleana continued, turning to face her father. Corvus said nothing, acting as if his daughter had never opened her mouth.

"Stand down, my King, and your lives will be spared. I will even arrange for a substantial cell in which you can contemplate what the High King has said. I assure you the debt will be payable and less than extortionate" Corvus added, trying to sound as kind as possible, a foreign and ridiculous concept to him and it was only ever used in a political discourse, in the pursuit of what he wanted. Ulfrik stood still for a moment, watching all the members of the court, noting how Eleana had tried to sway the court against Cythees' decision. "Once again, the hollow words of a High King and his father mean nothing. Your promise is void and I would let myself be torn limb from limb by a pack of wolves then indebt myself to your house so we can end up like the Lenglores or the Xanters. We spilt our blood for you to claim a right to that throne. We. Owe you. Nothing" He looked at the High King who stood with a grin emerging with perfect teeth lining his mouth. The King pointed his sword at Cythees "If you are so sure of your skill with a blade then I see no greater opportunity to prove. By both God's law and of man, I enact a trial by combat! Then we will see who must truly be punished for their transgressions, in the eyes of the eight!" he proclaimed, to which he heard gasps from the gallery.

"By combat?" the High King repeated.

"Aye. You should be familiar with this law. Was it not the same one you used to take the throne from our last High King? Now for my freedom and for the freedom of my man here, I ask for that same right, in the name of the Divines--judgment by the sword. What say you?" Ulfrik pressed. The time for diplomacy is over, was what he kept telling himself --they will never respect us, we are only used for the right time.

Cythees took a moment to ponder Ulfrik's words, a scowl drawn across his face. The nobles of the gallery stood idle, awaiting the High Kings decision. When that grin turned into a small smile, Eleana could tell that her brother had no intention of showing a shred of 'northern honor' as Ulfrik might.

"So be it! I accept the challenge. By the old rights I grant you this contest. I take it you will be fighting on behalf of yourself?" Cythees asked, nodding at Ulfrik who nodded calmly back. Cythees smiled as his eyes narrowed till it looked like they were completely shut "perfect" he muttered.

Ulfrik lowered his sword to his waist and looked at his friend. Dullever seemed restless but Ulfrik couldn't deny the lick of pleasure he felt, inside himself, at the thought of finally swinging a blade at the High Kings head. His father and kinsmen, slaughtered for this opulent oppressor and now they would be avenged and saved from their own poor judgment.

By noon, the bells of both the Gray Chapel and the Kings Keep rang into the air, alerting the city of the time of day, chiming throughout the skyline as their hollow rings echoed around the Bay of Gales. Observing the city from one of the high towers of the keep was Martis, perched on a window ledge with the sash's open and legs dangling out, totally fearless. Next to him was the mangy cat of the keep, hated or ignored by everyone except Martis. The feline seemingly only took a liking to him, rubbing it's messy and puffy, orange, fur against his arm and purring seductively.

It was peaceful and almost picturesque: the landscape of Kingsport. A deceiving sight nevertheless. The keep was the centerpiece, birthing the city before it and then out to the Summerplains that sprawled to the west and bordered on the east by the sea.

The door to the stairs below him opened and hit the wall with a bang. It was only when he heard the heeled footsteps on the stone did Martis know who it was. His mother emerged from the top of the spiral stairs, her hands holding her red skirt so as not to trip. Eleana's first words were startled when she saw Martis on the other side of the window "bring yourself in now!" Martis pulled a face of disappointment but still didn't move "in, now!" his mother repeated. The boy swung himself around as his mother quickly shut the window sash with a clamor, the sun that poured through the now shut window seemed to make her face glow when it caught the light. "So... what exciting events have transpired today? Has my uncle condemned a few more innocents to torturous fates" Martis asked sarcastically, swinging his arms.

"Actually, I've come here to bring you to one of those court affairs of which we both enjoy so much," Eleana smiled. Though she didn't believe in this contest between her brother and the King, she thought it would serve as a lesson to show Martis the true ways of combat. "What? It better not be another stupid sonnet from a bard or some noble crying about how the world 'owes' him" Martis complained.

"Oh, you might like this. You'll be one of the few who do" Lady Monthell said as she put her hands on Martis' shoulder. As she led him down the stairs she joked "I do wish you'd leave that damn cat alone. It smells like it's already dead"

"I'll have you know that Sir Claws is an excellent sneak. If only he could speak about what he's seen"

"He'd soon regret it, living here" Eleana retorted, wittingly.

The two arrived at the royal training grounds, sectioned off from the keep by a well-kept and trimmed hedge, taller than most men, it was as old as the keep itself, built by some of the first of the Quarthand line and made to last with the legendary iron-wood from Enk Forest itself so that time would never rot its circular formations. It overlooked the Bay of Gales with sight and smell as the warm, salty air blew its thick scent over the bay into the pit. Cythees stood in the center of the small arena, replacing his tunic for his golden armor-- glamorous and vain, imprinted with the royal standard. His black hair brushed his face as the breeze blew over the arena. On the observation deck above the High King sat Corvus, Saura and Jazar, all seated on an aisle of chairs under a red curtained canopy. Next to both of them was Sir Kellor and several of the Monthell guards, all perfectly positioned.

Cythees waited impatiently for his challenger to arrive, sword already drawn. The High King was one of the best sword masters of Kond, a title he clung to. He had removed his crown in place for a golden helmet with a carved eagle on its forehead, an insignia of the royal crown on his chest plate below it. He stood before the crowd, basking in their ignorance and his own. Then. The small chattering of the court dulled to hurried whispers as Ulfrik paced into the yard, his younger face with thick stubble and unkempt hair, turning him into the 'wild northman' the people of the capitol thought him so. His armor was simplistic but strong, with mighty shoulder braces and layered chainmail, carved with small tree insignias. A large plate of steel protected his neck and upper chest like an iron collar that was bolted to the insides of the armor. He was skillful and strong, Cythees was tactful and coarse.

The King's blue eyes pierced Cythees' own, the two took in every detail about each other, every weakness and slight. Cythees saw the bags under Ulfrik's eyes: tired from two weeks travel and no rest between. Something the well rested High King could play on. Ulfrik noted that Cythees' armor was made more for splendor than actual protection and wouldn't stop a straightforward attack, especially under the fleshy crevice of his arm. But something else lingered in Cythees' eyes: doubt. As one of the greatest swordsmen in Kond, Cythees was haunted by the knowledge that he was bested, by only several men, one of whom was the proud ruler of the Winterlands. His younger brother, the proud Christen and jewel of their fathers eye, had sparred once in the war before with Ulfrik, though that was when they were on the same sides but the burning fury of defeat still lasted in Cythees, forever since, had Ulfrik been praised as the only one left living to have beaten both the High King and his prideful brother who himself was learned with blade and waxed by youth.

Something was wrong, however. The place felt different, as if people were waiting in anticipation of something he didn't know of.

No words were spoken after. Ulfrik was handed his helm--pure steel, its visor embossed with the tree sigil of his house. The King placed the helmet over his head, his vision reduced to a simple slit of light for him to peer through. The two watched from huge, iron husks, sizing each other up. With every slight inching the plates and bolts of the armor creaked and groaned in the hot dry wind and the dust flew about the air with the eyes of the nobility watching them from their seats in the crowd above.

The champion of The Fold swung first and was immediately countered by Ulfrik. They were evenly matched, Cythees however swung and spun a lot more than his opponent whereas the hardened King who had spent the better part of his youth in the refining training pits of Ironmarch and the frozen reaches of The Winterlands to hone his own sword arm, Ulfrik heaved the blade above his head and brought it down with the crushing strength of a hammer. The fight was immense, one for vile glory, the other for cold justice. It was the likes of which the court had never seen, even Corvus, who as a youth had fought in the bloody War of Black Fields as one of its commanders. That war had claimed the life of his own

Lord brother, Cyrill, the pride of their fathers crooked heart. A silent heart that Corwell had passed onto his heir, Corvus.

They all watched as the Forrester King used his superior strength to cast off the golden shield to foist the High King to the floor, crashing in a great metallic thud.

Standing over Cythees, Ulfrik was ready, his armor notched and tightened, prepared to strike when, suddenly, a hand was raised in the air, startling the King. "Well!" Cythees shouted gleefully, Ulfrik raised a confused and furrowed eyebrow and saw how non in the court appeared alarmed at the near demise of the High King "as it is with ancient lore this duel was enacted it is with ancient law I should add to it!" the High King added to everyone's amazement. He then turned, looking at Ulfrik with a victorious smile on his face "I name my second to the pit; Sir Mord Hales" Cythees announced as he hurried to climb the ladder up to the courtyard.

At the announcement of the champion knight the crowd gasped in shock and flurried whispers once again filled the stands. Ulfrik knew why--a man doesn't earn the title of 'The Towering Knight' without first proving it to be true and Mord had done so. Ulfrik had only ever heard of the man before; knew he served the Monthells with his younger brother, Maxer, remembering the Massacre of Wolfenrad where the two had slaughtered most of the city in the closing days of the Civil War whilst hunting for a Quarthand Princess. He was convinced that the knight was at the family's seat of The Forge, not there in the capital. As the Kings Justice it was his blade that removed the head of royalist leader, Edmond Quarthand after he had been dragged screaming into the throne room and his blood made to spill over the quartz floor. The foot of the Gilded Throne was said to still be stained a light pink since the execution.

Their fears and elation were confirmed when a gate opened in the side of the pit and what emerged was little more than a brutish monster. Ulfrik watched, fists clenched on his sword, as a large, bulking man of muscle waded in. He was armored head to toe with Monthell steel and so wreathed in muscle that his chest plate seemed stretched under his bulk. From the slit of the visor a pair of dark hazel eyes peered like a frenzied animal. He must have been seven feet tall and as he approached the King, a small thud followed every footstep. The King drew his weapon closer to him as did Mord who pulled from his back a huge longsword, easily able to slice a man in half when wielded by a beast like him.

The red feather atop the giant's helm blew in the breeze, fanning out like a plume. Though it did help to dull the impression upon Ulfrik. Mord looked more like a proud peacock with that feather flying from his helm than a slayer of men. Though it would take a fool to dismiss the man as jesting--his heart was as hard and cold as chapel stone, the civil war had shown that, when he announced himself to be the brutish, murderous raper of numerous faceless maidens caught in his clasp. Ulfrik recalled the altercation outside Mule's Town, years before, where he'd stopped this monstrosity from strangling a barkeep for the simple crime of not skimming his ale. Ulfrik remembered the hatred and animalistic power in his eyes then, ready to attack, he saw now and now it was directed onto him. It was a cold and merciless rage that required no excuse to be let loose and after the war Corvus had set him with the task of finding and executing the remaining members of the Quarthand royal family and any extended family. Cythees may have been the one to begin the end for the founding house but Mord Hales was the one who saw to its complete extinction.

On the observation deck Eleana, disgraced with her brother's deception, hissed at him "you coward. You can't even fight the very battles you start. One glorious chain of retreats" as the High King slouched down in a chair next to his wife, a servant handing him a goblet.

"I've fought every battle I've ever started. Look at what I claimed the last time. This is an ancient tradition. I've done nothing wrong. Besides, if that mad animal down there kills the Forrester they can do nothing. Their love of honor and tradition will turn against them, it was by ancient decree that this fight was invoked" Cythees smiled as he began to strip himself of his armor. Drunk with glee and satisfaction, he smiled " besides…once he's dead perhaps the new child-king of The Winterlands will be more respectful and obeying of his liege in his father stead"

"You've insulted them and now you're trying to kill them. To what end? Prove a point? They will never forget. You think just because you know how to twist the rules they'll help you?"

"I think being High King will help me," Cythees answered, flicking his sister away with his hand. Martis saw and was about to object when he felt the gloved hand of Kellor on his shoulder, refraining him from the reckless action.

Ulfrik looked up at Cythees "It doesn't matter who you send in here, Monthell! Brute or not I'll still beat this big bastard!" Ulfrik said as he pointed the sword at Cythees, then at the towering Mord.

"You'll be lucky if you get to raise that little toothpick!" a booming voice shuddered from under Mords helmet, rolling out like thunder from behind a wall of metal. The giant heaved his longsword with enough strength that when he brought it down, missing the King, slammed into the ground and made an indent in the sandy floor of the pit. Ulfrik probed Mords helmet for weaknesses, tapping once as he slid out of harm's way. With every hit and slash that came from Mords sword,

Ulfrik feared it might knock the weapon out of his hands as the massive man swung with such fury and was quicker than one would expect for a man of his cumbersome size. The Lord of Ironmarch cringed as his hands grew sweaty with angst and anticipation before he returned to attack and swung for the colossus' head, but Mord slid the longsword down off his own and like a lion with a precious gazelle, grabbed Ulfrik's shoulder. Ulfrik felt his feet leave the floor as he was thrown aside, into the hard, wooden walls of the arena. He shielded his eyes with his arm as he felt them begin to burn with the earthy grit in them, distracting him. Forrester swung blindly as Mord tripped him up, sending him back to the dirt. "Some Lord...Prince...whatever the fuck you are" Mord roared as he brung his blade down over Ulfrik's neck but the sword never reached its target. the mad dog looked to see Dullever who had placed his sword against Mord's, holding it tightly with both hands away from his King. The huge man was enraged, swinging with his spare hand, which was the size of a child's head, aiming at Dullever who dodged it with relative ease. "How dare you interrupt a trial of the laws!" Cythees exclaimed, rising from his chair.

"By ancient decree both sides can declare champions, as King Ulfrik's only household knight here it is my duty to stand as that champion!" Dullever answered with flustered breath. Ulfrik looked up and saw the two men--warriors. One of skill and experience the other of rage and raw power. Dullever himself looked visibly shaken and though he, a man of many battles, would never even openly hint at it, a minute kernel of fear flickered within him. Mord was the Towering Knight and a man who took pleasure in his pains. "Then I name thee as my champion, Captain Dullever" Ulfrik smirked.

Above the two, Martis watched uncomfortably from the side of the pit, behind several people, Kellor seemed to find him. "I didn't know that Sir Mord was here," the boy said.

"He arrived with your grandfather a week ago. I see this is your first time learning why every man with eyes and ears is are afraid of Sir Mord"

"Yep. He's a strong'n"

"Aye and it's that strength that's earned him and his family quite the name"

"What do you mean? They're well known?" the boy asked. From birth he'd been meticulously made to memorize the great houses by his mother and then made to learn their each, individual, histories by his grandfather, but not this family, this one he had neer seen before, a rare breed that they were.

"Oh yeah, just not the way your imagining. You see there's Mord here, great big beast. Then his younger sister who, last I heard, leads a bandit clan that your grandfathers been after, murderers and scoundrels. She was robbing and raping back during the reign of the last High King, Morryg. And finally there's Mords little brother, Maxer, he's one of Kond's greatest and most recognised mercenaries and, most notably, first through the break at the Battle of Summerplains during the civil war. He earned himself quite a few kills that day, I should know, I was there. So yes. Quite a name they hold for themselves. A hardened bunch of bastards. Pardon my language master Monthell" Kellor smiled at Martis as the two watched on, both secretly hoping that somehow Dullever or Ulfrik would strike a lucky blow.

The pit was suddenly filled with the sounds of three blades all interlocking like a dangerous, metal puzzle game, clashing and bouncing off of each other so much that by the end of it both Ulfrik and Dullever's swords were notched. Their metal became worn as did their resolve for the trial to be quick.

Briefly, the goliath smote Ulfrik to the ground, leaving Dullever to fight him alone. The captain was a far better man at arms than Mord however, Dullever attacked, defended, attacked and defended, using quick techniques he had developed to suit his confining armor as no man could match Mord for raw strength. Even some beasts such as the great and mighty bison of Grasspoint would struggle to contend with his almost supernatural endurance. Court and crowd watched as Dullever swung at Mord's helmet, knocking it clean off, slashing Mords chin underneath. He fell onto his back as Ulfrik picked himself back up. Quite a large, thick stream of blood ran from his left cheek where the Captain had slashed him; however he felt little of it, the heat and the adrenaline were enough to block out the pain, though it was uncomfortable when the wind threw itchy dust into the wound.

The King looked at Mord, a burning fury in his eyes. Ulfrik lifted his sword, intent to strike down the beast on the floor. A quick flash of realization ran through Mords eyes and there Ulfrik saw him: a man. Short, shaved, black hair, heavy browed with a wide face. That face soon widened into a gasp as the King brought the sword into Mord's chest, retching into the plate and piercing the leather cuirass underneath. The Lord of Hale Hall groaned as the sword found its place in the thick muscle and tissue of his rib, spurting a small gush of blood up from the wound as Ulfrik pulled his sword up, almost taking Mords body with it as it stuck in his chest for a moment like the tourney victors flag.

Both men turned from their laborious conquest of the beast as the sudden noise of clanking armor and swords being drawn arrived along with three Kings Watch and several Monthell soldiers who fiercely crowded the pit and surrounded the three fighters. "What the fuck is this?" questioned Dullever as he watched the Monthells swarm around them. They both saw

Cythees as he rose from his chair again, this time with a smile painted on his face. "What are you doing, this isn't fair. The duel isn't finished yet!" Ulfrik protested, his hardened and heavy face blotched with mud and specks of blood staining the curly, blonde hairs of his beard. His cheeks red and his eyes bloodshot with dust and his wavy hair matted with sweat.

"Fair? Ha! I see two northmen attacking my lone champion and you ask me for equality? You have breached the terms of the duel and violated our sacred tradition" Cythees acted, pretending to give even an inkling of respect for the old traditions. "As such!" he continued "for your treachery and deception, I command that you be incarcerated to await the Gods mercy. May the eight Divines grant you forgiveness" the High King boasted, though sounding rather rehearsed when he mentions the Divines.

"Oh, not again" Jazar mumbled to himself, rolling his eyes.

"Guards! Take the prisoners to their accommodations to await further trial" Corvus ordered, giving a rather relaxed wave of his hand. As the guards approached both Ulfrik and Dullever tensed up and stood proudly vigil. The whole pit stood on edge, as if paused for a moment. Ulfrik was at an impasse, both he and Dullever were too tired to fight all eight Kings Watch, which would mean fighting eight of Konds greatest chosen knights and the Monthell soldiers behind them. Even if they tried to escape the pit, they wouldn't get far, the main gates were a thousand yards away and protected by the city guard and the archers of the Monthell infantry which, Ulfrik noted had been doubled since their arrival in the capital and he didn't doubt that that was what Cythees needed: an excuse.

The tension was broken when Ulfrik, sighing to himself, shrugged at Dullever and threw down his sword. The captain looked surprised but he understood that behind this outlandish action of his King was the desire for no further loss of life, or so he hoped, Ulfrik was a dangerous man when brought to anger and very few could be spared his wrath though he wasn't a particularly cunning man or one of plotting, his pride was hard to repair.

With a chuff, the captain placed his own sword in the dirt and saw to his King's ailing.

Martis watched from up high, estranged and somewhat disappointed. He wanted Ulfrik, who he had already grown to favor, to end Mord who was by now picking himself up, recovered almost from what should've been a fatal wound, knocking shoulders with Dullever as he left the pit, growling hard as his breath became labored and he limped out of the small arena like an injured dog, still ignorant and proud but as worn and wearied as he had ever been. When one unfortunate attendant tried to assist the knight, everyone watched as Mord picked the teen off his feet with one hand around the boys neck with a small grunt. The boy yelped before his eyes started to stream and the vessels in his cheeks ran red as air became hard. Both Ulfrik and Dullever watched with bewildered expressions to the man who had just shrugged off a stab to the lung now choking the life from a young squire.

Red turned to a deep and deathly purple as his face grew cold and the attendant spluttered just as that one hand crushed his throat. His red eyes rolled over white and Dullever and Ulfrik saw the terror of the Fold before they both felt the cold sting of metal shackles being placed around their wrists, even through their leather sleeves the cuffs bit into their skin. As the two were pulled away, Eleana watched her brother with disgust as she saw his teeth show from a victorious grin as the two men were led away and the attendant's lifeless body was casually dragged to one side. How could he not envision it all as his victory?

"Lady Monthell!" she heard Jazar's distinctly honeyed voice

call. She turned to see him behind her, walking calmly toward her so as not to draw suspicion. He was adept at remaining invisible and glided over to her without anyone from the court taking a second glance at the Lord of Spies talking with the High King's sister. He grabbed her arm and pulled her closer to him, so close that she could see the red veins in his eyes and the small, twisted braids of his beard. "Meet me near the old alchemy laboratory in a few hours. Near. Not in"

"The alchemy laboratory? The one here, in the keep?"

"No, the one in Ushkin. Yes, the one in the keep" Jazar replied sarcastically, nodding once as he returned to the High King and Queen who were already starting to leave with their meager victory. Eleana rested on one of the supports for the canopy as Martis and Kellor approached her. Sensing them behind her, she spoke very lowly "I suggest you stay ready tonight. I can feel it"

"What?" Martis asked, with concern and slight panic as for his mother to be so cryptic was uncharacteristic of her.

"I don't know. But the two of you had better keep your eyes open tonight. Something is happening that won't soon be forgotten. A dreadful storm is going to break, I fear. And Divines protect us when it does" she sighed "Cythees has done something that cannot be so easily erased and I fear those consequences will strike us first. Be ready"

"Mother. Be ready for what?"

"I don't know yet, Martis! But whatever it is, it will destroy us and I sacrificed too much the last time to do it again. Whatever happens, we leave, soon" Eleana returned, sounding agitated at her son. She turned and rested her hands on his shoulders "remember when I told you that you are the only thing that I have left?" she nodded with as cheerful a smile as she could muster, though by now it was almost a part of her cognition to act like that, to keep calm and unseen. Her son nodded. "I meant every word and as a mother your safety is paramount to me, above everything else, your survival is all I need in this world. So when I tell you something is awry it is because I fear for you first. Everything I gave up was for you and your cause" she put her hand on her son's shoulder, her fingers brushed against his golden hair. Lady Monthell then looked to Kellor "I'll see you tonight for supper. Keep a watch over him, please"

Kellor frowned "so be it"

Chapter 13 - A Last Salvation

A few hours dragged by since the pit fight, with all the court returning to their own chambers and offices about the Kings Keep. The night patrol had moved in and the many rooms and chambers emptied and filled with the quiet stillness of the day's end. Now with the early stages of night descending on Kingsport the corridors of the royal keep were wreathed in shadow. As the torches burned in the old stone corridor of the disused alchemy laboratory, Eleana slid through the dark, passing the vacant rooms of the laboratory where empty bottles of liquids unknown sat and barrels of nothing but dust and cobwebs lingered in the umbra. Using her detailed knowledge of the keep she used the mental map she had formed in her head after almost a decade traversing its passages to move quietly through the empty halls. She could tell why the tower was in such a state: having been the original alchemy tower that was built by Morriard Quarthand, a skilled alchemist and Konds cruelest High Kings. Clearly the place hadn't been touched since he had blown himself up at its summit two hundred and fifty years prior. There he had performed all manner of experiments and some of their corpses still lingered in the dark, watching Eleana with hollowed, eyeless and worm-ridden holes and gaping, soggy mouths.

Orange shafts of torch light shone through rusting bars from the level above and were the only guide for Eleana to see where she was going: an old door at the end of the dusty and dank underbelly of the keep. She approached the door, putting a hand on it to push it open, but it didn't budge. She tried again and the door simply shuddered. "Struggle all you want. I had some of the best locksmiths in the realms craft the keyhole of that door " she heard a voice from behind her say, Eleana flung herself around as she jumped back. Illuminated by the glow of a second torch, Jazar emerged from the dark as he jingled a set of keys in front of Eleana's face. "What did you want to speak about down here, anyway?" Lady Monthell asked, rolling her eyes as to how Jazar had scared her.

"Not out here. Come. We'll speak in my office"

"Not here? Wait, your office, then why are we down here?"

"Not that office. This one is much more of a secret, my favorite kind" Jazar stated as he fixed the old key into the rusty hole in the door and turned it twice as Eleana heard several clicks from behind the door, it reminded her of a strange device she had heard of that was being crafted in Argus: a clock, they seemed to call it.

The Lord of Whispers, in his exotic orange cloak and robe, opened the old iron door as it scraped the stone beneath it. As it swung open it revealed a tiny corridor that hosted nothing but another door at its end. Eleana could tell that this part of the castle was older than anything she had ever seen, the stone was gray and uncoloured, unlike the rest of the massive keep that was comprised of its signature subtle yellow stones, all beautifully crafted, but these walls were old, mossy, chipped and ridged.

"So, I take it that having an office down here was for security reasons" Eleana surmised as Jazar led her and himself to another door.

"Why do you ask?"

"Well I doubt it was for the view"

"Well you're quite right. People spend so much time these days looking forward that they forget to look back, as so many of these rooms and tunnels have been forgotten for a long time now. It was a while before even I knew of their existence" he pushed against the door with his shoulder several times "In truth I stumbled upon them whilst trying to find a way to move items of interest about the castle without anyone noticing but the place serves well as a safeway too" Jazar said, flipping the handle to the smaller door as he let himself in. The two removed their hoods as Jazar shut the door. "I assume you have some speculation as to why I asked you down here, my lady?" Jazar smiled, putting the torch up onto a clamp on the wall making its orange glow shine across the room. Eleana saw the not so large office in its entirety. No windows, no scents resting on high shelves, no carpets, no natural light. The roof of the office curved downwards towards the floor which was made of old and wet stone. The only things that hinted of the human world was a desk and chair, full to the brim with paper, logs and scrolls and a dusty fireplace at the opposite end of the darkened room. "Love what you've done with the place" Lady Monthell sarcastically regarded.

"What do I care? Even the rats won't touch this damp shitbox. The whole place has been left to mold now for well over a hundred years. Perfect" Jazar simpered. He was right in his guess. The halls had not seen any souls pass through since the alchemists and battlemages employed there had wandered there. "I imagine that after High King Morriard's death his replacements tried to bury most of his reign as they did this tower" The spymaster said as he took a seat.

"So, what do you want this time, spymaster? Maybe this time you want me to assassinate my father or sell myself to a Jea'Ikan pit fighter?"

"Unfortunately nothing so entertaining" Jazar retorted with a friendly smile and Eleana threw her torch into the fireplace, the light went out for a split second before setting the wood on fire and soaking the floor in the same light as the torch on the wall "the time has come, sadly. I was hoping both of us could help to stop it from occurring at all but it appears we've failed"

"Failed at what?"

"Preventing war. It's why I wanted you to try and curb Cythees' impulsiveness, I knew he wouldn't be able to help himself which means it's only a matter of time. Your brother has thrown himself into a hole that's hard to climb out of. He thinks that this charade is a display of dominance. That once the Forresters have paid for their king's safe return then they'll all forget about it and move on, but they won't. Cythees will...has, indefinitely, started a war, again, he seems to enjoy them. The Winterlands won't stand for it when they hear of this. Because of the Quarthands own neglects they switched sides halfway through the civil war and fought for Cythees and even then they questioned their decisions, now those doubts have been solidified, it seems. Cythees has done to them exactly what the Quarthands did: insult them without cause" his voice fast and worried, not its usual quiet and sensual tone.

"And how are they going to hear of this? My father has decreed no word be sent to them" Eleana asked Jazar, though she knew the answer. As did the spymaster who looked away from Lady Monthell, unable to say what he would be forced to do. She knew that Jazar wouldn't allow himself to stand by and allow the realms to fall into war or allow a not so innocent man like Ulfrik to suffer for it. "So, what do we do?" she asked.

"You need to help me. One last time. One last time and I shall guarantee yours and Martis' safety. But we have to do it tonight"

Eleana nodded her head, awaiting with wide eyes, as to what to do. "I need you to free the Forrester boy and his friend from the dungeons tonight" Eleana jerked forward as her full attention was directed at Jazar.

"Are you suffering from a delusion? Me? Break a convicted man out of the royal prisons?"

"A falsely convicted man and you know it"

"I know many things but I seldom act on them, Jazar. Do you know what you're asking? You're asking me to put Martis in the center of the storm I've done everything to keep him out of. We'd be in more danger than we've ever been in. No, I..."

"Tonight, there's a boat sailing for the Jea'Ikan coast, there you'll have an entire country to decide where to start a new life. A new *free* life with you and Martis. But you have to leave tonight. Once Ulfrik's set free Cythees will look for the perpetrator and you'll be first on his list when your absence is discovered, you've already spoken against his decisions several times in the last few days"

"Because you told me too!" Eleana rudely pointed at Jazar.

"I know. I placed too much faith in Cythees' loyalty, perhaps not to you, but to his family. It seems, however, that his pride will not even let him assail to those heights and I was a fool to think otherwise" he apologized as he held his hands up.

"Can't we just send a guard or one of your spies to set the poor wretch free?"

"I don't trust the words of any of the keeps servants and if a guard were to leave their posts to free the King then someone would ask questions. But if you're not here for when they start asking questions then you're already free and perhaps, out of the two of them, Ulfrik could be more inclined to make concessions. He actually fought in the last war, unlike your brother, he knows its cost and may be more averted to being involved in another" Jazar answered, cutting off any hope of avoiding the jailbreak for Eleana.

"Now I can arrange for the guards on patrol at the dungeons

to be busy with other things then you'll need to get in there and take the two of them out to the main courtyard. I'll have a group of horses waiting for you. You and Martis ride to the docks and you're away" the spymaster instructed, laying things out to Eleana so calmly that it was quite clear that this plan was incredibly premeditated, Jazar had planned for everything.

"You promise everything will go as planned?" Eleana said, clutching her hands together anxiously. Jazar calmly put his hand on Eleana's.

"No. I cannot. No plan is truly foolproof but I can promise this: if you do not leave with your son tonight then you may find yourself in of those cells and for a much longer sentence or perhaps you will be sent away to be married off to another fat lord and forced to be used as nothing but a broodmare. You have one true choice"

"Is that a threat? Jazar"

"No, my lady. That is my promise, the only one I can guarantee. I know what it's like to feel alone in a place so full of people. I only desire order and if I can help someone else achieve it themselves then I've done more than many did for me. More than I have done for others before. Besides, you and I may be the only ones who know the true value of that boy of yours and that... may come to serve us later" Jazar answered, rather genuinely.

Lady Monthell raised an eyebrow. She went through a flurry of feelings towards the lord: contempt, suspicion and distrust, she didn't fully understand Jazar but she knew that both were in this now together but something else hinted at her that maybe the shady spymaster was telling the truth. Perhaps it was the look in his violet eyes or the expression on his face and for such a mysterious and isolated man he had spoken to her the most. She primped and dusted herself, brushing her blood red skirt and the black cloak she wore over everything else, her hands shaking as she reached for the handle on the door. "So. Can I ask this of you?" the Lord of Spies requested. Eleana didn't reply, simply nodding very slowly with an expressionless face. "You know I wouldn't ask if I didn't have some faith in you, my Lady. Or in that boys birthright as we, like so few, do" Jazar regarded Eleana with a smile.

"No, he wouldn't" a third voice said from the darkness. Jazar and Eleana both jumped as Lady Monthell slammed the door shut with enough force to make the dust leap from the ledge above the door. They both watched as the figure of Darian Darianth emerged from the shadow, his perfect face smirking victoriously. Eleana looked into his eyes and could see something unnerving about them, she didn't know if it was the orange glow of the torch light or the shadow around him or both but in a certain light, or lack of, the imperious steward looked devilish as his eyes glistened. "So, this is what you've been doing for the last few weeks: turning the High King on his sister?" Darian smiled as he spoke to Jazar.

"The High King and his sister never required much assistance in that regard" Eleana spoke, cracking a powerful scowl at the steward, who smiled back. Darianth slithered out of the dark, revealing his lavish green tunic and high boots. "It appears that the nights must get so boring for you. How'd you find this place?" Jazar asked, unconcerned, for the time, that Darian knew of his plans, as if the spymaster expected as such from the steward. "Tut, tut, Jazar, as Lord of Spies you should know that it's not just the walls that have ears in this place. So too do those who fetch your water and wine and uncover certain maps pertaining to hidden passages" Darian replied. Jazar smiled, though not an endearing one, as if he were thinking, admiring Darian's tenacity.

"So. You've proven to be a real bloodhound, Darianth, you've sniffed us out. So, what do you plan to do with this information?"

"As loyal steward I must inform the High King"

"You lie," Eleana slandered, "the only person you're loyal to is yourself. You didn't come here to catch us did you? You came here because you could. To prove a point. It's all just a game to you isn't it. Well I can assure you, Lord Darianth, that the survival of my son isn't"

Darian sniggered, showing his near perfect teeth underneath dark lips. "My Lady, everything is a game. Life is the biggest one but so few know how to play. For example: how will I benefit from telling the High King, your brother, of your treachery? Relief? Well that would be momentary. Perhaps satisfaction of finally undermining Jazar? Well then that would mean that the most exciting game of all would be over so it can't be that. No. I wouldn't gain much from turning you over to the High King would I. So, you were right, indeed. I'm not here for personal gain, I'm here...to prove a point"

"And what point is that?"

"Nothing lasts unless we make it" Darian smiled again, looking at both Jazar and Eleana who appeared rather uncomfortable.

Jazar lifted a subtle yet calming hand at Eleana, hoping to relax her in Darian's presence. The spymaster then looked to his rival and continued "of course, you won't tell anyone anyway, will you? Because you know what I know. You know what they all suspect. And unless you want their suspicions to be confirmed, undeniably, then you will keep this meeting strictly in confidence" Jazar commanded, standing from his chair, his face emotionless and cold and so still. Eleana had never seen Jazar in his element, not like this. It was unnerving but as an ally, to see it was admirable.

"Oh. Is this a side of you I've rarely enjoyed? You've become rather defensive, my friend"

"Oh no, friend. If I were you, I'd be on the defensive. Especially when it comes to rumors, one rumor in particular"

"Care to enlighten me?"

"It details a steward having…inappropriate relations with a certain royal Queen. It would be a tragedy if somehow that rumor was given merit by…an unknown source, say… me" Jazar answered, mocking Darian with his theory.

"Careful, Jazar. Playing the same card so many times can leave your hand weary" Darian warned as his face changed from an arrogant smile to a concerned frown. There was a pause before Jazar raised a simpering hand to the entrance "I trust your many 'eyes and ears' can aid you in finding the door" the spymaster patronized. Proud with himself at the snide comment.

Darian licked his teeth and fidgeted for a reply "It's getting late. I should be going" he answered.

"Perhaps that would be best" the spymaster uttered.

Eleana smiled at Jazar, though he was busy keeping his eyes fixed on Darian. Both Jazar and Eleana didn't speak until the furtive steward had left the room and the door had been closed behind him.

"You shouldn't trust him," Eleana warned as she exhaled anxiously.

"Trust has nothing to do with it. Darian is a necessary evil and a beneficial one to those who can benefit him. He won't tell the High King"

"You believe him?"

"He may twist the truth but he's no liar, at least, he's never been with me" Jazar said, turning to look at Lady Monthell once again "you should go. I suspect we won't see each other again, so this is goodbye, I'm afraid" the spymaster whispered, squinting as he smiled as kindly as his general awkwardness would allow. Eleana pulled the door ajar and stepped out into the corridor, making sure Darian had gone. Once making sure that the rats were the only inhabitants of the tower, she cast open the door. Looking back one last time, both the two associates glanced at each other one last time "Jazar" Lady Monthell murmured. The spymaster turned as he sat himself back into the old chair "thank you" he heard her say as the door closed one final time. In that moment Jazar felt something that he thought he wouldn't, couldn't even: understanding. He wasted little time savoring the moment as he quickly grabbed a nearby quill, dipping it into the inkwell and scrounging for a piece of parchment.

*

A fog rolled in off the Bay of Gales, creeping over the still water of the docks and smothering the city. Vacant ships bobbed up and down to the tune of the buoy bells. Most of Kingsport's people had fallen into the brief comfort of their homes or the inn whilst dogs from all around the city barked indiscriminately as the more shady inhabitants moved through the alleys and back ways.

Young Martis was lying in bed, his nightshirt on and tucked under his sheets. There was a breeze rustling through the balcony curtains, distorting shadows of the candles, making them dance and flicker on the stone floor as playful phantoms. The boy turned over on his side, willing himself to doze. He sighed and flipped, again, towards the balcony and his dresser but sleep would not come. Leaning forward, he pulled back the dresser drawer and revealed something of comfort, something valuable to others but priceless to him, a large ruby. It was the only thing his mother said his father had left him before he left them. The older Martis got the less that story seemed to mean anything to him--a poor excuse for a fathers absence, he thought, but he still found himself drawn to the jewel, pondering what history could be attached to this lonely stone. In its vague surface he could see a reflection: a hollow image fading into the dark.

He could see on its sides that the stone was once rounded and had been part of a pendant or some such piece of jewelry. How and why his father, a man who he had been told was a merchant trader, had come by it, he didn't know. He had also always reflected on how Cythees would never tolerate the mention of the father, as if the name were cursed or somehow would breathe life back into him and even his mother would not allow his mention often. Which was made even more so odd as Eleana had once hastily stated he was a noble of Kingsport and even Cythees would not be so foolish to insult one of his beneficiaries.

Whilst Martis gazed upon himself in the stone he heard the sound of two sets of footsteps marching towards his door. He put the stone under his bed sheets and rolled over, feigning sleep. When the door creaked open, the light from the bright torches in the hallway cast two shadows on the dark floor of Martis' room. He cracked open his eyes slightly as he saw his mother with Sir Kellor standing behind her. "I know you're not asleep," she announced as Kellor carefully shut the door behind her, making sure not to create too much commotion. Martis gave up as he sat up "How did you know?"

"Because you've slept on your right side facing the breeze since you were born, you never sleep on the left" Eleana replied before grabbing some of her son's clothes off the floor and launching them at him "put those on, we're leaving" she ordered.

"Wait a minute. It's the middle of the night? Mother. What's happening?" Martis inquired as he threw back the sheets and got out of bed, feeling his feet touch the stone floor which felt like ice in comparison to his softened bed. When his mother saw the stone laying on the mattress she quickly stopped gathering her son's things. She froze. Then she smiled warmly. Eleana reached a hand out and grasped the stone whilst Martis hurriedly put on his clothes, nearly tripping over his boots.

Eleana held the precious orb in one hand, stroking it with the other, feeling its smooth surface as her fingers ran across it. "You had best keep this as well. Everything else we leave"

"Where are we going?"

"Come on, let's go" Eleana said tautly as she let herself out of the room and waited at the end of the corridor, whilst watching to make sure the guards Cythees had 'granted' her had not realized where she was. In the light Martis could see his mother was garbed in a large black cloak that had been pinned together by her eagle broach. She didn't look right, he could no longer see her full face for she was concealed with the hood with only a single strand of curled hair running down the middle of her brow.

"Oh and take this" Kellor grumbled "hope you've been paying attention to our sparring lessons" he said, handing Martis one of the swords he had seen hanging in the armory. "But I hope you won't have to use them" he muttered. It was a simple blade, nothing to it, he thought. Its sheath was more decorative than the blade with white stripes running diagonally down it. Once Martis had packed what little he could find in the flurried situation he, his mother and Kellor darted down the back stairs of the palace, with the old knight leading the way with his sword already drawn. They snuck around, keeping to the outskirts to avoid detection from any guards. It felt like days as they skulked around every hallway and stairway, every guard barrack and kitchen, through the royal apartments, past the throne room and down into the dark. There footsteps rang out down the hall as Eleana prayed to all eight Divines to silence their movements as they ran through the stoned corridors and lofty halls, past the statues of the various Quarthand kings, and out into the main courtyard. With every turn of every corner and every flicker of the torches, she envisioned a servant or guard catching a glimpse of them.

As they passed the armory, Martis saw its doors were open and inside he could see the famous dragon skull, the only one on that side of the world, taken from the last Champion Riders after their failed invasion. In the stillness of night it looked even more menacing; perched up on the wall, moonlight cast over half its face, its fangs bared and its eyes filled with shadow. Its huge size of almost eight feet tall, Martis could only imagine what the rest of the beast would have looked like when it was alive, before its skull was adorned in that very armory and its rib cage sent to Swords-Wrath to serve as the keeps archway: Ithilax, The Sapphire Dancer, as it was named. The last dragon. The great blue dread that felled hundreds of thousands and rebuilt the imperial legions-- now an ornament on the wall.

It wasn't until they actually made it to the courtyard, through a small passageway that Kellor knew of, leading them through the gilded gardens on the second floor, that Martis saw three horses all standing, untied, outside the stable, their breath visible in the cold night air. Eleana grabbed Kellor's shoulder with one hand, holding her skirt above her feet with the other "wait for me. I won't be long and keep him safe" she said as she turned back, towards the dungeon tower entrance to the right of the massive keep. Kellor tried to call her back but to make more noise than a whisper would have attracted the attention of the night watch. He saw his lady disappear into the shadows of the looming keep just as a patrol approached: a single city guardsman. Kellor pushed Martis behind a horse who grunted at the rude intrusion. Martis stayed hidden as the guard marched past. Kellor smiled at the lone sentry as he pretended to tend to the horses, the guard paying him no mind as he passed by.

Whilst Kellor was entertaining outside Eleana had run down into the bowels of the keep, to the dungeons. Back through the plaza and into the servants kitchen and quarters, through the shimmering gallery and across the outer bridge to the prison tower. Past rusted cages and rooms of ancient torture, she found the main wing of the dungeon. She pressed herself, tightly, against the wall. She could smell the blood and the urine of all the unfortunate souls of the keeps confining bars and it stung her nostrils with its foulness. Peaking round for the jailor, she half expected to see him but as she slunk her head around the corner she saw only the prisoners asleep in their cells. She smiled as she recalled Jazar's words, running for a nearby table and rushing to grab the keys she raced down the aisle, her heels ringing on the cobblestones, looking in every darkened and putrid smelling cell until she got to the end cell, tucked against a rotting wall. Peering cautiously inside, she saw both Ulfrik and Dullever, very much awake. Both sat on the stone benches with their heads in their laps. Ulfrik looked up with tired eyes and a pale face. The King looked in amazement and confusion as Eleana unlocked the cell with trembling hands. "What are you doing?" he asked with wide eyes.

"Clearing my conscience" Lady Monthell whispered, brushing her uncombed and sweat soaked hair off her forehead. "Come on!" she bellowed as she nearly dragged Ulfrik and Dullever off their feet. She led them back to the courtyard where they saw Kellor readying the horses. She pointed the two fugitives to the two spare horses as Dullever nodded in thanks "this was a very dangerous thing for you to do" Ulfrik assured Eleana.

"No more dangerous than it was for me to stay. Don't go and die and let this all be for naught. I'm doing this in hopes you'll remember that we have just come out of the clutches of war and I do not wish to see it again" she replied as she nodded at Ulfrik before the two parted ways. "Come on!" she shouted at Kellor who was about to help Martis get onto one of the horses when they heard a guard call out from one of the higher walkways. The three heard as guards from all corners of the keep began to shout as those shouts also began to rise up from the dungeons at the realization that two prisoners were gone. A small horn blew an eerily high pitched blare into the night from somewhere in the keep, invoking panic among the escapees. "The horses'll draw too much attention to us! They'll ride us down before we make the gate! Into the city!" Kellor advised.

"Go! Run!" Eleana shouted as Martis, Kellor and herself began to flee as a gaggle of alerted, ready and armed archers gathered on an overpass above them. They aimed for the King and his captain who reared their horses and set off for the main gates to the city below. The Monthell archers furiously knocked their arrows, drew and fired. The first barrage landed and splattered in the mud like rain drops. Ulfrik yanked the reins of his horse as the archers prepared another barrage. One archer took his chance, letting loose his arrow on Ulfrik, though it missed the King it headed like a bloodied dog towards Martis. His mother noticed and flung herself in its path. She gasped in sorrow and pain as her air was stolen from her. The whole courtyard stopped. Martis watched his mother as she too looked at him with shock and then terror as she looked down to watch a red stain envelop her chest, at the tip of an arrow head. Eleana gulped for breath as she felt the bolt had stuck itself deep.

Silence briefly. The night's wind blew a lifeless breeze through all their souls. Martis stood in the mud with his mouth open and his eyes wide with grief. He watched as his mother held out a weakening hand towards him as tears began to weld in both their eyes. The boy watched as his mother, his closest friend, she who cherished and raised him fell to the ground. The moment her body went limp and hit the ground a deafening scream erupted from Martis' mouth, almost inhuman, and so quick even he barely knew he had uttered it. He felt his rage and sadness pulsate around him like a wave fit to wash Kingsport away. Like a pebble in a great ocean.

Kellor saw what he had to do. Instinctively grabbing Martis and throwing him over his shoulder-- a heavy sack of grief. Martis kicked and screamed as he held out his hands for his mother's touch but it never came again. The old knight took Martis and himself down through the southern gate, down the street that led into the main city. Kellor's eyes were set on the docks and the welcoming white sails.

In the ensuing chaos and ruckus, Corvus and a small retinue of guards had made it outside. The old eagle stepped forth, recognising the body of his daughter laying in the mud. He knelt down next to her and flipped her over and when he saw the look on her face, when he knew what the cost was, he placed his hand on her cheek and felt as they grew ever colder before he closed her eyes. He didn't show his emotions, if ever, certainly not in front of such low company as servants and soldiers but though his face expressed only minor sorrow, like one would the loss of a prized piece of clothing or jewelry, he allowed one small, secretive tear to emerge. It ran from his eye, through each wrinkle and line on his face before hitting her soft neck. She looked so much like her mother in the gloom, their slender faces and perfect lips the same and the peaceful look on their eyes matched, as well as Corvus could remember. Yet nothing tugged within him, no inkling of remorse or doubts as to his principles. The grief was a new shield against the callousness.

He glanced up as two soldiers slowly approached him, like wolves approaching the lone bear, they were cautious, if not frightened of his reaction. No one, not even he could have known what he would do. For the first time in decades, the King of The Fold knew not what to do for this was beyond his calculations, his plans and desires for control were washed away with the largest of his losses. But he knew what needed to be done. Corvus let them take her, they picked her up as respectfully as possible, carrying her back into the keep as her father rose. He looked at the great gate and the fleeting glimpses of the two men on horseback riding through the city and he scowled, harder than he ever had before in all his sixty-eight years, so hard that his brow started to ache. It was a look of anger, a look of pure hatred and lust for payment of the debt. Before all was done, he would arrest his own family's future and send theirs to oblivion. He knew from his time as squire to his successful service in the War of Black Fields, only Cythees or Ulfrik could live at the end now but not both.

Chapter 14-The Red Plains

Blood red clouds dominated the horizon over the mighty dunes and wastelands of The Red Plains. The great canyons filled with sand and dust that blew in huge heaps, blocking the vision of Tarith's scouts as they pressed on into one of the dust storms that the country-wide desert was known for. The wind battered their bone-made helmets and their thick armor made of crocodile hide. Every step each man took felt like a piece of them had been forcefully chipped away as they waded, blindly, through the sand and dirt. Even the horses seemed to struggle from both the heat and the confusion as they heaved and huffed against the weight of the caravans.

Tarith was a few men down the line, his grayish-blue hair tangled from the wind and blinded him with its tendrils as did the sand that flung itself at him. For every setback they had faced in the three days since they had left Arden behind them, Tarith could sense that they were nearing their destination, he knew they were getting close because of the building satisfaction he could feel growing within him, like he had been to this place before, maybe in a dream of sorts. But he knew he would know where the company would find the crater. Low on water and lower still on food reserves it wasn't just destiny that drove the young Malacender on.

The morning sun that rose over them had baked the earth to a thick and crumbly mold, making the horses trip and stumble in crags left behind. "We've been marching through the night, your benevolence, I suggest we find a place to camp till the storm passes! Else I doubt any of us will see the crater!" Lo'atal boomed over the wind, from behind his prince. Tarith looked to his left, he could vaguely make out the silhouette of Amira riding next to him though she was only a few feet from him the sands created a confusing miasma. Tarith, not wanting to stop but recognising the threat turned to his General "so be it! At the edge of the canyon, there!" the Prince ordered, pointing his finger towards what appeared to be a ray of pure sunlight creeping through a clef in the rock. Within an hour the company tiresomely set up a few tents dotted around the opening, still being taunted by the sands that coughed up old bones and armor that some of the more eccentric Osh-Venn took as trophies. Though they numbered up a hundred strong, having lost some in the Citadel of Poison, most Osh-Venn braved the sands, training out in the feisty and desolate winds of the ancient land of ancestors.

As Tarith and Lo'atal laid the map across the table of one of the tents they could hear the men struggling with the other tents that were ripped from them by an unforgiving and dry wind that angrily snapped at them and blew the sand against them. The plains truly was a harsh and arid place and it was no wonder that in hundreds of millennia they had never been settled successfully. The General ran his fingers across the eastern edge of the Red Plains. There on the map Tarith could see the whole world of Lakir, what the men in the west labeled Manaheim. From Kond across the Sea of Swords, Antara in the far north and the Uncharted Lands in the south. There to the east, however, he saw a very familiar land, larger than the other continents by thousands of miles. He could see the vague outlines and names and saw how vast the Red Plains were, stretching for hundreds of miles outwards and buffering between Mundiil and Argus. "We are close, your benevolence.

Imagine--all the great heroes of old, the Harbingers of the past all traveled this canyon to find their own destiny. Vulun, Visalia, Fotia, all of them passed through these perilous caverns" Vacile said in his usual crazed and admiring voice.

"We're close?" Tarith asked.

"Aye. This time in a few days we should have made our way into the very heart of Dragontooth Crater"

"I don't think you've told me what I'll be expecting there, Vacile"

"No, my Prince. I haven't because I do not know myself. Each Harbinger reports something different when they get there and it is unknown to me what you may find" the curate answered with a mad look in his eye. "All I can tell you is that by tomorrow we may be standing there ourselves"

"Vacile…" Tarith started but soon recoiled in embarrassment. Vacile, though half maddened by age, cared deeply for the young man who he had watched come into the world. "What is it?" he asked. Tarith hesitated for a while before confiding.

"Ever since I was a boy I heard of the legendary Emperors and Empresses who went into the crater and came out with…with…certain boons of Ornagoth. Is it true? Will I.…"

"Ornagoth has given you this chance, this gift, a gift he hasn't bestowed since the last Harbinger six centuries ago"

"The last Harbinger was Fotia Iron-Crown"

"Yes?"

"And she tried to conquer the world in the name of unity"

"She used her power as she saw fit and what her reasons were for attempting such a thing were known only to her. You must improve and use your power how you see fit. Fotia believed she was serving the Empire when she invaded Kond and that she was adding to her forefathers legacy but in reality she was only serving herself, whether she knew it or not. To pursue one's destiny is the highest calling but so often does it consume us and warp even our purest goals. Doing nothing is sometimes the best thing to do though almost always the hardest" Vacile said. Tarith could feel something different, he could see it in Vacile. Rather than the look of a mad bird, all frizzy and ragged, Vacile had understanding and wisdom in his glassy eyes. Tarith leaned forward to say something else but the two of them and Lo'atal were interrupted by the sound of the tent curtain shimmying open. All three men turned to see Amira standing between the parting. "May I have a word with his benevolence?" she asked politely in her youthful voice, sounding as calm and as elegant as she looked.

The Harbinger looked around the tent at his two friends before nodding to them. Though Vacile left without question, Tarith saw the look on Lo'atal's face; an unmistakable look of caution, distrust and annoyance. It was directed towards Amira, who tried to ignore him as she felt two sets of eyes on her. Tarith pressed and nodded more evidently towards the exit. Eventually, the Osh-Venn General relented and left his post at the Prince's side.

"That Osh-Venn's like a dog with its favorite toy--not letting anyone else touch it. Not...sharing. I'd admire it if it wasn't irritating at times" the Princess commented, pointing her thumb behind her in Lo'atal's direction.

"He's Osh-Vennisian, they are stubborn and loyal to a fault. I could ask no more of any of the brave two hundred men just like him, that have followed me. They all volunteered. They've served as the backbone of the Empire for a few thousand years and *he* is the most stubborn and loyal one I've ever met. He can be...protective of me at times but thats because the man takes his duty seriously"

"Which is incredibly surprising due to the way you handled a sword back at the arena. He should only be working half the time. Not amazing but better than what I'd expect for a spoiled Prince of Ushkin" Amira smiled as she slowly approached Tarith, a devilish look in her eye as she was mere inches from him.

"It was Lo'atal who trained with me when we were boys?" the Prince smiled pleasantly.

"That great bumbling beast outside?"

"That great bumbling beast is the reason both of us are still alive"

"Well you certainly travel with a... strange retinue of people next to the mad scholar as well. Are all Ushkinians this strange?"

"Just the good ones" Tarith smirked as he felt Amira's breath brush over his face and smelt the scents and perfumed she bathed herself in.

"I should be thanking you. It was rude of me not to before, I see that" the Princess bantered.

"And why would you be doing that?"

"For rescuing me. It's the first time anyones gone that far for me. Well, since Sadeeb" the Nadenian Princess answered as she inched herself closer to the Prince, almost knocking into him, he could see how silky her skin had become, glistening with sweat from the midday sun. "Why did you?" she asked so calmly and so peacefully it was almost a whisper. Tarith looked down to her, his silver eyes watched at her--the great jewel of the desert. "I know how it can feel to have others make decisions for you. How...powerless the feeling is, to think you cannot do anything to stop it and that your choice is made but your voice isn't heard"

"I really hope your telling the truth about that"

"Have I done anything to dissuade you from trusting me?" Tarith bantered.

"No. If anything…" her hand started to reach for his own "you've done the very opposite but still, why save me? I owe you nothing. Two countries that share an ancient rivalry with two different people entirely"

"I see no reason for such menial differences to stop two peoples"

"Perhaps"

"If I were to tell the truth, as I sometimes force myself to, I don't know yet why I saved you. Maybe you can show me why, soon" the Prince whispered tenderly as he felt her soft hands run up his forearm to his bare biceps--warm and polished with the day's heat.

"Maybe…" she answered as her lips parted.

The two didn't speak after that, words were not necessary at that moment. Tarith meekly started to wrap his hands around Amira's waist, the urge was almost instinct as she pressed herself closer still. Their eyes met just as their lips were about to. He could feel the heat from her, it was welcoming and differed from the raging heat of the waste, it embraced him and filled him with desire. Tarith slowly slid his hand up Amira's arm, fondling for the strap on her armored dress but as he was about to pull the strap down off of her, he felt her quickly push herself off him and a look of realization drew across her face, as though awakened from a deep slumber. "I, I shouldn't have done that. We shouldn't have…that was wrong. Very wrong. I should know better. Forgive me, I…" she reasoned, though with some regret for that desire also flickered the same flame in her as it did him.

They both stood in awkward pause for a moment, unsure of what they might say to ease the other.

The curtain of the tent swung open again, intruding on their audience. They looked at each other forgivingly as an Osh-Venn's head poked in and then quickly turned, begging for forgiveness.

"It's alright, my friend, what is it?" the Prince passively held out his hand.

"Pardon, your benevolence, but the scouts have found something. Something they think you should look at"

"Like what?"

"It's best you see for yourself, my Prince" the Osh-Venn said as he left the tent rather awkwardly. The Prince turned to follow and for a moment, that encounter with the Princess was no longer so pressing and he only recalled back to it after he'd left the tent. He cursed himself as he followed his man, pained and slightly angered by his own naivety with Amira and shocked at himself at how quickly it took him to lose the composure he'd been thus far successfully feigning.

The Osh-Venn led him to Lo'atal and Vacile as well as several dozen other Osh-Venn warriors. "What is it, General?" Tarith asked, not paying attention to what his compatriots were looking at.

"We may have reason to believe that we aren't alone in this canyon, " Lo'atal said in a low voice, keeping his eyes fixed on the ground. Tarith followed his gaze to the floor. When he saw what they were all looking at. His mouth dropped open in surprise and woe. It was a trail of massive footprints, similar in shape to that of an elephant: circular feet with four small toes, but these footprints were much larger than any elephant--they could've fit three men in at least. "What. by Ornagoth's breath. Is that?" Tarith asked slowly, his mind in shock.

"Sand vipers also known as ash wyrms" Vacile answered, sounding more amazed than anybody else at the discovery.

"I didn't think they ventured this far west" Lo'atal uttered, none of them moving their eyes off the sight.

"They do when they're hungry. They normally feed on wild horses or anything else that's foolish enough to meet them out here" Vacile answered. The group stood still and silent for a moment before Tarith leaned towards Lo'atal and put a hand on his shoulder "you may want to put an extra man on night watch" the Prince whispered, shrewdly. The General turned to him with an obvious look on his face.

The night in the camp was restless for most. Few of the Osh-Venn dared to drift into sleep after they'd heard of the discovery of the ash wyrm's footprints, threatening to snatch them from slumber and drag them to the dry depths of the Red Plains. For the safety of the camp and to set the men's minds at ease, more fires had been lit than normal and had been spread in a larger vicinity around the depths of the canyon, bleeding red light that crept up the stony walls. Tarith was squatted next to one of the fires. Alone. He still wore his centurion armor, though without the boots and braces, the sand on his bare feet soothed him, making him think of the sanded roads near Ushkin. His mind wandered and played on thoughts of his parents, his people and what he would bring back to them, or what he wouldn't. From the subtle sound of rolling sands and small chunks of stone plummeting into the canyon, he heard sandals clapping against the red rock. "What are you doing out here, Tarith? Get some sleep" the General ordered as he approached his friend, crouching opposite him on the other side of the fire. "I can't rest yet. I just need to think"

"You don't need to 'think' you need sleep. The men will keep this place safe; they don't fear ash wyrms. Each and every one of these men I would trust with my own life, having trained a great many of them myself. You are the Prince, stop thinking like a soldier. Besides, I doubt you will be sleeping alone tonight" the General smiled. mischievously.

"I am not concerned about the ash wyrm's, I... wait. Who told you about…"

"People talk. I must confess that I only came here to tell you she's in the tent, waiting for you" Lo'atal revealed with his iconically literal tone. "Want me to take her out. I could 'accidentally' mistake her for an intruder and kill her for you if you want"

"No…" the Prince smirked. The two knew each other better than anyone else, Lo'atal always seemed to be the older brother Tarith never knew he wanted, growing up the only child and with a heavy future ahead. The Prince asked "I thought you didn't like her?"

"I don't," Lo'atal answered as bluntly as possible. Silver-blue hair blew across Tarith's chiseled face as he smiled to himself at his friend's honesty.

"I just needed five minutes to myself without someone telling me what's destined for me or what my ancestors did, good or bad. No less than a month ago I was a Prince to an empire, no different than the thousands who came before me, now they say I will be Champion Rider, heir to the Empire, savior of men"

The General sighed. "It's a destiny I would not have wished to have pushed on me. Then again our paths have always paralleled but never seemed to join" He spun his knife by its pommel in the dirt "it's my job to put myself aside for others but be careful not to shrink from what you could be. You never heard about those who denied their power did you? Then there are the ones who misused their power, had to be put down by men like me and you don't wanna end up like them either"

Tarith eyed his friend and saw with the light of the fire it was visible that the gray war paint that doused Lo'atal's entire body was starting to crack with the heat. "You need a new paint job" Tarith bantered as he pulled himself up off the ground and wandered to his tent "Good night, my friend. Rest with ease" Lo'atal bid the Harbinger. The General watched as his friend became another shadow in the camp. He then brushed a few pebbles from aside him and laid flat out on the stone, comfily warming himself by the fire--a lion--unconcerned about his whereabouts. He shut his eyes and waited for sleep to find him. As the night went quiet and the sound of men shifting barrels of weapons and food became more and more distant, Lo'atal didn't realize how the small pebbles and tiny fractals of dirt seemed to jump up and down, as if vibrating, shuddering from a massive force...or movement from below.

Inside Tarith's tent, the future Emperor lay, his cloak off and his armor already scattered around the short statured tent, standing with almost nothing on. Idly he pulled out his dagger, stabbing it firmly into the table and twirling it till it carved a tiny hole into the small map. He looked around, seeing the shadows from outside move and fade with the firelight. He sat there for a while, admiring the small blade, finally allowing himself to relax for the first time since he left Ushkin weeks ago. Even more soothing was the lone crickets that must have been sitting outside the tent somewhere, chirping it's only note.

He could feel his eyes growing heavy, the weight of the day's trek and the wind of the desert dragging them shut. The royal's head started to bob as his drouse became unbearable and he felt himself ready to fade into the dream lands when he felt the swift draft beside him, he snapped from his slumber and pulled the curved dagger from the table, holding it to the throat of the silent prowler. He was only half surprised when he saw her face looking back at him as she gasped. "Why is it every time we meet, you point something at me?" she whispered.

In the light of the candles, Tarith made out her slim figure and how she had now let her hair down so that it now fell to great lengths almost to her hips like a fine, black, drape. A simple but fine green, silk, night gown adorned her and it was less than modest in emphasizing her bosom as, no doubt, she had wished.

"I'm trying not to make a habit of it," the Prince grumbled. "Why are you here? I need sleep I'm afraid, Princess. I'm sure we have made your accommodation sufficient"

"Of course. But I felt I had to speak to you about earlier today…"

"Nothing happened earlier today. It was merely the excitement of all that has transpired. We both know that" Tarith cut her off. "Don't we?"

Amira rolled the long sleeves of her green night dress around her wrists "that may be so but I felt I had to speak with you"

"Concerning what, Princess?" Tarith restlessly turned away from her, finally lowering the dagger.

"All this. We may be on the brink of a war if my father calls all our forces to him. You insulted him"

"*We* insulted him. You also defied him if I recall and if he's going to, can he wait until tomorrow?" Tarith sarcastically smirked.

"You don't appear to be afraid. Why?" she questioned.

"I suppose not. Your father never struck me as a fool. Ignorant? Yes. Greedy? Yes. Ugly both inside and outside? Definitely but not foolish, how else could he orchestrate an attempted breakaway from the Empire?"

Amira shot Tarith with a powerful, sharp look. Disappointed and angered. The Prince read the look and receded. "I understand he is still your father but I myself hold no love for the man, no semblance of tolerance"

"I understand. I told myself all those things when he tried selling me off, when he tried having me imprisoned; he's not my father, don't think of him as thus. But, perhaps I will never be rid of him. A part of me will always love him even if he doesn't recognise me anymore"

"You know he will never let you back" the Prince stated as he stood next to the bedroll laid out for him. "And, as I said to the General the day we met you, he clearly has some friends inside the senate who are going to make life difficult for me. The real war, if there is now going to be one, will be fought there" He pressed the clip on his sash and the red drape around his shoulder fell to the floor, Amira watched him. Watched him unclip the straps on his iron armor until it burst open to show bare flesh, strong and muscular. As his back was turned to her, like a lynx, she crouched slightly as she crept towards him with muffled steps, padded by her soft feet on the sand, her eyes narrowed as she saw her prize. By the time the Prince turned she was positioned so close to him he'd have knocked into her had he chosen to move. Again they could see the deep features of each other's face, silver eyes on green. A handsome, chiseled and structured face peered at the beauty of a soft and short one. He could feel her. So close to him that she was trembling, her breath running over his lips with a flirtatiousness and subtle warmth .

"This is a change from your usual serious exterior," Tarith said gently murmuring. She could see how his silver eyes nearly glittered when one looked closely enough.

"Yes. I noticed you watching my exterior" the Princess smiled as she ran her fingers through his hair. Tarith smiled as he felt himself pulled onto the bed. She was ready to pounce, not being able to hold it anymore when she felt his hands gripping into her arms and pushing her back "Amira. No. I can't. Just as you said…we should know better. I can't let this continue in good conscience, no good will come of this. Not for what may happen"

"Oh something will come of this. And I'm sure its going to feel good" she smiled before running her hands across his scalp and into the smooth streaks of his hair. "This doesn't have to be for politics. Fuck the Empire, fuck my father" she added as she finally got to feel it: her lips against his, soft and silky. "This may feel good but then what, how will…"

"Forget what they have to say. I'm fed up of listening to what the world thinks of me and I'm fed up with being told what to do. I'm not fates pawn. Are we one in this?" she asked. Tarith stopped as did his seducer. They were aligned and joined. "Family is what? A setback. They tie you down and break your heart" she continued as she softly stroked a stray hair away from the Prince's eye.

"You can't just throw it all away so quickly. Not after so brief a time"

"It has not been brief. Not for me. Every year, every time, I wanted to walk away from it but I had no where to walk to. Now, perhaps I do: wherever I want"

Tarith sighed as he felt himself ready to tell her about the shadow over his own family. Her welcoming demeanor told him she was ready to be told. Tarith drew a quiet and steady breath as he confessed "I haven't told you much about my own family, have I?"

"No"

"Well since you are now a castaway yourself perhaps I may alleviate that sadness or burden with my own family's cast off. I'm not the only child of Tephus and Cassandra. Before me came my brother"

Amira's eyes fluttered in shock, as though she had been suddenly and unexpectedly struck. "A brother? You- you- how could anyone not know?"

"Oh many know but most have just forgotten or turned a blind eye. His name was Tarren. I have never met nor seen him so I'm afraid that is the extent of the knowledge I have of him. Most others within the Empire have just forgotten he was once the heir"

"Heir? He was the eldest? Few would turn down the chance to sit upon the Fanged Throne and call themselves Emperor"

"I cannot truly say. Only from what my mother told me. My father does not speak of him. There are no tributes, no statues or reminders of him. No indication he ever even existed. Nothing. No memory. Not even the dust to claim he stood on" Tarith relayed as his face sunk in anguish and a deep, insatiable regret "it started after my birth. Everything changed. For this whole family, for the whole Empire! The moment my father saw those wisps of silver hair he knew that this is where I'd end up. So he devoted his time primarily to me, training me in swordplay, statecraft, ancient history, law and geography and Tarren..." Tarith sighed "he was forgotten by my father. He may have been heir apparent but not when presented with another male heir who showed the telltale signs of Ornagoths chosen few. My father and him started arguing after that, he was sixteen years older than me. Until one day he just left, rode out of Ushkin, never to be seen again. It must have broken both their hearts, well, my mothers anyway, perhaps it was what my father was aiming for: get him to finally get up and leave and make room for me. Perhaps not, my father he is, but an

Emperor before that" the Prince sighed as Amira pressed her head against his chest with a sigh of her own.

"I don't think you can claim the blame for that one. Least not for the crime of being born. But I did not know our fathers were so similar, they might benefit from talking for the sake of their countries and at least your father got the child he wanted. Mine wasn't so fortunate"

Tarith paused. "I'm sorry for what happened in Arden, it wasn't my design. And I'm…sorry about ruining your evening with my own family's woes. I…" he was shushed as she placed a finger across his lips.

"See…" she smiled "I told you we were one in the same. I'm tired of running from this pain, I'm tired of acting as my station demands. And so. Are. You"

The moon rose and sank. By early morning, the patrols were already gathering. Most did this in next to nothing as even in the early hours the temperature was humid and the air stuffy and stifling every breath, making the Osh-Venn drench themselves in sweat as they moved sacks of supplies from one horse to another, others falling over their own tired feet whilst they dressed themselves. The General marched through the camp, aiming to find Tarith before day had come in full force. He appeared puzzled when he saw the young man wasn't sparring with the men as he would normally be doing at such a time in the morning. He was confused when Tarith's head emerged from the tent next to him. When the General realized what Tarith had committed, his face flicked from minor confusion to a look of astonishment and impressed that Tarith had never seen anyone give before, it was almost unnerving. "Sleep well?"

"Oh please. Like you expected me to do any different"

"I have no expectations of you, you're my leader. But my, my, how quickly ones priorities change from an enemy to a lover the moment a pair of tits come bouncing into view" Lo'atal murmured to the Prince, turning his back on him whilst he got dressed in full view of the camp, quite comfortably.

"Yeah because you would choose to train rather than accept the appreciation of a beautiful woman" the Harbinger crudely remarked.

"Oh is that what those noises were!" Lo'atal intentionally shouted and smiled belligerently. "Because we Osh-Venn call that something else" he added as his troops scurried around him.

As Tarith dressed himself, pulling his normal, thin red tunic on, he was about to speak again when Lo'atal's hand lifted up, shushing the Prince who looked around to see that whilst most of the Osh-Venn were still performing their chores, some had taken to listening, as if paused or frozen in time with their ears glued to their surroundings--listening.

"What in Aeron's name is that?" Tarith asked. As he fixed the iron buckles on the back of his armored cuirass he felt it, as did all else. A shudder. Emanating from the ground and vibrating through their feet as if the very bones of the earth moved against themselves. As the vibrations shuddered the ground, barrels and pikes resting on tents started to fall in heaps, stones started to crack and debris from the top of the canyon plummeted down with splintering crashes. Lo'atal pushed Tarith back and quickly placed himself between the Prince and the epicenter of the quake. The earth moaned as a deep roar from its great pits echoed through the land which began to open slightly, not like an earthquake, the sand and dirt and rock fell inwards and was then spat back out by something large. Lo'atal drew his sword as he called in his own language to several other Osh-Venn who approached with weapons of their own. They watched as a crocodilian snout poked from the ground, its yellow teeth curling over its lower jaw as its hardened, chalk white skin was shown. Two clawed feet pulled the monster above ground as it revealed itself to be an ash wyrm. Its two chameleon-like eyes twitched with a feral madness at both Lo'atal and Tarith as it started to tower above them. Its scales were worn and dusty and veterans of hundreds of attempted hunts as its many scar's stood on display as a mangled mass.

The whole camp watched as the animal pulled itself out of its sandy tunnel underground, rearing up on its back legs and rising so high its snout covered the light of the early rising sun. It was a true hunter of the wastelands. The ash wyrm released a low, guttural grumble, deep from within itself. Even on the ground Tarith caught a scent of its breath: a thick musty smell, like wet earth, followed by the stench of dried and decayed meat. They all watched as the wyrm's mouth opened and it unleashed a dreadful roar, so powerful and so brutal Tarith felt it almost knock him back. He heard Lo'atal scream angrily at the beast as he and several other Osh-Venn charged the creature who cast most of them aside with one flick of its barbed tail, casting specks of blood all over the tents as the soldiers heads were scattered to the wind in clumps of bone and wet, bloody tissue. The Champion Rider drew his own sword as the wyrm snarled, casting its head towards him. It stretched out a long, clawed hand in an attempt to swipe at the Prince, catching his hip, Tarith felt its large claw seer through the thin leather, cutting it into ribbons and savagely tearing into him, he let out a gasp of pain as he fell to the floor.

The sky went dark for a brief moment as the ash wyrm opened its jaws as it lunged at Tarith, creating a whirlwind of dust and sand as it moved with surprising speed. Tarith shut his eyes, but the sharp teeth piercing his rib cage never came. He opened both eyes as he saw Lo'atal had driven his sword into the animal's lower jaw, a thin trail of blood spurted out from the beast's mouth as it groaned and rose up again, keeping the sword wedged inside the fresh wound. The splintering pain didn't deter it, it retreated only briefly as it lunged a second time and Amira's spear met its eye. This time the beast screamed in agony, turning around and flinging its tail. Tarith heard a crack as the General howled in pain as he was flung into a tent by the whip-like weapon. The Osh-Venn and their leaders gazed in shock as the ash wyrm cast itself back into the sandy depths again with its tail wildly flailing about.

Arrows soon followed in its wake as Osh-Venn surrounded the opening and pelted barrage after barrage down into the cavern where the beast had emerged, cheering and clamoring with angry voices. Again, however, the ash wyrm drew back up. It snatched its jaw forward and clenched in it a soldier, barely dressed and out of his tent. He screamed in helpless agony as the animal, now frenzied, whipped its head from side to side, launching parts of its victim all about the camp and splattering in messy, clumps. Then it began to roll like how Tarith had seen the great crocodiles of the Bhagon River do so. The spiny ridges on its back dug into the earth as it began to flatten tents and pressing them into the sand like huge stamps, disappearing momentarily amidst the dirt.

It's tail wildly flew over Tariths head as he dove to the ground whilst the men tried to subdue it though only in vain as the beast was as cruel as it was as cunning and thrashed its tail every time someone dared intrude on its space, hissing at them with rows of curved, serrated teeth. The Prince, enraged and emboldened, looked for his blade and found it resting between the rocks. His fingers wrapped around the cold hilt just as the tail came back down as the wyrm turned again. Tarith raised the blade and felt it pass through the thick muscle and tendons of the beast's tail, lodging into the bone.

Everyone took for shelter as the maddened monster scratched at the earth and skinned the men it could find with such animalistic and basic rage as it turned to Tarith: the source of its pain. It bared its teeth into a malicious and calculating smile as it lunged for the Prince who lay in the dirt, bewildered and now disarmed. It's one good remaining eye spotted Amira who lept from the top of the war table, spear in hand. The wyrm couldn't turn fast enough to catch her in its grip before her spear found its place in the soft, rubbery heart of its last remaining eye. It roared as it retreated a final time, blinded and crippled, the wyrm relented and was prodded furiously by angered spearmen though their tiny barbs did little against the monster's scaly hide. It flipped itself back into its dusty hole and folded itself back beneath the waves of ashen soil as the ground healed back.

Lo'atal sat, hunched against a rock, holding his chest. Both Vacile and Tarith rushed to him. They tended to him, as some of the Osh-Venn flocked to him as well, concern between comrades not found in most other places of the world for the bond between an Osh-Venn is brotherly. The old Curate knelt down as he drew his fingers across Lo'atal's chest. The General winced. Vacile prodded his ribs sharply "fractured rib cage. Keep his movements to a minimum. I may have a tonic that will numb the pain but only rest will heal this. Help him and fetch some Harpcluster from my tent, the yellow plant petals, I should have some crushed and soaked. They will dull the swelling" Vacile ordered as he clicked his finger, summoning two Osh-Venn who hoisted their General up onto their shoulders. "We can't stay here, with that beast still out here" Tarith said as he turned to Amira, ignoring her aid in fending off the savage animal. The Princess stood back, slightly let down by her lover's response. "Gather all the men. We move to higher ground!" Tarith ordered, shouting hoarsely to the back of the camp.

"We shouldn't move, not in this weather, not with the General like…" An Osh-Venn stated as he was cut off by his Prince.

"We go now! Make for the crater, Vacile, do you know the way from here?" Tarith ordered the soldier before turning to the Curate.

"Of course, your benevolence. It's a two day ride east, into the thick of the Red Plains. We'll certainly know it when we see it. It lies just before the Wall" Vacile answered, somewhat calmed and timid after Tarith's outburst of sternness.

"Good. Right. Get moving!" Tarith shouted, desperate to keep time. Lo'atal's injury had awoken something within him, something automatic, something instilled within him: responsibility. Both Vacile and Amira watched as their Prince stormed to the front of the camp to hurry the men, their eyes met when they looked at each other in surprise at Tarith's quick temper. Vacile smiled a toothless grin at the Princess before following Lo'atal who was being helped onto a horse already as his own mount was far too large. Amira wondered why the old man had looked at her so strangely, when she looked down, her answer was rather clear, and not just to her. She had nothing on, no undergarments, nothing. When the ash wyrm attacked the fighter within her switched on as intended: a honed instinct, disregarding her undress and had proceeded out into the open, naked. She hurriedly covered herself with her hands as several of the Osh-Venn could not help but stare at the finery of her figure. Her eyes were what they missed, at first, staring both of them with a building fury that soon quelled their lusty and simple thoughts and drove them away in silent embarrassment.

Tarith approached the horse Lo'atal was put on. The General sat, not quite upright in his saddle, clutching his bleeding and swollen chest that the Osh-Venn had managed to quickly wrap in gauze. The Prince placed a hand on Lo'atal's leg in comfort.

"Are you alright, my friend?"

"Well its less than fucking pleasant if its the healer whose asking. Been a long time since I've felt pain like this, what a bitch of a monster. Udar (damn). I think I know what I'll be doing once you've found this crater" Lo'atal awkwardly twisted himself in the direction of the sand vipers hole "coming back to kill that fucking rock sucker!!! Udar!!!" he shouted, his voice cutting off as he clutched his chest again.

"Hold off on that for a while. Rest, withhold your anger for now. That's an order, General" Tarith bantered.

"Time to move out everyone, zes gren! zes gren!" he ordered, shouting to move. To his call the men seemed to quicken their pace tenfold, sliding on their skull helmets and scaled armor. Within an hour, two hundred Osh-Venn had left what had once been their camp. Tarith, Amira and Lo'atal headed the line, on horseback, as they marched on to fates path.

"I've never seen you like that before, not even at the arena," the now-dressed Amira whispered as the horses cantered hastily over scorching sand and dirt. "We had won. We could've killed that thing if it came back. Why did we leave?"

"Because there are some aspects of nature man was never meant to conquer and every now and then she likes to remind us of our place. If not that then something worse would've found us and less prepared. I don't want to try our luck or gamble the mens lives to nature" the Prince answered grimly "But I appreciated your help, of course. In fact I noticed most of the others appreciated it as well" he added, smirking to himself.

"Yeah, very funny" Amira replied, she wasn't amused and seemed disappointed in Tarith for the comment.

"I thought so" the Harbinger answered back as they now past back out of the canyon.

Chapter 15- A Pup Leaves The Den

Kellor dragged the depleted Martis through the back allies loaded with filth and littered with the drunk and drugged, over the cobbled streets of Kingsport and through the stinking fish market. The old knight didn't know what kept him going, yet didn't falter. The weight of Martis, half conscious, exhausted from crying insatiably, on his shoulder and the sores on his feet from running so long, caused Kellor to stop once in a while for breath and contemplation. His white beard was matted with sweat and his brow dripped with every step. The docks were in his sights, another ten minutes and they'd be there. He pushed his way through all the traders with shaking hands as some onlookers watched with puzzled faces. Adrenaline coursing through his blood, the likes of which he'd only felt during the War of Black Fields, out high on the battlefield, the bodies thick and sweaty, crowded and packed until every breath was filled with pain and labor.

Martis saw them through blurred vision, whether it was from the tears still in his eyes or the lack of sleep as he and Kellor had been maneuvering through the city, he didn't know. All he felt was the nothingness. An absence. No longer was there any flicker of hope or a yearning for the world as a young boy would hold, his mother was gone, his uncle had won. All had been in vain for them, all had been lost. The fifteen year old felt every jolt as Kellor moved, the old man's armor digging into his side and the smell--it was all around him. He had smelt the stale, dank stench of unwashed people before but this time he didn't know if it was the people of Kingsport or himself. Dry mud was splattered all over his face from the stables making him smell of earth and salt from the market. His clothes were tattered and worn. With every step the knight took Martis felt him become weaker, his aged body quivered now with every step but he never gave in. "Kellor. Enough..." Martis groaned. At first the sworn protector didn't hear him but when Martis piped up his croaky voice the knight released him, nearly dropping him head first onto the stone street.

"What is...it?" Kellor panted, harshly.

"What are we doing? The ship will have left by now. There's nowhere to go...we have to...stop. I can't...we've gotta go back, we can..."

"No, my Lord. There is no return. Those vipers will take what's left of you if we don't go. There's plenty more ships at the docks," Kellor conceded. Martis relinquished and didn't even attempt to haul himself up from the ground. "We have to keep moving, is what we have to do. Come on" the knight spoke to him--no answer, Martis was alone with his grief, freshly burning in his heart. "Get up, boy! Martis! Come on." Kellor implored, grabbing Martis by the dirtied scruff of his tunic and picking him up, almost tearing it off his body. The house knight steadied the boy and looked him head on, his head lowered to eye level with the resigned boy "listen to me, look at me, boy. So long as you live from now on they will never stop looking for you, never stop hunting you. How long can the hare outrun the wolves if he refuses shelter or help? And they are wolves, Martis"

"I don't want help. They need to die! All of them, all of them! They...killed her. They have to pay. He has to pay. I hate him!"

"And they will. But you can't claim vengeance at the end of a rope" Kellor yelled, trying to stoke the urgency into the boy but he still continued to look through and past his old friend, the blank and vacant look spread across his face, lifeless and as still as set stone. The two had barely noticed the gathering commotion behind them. When both turned their heads, they saw a group of soldiers, Monthell soldiers, on horseback, riding through the street, some knocking over people as they thundered past with a noise to drown out even the bells of the Gray Chapel. Kellor saw that at their head was Sir Mord, healed already from his duel. The great big knight was searching for the two of them, probably on Cythees' command, he worried.

Kellor turned back to Martis frantically, grabbing both his shoulders. Martis felt the old knight's breath on his face and saw the panic in his eyes. "My lord, do you still have the jewel?"

"Yeah... why?"

"Keep it with you. Listen..." Kellor said as he pointed down the street, to the west of the docks. " I'm sorry, Martis but I can't stay with you. I'll tell them you're heading for the docks, it's what they'll expect. Don't go there. Not yet. You take yourself and go and find Marcus Yony, here in the city. Got that? Marcus Yony. He's...well connected "

"No Kellor. I can't..."

"Listen. Our time here is done. You must learn now, son. Let the boy die, he must, so that the man can be born today. It shouldn't be like this but it is. This is over. Now you have a sword and you know how to use it and plenty a man can survive on that. Stay out of sight, stay sharp and I swear by all eight Divines I will find you. Find Marcus, he'll help you, tell him who you are and him alone" Kellor said as he peeked around the corner of a house, looking for Mord and his pack. "Go, Martis. Go. Now!" the old knight hissed, pushing Martis down the street though the boy tried to resist and pushed back.

Martis ran and ran, Kellor watched him all the way till he was sure no one would spot him among the mass populous of the city's people. Sighing to himself and feeling almost satisfied with what he'd done, the old man left the shadowed safety of the corner and went and stood in the center of the street. He saw the huge knight pick him out as his head thrashed from side to side in search. He heard the thundering of the hooves on the cobbles as Mord approached, broadsword drawn and visor down. The horses quickly surrounded Kellor, like a herding dog with the sheep. Their red coats flapped as they reared and snorted into a circle formation. He listened as Mords booming voice erupted from the helmet. "Where's the boy?" he commanded.

"The docks. But you won't catch him, you're too late, dog. You may tell your master that" Kellor replied, glancing at all the horsemen one by one.

Mord looked to two of the horsemen and growled "find the urchin. I'll bring this one back with me" he tugged on the reins of his horse as it snorted angrily. "I can't wait to see what the King does to you for this" he added, sadistically, and though Kellor couldn't see his face he knew Mord would be smiling crookedly under that metal mask. "I don't fear Cythees or his pettiness" Kellor retorted. Mord leaned forward in the saddle, crushing the stallions neck. "I wasn't talking about that King"

The old captain of the guard lowered his eyes and felt as the fear finally reached his heart with a shaking thud as the words all but confirmed his expected fate. One of the Monthell soldiers clambered down and bound Kellor's hands behind his back with a pair of cold, half-forged manacles. He felt the course metal scrape his wrists as he was dragged up and seated onto the horse. Kellor allowed himself one last look at the docks, partially hoping to see Martis concealed within the crowd, though no sight revealed itself. The old knight smiled. Martis was safe and the knight had done his duty.

The boy had made his way further into the city, perhaps the eastern quadrant or the souther, he surmised from the putrid smell of sweat, fish and animal excrement the further he went into the streets. Martis never glanced back, he knew he couldn't for the urge to go back to Kellor was compelling enough and on the streets he knew he had no allies. This world was a foriegn one, its stone maze spread right out to the docks to the east and the Summerplains to the west. Foolish, he thought, that he never attended the walks about the city with his mother when she had been escorted, perhaps then he would have been more savvy to the roads, houses, shops and back alleys. He asked around from shopkeeper to store vender to merchants and sailors but the ones who didn't ignore either answered in a tongue Martis wasn't familiar with or replied only to tell Martis to leave. It felt like days as he plodded over every cobble, he could feel his strides becoming heavier, like a weight on each foot. Tired and severely defeated, Martis contemplates giving up there, rolling up into a ball on the warm stones and allowing the world to have its way with him, until. Something caught his eye, or rather, at first, his ear. He heard, coming from his right--a ringing, a call. He was firstly surprised no one else could hear it, looking to see their distracted faces continue ambling on with their tasks. Turning to where the ringing was coming from, Martis saw something abstract as far as scenery in Kingsport went; a large, black wolf-dog. Its eyes were a deep yellow and both peered at Martis from around the corner of a building. Whatever it was about the animal, Martis felt something different about it. An animal like that would never venture as far south as Kingsport, the furthest Martis had heard of wolves was in the hills and dense forests of the realm of Grasspoint. But it was the way the dog peered at him, with almost human eyes instead of that of a potential escaped wild beast. And it smiled. In a very strange and eerie way, the skin on its mouth stretched upwards like a devil and yet it passed so freely among the people who blindly carried on around it as though it were never there. Martis watched as after a few seconds the strange creature turned back around the corner and disappeared. Something awoke in the already adventurous Martis, a simple but strong feeling to follow. He wandered over to the corner of the house and, looking down the street where the creature should have been sauntering down, saw nothing but people. It was only when his eyes searched for the beast did Martis see what he needed to see though he himself didn't know. A sign, hanging above an old inconsequential building, was some sort of merchant's store as the sign read 'Yonys general goods'. The boys eyes narrowed as he questioned if this was the Yony Kellor meant? And the more prominent question; where had the wolf-dog gone and why was it there in the first place?

Martis' thoughts were quickly interrupted as a patrol of city watch marched past. He heard them first, their armor gleaming like the summer waves on the bay and clanking like a barrel full of knives. Martis pressed himself against the wall of the house, putting his head down low, to the ground as the batch of men moved past him. Martis knew that he had to move, with both his family's soldiers looking for him and now the city watch. It wouldn't be long before he would be recaptured. Turning back to the store with panic and desperation, almost tripping over a rogue cobble with delirium and fear, he quickly and discreetly crossed the street to the merchant trade. He could still, easily, see the Kings Keep and felt as if eyes could be bearing down on him from every tower, every turret, balcony and bridge.

As he got closer to the shop he thought it best to not simply use the front door, better to avoid attracting unnecessary attention, he thought to himself. Approaching the side of the shop, he found a sash hanging above the entrance to the shop's store room. Martis saw no other way, he had snuck through the empty confines of the keeps halls and through its walls but not through an entire city. Pulling back the purple sash Martis stumbled into a few boxes, loaded with old nets, making a small thump as his boot hit it. He jerked back, cowering behind a large, steel cage. Paying no mind to the construct at first, only when he heard the chirps coming from inside did he see the vibrant beak of several toucans hopping around inside. Martis smiled at first, enjoying the innocent company of the birds but soon frowned when he saw them in the cages, confined and limited in flight.

He was about to reach out and open the cage door when a startling voice called to him from the top of the stairs to his left. "Lovely birdies aren't they?" it asked in a foreign accent. Martis bolted upright to see a figure standing at the top of the stairs, concealed by a vale of morning shade. The boy said nothing, hiding behind a box, hoping against reason that he had imagined the voice and the person. "Well come out then, boy. Before I come over there and relieve you of those thieving hands" the man said pompously. Martis felt insulted at the accusation and went and stood in the middle of the store room, his hand on the bronze handle of the sword Kellor had granted him "it would be better for them if they were not in cages. Don't you think?" the boy asked. When he did he saw a smile creep over the man's face, he could see a gold tooth glistening in the dim light. "My dear boy. Most of anything that lives spends its life in a cage but some are just more visible than others" the man said as he stepped into the room to join Martis "put that down. You won't be needing it" he ordered, referring to the small blade Martis was about to draw. As the man approached Martis he saw the exotic owner of the store. He was dressed in ornate and puffy merchant clothes, his jerkin was a mix match of browns and yellows and greens, looking more like a jester. The smell of perfume over sweat followed him when he swapped from his left to his right foot when he stood still. In his right hand was a cane that appeared to be years old, its pommel was carved in fine steel and into the shape of a gull's squawking head. His short, black, upward hair was clearly unkempt as was the curly, scraggly beard that called the tanned skin of his chin home. His eyes were a dark brown and beady, gazing at Martis with question and curiosity. "So, what do you want, boy, if not to steal. Gold? Ha. You'll have to earn it, if so" the owner implied.

"Actually, I'm trying to find a..." Martis stopped, wise enough to know not to mention names to strangers.

"Spit it out boy. Who?"

"A mister Yony. Know him?"

To the question the shop owner tilted his head, as if not understanding what the boy in his shop had just said.

"Oh, so you're simply a messenger. It's okay you're just not the usual one. Well you can tell Grimvar I won't be selling anymore to him; he's cost me a lot of coin and those girls they...."

"No! I'm not a messenger. My m...my friend told me he'd be able to help me" Martis said sheepishly, not wanting to mention his mother, she'd been dead only a few hours and the boy's mind and heart had still to accept her absence in the world. Every memory that flickered through his mind of her breathed life back into the hurt and pain like a torturous reel.

"Who's this friend?"

"Why do you want to know?"

"You're in my shop, I don't know you and I don't deal with people I don't know. I deal in procurement of not just goods but the more...costly types of merchandise as well" the stranger grinned.

"Sir Kellor. I doubt some lowlife like you knows…"

"So, he still remembers me. After all this fucking time!" the stranger laughed. It took Martis longer than he would have liked to figure out what the man's sudden outburst of joy meant. Martis faltered as he spoke "no. Not you. Your Marcus?"

"Oh yes. It would appear that fate has truly led you here" Marcus remarked, placing an oily hand on Martis. The young Monthell receded uncomfortably at his touch "how did you find me? Where's Kellor then if he sent you? " Yony enquired. Martis, remembering the wolf, answered "Yeah…something led me here" he mumbled.

"And Kell?"

"He stayed behind. He's not coming…or he's…dead, I don't know which"

"Oh. So that's all his doing: all that commotion out there. And here I believed today was going to be boring" the trader muttered as he walked over to the sash and pulled it back, poking his head onto the streets to watch the guards and soldiers running up and down the streets."So, who are you?" Marcus asked before throwing the sash back and pulling a crate between his legs to sit on. "You're not mine are you?"

"No. Gods I hope not. No. I'm…my name's Martis. Martis Monthell" at the answer Marcus' mouth dropped as his eyes widened and his nostrils flared in shock, becoming two large holes in his head. Martis grew confused, wondering if he had said something to offend the shifty merchant.

"Your Eleana's. Where is she? Did she send you? With your grandfather here in the city she should know better. He'll…"

"My mother's dead," Martis interrupted, looking to the ground, noticing two rats squealing in the corner.

At the news Marcus also looked, regrettably, at the ground. "We always knew something like this would happen. That things would boil over. Me and Kellor warned her but she wouldn't listen. I told her. But I'd expect it from her. She always kept herself there to keep you safe, not that there are many safe places anywhere in Kond but..." the merchant growled.

"How did you know my...her?"

"Ha. I was a trading partner of her late husband; Bursley Wentworth. You remember him? Mind you, you were only little. Four, maybe? I was also the one who helped her with his 'tragic maritime accident'. It is dreadful when one tries to sail without the proper hull. He was never a kind man to her nor was he a fair trader so we were all more than obliged to help her" Marcus smiled rather sadistically. Martis scowled, surprised at the lengths he never knew his mother had gone to. "Your saying my mother was responsible for that?"

"I'm saying nothing that you didn't already suspect. You knew he wasn't your father, you strike me as a smart whip" Marcus smiled cheekily. "So. Young Martis, what is it that you want?"

"I need to leave this city. Now. Kellor said you'd know how" Martis rushed, waving his hands around in a flurry of emotion. Marcus simply acknowledged him and swiveled around and began to rummage around in an old shipping chest behind him. "You're not going to ask why I want to leave?" Martis pondered, furrowing his eyebrow. As Marcus searched in the chest he replied casually "in my experience the fewer questions asked the fewer heads are lost" something that gave both a strange sense of comfort and displeasure to the young Monthell. After a few seconds Marcus pulled out an old, dirtied tunic and some worn boots, holding them in front of Martis "What the hell do you want me to do with these?" the young boy asked.

"Isn't it obvious? I want you to paint a picture of--put them on you fool" Yony replied sarcastically.

"Why?"

"Because someone who doesn't won't to be found by the Monthell guard shouldn't be stupid enough to wear their colors" Yony replied. Martis, minorly hurt by what Marcus said, put on the simple clothes as quickly as he could be bothered. Once they were pulled over him to the point where he could feel the course boots rubbing on his heels, he looked at Marcus for a reply. "Great. Now time to get you to a ship" Yony answered smugly as he turned for the stairs, expectant of Martis to follow. But the boy didn't move. Behind him Marcus heard him ask "How do you know I'm telling the truth? How do you know I'm really who I said I'am?"

To the question Marcus smiled as he ran his fingers through his frizzy hair, turning around and saying "You should be more careful of the things you drop for others to pick up. No mere beggar or common-born boy has this" as he produced the same ruby Martis had taken with him from the keep. Looking shocked, the boy ran to Yony and tried snatching it back but the tall man quickly tucked his hand back into the silk confines of his vibrant clothes "that wasn't yours to take"

"No but the Divines deemed it was mine to find. That's how I knew it was you"

"How? It's just any old ruby. My mother gave it to me. She said it was what my far…"

"Your fathers, yes?"

"Yes? How did you?"

"Best I keep it. Wouldn't want it giving you away. I'm not the only one who knows what this is and besides it's a rare find.

Brings in more gold than you could imagine"

"You can't! It's mine! Give it..."

"Think of it as payment for saving your life. Now come on. Time to get you to a ship, your uncle will be leaving soon" Marcus said, putting a hand on Martis' shoulder and nearly throwing him up the stairs into the main shop which was just as dingy as the store room. "My uncle? How do you know my uncle, he's at The Forge?"

"Not that uncle" Marcus replied, opening the cracked wooden door to the shop, leading Martis back out onto the hot streets of the city. Martis knew that if Marcus didn't mean his uncle, Christen, handsome and wise, it only meant his other uncle, Drake. Of whom Martis had only ever heard his mother speak of a handful of times, often in regret. He'd also heard tales from the Monthell soldiers, most expressing secret admiration for Drake, however those more loyal to Corvus and his circle would show resentment or simply never discussed him at all. 'The lone eagle' was what some had slandered him--a renegade who rebelled from his father at a young age and had since left his royal lineage behind to pursue a life on the waves.

It took several more minutes before the merchant and the runaway arrived at the docks of Kingsport, stretching along the entire eastern side of the city, straddled by small islands and sand banks across the bay that acted as a gateway to the Sea of Swords. All manner of vessels lined the waters from small fishing dinghies to large spice ships from the other side of the world and onto the great war galleys that anchored just off the coast. All bobbed along like driftwood on the currents and their sails blew calmly in the last of the summer breeze that sprawled in off the sea. The two vagabonds weaved themselves between sailors and stacks of crab cages as tall as them, once or twice Martis lost sight of Marcus through the thicket of the bodies crowding every cobble and through the cracks between bodies could've sworn he saw flashes of black fur and four legs trotting alongside him.

When the boy finally caught up with Marcus he found himself at the end of the docks where a small sized ship was moored. He read the vessel's name 'The Mad Dog' off the stern with difficulty as the once golden paint had faded with salt and time to a browner color. The sails of the ship were a tattered and dirtied white with several small holes dotting them. "This is where I must leave you" Marcus said, turning to the young Monthell who appeared rather confused at what the merchant had said. "What do you mean? People will know you've helped me"

Yony smiled warmly. "You certainly have that same streak of compassion she had but I'm not a rookie, boy. This isn't my first time smuggling more...live cargo. You'll be safe. Now. Get on board" he shoed Martis up the gangplank when another man came walking down. Martis gawked at him, the face seemed familiar: piercing blue eyes, just like Cythees', spiky and messy black hair along with a perfectly kept and trimmed beard that was thinly strapped to his face and with the same small nose as his mothers that was squinted as the wind blew salty air at him. He looked at Marcus as he placed a hand under his belt buckle "I hope you aren't planning another stow away" the man joked. His voice was welcoming and smooth but boomed with the confidence and control Martis remembered of his grandfather.

Marcus smiled as he pushed Martis up the gangplank "more of a rescue and run operation" Yony replied with a grin.

"This is the last time I'm saving one of your little cretins, we're getting too crowded as it is" the captain spoke over the waves that were rising with the morning tide. "You're lucky we're still here. Bo forgot our cargo again so we had to lay over" he added as he ran his gloved hands through his hair.

As Martis walked up the gangplank he looked back to Yony "give me back the stone. It's mine" he hissed.

"Best you forget about it, son. Trouble you don't need right now" Marcus replied just as the man helped Martis on board. "Good luck Captain" he bid as he tossed the sailor a satchel of coins.

Martis looked at the captain, now more closely, the blue jacket he wore that was clearly as old as him and the dirtied tunic strung together underneath that, stained with ale and gull. "There's a small cabin below decks, it's yours. Go on. Don't let the crew see ya, they'll think you're a stowaway which means they'll have some fun with you. Go" Drake said, flicking a finger towards the cabin door.

Martis sheepishly nodded his head before ambling onto the ship. He looked out from the deck and saw the splendor of the capitol for a final time. He may have wished to leave that place more than ever before, alone and fearful, but he still felt the lump in his throat pulsate with sorrow as his home it was no more. He was free of the gilded cage but now cast out to sea and the strange world beyond. Martis sighed and sniffled as he opened the door to the lower deck, the scent of ale and fermented fish stifled him as he retreated into the ship, taking refuge behind one of the fish barrels. When the door shut behind the boy Marcus quickly made his way up the gangplank, taking quick, almost comical, steps. "What do you want me to do with the stone?" he asked the captain with a concerned expression as his eyes widened.

"Keep it, sell it, bury it. Do whatever with it but make sure no one ever sees it again, only a handful know what it represents and I don't need the boy finding out. Anyway, Where's Eleana?

You know it's a good job Kellor told us what he was doing or we may not have found them. You'd better keep an eye out as well. Kell said that shifty bastard, Jazar, knew about their escape too. He's supposed to have gotten a boat already lined up for them but there weren't no way that was happening. If he knows then..."

"I'm fine. I've been under their noses for fifteen years" Marcus laughed. So... where's lana? Where's my sister?" the captain inquired.

Marcus slipped the stone back into his satchel before shifting his head in the direction of the cabin "best you get the boy to tell you. It's not my place. Perhaps the two of you can find solace in each other, besides, you haven't seen him before, right? Not the first thing I'd like to have to talk about with him but…" Marcus said, smiling more simply this time before turning away, heading back towards the city, keeping out of the eyes of the city watch. "Keep safe!" the captain called to Marcus, who waved once before disappearing into the crowd. The seafarer stood for a moment, on the deck of the ship, even with the sun beating on him from above, it did very little to dull the cold and numbing feeling of certainty. He knew what had happened, he could feel it, though he hoped against it, he knew the rules of the game his family played. A sailor in tattered rags and a sea cap approached the captain. "Your orders, sir"

"Cast off. There's nothing here for us anymore"

"No, sir?"

"Not for me"

Back up the hill, inside the Kings Keep, a small entourage of Monthell soldiers escorted Kellor through the castle's corridors, past the already unforgiving eyes of serving girls and other royal workers, people Kellor had known for years on end and now he could feel their anger firing at him with every look, the blame which he knew was rightful. The news had already started to spread of Eleana's death, Cythees would've made sure of that, to take blame off himself for having the murderous soldiers follow her in the first place. Several times Kellor felt like relinquishing all his hope, letting his boots drag along the floor as the soldiers dragged him to Corvus' office. When they threw open the door to the room Kellor saw all the shutters had been closed, no one had opened them since the previous day, and Corvus, stood, arms behind his back, staring at the blank window in front of him. He had dressed himself as respectfully as ever, no death or blow would stop the King of The Fold from appearing as regal and powerful as he was. Standing close to the vacant and empty fireplace was Mord, his tall figure looming with a presence as ugly as his features. His black hair was thinly shaved to his scalp, his egg-shaped face covered in scars and scratches from all manner of opponents over the years and were just as pronounced as his bulging eyes like that of a bulldog. His chin was host to a manner of bumps and marks that were half covered by stubble and grime. The brute never showed much emotion, standing like an abstract statue, a monument of feral strength, until bade otherwise.

Among the shadows, Kellor was placed in the center of the room, his shoulders still being clenched tightly by the soldiers.

Though he wasn't alone in that room Kellor felt it; the pressure beating down on him, he felt certain he knew what was to become of him. He had served Corvus for nearly fifty years and the King of The Fold only ever had one punishment for traitors of any kind, from the War of Black Fields to the Marauders Invasion. But the old eagle stood silent for a moment, the room stood still with him, the wind wrapped around the high tower, knocking on the shutters. Till finally Corvus spoke a few gray words so quiet and slowly that it would've been easy to doubt if he had spoken at all "Get out, all of you"

A Monthell soldier sheepishly stepped forward "Are you sure, your gra…"

Corvus snapped around to face the man before he had time to finish, his blue eyes scowling for the first time in years, wrinkling his balding forehead more than it had ever been for he was not a man to allow even a fraction of true feeling to leak out but his daughters death had shaken him enough so that his patience was worn to an all time thin. An asset had been lost and a stake in the game was at risk because of it.

His saying nothing was all it took to air his command. They nodded in submission as they discreetly left, throwing the chain connecting Kellor to his manacles to the floor. Only Corvus, Kellor and Mord remained in the room, all three standing still. "Do you know what has happened today?" the Folds King asked, watching Kellor intently, a certain anger brewed behind his eyes as if waiting for Kellor to say the wrong thing to unleash itself upon him. The old knight hesitated for a moment before stumbling forward out of tiredness "a tragedy, my King. One I…"

"You've betrayed me!" Corvus interrupted with an anger Kellor had never seen before. Corvus was always an intimidating man but seeing him in such a way made Kellor fearful, an emotion he hadn't felt in decades. "Corvus I never meant to…"

"Do not speak my name! Do you know what you've done?"

"Nothing I would've advised against given my judgment"

"Judgment!? Your duty isn't to make judgments! It's to serve, something you've failed to do and though this is the first time you've failed me, understand it is drastic enough to be the last as well! Your lucky I don't have you dealt with, you certainly wouldn't be the first and by Oldir's grace you would certainly be deserving" As the words quickly left Corvus' mouth the office doors opened again as Cythees threw them open, stomping towards Kellor with a look of anger so malignant and harmful the old knight raised his hand over his face, expecting a blow. "You bastard!" the High King roared "everything my family has done for you, given you a home, a high station as captain of the guard, respect and after all that all you do is kill my sister!"

"The only help she was granted in that was by the arrow that pierced her heart" Kellor retorted, letting go of all decorum at the mere sight of the High King. Cythees drew back, anger and now surprise on his face at the gall of the underling. He drew his golden hilted blade from its bronze scabbard and raised it at the man who had once helped him develop his sword techniques "Cythees!" Corvus roared from the other side of the office. Cythees looked to his father and healed, lowering his sword yet keeping it free.

"I'll have you executed for this, I'll have you stripped and whipped through the streets! You will beg for death before I'm done! I..."

"Enough!" Corvus shouted, his voice horse. having rarely been raised. "Mord take the High King and escort him back to the royal apartments" Corvus ordered.

"I will not. How dare you. I'm the High King of the lands, father! And I will be avenged!" Cythees raged.

"Must you be so belligerent? Fool! Remain in your chambers and we will speak later!" Corvus retorted with his final threatening command, his voice just under a shout as he tried to regain his lost composure.

Mord approached Cythees, placing his arm in the High King's way as he tried to guide him out of the room, almost carrying him out of the room as he screamed at Kellor like a scorned child. As Cythees left he turned to utter his piece but was silently halted by the stern and almost resentful look his father bade him as he left the room.

It was whilst watching this spectacle, that Kellor finally wondered: had Corvus always wanted this? Kellor was with his King the day Morryg insulted him to the courts for asking for aid against a band of cutthroats several years ago, they had ran across the entire south and the other Kings had absently looked to Corvus to end them. Morryg had sealed his fate there, Corvus withdrew royal funding and the city fell to ruin as his allies in the crown territory also turned away and refused Morryg's command, the riots started as starvation crept in and, within the year, Cythees arrived to challenge Morryg to the duel that would end the Quarthand dynasty. Corvus was a man of cunning, determination and commitment, it was almost impossible to believe he had not orchestrated it.

Once the door was shut the King immediately resumed. "Not only have you contributed to the death of my daughter, the Lady The Fold, you have contributed to the death of Gryff's wife thus destroying any hope of finalizing our grip on The Highfelds!" Kellor looked to the floor in disappointment of both himself and Corvus, however much he expected it. King Monthell never cared for any of his children the way a father would, rather the way a collector tends a prized possession; jealous and grasping in their keeping.

"So then, will they give me a final prayer to speak? I'd prefer to get it over with soon. If the Divines wish to call me home I shall return to them with…"

"You'll meet your 'Divines' in due course but I won't be ordering for the block today. But make no mistake--you are no longer captain of the guard. I'm demoting you to officer and I'll be sending you back to The Forge where you will remain for the rest of your failed days. I'm sure Christen will have…other uses for you" Corvus instructed as he calmed himself back to his normal collected demeanor and sat down at his desk, reaching for his quill which sat in its murky inkwell. "I'll send word to Christen to expect you" he muttered.

Kellor let out a sigh of immense relief that was quickly hushed by the realization of what would happen to him once he was at The Forge, he imagined things wouldn't change much and already knew that the looks of disgust people gave him would become that of a common occurrence, etched onto their faces as if sown, fixed, tapestries. Whilst Kellor saw that Corvus was focused on the letter, he let loose a single tear which ran down his wrinkled eyes and into the mess of his wiry beard. He raised his head to Corvus, peering at him, still with the monumental respect he felt for his King "why are you letting me keep my head? I'm a lowly knight, a boy who grew up in the slums of Rothbrook. I'm expendable to the house of Monthell"

Corvus stopped writing, slowly raising his own head "the only reason you still breathe is because of the dedication you have shown to this house in the five decades you've served it. Your talents in battle are the only things I have use of from you now. Which once again, thanks to you, we may all be seeing before the end of the decade. Had it been anyone else you would already be swinging from the palace walls. You've shown skill in those years and all of that has been betrayed by your lack of sensibility and a misplaced sense of authority and that is the only explanation I owe you. Now. Go. If I ever see you again

I will grant you the just end that you deserve" he answered coldly, returning to scribbling on the parchment. Kellor turned for the door, he felt his steps become lighter as he knew he would continue to live, by Corvus' wish, but those steps suddenly stopped when he heard the King of The Folds voice call "oh, and one more thing!"

Kellor turned as another tear fell from his aged face "should you contribute to the harm of any more of my blood or even conspire or think of going against the survival of this family in any way I deem so...I'll have you killed in such a way you will beg the Divines for reprieve" the old eagle threatened, his face grim and serious as he stared at Kellor. How Corvus was able to so eloquently hide from his own guilt by placing others in front of it both astounded and enraged the old knight to depths he had never felt. He couldn't think to say anything but to bow his head and leave for The Forge whilst he still could.

The office doors slammed shut. Corvus shook his head as he returned to his papers a second time.

Chapter 16- Heritage of The Dunes

A day's march had left the troop of Clan Malacender wearied as they drearily approached a large opening, a valley of sand, black in the night as the day's light had all but drifted away. They were left navigating a sea of earth under a sky of so many stars, dotted so precisely and yet so randomly. Spread across the desert, the Osh-Venn carried themselves on either their horses or the ones injured by the sand viper were carried on each other, like a colony of ants, trekking dangerously across the Red Plains. Tarith, Amira, Vacile and the still injured Lo'atal led the vanguard against the blistering sand as temperatures had already begun to drop to an uncomfortable cold.

The moon shone a bright opal white in the sky, so close, like a guiding light and yet so hauntingly as if keeping an eye on the two hundred men below, the likes of which Tarith couldn't remember ever seeing before. Amira was fixated by it, her eyes lifted to the sky, forgetting where it was her horse was taking her. Vacile rode next to her, keeping an eye on the General who seemed to be slouched in his saddle with a hand resting on his chest.

The Prince, however, was riding a few feet in front, trying aimlessly to navigate where to go. Cool sand flicked up from his horses hooves and ran up his bare legs. The desert's remoteness appealed to Tarith, he felt most at peace in the great expanses of the world, here he was untouched and for the first time, thankfully unwanted. Wandering through the jungles back home brought out a similar feeling in him. By his side, Vacile rode up. His blue hood gently flapping in the breeze rising over the dunes "we should be within closing distance of the crater by tomorrow's end if we keep this pace" Vacile said towards the Prince whose eyes still stayed fixed up ahead, watching the sand and stone glitter under the starlight. "So…" the curate added as he tried to alleviate the quiet "this is the edge of the empire, few of our people have ventured beyond these confines. I suppose when half the world is yours there are few places to go where one's influence can't be found"

"Do you ever shut up?" the Prince cut his curate off. Vacile, a man of respect, silenced himself and lowered his head with embarrassment. They both sat in awkward silence for a moment "I'm sorry, Vacile. I didn't mean that and I was out of line. Sorry. I was just enjoying the calm, that was all" Tarith apologized.

"Of course. I understand your benevolence. I'am prone to bouts of self indulgence especially when you have been studying these kinds of events since childhood as I have. I've heard all these stories, read the reports, books, scriptures and scrolls but to see it for myself is something else, even too see it so late in life. I never thought to be a part of such legend, least not at my old age"

"Well stick around and you might just get to. If we ever reach where we're going"

"Oh we will, my Prince. There's your proof…" Vacile stopped his horse before Tariths, whose own waded a bit further on before the Prince looked back to his friend who was pointing out to the depths of the horizon, shimmering across the darkened curve of the earth.

Tarith followed his gaze and saw what Vacile was watching: a great wall. It spanned the entire horizon from left to right. It was almost half a mile from them and still Tarith could make out its immense size--almost a thousand feet of orange stone and dusty bricks, carved by the ancients thousands of years ago. Seemingly perfectly placed, at the very middle of the wall was a huge spacing, large enough for four of the great Argustinian war floats to pass through abreast. Its lone figure stood as a highlighter to the night sky and a monument to the great days of old, calling back to when the largest dragon flew the sky and when its first Champion Rider walked the lands.

"Yeffrae's Wall" Vacile sung with a smile "the first bulwark against the armies of Argus. This wall is as old as the empire itself" he added. Tarith stretched his hand into the cool vapors of night and halted the march. Both Amira and Lo'atal rode up to their Prince, at first unaware of the architectural masterpiece before.

"Lo'atal. Keep the caravan here. Tell the men I wish to ride alone for a bit, let them stretch their legs. We have been riding for long enough. Make camp here tonight" Tarith ordered.

Vacile cautioned "Would it not be better to push forward, as beautiful as the wall is it isn't why we are here. You should focus on…"

"If my destiny is waiting for me to claim it then it will have no quarrel with waiting a little longer" the Prince sternly ordered his court and attendees as he flung his head back to address them. Lo'atal wearily nodded, still holding his chest, he turned, slowly. Even Vacile's alchemy did little to null the pain as he still felt it throbbing through his chest with a burning scorn once again.

The Prince jarred his horse, the stallion snorted impatiently as it was made to trot on down the dune and across the dried stone and through the hollowed bones of previous victims of the Red Plains that were coughed up when the wind blew the old sands away.

After a long sprint the sand finally leveled out back into the baked and fractured earth. Ahead of the flattened land, bare and lifeless in its ancient menace. Tarith halted his horse in awe of the wall's enormity. Its shadow already had covered them a few minutes before he had arrived at its base and its almost prehistoric stones rose high enough to spitefully blot out the moon which left its light to carefully flow through the large and only opening. Prince Tarith looked up to the right side of the wall where he thought he saw a lone construct, hewn from the same orange stone though he had to draw the horse back a few feet as he couldn't adjust his neck to gaze. Atop the wall was the large, carved, statue of a woman that must have been atleast twenty feet tall. Her arms held out in a warm welcome and a circlet of flowers about her hair that was masterfully crafted to show as being blown in a bygone wind. "Yeffrea" Tarith greeted her. Two silver eyes looked up to the smooth and stark eyes of a long departed soul, one Tarith felt that, going by her profile up on the rock, she would have been one of the greatest and most graceful beauties of the ancients.

The Prince smiled up at Yeffrea: staring out, back to her homeland. Finally, something settled within the young man, his fear cast aside as surety filled the hole. He was so infatuated with the stone woman that he didn't see nor hear the living one ride up to him, Amira had followed him to the wall whilst camp was being pitched. The headscarf she wore to keep out the sand blew gently as it reached out its silky waves across the desert air. Her leafmail armor, bronzed and golden, shimmered as she passed through the huge shaft of moonlight coming from the wall's mouth. The Prince did not turn "Beautiful isn't it? Yeffrea's wall" he asked. Amira pondered. "It is certainly a marvel of stonework and engineering. I have yet to see it for myself, even us Nadenians do not venture this far out into the wastelands"

Tarith grinned in amazement "this is not the work of any mason or crafter among men. Once this was a huge mountain ridge, tens of thousands of years ago"

Both now looked up at the colossus. "Then what could carve so fine and so immense?" the Nadenian asked her Prince. Tarith once again smiled with reverie as he looked to her and muttered the word he had dared not to speak yet "dragons" and sure enough when Amira looked to the wall's heights she could still see the scorch marks left by the beast. Timelessly etched into the top of the wall. "Why? How?" she asked, climbing down off her horse to bask in the size of the palisade.

"Up there" Tarith nodded towards Yeffrea "do you know who that is"

"No. If I did it's lost to me now"

"Well her fate is tied to this very wall as is the reasoning for its being here. Her name was Yeffrea, warrior wife to Stun, the first Champion Rider. She was the first Empress in all our history, together the two of them forged Ushkin into a single country and their children later finished off the empire for them" Tarith lectured with his lessons from Vacile. "This was back when Argus had still not accepted that we were as a united people. Still seeking to infringe on a few lonely tribes. So many stood against them to prove Mundiil would never be theirs again and so many fell. Argus thinks its advancements in engineering and culture give them a right to take as they please. My father always said that this still rings true. So every year Argustinian war parties would climb the ridge to attack Nadenia and Ushkin and after Yeffrea was killed in one of those attacks, great Stun and Numinex carved the ridges ascendable gaps into Yeffrea's Wall, naming it in her honor. He set guards to watch over the wall as a bulwark against Argus until he'd thrown them back. Or that's how the story was told to me. Whatever it was that he did here, it was definitely for his love for her"

"Soaked in fire and blood" Amira responded with a murmur.

The two looked at each other, both in astonishment.

Imagining Numinex, the largest of any dragon to exist, his wings alone covering entire towns, his claws able to pick up two or three Notholi elephants, his fire that knifed through mountains and the vacuum he made as he passed overhead ripping trees from their roots. "So this is loves extent" Amira murmured.

"This is love's aftermath. Stun used this as a demonstration of his power and it was a warning to all the noble houses and councils of Argus: to test the eastern dragon is to bring ash and ruin to all one knows"

"It would appear the message was successful. Borders have been drawn and agreements settled and the wars of old are over" Amira put forward. "Now we make war on ourselves and others within the empire instead. But it's what strengthens us" she added. Tarith demurred at the truth levied by Amira's words.

"No. If you sharpen a blade too long it grows brittle and shatters. The same with empires" He grasped the reins of his horse and gave it a tug "not for much longer". "The dragons of old, Stun and his wife. My ancestors. It all meant something-- it founded the greatest and largest empire mankind has ever seen. One that has stood for twenty millenia. It has survived armies, invasions, oblivion itself and it still remains. It shall not falter on my watch. It can't. This is it, what its all for: history, remembrance" he pledged and with his oath cast, he rode back to his camp, his shadow cast with the moon and reached out as long as the walls. Leaving Amira still within its darkness.

The Fire Prince arrived at his camp, enlightened by his new sensibilities. The air was stiller and calmer now and the eyes of history that pressured on him were no more.

The Osh-Venn had not bothered themselves with setting up the larger tents, choosing to set up Tariths and the main garrison tent with the rest of them making a huge congregation with bedrolls and blankets and fires and hammocks that rested from the odd dead and dried tree. Nearly two hundred men sprawled over the sand dunes at an empire's end and bathed in the silver light of the stars and moon.

Though for sleep, Tarith could get non. As he lay in his tent, alone, he couldn't find respite from the day's long trek. He wandered outside several times to intrigue what the rest of the men were doing though most were simply already asleep. He even strayed outside of camp to moon-gaze. The heavenly body was so close to them and filled the night sky and it lingered so close. Several things were what kept him from slumber: the suspense of what his trip to the crater would bring, Amira's yearnings that he did not know were true or not himself and mostly, the pain thrashing inside his head that had been apparent into the evening and only got worse throughout the night. Back inside his tent Tarith clutched at his forehead and smothered his face into the covers of his bedding for even the candle light was getting so unbearable to his aching eyes.

He lay flat on the bed, his eyes shut for at least another hour before his plagued rest was disturbed again by the sound of the curtain brushing open. "You should know better than to disturb a Prince. Whatever it is begone. It can wait till the morning" Tarith grumbled with his eyes still shut.

"Perhaps but by then it will be too late" Lo'atal low tones rumbled through the tent. Tarith opened one eye. The General took a seat next to the map table, pulling the chair close to Tariths bed who noticed that Lo'atal was no longer holding his chest and though the redness of his raw skin still showed from under the gauze, the General seemed more at peace. "Could this not have waited until the morning"

"No. Well then I won't keep you. Vacile just reminded me that your father bade me to give you this if we made it to the crater.

I'd almost forgotten given everything we've been through in these last few weeks" Lo'atal mumbled as he produced a small cloth satchel, strapped to his bone and leather belt. Unraveling it as a small ring fell from its contents--pure gold it was and in the shape of a writhing dragon, its barbed tail looping several times. Tarith sat up at the odd piece of jewelry. "And this is?" he mocked as he plucked it from Lo'atal's palm and held it to his eye, examining it with his finger. "From what your father tells me it is the Band of Forebears. Something passed down from every Harbinger. I've been holding onto it for some time now. I didn't think it best to give it to you until now as I've seen how much this trip has already taken out of you and I see how it is affecting you. I did not wish to go adding to your stresses"

"Don't be foolish. It is merely a ring"

"Not just any ring. You are one of now seven people to have ever worn it. It's the mark of more than an Emperor" the General answered. Tarith slipped the ring onto his index finger, the cold gold gleamed as it proudly adorned its next rider's hand. "Then I'll wear it with honor, ' Tarith replied with a nod.

"Look…" Lo'atal said as he threw the empty satchel onto the table. He scratched at the stubble forming on his face that pushed out from the cracked body paint which by now had crumbled into nothing and the man below it showed. His skin actually was more tanned and darker than Tarith knew and the ceremonial symbols on his forearms were not mere paint either, they were the tattoos of the Gasharo, an honorary group of Osh-Venn warriors, enough to stand out from the usual war-like people, sworn in defense of the great sun god's name. "I may have been…impulsive in my judgment of the Princess. Though I can't withdraw it for her father, big fat bastard. I simply, was too misguided"

"You understand you weren't the only one with suspicions about her? Her people have never been the most welcoming.

I myself have only just begun to trust her as something more than a deadly assassin or a deceitful killer"

"Of course, but there has already been talk from Arden and the other Nadenian holds"

"What talk?" Tarith asked as he sat straight up, dangling his bare feet off the bed. "Talk of revolt. Several of our men who lingered in Arden joined back up with the troop yesterday. They said they had to sneak out of the city, claimed it was on lockdown and the Sultan had called his councilors for a vote"

"A vote for what exactly? No, wait. I know already don't I? I've been a fool" Tarith cursed himself wearily. "I've given him the excuse he's been looking for for almost twenty years. The Prince of the empire seemingly kidnapped the Princess of Arden. They'll have raised their armies before the months end"

"Not necessarily, my Prince. There could be a way to avoid this before it starts"

Tarith looked at his General with a look to proceed.

"I will never fully trust the Princess. For I cannot be sure of her motives but she certainly has a more…open approach to you. She would listen to you perhaps more so if she were to be made your wife" Lo'atal suggested and braced for Tariths answer which came as he expected.

"Oh not this again. I spent one night with a woman. Nothing I have not done a thousand times before. I didn't marry any of them!"

"Non of them were the Princess of Nadenia! A nation that is on the brink of declaring war for independence within the empire, something that cannot happen now" Lo'atal commanded. "It is only my suggestion as your counselor as well as your military General who has seen the face of war before. I've killed men, sent them to early graves. Some deserving, some not. Perhaps it is sometimes necessary, war, but that does not make it any less painful for those left in its wake. Tarith, listen, you're someone I can call my brother-- you may be the first Emperor in hundreds of years who might actually have a legacy before him. You could ensure the empire is kept whole or you can watch it begin to fracture and its breakup may not be complete within a single lifetime but the rocks will start to fall on your watch. Take the girl as your wife and perhaps that can be avoided"

The tent fell silent for a moment as Tarith pondered and Lo'atal stewed. "I will...give it some thought in that case. It may help solidify our relationships. Or divide them even further. Our own people might not favor it. It may do nothing but further worsen things" Tarith murmured as he held his head again and rested back into the cushions. "Until then, however, that will be all...General" the Prince ordered to his faithful. Lo'atal sighed as he pushed his great bulky body back up from the chair and, with one last nod, he rejoined his brothers outside. He knew Tarith, knew how easy it was for his curious mind to be distracted or how he allowed it to be, which stopped him from grasping aspirations of the future.

By mornings hot light creeping through the break in the tent, Tarith had still failed to gain enough sleep to call it a good night's rest, for the pain at his mind's center still remained and was far from quelled when the morning summoning drums thundered to the tune of soldiers forming ranks. Tarith drearily pulled himself up, squinting at the scorching, early rising sun of the Red Plains burning hot down on them. The Prince thought to himself that if there were such a thing as the great burning oblivion he had heard the people of Kond claim to exist for evil ones after death, this would be an equal rival to it. At least in Ushkin City the forest was humid but the falls of Tashi were all the city needed for its cooling water--the lifeblood of the cities of northern Ushkin but here there was no such luxury for no water, well or oasis must have existed there for a hundred miles in any direction.

Half-dressed, Tarith made his way across the sands to give the order to Lo'atal. On his way there he noted how tall some of the dunes were, looming with great majesty like fragile mountains, some as tall as Ardens chief palace and fighting against the sun. The land was certainly beautiful in its own right, he thought, a shame that it also boded ill for anyone staying in it for too long as he had also noticed on his way across the plains: dried and old bones, brittle in the sun, thousands of them littering the sands.

"General" Tarith called to his friend who was already training with his men who he saw had washed the remainder of his body paint off and had let his black hair down from its bone pin. Without the paint the General's face seemed even broader than with it, making his small eyes even more pushed back and beady in his head. "Oh. Good morning, my Prince. Don't worry, we'll be moving out this afternoon. I've spoken to the old man, the scholar. He believes we're close"

"That will be unnecessary. If we are truly close I won't need the whole troop. Just you, a handful of the men, the Princess and that 'old man' tell the rest of them to finish setting up. It's time, Lo'atal" Tarith ordered as he turned to go back to his tent. "Do you really believe this?" the General called. Tarith turned on his bare heels, feeling the soft grains of sand massage the souls of his feet.

"I've come too far and gained too little to not, at least, find some meaning in all this. Who knows? This may all have been a waste of time and my prophecy could've simply been misread but there's only one way to know" the Prince answered.

For the entire day, since they left the sea of dunes, the headaches simply became more dramatic and wrapped around his head and pulsated with every movement of the horses. The weakness and fatigue that took over because of it was almost enough to slump Tarith from his horse until the old curate rode alongside him, who didn't seem to notice, given his distraction with the headache "we must be close" the old man muttered.

"What did you say?" Tarith looked up and squinted.

"Are you having head pains?"

"Yes, why? Don't tell me this is all part of Ornagoth's plan, ridiculous. This is just a headache brought on by nearly a months travel with little rest and stressful situations"

"Maybe. But it is certainly coincidental. Reports of Fotia Iron-Crown *and* Arvagnr, two Harbingers, also claimed to experience them just before they hit the Crater. Do tell me what the visions are like, should you have them, your benevolence. It's just that curate Azeron wrote a study on the effects of the canyon on Champion Riders and…"

"Vacile! I'm fine, there just headaches!" Tarith sputtered in a moment of immense irritation.

Vacile suddenly stopped riding, looking dead ahead, across the sandscape. "By the light of the moon" he said, pointing an old and rigid finger dead ahead. Tarith looked through blurred vision from the sand and saw, on the very edge of the land, on the border between earth and sky, a massive dip in the earth. Big enough to swallow a small army within its sands and still have room. It sat alone; a barren land from north, east, south and west. Dotted around the sinkhole were several old, dried up and dead trees all sitting randomly in the sands, like ancient bones grasping for the surface, their spiky branches casting twisted shadows below them where once a proud oasis lay. "That's it? We're finally here? After all this" the Prince murmured in disbelief as he cast his eyes towards the crater that danced in the desert mirage. The Champion Rider turned back towards the Osh-Venn "the crater, boys! We've reached the crater! Come! We're nearly there and on this journey, that you've shared and aided in you will all be remembered as the brave Osh-Venn who walked on sand and stone and forested floor with the Dragon Prince! My brave two-hundred! My brothers-in-arms!" Tarith declared before tugging on the reigns of his horse, galloping off into the sand dunes as the men behind him cheered as their own spirits rose in relief, loyalty and awe at the simplistic view of their long-saught destination.

Amira followed closely with Lo'atal and Vacile bringing up the rear, the horses leaving massive, calved dust trails in the sand, looking as if a much larger beast had dragged its claws and raked the earth. With every great leap the horse took Tarith felt the pain in his head subside and be replaced with the sense of satisfaction, the belief that he had achieved one of history's greatest feats. He could barely see through the strands of his silver hair that had grown considerably since they had left his homeland weeks prior. Through each flicker of each silver lock he drew closer to the pit until he thought he and the horse may fall in. Finally, he thought, as he drew up at the precipice and peered into its mouth.

Looking down, Tarith saw that the dip was deep, deep enough that only a fraction of the sun's lights peered into the sink of the earth, illuminating a hard and cracked, salt floor. In the pinpoint of the dip was a small stone tablet, inscribed with the ancient tools of the first people to set foot there twenty thousand years prior--Stuns disciples, they who told his stories and even aided in the construction of the black Obsidian Pyramid thousands of miles back west. The crater was a relic, almost out of place even in such a desolate land, it seemed almost too old to comprehend that for twenty millennium only six and now seven of his people had made the journey for their greatest judgment and here the tablet still lay alone and unblemished after all this time.

The Harbinger led his people down the slopes of the mound, which gave way with every step and rolled in large waves, till eventually they reached the weathered monument to the first Champion Rider, the Ambassador for Ornagoth. Amira watched as Tarith slowly caressed the tablet like he was in a trance, enthralled by the ancient stone. The Princess of Arden pulled down the green bandanna that covered her lips and nose from the elements and asked Vacile "what's it say on the tablet?"

The old man looked quizzically at her and then the tablet, reading from it as Tarith circled it impatiently under the eyes of all his men who watched from above, along the craters rim. At first even the curate was confused as even he, a man who'd dedicated his life to the lore of the dragon empire, couldn't decipher the ancient Ushkinian Hieroglyphics. "This writing is old, your benevolence, very old. It's using the old Ushkin language. A language the old monks adapted from the Osh-Venn, barely taught these days, few know it and fewer still can recognise it. The key parts are legible, though, let's see. It says: 'herein lies the great shrine of our Lord…those chosen to enter shall see the door, those chosen shall see the way. The Father of Jaq'iv, his chosen messenger on Earth, lay these words. By his breath he gifts his Harbingers onto us. Here lies the bastion of…" Vacile went quiet as a shaken look took hold on his face.

"What? A bastion of what?" Tarith asked frantically.

"A bastion…of the fire breathers" Vacile answered, staring off at nothing, a glazed look in his eye. Both Tarith and Amira looked at each other with surprise etched onto both their faces "by Sal Uran's hand" Lo'atal coughed "you really were telling the truth, Vacile" he spluttered.

Everyone turned to Tarith, all waiting to see what their Prince would say but the Harbinger stood there, in realization of his role, he felt, suddenly, a lot smaller. "It...it mentioned a door and those chosen could...see the way. I'm chosen aren't I... this tablet refers to the Champion Riders, it must" the young man murmured as a large ball gathered in his throat, formed from the fear, hot fear he suddenly felt.

"Yes, my Prince. I believe it does"

"Then where's the..." Tarith went quiet as he held his head as a sudden pain rushed through it again. It was far worse than the pains he felt on the way to the crater, like a hot blade being dragged, slowly, over his forehead. He fell to his knees as Amira and Lo'atal rushed to him, the General, pushing the Princess aside. "My Prince? Tarith? What is it?" Lo'atal asked, forgetting the pain he felt himself. The Prince ignored the reassuring hands on his back as he looked at the sandbank, his vision began to blur as he saw the sand begin to move. At first it moved with subtlety, like water over rock, but quickly turned into a raging avalanche, falling down to Tariths feet.

The Osh-Venn stepped back, one of them grabbing Vacile as Lo'atal rushed to grab Tarith, almost throwing him back onto Amira before a sudden burst of wind knocked the Osh-Venn General flying across the pit. He reeled in pain from his ribs as he pulled himself up, agonizingly. The entirety of the small army watched as the bank slide came to a sudden stop, the hissing of the moving sand silenced. For a second they were all covered by a thick blanket of dust that hazed their vision and impeded every choking breath, however, once the dust had settled and the Osh-Venn had collected themselves, pulling themselves out of the sand, their bone masks pouring the desert's confines out of them. The men all stood in awe at the sight of a small opening within the bank. It wasn't any grand, golden threshold, it didn't even have one. It was as if the sand had simply parted and the darkness within was actually a tunnel made from the very desert itself. The land had made a passage within itself though it looked as though it had always been there for the ground beneath it was not cracked or withered with age but was a fine, white, stone. "Get me a torch and leave me!" The Champion Rider commanded.

"Tarith, have you lost your mind? What in the sun's name do you think you're doing?" the General questioned, moving towards Tarith before a dreadful shooting pain ran down his chest.

"Do you fear that I won't return?" the Prince asked. Lo'atal silently relented, breathing out a deep sigh in defeat. Tarith smiled as he glanced at the bank entrance, its toothless, sandy mouth pried open. "Vacile" Tarith stated as an Osh-Venn handed him a lit torch, its flames illuminating his handsome face, freeing it from the shadow of the dune though still, he could feel the heat now boil at his skin as the day's assailed. "I do hope you make a good retelling of this" he jested.

Clutching his golden hilted sword and drawing it into the fresh air of a new day, the blade singing as it was unleashed, its cold, white blade glimmering. Tarith brazenly strutted into the opening, listening intently to the murmurs of voices becoming quieter and quieter as he ventured further into the small tunnel. Throughout his trip he had felt mostly in control, if not seeking aid from his advisors, however there in the crushing black he felt more like prey wandering into a predatory lair. It wasn't long before Tarith noted something about his footsteps; they were no longer pressing down on the soft. They were being held by solid stone, something he would never have realized if he hadn't looked down at his boots to make sure he was still walking at all in the disorientating shadow. Turning around he saw that there wasn't any light shining from the entrance he had just come through, even at the peak of day that was nearly approaching, only a crude imitation that wrapped around the bend in the tunnel but Tarith never remembered shuffling round any corner where by the light wouldn't be able to go. It was though the sands themselves had shifted and sealed back up in protection of the Prince or in his eternal imprisonment beneath the earth. He heard as the voices from outside vanished and all turned to silence in the sands.

Led only by the torches light now, letting his feet judge the surface, he stumbled several times like a baby taking its first bumbling steps. And then he saw it. The heart of the desert. A shaft of golden light shining down upon an overlook that sat, poised, over a gaping drop off below. When Tarith looked, first at the light, he saw there was no opening for the ray to emerge, it was as if the light beamed through the sands of the Red Plains, hitting the thin overlook, illuminating it, embellishing its chipped features of old limestone. Followed by the drop off that seemed much more like a void, reaching out into another starless world with no end. Tarith could feel it around him, the size, the enormity of the place he was in. It was like an aquifer but with no water within or a palace without people. Just stone and darkness. He soon recognised some sort of monument at the end of this thin walkway of stone, approaching it slowly, kicking sand off the stones, watching it fall into the endless chasm below and fade into the dark, he felt colder the closer he drew upon the end. When he did finally reach this monument, he saw it to be nothing but a stone bowl with two very large, plain rocks in it. Examining them, Tarith saw the rocks appeared to have been carved to resemble ovals. He felt a certain pull toward them, an irresistible urge to take them, like a thief in someone else's horde. Stretching out his naked fingers to grasp them, he could feel warmth emanating from the rocks, as if they'd been laid out in the sun, however when he grasped them firmly in both hands he quickly felt them become scolding hot, like magma stones from the heart of a volcano from En Jepo, far to the north. Tarith had seen a magma stone on a visit there and imagined they'd feel like the rocks did in his hands. Quickly dropping them to the ground, hissing in pain.

The moment the egg shaped rock hit the dusty ground: noise vanished and everything went dark as his torch was blown out and the world was swallowed in the silence of the void.

But another feeling resided within him as all went dark; a change in place, as if his world had folded onto itself and he was left in its creases. His body lay still in the dark whilst his mind drifted, Tarith could feel it, he was conscious but cast adrift. For a brief moment the darkness lingered, till he opened his eyes, though he could not recall closing them. He found himself standing in the familiar tall grass just outside of Ushkin City. He could feel it, which was the most surprising to him, he wasn't in a mundane dream but rather something else. As his vision began to clear and the fresh, bright light of waking eyes vanished he could see the low hanging trees of the western entrance to the city, their vines and leaves kissing the grass. The wind brushed over his face with a calm stroke as Tarith looked to the cloudless sky, a sky he'd watched his entire life. His serenity was momentary as he looked back down, away from the sky. He was now much closer to Ushkin, almost within the threshold of its carven gates, the city in view but not the one he recalled. Ushkin was in flames. Smoke choked even the Obsidian Pyramid, wrapping around every building as the flames lit the black, ash-filled sky that coughed pieces of charred wreckage in every direction. Tarith stood in the husk of the once great capital city of the empire, his home, the house of his clan and home of the dragons of old. He stepped forward, intent on rushing into the fallen buildings and burnt streets but his vision blurred again and he felt himself be moved or picked up and whisked away as if he were traveling to these places in reality but he knew his mind and read these visions to be idle memories, changed from his recent experiences. That was the Prince's theory until he opened his eyes a second time to find himself in a place he was unfamiliar with, a foreign place yet unlike any other strange land within the empire he had heard of.

He was stood on the pier of a large port that held several dozen ships in its quays and one or two spice ships on the horizon. The sun was held high and hot in the sky as Tarith saw it beaming over a large city, smaller than Ushkin by half, on its only hill the port city seemed to have a massive keep, tower after tower rising above all else like golden monuments of ancient power and halls and open corridors intertwined around and between the towers that seemed to grow from the hill, with the houses and manors of the cities inhabitants, twirling up the hill just below the keep. The palace stood on a large street that bled into the rest of the lower city.

Then, as this quick premonition had taken shape, so too did it begin to fade once again, and as it did Tarith heard a voice call to him. It didn't come from a particular direction but rather was displaced and radiated all around him with a commanding boom "herein now the crown of scale, of fang and of flesh is renewed with a worthy brow to sit upon " it stated with a voice that seemed compiled of more than just its own, layered with the tones of disembodied beings. In that instant Tarith felt a powerful presence join him in the dream world, one he'd heard before and knew it almost without effort. This godly voice erupted from the mouth of the chasm, of which the young dragon Prince was sure. It was both a herald and a warning. Tarith felt himself smile as the dream abated and he was revoked back into the mild climate of the cave, like a new-born, the world seemed cold to him and different. He stumbled as his feet became adjusted to the floor beneath him again, uneven, grabbing onto the stone bowl to stop himself from falling at the adjustment of the ground. Pulling himself up to look at the bowl again he saw something, something that wasn't there before. Several things. The first thing the Harbinger observed was a small piece of perfectly crafted gold, a fragment, shimmering in the resplendent light that still shone on the monument from above. Staring closely at it, Tarith saw the tiny chips on either side of the fragment, as well as three small rubies in its center. The jewelry couldn't have been bigger or wider than Tariths hand as he soon realized as he picked it up in just the one, caressing its rubies with his thumb. It wasn't in the sacred bowl when he arrived, just the two rocks but something had changed, not just the amount of things in the bowl but the rocks themselves.

Tarith held one of them, this time with no fear of the pain it could cause. Looking closely at it, the Prince noticed something about the clump of dust and earth. They were no longer rocks, they'd become speckled and felt slightly lighter in his grasp, their surface was now brittle like paper and when it moved Tarith felt something slosh around inside it. Placing the fragment into a small satchel on his belt and placing the egg back in the bowl, Tarith watched as the new rocks-turned eggs seemed to move, a tiny shudder almost undetectable as something stirred. The Prince squinted as he drew closer to them as he saw both now move, shuddering as if someone moved the bowl they were in. He watched as the shuddering became more violent and relentless, vibrating with an inhuman force. Tarith's young face coiled in confusion as he saw an oily clawed nail break through the shell, pulling itself out, revealing four scaled legs, tiny and fragile. They chipped and cracked away at their eggs, bursting out of their warm nursery. The legs flicked outwards in kicks, spitting fluid, and were attached to a small leathery body that hosted two membraned wings protruding from the shoulder bones of these creatures as both pulled themselves out. Tarith drew back as he witnessed the birth of legends, folk stories and fears all compiled into that moment and saw the renewal of mighty creatures not seen since the last age. Could this be another dream or absentee sign from the Lord, he pondered in shock as he watched. He remembered the old tales told to him by his father and mother both and facts he'd learnt from Vacile about the mighty fire breathers, gifts from Ornagoth. Still though, he felt as though such an event was only seen in the pages of old history books and almost felt unworthy to look upon its actual making. In that void he knew more sets of eyes watched him then his own could see and felt as the tides of fate now shifted to him. His face still with astonishment as he gazed upon the first dragons seen in the world since the last era. Their miniature bodies shook the embryonic fluid off their wings as it clung to them like webbing and their tiny screeches were already deafening as small puffs of smoke came from their toothy mouths. The seventh Harbinger stood, a dragonling on each side. He saw that one of the two was a fraction bigger than the other, his scales were a deep blood-red and his eyes glowed with orange light that illuminated the scales around his snout, showing two short, little, black horns on the top of its head that curved inwards like a scimitar, with a smaller set of horns on the bottom of its chin. Running from the top set of horns all the way down to its barbed tail were two black stripes that ran down its neck, across its back and joined at the tail, similar to what the tigers of Surcami looked like, Tarith thought.

The smaller of the two had much lighter scales, almost yellow or gold in color, with tiny little black, stubby horns on the back of his lizard-like head. Its scales were yellow but the webbing of its wings were cream splashed with black specks.

Though both were only as big as the flying squirrels Tarith had seen in Ushkin's forests, he could feel their weight on his hands and the tiny, pin-like claws pushing into the tips of his fingers as they glared at him, flapping their wings whilst simultaneously screaming and clicking to each other. He watched as they scurried up his arms like little mice, both taking a position on each of his shoulders, casually wrapping their tails under the leather straps of his armor--imprinted on him.

They looked up at their master, screeching at him as they did, and as their new cries rang in his ear with a dreadful pitch, he felt the warmth of tiny fires on each side of his face, a pleasant and newborn warmth, fragile and young.

Turning back again, Tarith saw the opening he'd arrived through, the once black and seemingly continuous dark was now, once again, lit by bright beams of golden sunlight. The Champion Rider proceeded back through the opening in the dunes, finally emerging back into the world of the living. Familiar light of the world stung his eyes after such an episode in the dark. Emerging with more than he went in with, the light pulled back over Tarith's face showing him and the dragonlings. All the men he'd traveled with, strong warriors from the volcanic reaches of Dush'Uul now fell to their knees, as did Amira and their General as the future Emperor appeared with two squawking dragons. Looking on with shocked faces some Osh-Venn even bowed their heads as well, in submission, their scaled armor and bone helmets clicking in unison like a gothic orchestra as they lowered their heads to the sands. The Harbinger watched with bewilderment, more at himself than the loyalty shown by his men but though his face projected surprise he couldn't shake a feeling of consternation that fixed itself within him but instead of ignoring the feeling, with the two mighty beasts that hissed with every breath on his shoulder, he felt it become a part of him, being molded by it though it was always a part of himself he'd kept hidden and denied. His vanity hadn't been rewarded but rinsed from him and replaced with one, unknown directive. A small crack of a smile crept across his flawless face as he raised his head to the cloudless sky as far above, resting above the dunes, the purifying light of a new day shone down on the crater, washing over the people as it cast their shadows to the sand. The dark hushed away as the light spread on the backs of dragons.

In the far northern region of Antara, within Vaskuul's temple, Gravis sat. Alone. He had just finished a bowl of stew, the first proper meal he'd eaten in the weeks following his escape from Jorrvanskar. The beautiful smell of cooked rabbit provided him with a small comfort, recalling his own stronghold and its own simplicities. Below him, in the lower chambers of the temple, he could hear the other All-Seers chanting in the old, ancient tongue of the hardened people that rumbled through the temple, coaxing the favor of the All-Maker. Every so often they were interrupted by the dripping of melting snow that peered through the stone rafters above Gravis' head.

Then. As he gazed around, realizing his apparent isolation from any other people, a thought pulled at the old ranger's consciousness. He looked at the small, blue flames of the seeing brazier, stood just next to him, in the midway mark of the room, in front of a central stone pillar. It spouted its small flames that illuminated the surrounding area with a blue tint, as if everything were submerged, deep below the water. Similar to the one he had at Jorrvanskar though this seeing scryer was much larger and grander than his own, with its perfectly crafted carving along the entirety of the rim. The Arch Seer's scryer was older and further reaching in the vision it provided its users though only Fanatiker, the Arch Seer himself was permitted to use it, by some long tradition or assumption, perhaps, the Arch Seer was the most gifted as Gravis recalled, but he knew that he had to understand whether what he suspected was warranted or not, meticulously placing his fur gloved hand within the flames, closing his eyes.

His mind wavered for a moment, rippling like once still water, he was carried to a vision. Placing his trust in the patron of Antara he allowed his God and guide to show, through the fire, something occurring, something in the present moment, though not revealed to him, he knew. A cold, hard shiver ran down his spine as Gravis recognised the familiar rooftops of the small, stubby huts of Jorrvanskar. However, the vision the All-Maker granted was altered in several ways: Jorrvanskar seemed to be in the heart of a raging blizzard, something not rare for the far north-west of Antara but certainly not how its inhabitants had left it. As if nature could wait not longer to strike in the absence of man. The second difference to what Gravis knew of his home was the sky. What was once a blotchy, gray, clouded sky that dimmed the light enough for the ice moss to grow, had been transformed into an icy blue, like the polar lights that beamed over Vaskuul on certain nights but these lights were bright and didn't just occupy part of the skyline but all of it. A vibrant and bright blue that tore its way across the sky, beautifully piercing across the globe and down to the horizon.

But the third difference, however, was what sent fear into Gravis' mind, like a cold dagger, taking up all thoughts. Such primal terror, he had never felt before. Around Jorrvanskar were hundreds, if not thousands, of people. All motionless, staring up at the blue sky above the blizzard, which hid most of their features. But their eyes, he saw their eyes, like jewels; glassy and almost carved into their heads. They were white eyes that gleamed out of the blizzard and looked to the light. Then, with nothing but the sound of the violent breeze around them, all of them turned their heads from the sky towards Gravis. Though they couldn't see him, Gravis knew through them, they could sense a shadow and a veiled man walking amongst them. He heard the bones in their partially visible spines crack as they turned their heads and some of them had jaws so loose because of the rot that they hung as they stared with sunken eyes or sometimes no eyes at all, simply hollow sockets, reflections of the void. Grim statues. The ones that appeared closer to him had their remaining skin bleached white by the sun, looking like painted ghouls, resentful but trance-like.

Then the array of bodies looked up to the monument, the same one Gravis had communed and lived in for many freezing decades. On the curved, stone roof, a figure slowly paced over it. It was the same dark figure Gravis had seen in his vision, the vision of fear that drove him to where he was now. He felt the quick and unpleasant sense of vulnerability spread itself over him with its unwanted tendrils as he saw the enormity of its overlord. The great armored figure stood upon the temple, like a conquering beast, its dark hood resting above its cruel, cursed eyes. The torn and ripped cloak behind him whipped and flew in the current of the wind like a flag heralding doom. Gravis watched as it raised its armored and spiked fingers into the air and then stood silent for a moment, posed like a monument of death. The blizzard parted like waves and as it dissipated it left a huge path in the wake, the very snows were under its command. Then came the marching and the clatter of ancient and rusted weapons, axes and swords being dragged through the snow and the feet of other fell creatures: frost trolls. Even uglier in death than in life, their pitch black eyes turned a rusted green with decay.

Gravis felt it. Darkness was marching on Antara. The One, The First Enemy brought with him ruin and unlife. A promise he had made in the moment of his creation: a promise of a cursed existence to any unfortunate soul ensnared. Something had awoken.

The last storm had come.

Printed in Dunstable, United Kingdom